HEART OF IRON

HEART

OF

IRON

by
C. M. Alongi

author's note

On February 3rd, 2023, I uploaded a silly little skit inspired by a Tumblr prompt that asked, "What if the Fae ran a coffeeshop?"

Having been on TikTok for a couple of years by that point, I knew that this skit would likely go mini-viral. (Relatable food service + the wish fulfillment of telling a customer to shut up? Yeah, that was gonna connect with fans.) However, I figured that I would only get three or four skits out of the idea before the interest died, and I'd have to move on to other pursuits.

Spoiler alert: the interest never died, and CaFae Latte—as it came to be known after the third skit posted on February 5th, 2023—has been going strong for over two and a half years at the time of this book's publication. (And no, you do not have to have seen a single TikTok to read this book, or vice versa. Think Marvel Comics vs Marvel Cinematic Universe: same characters, similar rules, different stories and details.)

It was only six months into the life of CaFae Latte that I was able to quit my food service job to create content and write books full-time, something that I didn't think would be possible until I was well into my thirties. (I put in my two-week notice on my twenty-eighth birthday.) And while yes, I take pride in my work and the skill it takes to create these stories in all sorts of mediums, at the end of the day, the book you're about to consume—hell, my *whole career*—is possible only because of you. My fans.

The money that was used to hire editors, the cover artist, formatting, promoting, all of that came from you. I ran a Kickstarter in February 2024—celebrating CaFae Latte's first year anniversary—so I could publish this book in as high quality as possible.

(At least, from an objective publishing standpoint. I haven't seen the Goodreads rating yet.)

I also invested a lot in sensitivity readers. I am queer—specifically aromantic and asexual. But I am also cisgender, not nonbinary like Jennifer Charles. I am white and neurotypical, which means I am not black or autistic like Nicole. (I *am* a Nichiren Buddhist, which is why she is, too.) No matter how many times I do it, it's always a bit nerve-wracking, writing such different characters from groups that my ancestors have—shall we say—not treated particularly well.

Luckily, I have the best fans, many of whom are in those groups. And they were instrumental in helping me make sure that my portrayal of these characters are as accurate and respectful as possible. If I missed something, please let me know. But I wouldn't have even dared attempted it without my audience cheering me on.

So from the bottom of my heart, thank you. Even if you didn't put a penny in the Kickstarter, or you borrowed this book from a library or a friend, the simple act of reading (or listening to) my work and sharing it with others is a gift, one that I will never take for granted.

prologue

War did not leave much time for construction projects, even for those as vital as running a new country. Thus, the Senate met in a cave for their first official meeting.

The caves had once been a goblin city, abandoned when the fairies invaded their lands centuries ago and the goblins decided they would not be serfs or war fodder for their new conquerors. Most of the caverns were unusable, accessible only through tunnels that a human or fairy had to crawl through to access, if they could get to it at all. That had been excellent for security and secrecy; when Violet would meet with other leaders of the rebellion, they would crawl through tunnels built for creatures half their size until they reached a large, open cavern that had likely been some kind of market square. By candle and torchlight, they would pour over maps and letters, planning their next move against half the world. The only reason it hadn't worked for the goblins was because the fairies had been able to cut them off from their food supply, starving them out of their own city.

Now, human and goblin (and the odd dwarven) builders chipped away at those tunnels every hour of daylight, expanding them so they could have access to the underground city within. To build something new atop the old ruins of rebellion. Already, they had created a hallway large enough for Violet to walk upright to reach the Senate's chamber, although the dust had to be constantly swept off the rock floor. But the builders hadn't gotten to the chamber itself yet, leaving the large space bare and lit with torches. Everyone stood on the floor, the exception being a handful of elderly and disabled who needed chairs carried in for them. The eight goblins that had been elected to the mostly-human Senate were in the front so they could easily see, as none of them were taller than a man's waist—even with the horns. Dozens of torches bathed the eager members of the Senate in a warm glow reminiscent of a sunrise. At odds with the orange light, the chamber still smelt of damp stone, despite the best efforts of the sage incense.

"The first *official* Senate session of Gialdon has begun," the Speaker announced from a lectern someone had scrounged up somewhere. Though she knew she wouldn't be here for the second session, Violet smiled at those words.

There had been a lot of controversy over how, exactly, the new government should function once humanity, goblins, and other mortals had freed themselves from the fairies' rule. It had been widely agreed upon to avoid royals, emperors, and tyrants. No one person or family could ever have too much power over others, and laws against serfdom and slavery had been among the first penned.

But that had been about all they could agree on in the last weeks of the war. Finally, a handful of humans who had grown up in the Mortal Realm and had heard of some of their ways suggested using the system of one of their most ancient and revered empires: Rome, specifically the Roman Republic before the Punic Wars. The new nation of Gialdon was divided into provinces, and people of those provinces ran for a seat in the Senate, filling thirty seats, with the Speaker (head of the Senate and domestic affairs), Chief Counselor (head of foreign affairs), and Chief Commander (head of the military) being the most senior and powerful positions, and half a dozen scribes standing on the edges transcribing everything. It was similar enough to a goblin Counsel of Elders that they agreed.

Unsurprisingly, the vast majority of those voted into the Senate had served as officers in the war, which scholars were already calling the War of Gialdonian Independence, or the War of Human Liberation ("*Mortal* Liberation," the goblins would correct).

There were a thousand ways it could go wrong, but that was true of every country. Violet was cautiously optimistic.

"First order of business," the Speaker said, rifling through his papers. The fairies had called him Dirt when he'd been born in their chains. During the war, he'd taken on a new name: Aster. He had done very little direct fighting, instead handling correspondence from spies and allies, supply chains, and diplomacy. One of the few Senators not wearing armor, he was instead clad in comfortable linens and furs against the damp chill of the cave. His long brown hair was pulled back in a bun, and he usually had a smudge of charcoal around his lips from where he'd place the pencil in his mouth while shuffling through his papers. *Ah, yes, there it is already*, Violet noted.

Aster triumphantly held up a long scroll. "The Kingdom of Ivae has signed the peace treaty!"

The entire Senate erupted in cheers, their joy bouncing off the stones in an eternal echo, and he had to shout to be heard over them: "They have recognized us as a sovereign nation. They will not steal or enslave our citizens, and all their active troops are already being removed from our lands. The war is officially over!"

Violet grinned, leaning against the wall as the Senators whooped and cried. It wasn't a surprise. There hadn't been any fighting in the last several weeks, as Ivae had thrown up the white flag of truce after losing what historians were already calling the Nine Days' Campaign. Still, it was nice to see it in writing.

Aster let the Senate go for a few moments before banging the gavel on the little lectern. "All right, all right, order. Honestly, you'd think you were all surprised."

"This is going in your book, right, Aster?" Chief Counselor Coral (birth name Twig) teased.

Aster rolled his eyes. "No, I'm going to write my memoir *without the damn peace treaty*."

Chief Commander Rat snorted. He was one of the few mortals who had not changed his name during liberation, wearing it as a badge of honor. He'd actually managed to escape serfdom in his youth, joining the underground freedom fighters that Violet had first hunted, then joined after Rat's hair began to turn gray. His knowledge and leadership had been invaluable, and she was glad to see him in the highest military position in this new nation. Even if they tended to get on each other's nerves.

The second and third orders of business had to do with foreign affairs (the dwarves wanted a renewal of their alliance, but that might drag the fledgling nation into a war with the giants) and infrastructure (a couple of mortal cities had popped up spontaneously throughout the years of war, but they had no organization, little oversight, and few good roads between them).

Finally, Aster said, "Next, the issue of Commander Violet."

The fairy left her spot on the wall and came out into the center of the now-quiet Senate chamber. She was not the only fairy in the room—there were a couple of kitryes, those born of human and Fae, among the Senate—but she was one of the few full-blooded ones in the new nation. And the most notorious.

Last night, she'd given her armor a good polish, the silver rings and iron plate setting off her lavender skin and deep purple hair. Two swords dangled from her waist: iron for fairies, steel for humans.

When she reached the center, she bowed. "Speaker Aster."

Aster grimaced. "Scribes, make a note. No bowing to Senators."

Violet chuckled, straightening. "Force of habit."

Chief Commander Rat, always to the point, grunted. "Half of my soldiers want to see you executed, witch. The other half wants you in charge."

"Then I saved us both a headache by not running for your seat."

Aster sighed and set down his papers. "Violet. This country owes you a debt it cannot repay. You destroyed all records of our full names, preventing our oppressors from effectively using magic against us, giving us a chance of victory. You helped Rat lead our troops, helped Coral and me bargain with allies, emptied your own stores to fund our war effort, provided invaluable intelligence of Ivae's inner workings, and were on the front lines of battle. We would not be standing here without you."

Violet nodded, waiting for the inevitable "but."

"However," the Speaker continued, his shoulders slumping a bit. "You are also the reason that we are in the Fae Realm at all. Our ancestors, our parents, even some of us living today were kidnapped from the Mortal Realm and brought here on *your* orders. And before you had your change of heart, you spent centuries putting down rebellions and liberation efforts that, if successful, would have prevented us from being born in bondage. The suffering you've caused our people is indescribable and incalculable."

The only sound in the chamber was the scribbling of scribes writing every word. All the Senators—friend and foe, human and goblin—seemed to hold their breath.

Violet did not react.

Aster swallowed, his eyes misting. He looked to the assembly. "As such, I move to have Violet, Commander of the Gialdonian Liberation Front, ex-Princess of Ivae, exiled from our lands."

The Senate exploded into cacophony. Thirty senators, some cheering, some enraged, others arguing. To be heard, and to restore order, Aster had to bang his gavel multiple times.

Throughout it all, Violet did not move, did not speak, waiting for the chaos to settle.

"Ivae's going to attack again!" someone shouted. "It's only a matter of time. You want to chase away our best weapon?"

"What's stopping her from betraying us the way she betrayed them?" someone else snapped.

"We need Ivae as an ally," Coral called, her voice echoing in the chamber. It was always impressive, how such a short woman could produce such a bellow. "I hate to say it, and you hate to hear it, but we need them either neutral or on our side. That won't happen so long as the Iron Witch is sheltering within our borders."

"Agreed," Violet said, the quiet strength in her voice silencing the arguments. "If I'm here, your chances of a second war with Ivae are much higher, and it'll be sooner rather than later."

She gazed around the chamber, making eye contact with as many Senators as possible. "I'll stay if you're willing to take that risk."

Rat grimaced. The other Senators were agitated, but had stopped yelling. Aster took advantage of the relative quiet to say, "All in favor?"

All but a few people raised their hands, including the Speaker, Chief Counselor, and Chief Commander. Aster nodded, unsurprised.

Coral addressed Violet, speaking as quietly as that booming voice permitted. "Please understand that we hold you in the highest respect. And I wish you could stay as an adviser."

Violet smiled. "Chief Counselor, I'm honored. But I've had quite enough of politics. However, before I go, I would like to make one final suggestion."

"Yes?" Astor asked.

Faster than a blink, Violet drew both swords and had the blades against Aster and Coral's necks.

Rat cursed, he and several other Senators drawing their weapons—too slow, too far away.

Aster held up his hand, quieting them while he glared at Violet. Coral swallowed, the skin moving against the iron blade.

Violet waited for the chaos to die down, for everyone to realize that she hadn't even drawn a drop of blood. She then sheathed her blades, this time moving slowly enough that everyone could actually see the motion.

"Get yourselves some bodyguards," shew said kindly. "If you die too soon, then so does your nation."

She walked out, patting Rat's arm as she passed.

§

"They *exiled* you?" Blue shrieked.

"Mm-hm," Violet said, putting the finishing touches on the thick wooden beads. It was tricky, carving runes into something the size of her thumb. She'd much rather do it on a larger item, like a wall. They weren't pretty, but they'd serve their purpose.

Yes, she'd told the Senate to get bodyguards. But a bit of magic wouldn't hurt. She'd leave these enchanted beads for them, explaining that they were imbued with good luck, something that sounded so innocuous and yet, again and again, had proven to be the difference between life and death, victory and defeat.

She could have put the spell on their persons. But that would require her to know the full name of everyone wishing to be enchanted and would continuously drain her energy until either the enchanter or enchanted were dead. Thus, it was best to pour the magic into an inanimate object, anchoring it with the runes that would act as a well. It'd be more exhausting *now*, but she'd recover more quickly. She could "load" each charm with a certain amount, ensuring it lasted anywhere from days to centuries, depending on how generous she was feeling. When the magic ran out, the charm would break.

"After everything you've done for them?!" Blue continued to rant. "Are they mad or just stupid?"

Violet blew on her carving and raised an eyebrow at the boy. Orphaned from the war, Blue was only a century old, equivalent to a seven- or eight-year-old human child. Violet had taken him in as a temporary measure, and now he paced the length of their tent, set up among thousands of others outside of the Senate's caverns, the gentle breeze carrying the smell of farm animals, mud, and manure. The sound of the military camp's organized chaos had soothed her to sleep since pitching the tent, people running and chatting and drilling—and now drinking, with the victory. She suspected that this mountainside would soon be transformed into a proper city, with permanent buildings rather than cloth tents and shanties. The original goblin caves within would serve as a good fallback in the event of a siege, or as storage for particularly valuable items or prisoners.

"Child. What do you see?" Violet asked.

Blue paused. His nickname was similar to hers, taken from his pale blue skin and tangled indigo hair. Fairies did not have freckles, but they often had a marbling effect of other colors that swirled across their skin. Violet had dark purple marbling across her lavender back and upper arms, usually hidden beneath her clothes. Blue's skin was pale blue, with marbling of light gray and ivory white, and it covered his whole body.

"...you?" he asked.

She pointed across the tent. "What do you see?"

He followed her finger to the backpack and trunk stacked on the floor. "You already packed?"

"I packed days ago. This exile was planned. We talked about it for weeks. I told Aster, Rat, and Coral that I was leaving when the war was won. That I was done with politics and war. They agreed that it was probably best if I left, given my ... controversial history. We decided to make a bit of a show of it."

"So..." Blue's brow wrinkled. "You ordered your own exile?"

"I wouldn't say I *ordered* it. Rat's the one who said I should never come back. Exiling me gives the Senate teeth. A show of real power. It also makes future diplomacy easier. Almost every other nation in this Realm is my enemy. Getting rid of me will make international relations more friendly. And," she continued, "I deserve it. You saw me help these people, yes. But that was only after centuries of causing them pain. If my leaving is what they need to heal, then so be it."

"Where will you go?" Blue asked.

"Well, if everyone in this Realm hates me, where should I go?"

"... another Realm?"

"Exactly."

"You're going to Earth?" he guessed, bewildered.

"Probably," she said. "I certainly know more about humans than I do about demons. Or angels. Or oni. Or any other number of other creatures and Realms in the universe."

"What ... what happens to me, then?" he asked quietly.

Violet smiled, hoping it was reassuring and not desperate. She'd never seen herself as a mother before, had only taken in Blue out of a sense of duty, so he wouldn't starve or get killed before they found a better match. Now, though? She didn't want to consider her life without him.

But that was not her decision.

"That's up to you," she said. "I can find you a guardian here. One of the immortal kitrye can look after you and keep you out of trouble. Or you can come with me–"

"I'm coming with you," he blurted.

"Think about this," Violet warned. "There won't be any other fairies in the Mortal Realm. There will probably be very few immortals or magical beings at all. We'll have to keep our own nature hidden, for safety."

To his credit, the child pondered that for a few seconds. Then, "I don't want to be here anymore. I don't like all the memories."

Violet softened. She hugged the boy. "Then we'll leave tomorrow and make some new ones."

Approximately 200 years later...

a midwestern freckle

JC picked at the dent in the wooden kitchen table, watching their parole officer flip through her tablet and wishing for a cigarette. Someone had cooked a frozen pizza for lunch, the scent of burnt crust lingering in the air like a bad fart. The overly dramatic blast of some reality TV show in the next room mingled with the work-out music oozing from the basement, resulting in a headache.

Their parole officer, Mrs. Amanda Jackson, frowned at JC's outfit over her tablet. "Interesting clothes, Mr. Scott."

"Pretty sure I told you to call me Jennifer Charles, Mrs. Jackson."

"Right. Sorry." She turned to the house staff, Brandon. "How is he settling in?"

Brandon was in his forties. Halfway house staff either bailed within a year or stayed forever, and he'd chosen the latter. His balding head and beer belly made it hard to think of him as a former Navy SEAL.

"*They're* doing great," Brandon said, stressing the pronoun. JC bit back a smile. The house had four staff watching the parolees (only two of them full-time), and Brandon was their favorite, even if he could be strict sometimes. "No fights. They're here by curfew. Biggest issue is finding them a job, but not for lack of trying."

"Also, I think the stove's trying to kill me," JC added. "Every time I turn it on it uses so much gas the first few seconds that it practically explodes in my face. But nothing's caught fire yet, so..."

Mrs. Jackson flipped to another tab, adjusting her thick diva classes. She had a twenty-something-year-old daughter going through beauty school and didn't mind being the girl's test subject, resulting in freshly dyed or cut hair every few months. She'd shown JC the pictures during one of their earlier meetings. This month, her hair was jet black with bright blue extensions that looked like police sirens, matching her blouse and navy suit.

"Your drug tests came back negative. That's good," she muttered. JC preened, just a little. They knew whenever they were greeted with a cup that the tests would be clean, but it still made them nervous.

"Job search not going well?"

They grimaced, crossing their arms as the frustration from the last two months bubbled up. "Lots of interviews, lots of 'We'll get back to you,' lots of nothing. I've got another one for today."

Mrs. Jackson looked up. "And you're wearing *that*?"

The black skirt from Walmart had eaten up the last of their non-SNAP money last month, the light fabric gliding across their skin like a winter kiss. JC had initially wanted the red one, but decided black was better. More professional, and it went with more of their tops.

"Yup," they said, popping the P.

"Maybe you'd have more luck if you dressed more...masculine."

They gave her a flat look. "You know that half the reason I went into drugs is because I was surrounded by queerphobic bullshit, right?"

"There's no need for that language, Mr. Scott."

"JC," they and Brandon corrected.

"Right. Sorry."

"Honestly, Amanda, almost everyone else in the house gets it right," Brandon gently chided. "It's been months."

"It's hard to remember," Mrs. Jackson defended. "Especially when that's not their legal name. I don't see *JC* every time I look up the case file. I see *Richard*."

JC rolled their eyes. "Whatever. And about the clothes, I'd rather go into the interview with all cards on the table rather than get a job with someone who's going to make my life a living hell."

"You're more likely to get calls back if you compromise," she lectured. "Not forever, but I can't imagine your insulin is cheap."

"Pretty sure the biggest problem people have with hiring me is the manslaughter and drug charges, not the skirt," they retorted.

She frowned, changing the subject: "Where is this interview?"

"Place called CaFae Latte, down in Bernier. I sent you the thing."

Mrs. Jackson scrolled through her tablet until she found the email they'd sent. Her mouth tightened. "Owned by fairies."

"Uh, yeah. It's in the name."

"Is that a good idea?"

JC frowned. "Why not? They're hiring."

"It's a Fae establishment. You know your history."

They snorted. "So *all* fairies are para-drug dealers? Wow."

"That's not what I meant," Mrs. Jackson said, frustratingly calm. "Just flipping through their website, I see they use a lot of magical ingredients in their drinks."

"Nothing addictive. They have to pass, like, eight FDA screenings. Hell, McDonald's has that Hellfire Bar-b-que Burger, and Dairy Queen's got berries from dryads for their summer specials. None of that is like marbles. You'd have better luck making meth out of pop."

"Hm."

"It's *Bernier*. Every dealer knows you *don't* do business there."

"Why not?" she asked.

JC shrugged. "Honestly? No idea. Every time a dealer tries to do business there, bad shit hits them like a truck. They suddenly get busted, or they get sick, or they get *literally* hit by a truck. The place is bad luck."

"One of my friends runs a halfway house there for recovering addicts," Brandon added. "Says it's the most successful place she's ever worked. No dealers. No gangs. Nothing."

"So, it's a small town," she said.

JC laughed. "Mrs. Jackson, small towns are where you go for the *best* shit."

Brandon nodded. "My only concern is how you're going to get there. That's a long bus ride."

"Beggars, choosers," JC said. They checked the time on their phone and winced. "If I want to make that interview, I've gotta get going."

"So, you do." Mrs. Jackson closed her tablet. "Let me know how it goes, and I'll see you next week."

§

St. Paul had a lot of buses and even a few trains, most of them running to and from Minneapolis like metal ping-pong balls. Yet only a handful of them went beyond the suburbs, and only one of those went to Bernier. The bus left for that town once every two hours. Its doors closed on JC's heels when they hopped on and used their pass to pay the fare—only seventy-five cents left on that card.

They secured their bike against the bus wall and sat on the felt-covered seat by the window, ignoring the weird crusty spot beneath their leg, and listened to music on their phone. They had to hold the cord *just* right, or only one of the headphones would work. Outside, St. Paul morphed into suburbs, and then into farmland.

It wasn't JC's first time in the area; they'd gone biking a few times, preferring hours of empty trails and burning legs to being cramped in a house with thirty guys. Bernier (the town, not the lake) was a Midwestern freckle, caught in the crosshairs of farming and industry, small town and big city. The town had just under 30,000 people, but it felt like only 300. A couple of highways met in the center for a smooch, but instead of U.S. 61 and MN-55, everyone called them Mississippi Street and 32nd Street, and while they were always full of cars, they were never truly clogged with traffic. There were few regular buses, but a lot of bike paths. Follow either highway out of town and you'd drive through seemingly endless stretches of farmland where all you ever saw was corn and soybeans and the occasional cattle ranch. Then suddenly, in the middle of those empty farms, MN-55 would take you straight to a Pepsi factory that employed a third of the town and reeked of stale metal.

Most importantly, it was clean. No gangs. No mobsters. It should've been prime territory, with a combination of the depressed poor and bored rich overlapping each other in a rough quilt. Plenty of spots to make deals, from the sleazy motel on Baker Street to the country club on the golf course just west of town. Yet everyone was warned against doing any business in Bernier. If you did, you were gone within a month. Dead or in jail, usually, though never for the same reason or, presumably, by the same person. Any goods used in Bernier were bought by the locals *outside* of its borders, and those were only small-scale customers visiting the Twin Cities for a fun weekend, not true dealers or distributors.

Rumor had it there was a powerful fairy witch that claimed the town as her own. No one knew why. None of the gangs—human or para—could really get a clear picture of her. They couldn't even agree on what she did, whether she ran a gang herself or worked for the cops. But ever since the Fae Migration in the '60s, Bernier had been clean of gangs and organized crime. Any attempt at influence, manipulation, or intimidation washed away within weeks, if not days. At least, that's what JC had heard.

JC didn't care about the witch, what she wanted, or if she was real. Bernier was clean. Bernier was protected from their old life in every way possible. Thus, Bernier was safe, if boring as all hell. There was a movie theater, a gaming store, and a strip of park along the Mississippi River. That was it, and JC didn't have the money for movies or gaming.

The bus stop was on one of the busiest, crowded parts of town, right by the river, just off the Mississippi Street highway and pale blue bridge. Hopping off the bus, JC collected their bike and bundled up their wide flowy skirt beneath their butt on the seat so it wouldn't get caught in the chain. They pedaled toward the river, to Main Street, taking it slow and easy, grateful that everything was flat with no major hills so they wouldn't show up soaked in sweat.

Main Street was, according to the informative plaques along the river, the oldest part of town. The old brick buildings spread from the shadow of the pale blue Mississippi Street bridge, which crossed the wide, calm river and spewed cars toward the Cities. There were half a dozen antique stores, a few restaurants, a yarn shop, a beauty parlor, some boutiques with price tags that made JC cringe, and the café. JC had applied for jobs at all of them. Only the café had invited them for an interview.

JC locked the bike on a streetlamp just outside CaFae Latte. It had some outdoor seating, cluttered with customers. The modern logo—a silhouetted winged fairy pouring the white letters of "CaFae Latte" over a lavender stain—clashed and yet somehow complemented the old-style brick building. A couple of tables were set near the windows inside, holding a few more customers, and JC breathed easier when they saw the Progress Pride flag sticker on the glass.

Although the bike ride had been chilly, their quickened heartbeat hadn't slowed, they were starting to sweat, and there was that edge of dizziness and slight throbbing of an early headache that warned them their blood sugar was dropping. Tempting as it was to go into the café and order a sugary drink, that was for people who had money.

JC went into the mini-cooler strapped to the front of their bike and pulled out the emergency pop they'd stashed in there for just this problem. They slurped it down, tossing the empty can in the recycling bin by the light post.

They'd gotten here twenty minutes before their interview. Normally, to give themselves a boost of confidence, they'd chomp on a marble or two. But the folks at Narcotics Anonymous would probably frown on that, to say nothing of the halfway house. Instead, they ducked into the tiny alley between CaFae Latte and the antique store and pulled out a cigarette.

Yeah, yeah, lung cancer, nicotine, heart disease, blah blah blah. Still better than marbles. No one ever went on a shooting spree on nicotine. Or picked a fistfight with a troll. Or tried to impress a date with a bike trick on a roof that ended in a dumpster and ER visit.

They let the smoke fill their lungs and watched the sunny street for a few minutes, until the embers went down to the yellow butt and they felt just a bit calmer. The sugar from the pop had also kicked in, keeping them from face-planting anytime soon. The trash bins didn't have any ash trays on them, so they had to drop the cigarette in the alley and snuff it out with their Goodwill loafers.

A couple of small sweat stains now plagued the pits of their polo shirt, but so long as they kept their arms down, it'd be fine.

They smoothed out their skirt, plucked the cooler from their bike, and went inside.

The smell hit them first, a thick blanket of coffee and espresso wrapping around them. On the second whiff, they caught the various teas lined on the wall in tin jars, and the lemon in the cleaner that must have been used on the dark wooden tables and chairs.

Considering who ran the place, it was a surprisingly ordinary café. It was just small enough to be cozy, with earth-colored couches and cushions. Framed photographs spanning every decade that cameras had been a thing cluttered the deep green walls, along with a handful of paintings and other bright artworks, mostly purple or lavender, like pockets of wildflowers in a warm forest. The entire front of the café was windows instead of walls, bringing natural light into the room and making the lightbulbs hanging from the ceiling almost unnecessary.

Behind the counter, a tall young man finished steaming some milk for the customer scrolling through their phone. Well, he *looked* young. JC honestly couldn't be sure, because he was undeniably a fairy, with that brightly colored, marbled skin and large pointy ears. In this case, he had light blue skin and gray-white marbling. Fluffy indigo hair peeked out of the bottom of his black hat, which he wore backwards, his bangs sticking out of the gap of the hat's back. To top it off, he'd covered the hat, apron, and even his belt with pins: ace pride flag, bisexual pride flag, "single AF," "totally Fae," "just stab them," a coffeepot on a stack of books, etc.

Honestly, if it weren't for the book pin, JC would've pegged him as a jock. Those arms and shoulders had been *earned*. Football, maybe? Or basketball?

He definitely wasn't a dancer. While he swayed and quietly sang along to the Miley Cyrus song bopping on the speakers, it was completely off-beat. And out of tune.

"Be with you in just a sec!" he called, spotting JC. The menus were dark brown with white lettering, and JC scanned a bunch of drinks like coffee, cappuccino, mochas, something called an Arcane Rush, a list of toppings that included cinnamon, vanilla, pixie dust, essence of hellfire...

JC went to the little display case, noting the cookies, brownies, and scones. A typed note proudly declared that they were all vegetarian, many were vegan, and almost half were gluten free. But they didn't think any of them were made in-house. They all had that too-perfect, too-uniform look of factory-made goods.

"Have a good one!" the fairy said cheerfully, handing over the finished drink.

"Thanks," the customer replied.

A jar suddenly appeared on the counter. The fairy waved his hand. "Ignore it–you already tipped."

Huh. Weird spell, JC thought. Most invisibility or glamour spells were used on people, or illegal goods. Not tip jars that vanished as soon as the customer walked away.

The fairy smiled wide and bright at JC. They couldn't tell if he was tall or if they were just short. Probably both. "What are we having?"

"A job interview."

"Oh, you're the two o'clock!" He glanced at the time. "You're early."

"If you're on time, you're late." This close, JC could see the nametag on the neck strap of the black apron: *Hello! My name is Inigo Montoya. You killed my father. Prepare to die.* They snorted.

"Boss is wrapping something up in the back," he explained, "but it shouldn't be long. Call me whatever; I've been going by Inigo today, but most of the time it's Blue. He/him pronouns."

"JC, they/them. You're a nerd."

"Excuse you, I am a *geek*. Big difference."

"Pretty sure the only people who care are dorks."

He snorted a laugh. "All right, tiny. You want a drink while you wait?"

They shook their head. "Nah. 'Preciate it." They hesitated, then with a mental *fuck it*, asked, "What are the chances that you guys will hire an ex-con? Because if the answer is none, then I'd rather not waste anyone's time."

He didn't look shocked, condescending, scared, or angry. He didn't even miss a beat when he replied, "Depends. Was that crime high treason, espionage, and/or murder?"

"Uh, no?" Well, it wasn't considered murder only on a technicality...

He snorted. "Bor-*ring*. You'd be the odd one out. What the hell are we supposed to talk about?"

They probably should've been alarmed. Instead, JC's shoulders lost their tension, and they smirked. "Your shitty dance moves?"

"I'm not hearing any complaints."

"Yeah, 'cause most Minnesotans are too polite."

"Blue! Where did you put those brownies?" someone interrupted from the back.

"The fridge with the glass door, bottom shelf," he hollered.

"And how many of them did you put in your stomach?"

He winced. "Uh...your two o'clock's here!"

JC bit back a laugh. Through some quirk of magic or evolution, fairies couldn't lie. But they could evade—usually better than that.

A woman came out of the back, giving Blue an unimpressed eyebrow. She was another fairy, with lavender skin and near-black hair neatly tied back in a ponytail. She wore her hat right-side forward, and somehow managed to look prim and proper in an apron and jeans. The mesh scarf delicately looped around her neck that shone with *gold* probably helped, same with the earrings, rings, and bracelets.

Unlike Blue, she did not have a nametag. JC knew better than to ask a fairy for their name, but since they had to call her something, they mentally dubbed her Bob.

"Is now a good time?" JC asked before Bob could ream into her employee. They held up their résumé, folded neatly and only a little wrinkled.

She took it. "It is an excellent time." Her eyes narrowed. "Assuming my employee can hold the floor without eating the rest of the goods."

"No promises!" Blue said cheerfully.

Snorting, Bob waved for JC. Tightening their sweaty grip on their cooler, they followed her.

the soldier

An excerpt from *Round-Ears: A History of
Gialdon and Humans in the Fae Realm*

T he War of Gialdonian Independence—or, the
War of Human Liberation—was a very long,
drawn-out affair. Its official start was pre-
ceded by years of guerrilla warfare from escaped mortal serfs who called themselves Gialdons, from the Fae
word *gialdis*, meaning *to break free*. ("Gialdon" would, of
course, be the name of the new nation, and "Gialdonian"
became the adjective. For the purposes of this book, we
will be using the historically accurate titles.)

Most history books acknowledge the official start of the war as the defection of the Violet Princess, later known as the Exiled Princess, from Ivae to the Gialdons. At the time, she was most commonly known—especially to her enemies—as the Iron Witch for her brutality in battle, iron armor, and "heart of iron." That title was apparently ill-given, as the Violet Princess reportedly found herself growing more and more sympathetic to the mortals that she had been ordered to subjugate and force into battle for centuries.

She has also been called the Traitor Princess, Human-Lover, the Liberator, the Hammer of Ivae (prior to her defection), the Purple Dragon, the Fire-Wielder, the Rogue Princess, the Violet Ghost, and dozens of other titles. Needless to say, even today, she is an extremely controversial figure all over the Fae Realm.

Despite being royalty and thus watched and recorded more than most other people in the [Fae] Kingdom of Ivae, little is known about the Violet Princess's thoughts and intentions, especially closer to the war. She was a private person who did not readily share her opinions, a trait likely encouraged by her political and military status.

She was one of several princes and princesses in the Ivaenian royal family, the youngest child of the king's youngest child, and thus far enough down the line of succession of immortals that she was largely considered an afterthought in her youth. She began military training early, most likely at the orders of her parents and/or kingly grandfather. Despite fairies' general disdain for death, the military still needed to be firmly in Fae hands, which was why the vast majority of the leadership positions—especially that of Chief Commander, the head of the entire force—were fairies.

The Violet Princess was known to be unusually good to the people under her command as she rose through the ranks, from lieutenant to captain to commander to Chief Commander. (Most immortals who reach the rank of Chief Commander are typically 1500 years or older, even if they have the advantage of being royalty. The Violet Princess achieved the promotion at the approximate age of 850.)

While other officers did little to improve their mortal soldiers' lives, the Violet Princess generously rewarded good performance and did everything in her power to get her regiments the best supplies, from weapons and tents to food and entertainment. She avoided collective punishment, often letting her soldiers choose the punishment of those who committed minor infractions, which had the added bonus of preventing her subjects from ganging up on her. And she was known to be incredibly respectful to foreigners—such as dwarves, giants, and trolls—as well as treating immortal kitrye (those with both Fae and human ancestry) as graciously as full-blooded Fae, something not typically done in Ivae's rigid caste system.

She also chose to endure the same hardships of battle as her mortal soldiers, from carrying her own tent and supplies to fighting on the front lines. When her captain asked about this decision when she was a lieutenant, she's recorded to reply, "How can I effectively lead [my mortal soldiers] if I don't know what they experience?" Other sources have recorded her mentioning that it would be faster and more efficient for her to carry her own burdens, rather than rely on servants.

In battle, most Fae officers stayed in the back, preferably in a higher position so they could oversee the entire scene like a chess board. They learned martial combat, of course, but that was more of a safety measure, so they could defend themselves in case mortals managed to attack them, although that was rare and heavily punished. Even when mortals managed to kill the commander of an enemy army—giving their masters a distinct advantage—those mortals were [magically] cursed, if not executed, for attacking an immortal. When a Fae officer did order the death of someone (always a mortal, never an immortal), they relied on their mortal soldiers to carry it out. If this was ordered outside of battle, they had mortal executioners, thus keeping their own hands clean. Fairies remained above death, always.

The Violet Princess rejected this notion. A skilled sorceress and one of the greatest fighters of her time with an edged weapon, she was usually in the thick of battle herself, fighting and killing the enemy alongside her enslaved soldiers. Supposedly, her grandfather the king once ordered her to stop the practice and stay in the back like a "proper" military officer, to which she reportedly replied, "I refuse to order anyone to do something I would not do myself. If you wish for me to follow that order, then everyone under my command will stay out of the fight."

This relative benevolence toward her soldiers and willingness to fight and suffer alongside them earned the Violet Princess a much fiercer loyalty from her soldiers than any other Fae officer.

However, for the vast majority of her military career, the Violet Princess was one of the greatest weapons used against human liberation in the Fae Realm. She led the suppression of countless mortal revolts and rebellions in her centuries of service and even ordered them taken from the Mortal Realm [re: Earth] to replenish her armies. Historians estimate that her orders are responsible for the kidnapping and forceful relocation of anywhere from two million to six million humans over her seven hundred years of service to Ivae—not including other mortal victims, such as goblins and dwarves. That figure also does not include their descendants born into bondage, nor does it include the orders of her fellow commanders and royals, both in Ivae and the wider Fae Realm.

The Fae's long habit of coming to Earth to steal mortals—preferably infants and young children, as they are easier to control—is long and varied, ranging from

Pied Pipers to elaborate parties in the woods to seductive women. Most of them were destined for the only thing "death-touched" mortals are good for in the eyes of the Fae: war.

Pictured *a carving from the Wooden Palace of Ivae, depicting a battle between the Fae Nations of Ivae and Riada. This piece is dated approximately 1200 CE, and the battle itself likely took place around 1100 CE.*

like a band-aid

"So, Mr. Scott…" Bob began.

"Ah, actually…" *First test. Let's see how she reacts.* "I'm nonbinary. Richard Scott is my legal name, but I'd rather you call me JC. They/them pronouns."

"JC, then," she said without missing a beat. This close, JC could see that her mesh scarf probably wasn't magical. Though it shimmered gold in the light, it wasn't actual gold, just blue yarn with something shiny put in the mix. The jewelry was harder to judge.

They both sat in little wooden chairs at a table in the very back of the café, right by the emergency exit. When JC turned around, they could see the front windows, but the wall and restroom jutted out to block Blue, the counter, and most of the rest of the floor. For all intents and purposes, the two of them were alone.

"How much experience do you have working in the food industry?" Bob asked.

They grimaced. "Not much. Odd jobs, here and there, which I listed."

She scanned the résumé. "Why were you working for them for such a short period of time? Nothing more than a few months."

Second test. "Because I was a druggie and either didn't show up because I was too high, or tried to steal from the registers."

Bob's violet eyes flicked up to meet theirs.

"The Anagram employment near the top is what I did in prison. They're a balloon company and like to hire criminals in lock-up to keep everything cheap," JC continued. "I did the baking program at the top while there, too. It's where I learned to make these."

They removed the lid from the cooler and pulled out three Ziploc bags: one with chocolate chip cookies, one with brownies, one with brigadeiros (a type of Brazilian chocolate truffle).

"They're all vegetarian, and the brownies and brigadeiros are gluten-free."

They hadn't been surprised when scouring the website to see that CaFae Latte was vegetarian. Most fairies were. Something about avoiding death.

They knew it wasn't usual, but proof of skill was the only thing they were riding on. They didn't have the job experience, barely had the training, and didn't even have a high school diploma. But they did have results.

Bob seemed very amused as she delicately plucked a cookie from the bag. "You know, in the Fae Realm, eating your food would indicate that I now work for *you*."

"Good thing we're on Earth, then. I don't think I could afford you."

She chuckled, taking a bite as she continued to look over the résumé. "So, you're—Mm. That's good. So, you're completely rehabilitated?"

JC pulled a coin out of their pocket and put it on the table. The green 60-day sobriety chip winked up at them. Bob picked it up with calloused lavender fingers and studied it. "Quite the achievement."

JC shifted in their chair. "It should be a three-year chip, but prison's not a great place to get clean."

Bob hummed in agreement.

They frowned. "I didn't mean to add that part."

"I enchanted your chair," she said, handing the chip back. JC quickly returned it to their pocket. (Another win for the skirt: actual pockets.) "Any who sit in it is compelled to tell the truth. Seemed only fair, as fairies are incapable of lying."

JC blinked, then stood and examined the chair. They found the magical runes carved into the wood on the bottom when they flipped it upside down and laughed.

"You only just now noticed?" Bob asked, trying the brownies.

"The whole 'I'm an ex-felon' thing is easier when you treat it like a Band-Aid. That and the non-binary thing." They returned the chair to its place and pointedly sat back down. "I'm still on parole and live at a halfway house in St. Paul. They're pretty strict on curfew, but they're willing to be flexible for work hours. Everyone knows that you take what you can get."

"We usually close our doors by three," Bob said between bites of brownie. "But we open at six in the morning, which means you'd be here by five to put everything in order."

JC tried not to squirm as they watched her eat. They knew they were a good baker—a surprising skill they'd uncovered in prison—but those brownies were tricky, and a bit too chewy even after a few batches. Gluten-free baking was a *bitch*.

"You haven't been out of prison long, then," Bob stated.

"Just two months. How long have you been here?"

"I started this café in the 1960s."

The pieces snapped into place. "...you're the witch, aren't you?"

"What witch?" she asked.

"The one who keeps Bernier clean. Everyone in my old life got so pissed that they couldn't deal here."

Bob smirked. "Enchanting the land itself is very difficult, but doable. If you go out to the town borders, you'll see seven strategically located stones, about chest high. They're almost impossible to find unless you're looking for them, and you'll forget their precise location as soon as you walk away—I enchanted them that way. They're engraved with spells of protection. I put them there when I moved here. Tornadoes avoid this town, floods aren't too destructive, violent crimes tend to be prevented or happen elsewhere, and should there be a war or invasion, Bernier would have the luck of faring relatively well."

"...huh. That explains it." JC frowned. "What are you doing running a café?"

As Bob raised a dark eyebrow, they added, "It's just, you seem a bit overqualified? You could be a general or make a living off the spells or even be the damn president."

"I could," she said, tapping a finger against JC's résumé. "But you're not the only one seeking a fresh start from a dishonorable past."

"...oh."

The two regarded each other. JC shrugged. "Eh. Legality's just a set of guidelines, anyway. Who cares if they're followed?"

Bob laughed. It was a melody. She folded the résumé back up and slid it across the table. "How soon can you start?"

JC paused. "Just like that?"

"You're obviously a talented baker, if you can create that quality with so little training. I'm curious to see what you can do with proper support. My ward and I are good with drink, but woefully ill-equipped to handle any form of baking or cooking. All of our foodstuffs are bought ready-made. We tried making the shift to an in-house baker a few months ago, but she had a family emergency and quit unexpectedly."

"Uh..." They could not believe their luck. "Full-time? Part-time?"

"Full-time, with overtime pay as needed and health and dental included. Typically, I would offer $20 an hour to someone just starting out, plus tips, especially with your lack of experience. However, with your unique status, I would like to provide an alternative option."

JC's brain actually stuttered at *twenty dollars an hour*, but immediately went back online with a sense of wariness. "What?"

Bob tapped the folded résumé. "You cannot legally change your name while on parole, can you?"

"No. Not until ten years *after* parole ends." That was thirteen years from now. Not that they were counting.

"How would you like to change it now?"

JC hesitated. In their experience, fairies were all about fair exchange—or at least, what *they* saw as fair exchange. It was a cultural thing. *You scratch my back, I scratch yours*, except some of them decided to rip out a pound of flesh. They were very similar to humans, in that way, giving as little as possible while taking as much as they could, all while singing "a deal's a deal."

"How?" they asked cautiously.

"Magic is, at its root, the ability to bend reality," Bob lectured. "Minor magic tweaks or nudges it in certain directions. Major magic twists and bends it until it's almost unrecognizable. So long as it doesn't break, we're fine. Wiping out your legal, dead name, and replacing it with your true name would be somewhere in the middle, and cost a fair amount of energy on my end. As such, instead of twenty dollars an hour, I'd put you down to nineteen for the first year of employment. Your other benefits, such as health and dental, would remain untouched. And if you decide to leave before the year is done, I would ask for monetary compensation or some other equivalent."

"You can do that?" JC demanded.

"Yes. Additionally," she continued, "your dead name will be completely erased from existence. No one will remember it, except for you, me, and possibly any other fairies you've told. Not even your parents will remember calling you Richard, or any variation thereof."

"But you would have to know my real name to do this," they realized aloud.

"Yes. Even though Richard Scott is your current legal name, by definition, it is dead. It holds no power over you. Thus, at the moment, you are completely safe from any spells I would cast on you directly."

JC crossed their arms, thinking. Everyone learned as early as preschool to never let a fairy know your true name. It was like giving someone your Social Security number: share that with the wrong person, and they can fuck you up. That was why so many people had one, two, even three middle names, and they were locked down tight, as hard to get as medical records.

They thought of the skin-crawling shudder that went through them every time Mrs. Jackson called them Mr. Scott and all the countless job interviews in the last two months where they'd had to correct the managers—often multiple times in a single thirty-minute interview. All the slimy, condescending smiles and looks of confused disgust. And that was before they got to the arrest record.

Their life was already fucked, so why not add a deal with the purple pixie devil?

"You got a pen?" JC asked.

Boh plucked one from her apron. On the folded back of their résumé, they wrote *Jennifer Charles Maria Frederick Scott*.

"Jennifer Charles is my full first name," they explained. "No hyphen. I want Maria and Frederick to be my middle names, and Scott is my last name. No need to change that one."

"Maria. You have Spanish or Italian ancestry?"

"My grandmother was half Mexican. Did you know that, even if you get out of prison early, if a condition is to stay at a halfway house, you have to pay a hundred bucks? And that's before rent."

"I did not know that," she said. "But I can't stay I'm surprised."

"Well, there was no way I was going to be able to do that. The rest of the family wanted me to keep rotting in prison, damn what the parole board says, but my grandma...she got me out. Pulled some of her life insurance money early to get me to the halfway house and a few months of rent and groceries."

"Quite the gift," Bob said. "Is she still alive?"

JC shook their head. "Heart failure. About a week after release."

A small consolation was the fact that she got to see JC get their white 24-hour chip. She got them a cake that read *Felicidades, Genoveva Carlos*, which is what she called her grandchild when they finally came out as nonbinary, always reverting to Spanish to keep that part of her heritage alive.

"I want to be named after her, at least a little," they said, clearing their throat so their voice came out steady.

Bob's face was immeasurably kind. "Naming yourself after someone is one of the greatest honors you can give them."

JC cleared their throat again. They were not going to break down in a goddamn job interview, even if they had just gotten hired. "So...tomorrow?"

"Tomorrow. Come at ten in the morning; it'll be suitably quiet enough to get you some training."

"Cool. Uh..." They hesitated. "I've been calling you 'Bob' in my head. You got a different name people use?"

She chuckled. "Most everyone calls me Violet, but Bob works well enough."

§

JC was at Walmart when it happened.

They stood in the freezer aisle, frowning at the price of the frozen meals. They had ten dollars and twenty-three cents to stretch until their first payday, all of it SNAP. There was nothing else in their bank account. (Which meant they couldn't restock their cigarettes until payday, either, unless they bummed off someone else.) The frozen pizzas were bigger and would last for several meals, but the crust was made of cardboard. They could probably make a pizza from scratch, but that would cost a few extra dollars, and there was no guarantee they could actually pull it off. Alternatively, if they got a couple bags of frozen vegetables and some boxes of pasta, they could make a veggie dish that lasted about a week...

There was no way to describe it, other than the feeling of the air popping around them, and they could have sworn they heard an echo of Violet's voice, whispering their full name from three towns away.

JC jolted. The old man examining the chicken pot pies gave them an odd look before going back to ignoring them.

For some reason, JC instinctively reached for their wallet. They didn't have a driver's license. Driver's ed had been too expensive, to say nothing of a car. But one of the first things they'd done out of prison—in that hazy, surreal week—was get a state ID.

The photo was the same: bushy brown hair that had been chin-length then and now reached for their shoulders; a lack of beard showing off the gaunt cheeks and bags under their eyes because they'd just gone through withdrawal again; and either their health had been in the gutter at that time or the lighting was really bad in that office, because their skin was *pasty* white.

State of Minnesota. Residential address in St. Paul. Still a donor in case they got splattered on the sidewalk. But something had changed.

The most obvious was the name: *Scott, Jennifer Charles* was boldly typed in the middle of the card as if it'd always been there.

Violet had even changed the sex from M to X, which JC hadn't thought of.

No middle name. Those were too risky to put on IDs. They were only on birth certificates and Social Security cards, and JC would bet that those had been changed, too.

That old man probably thought it very odd that a fellow customer was crying in the frozen foods aisle. Even odder that they were smiling.

JC could not wait to go into work tomorrow.

tall metal teeth

The Mortal Realm reeked. Red Wolf had only been here an hour, and already he choked on the stench of mechanical fumes and human filth. Why the humans in the Fae Realm were so annoyed to have missed out on *this* was beyond him. It seemed to get worse every time he was forced to visit.

It used to be that Fae portals were near impossible to find and were controlled exclusively by the Fae. Now, the humans had built "airports" around them, as large as a palace and nowhere near as grand. While some portals remained hidden–especially those that spontaneously appeared or disappeared due to chaotic magic–they were increasingly hard to find and riskier to use.

At least this horrid "airport" was easy to navigate, and Red Wolf's party had found their human contact–Steven–waiting for them outside with a shuttle just barely large enough for them all.

"Eyyyy, you must be the wolf-man," Steven greeted. Red Wolf had rarely paid attention to mortal fashion, and apparently neither had Steven. The tank top was too tight and the coat far too big. So impractical, especially at the start of summer.

"You may call me Red Wolf," he said, adjusting the crimson cloak that he had glamoured into a jacket to better blend in, but still be identified by his mortal host. As a matter of fact, all of his six fairies had glamoured themselves to look like humans, though none of them liked it.

"Well, let's get you going," Steven said, ushering them all into the small bus, gray exhaust puffing out of the pipe in the rear and tickling the back of Red Wolf's throat. "Boss is gonna wanna double-check with you guys, get you all sorted out."

"And Michelle? My understanding was we would be working primarily through her."

"You will, you will," Steven promised. "But it's the Wolverines that's housing y'all, making sure you got everything you need. Michelle's not from around here, but we are."

One of Red Wolf's two lieutenants—Piper—raised an eyebrow and casually drifted his hand toward his coat pocket, where his pipes were hidden. Red Wolf shook his head.

"Careful with those," he said in Fae, ignoring Steven's frown at the foreign language. "They're outlawed in this Realm."

Piper pouted. "Poo. No fun."

"You'll have plenty in due time."

The fairies got their belongings and themselves on the shuttle, dropping their glamour as soon as the doors closed. All of them were bright spots of color, leaving Steven looking bland and earthy in comparison. Red Wolf himself had originally been nicknamed Harvest Moon, not just for the time of his birth but because his skin was a mass of orange, brown, deep green, and even some red, the colors of harvest. Even without that, he tended to draw attention to himself, being over six feet tall and well-toned after centuries of combat.

Red Wolf's first lieutenant—Black Dove—huffed as she took her seat, her plain summer dress melting into its true form of sorcerer's robes. They were ivory, offsetting her pitch-black skin with beautiful silver marbling curling up her neck and left cheek, as well as the back of her head, which she kept shaved to show it off. "We could just fly there."

"The less attention we draw to ourselves, the better," Red Wolf reminded her, still speaking Fae. "And I don't want anyone seeing your wands." Fairy wands were largely outlawed in the Mortal Realm, and while Black Dove was trained to glamour herself into any creature imaginable, doing it to others would require either their true name, a piece of their body (plus that of the animal they were transforming into, such as a cat skull or bear claw), or a druidic wand—which she did have, tucked deep in the pockets of her ivory robes.

Steven adjusted his oversized coat. "So, what brings you to Earth? Boss was skimpy with the details."

Red Wolf flickered his gaze from Steven to the mortal driving the bus.

"Don't worry about Carl; he's with us," the mortal assured him. "Aren't you, Carl?"

The driver snorted. "You don't even want to know the shit I've carried in this thing."

Steven held up his hands in a *See?* gesture.

Red Wolf glanced out the window, a forest of concrete and metal passing by. "I'm here for justice. Someone here dealt centuries worth of pain to me, my people, and my Realm, and thought she could walk away."

The last two centuries had been nothing but frustration as Red Wolf had used up every favor, every ally he had, to try to get this mission approved. He should have been in the Mortal Realm at the head of an army, not a mere half-dozen fairies willing to risk a traitor's fate for this.

Ah, well. If there was one thing immortals had in spades, it was time.

Steven snorted. "Putting out a hit's too easy?"

"If you're implying assassination, fairies don't do that," Red Wolf scolded. "We're not barbarians."

Steven held up his hands. "Aight. Your money."

The rest of the drive was largely silent, and mercifully short. Steven's people awaited them in a bar, grimy and built low to the ground, utterly unimpressive compared to the tall metal teeth of the city beyond.

Black Dove stayed with the others. Red Wolf picked up his small suitcase as he and Piper followed Steven inside, casting their glamour as they did to pass as human. Piper's unusually pale, yellow skin—with flecks of a darker wheat color swirling along his arms and fingers—darkened to mortal peach. His hair—already earthy brown—remained unchanged. Both of their pointed ears became small and round, and Red Wolf's swirl of green and orange and brown over his skin became boring peach. His long dark hair was shortened to match those of the male humans around him.

The inside of the bar was just as grimy as the outside. Nobody had deep-cleaned it in ages. Something smelled sour and borderline rotten. Besides the bartender, there were only three men, all about Steven's age, sitting at a table in the center of the room, nursing beers. They were a trio of jeans, T-shirts, and baggy jackets, despite the summer heat, all reeking of tobacco smoke and gunpowder. Red Wolf quickly picked out their leader, Lance, despite having never seen him before. Leaders carried themselves with much more confidence and assurance, while their followers typically tried to copy their behavior.

"Yo, Boss, I picked 'em up," Steven announced unnecessarily.

Lance barely looked up from his cards. "You got it?"

"Are all mortals this rude?" Red Wolf huffed. "Most people would offer at least a greeting."

"Figured you wanted to save time."

"Time is rarely an issue." He dropped the suitcase on the table.

Lance motioned for one of his men to look. He unzipped it, revealing dozens of packets of marmair seeds—seeds being much easier to slip through security than the actual flowers.

"These'll grow?" Lance asked.

"Assuming you plant them in good soil, give them plenty of sunlight, and water them regularly, they'll grow," Red Wolf promised.

"They're not tampered or spelled, are they?"

"No."

He grunted. "How long you staying?"

"At least a month, possibly two," he answered. "We'll need escape routes in case our original way out is blocked, law officers to bribe, and a secluded place out of the way where no one asks questions."

"That'll be the Loon. It's a motel run by my brother. Michelle's already there," Lance said. "Don't poke your nose in other people's business, and they'll do the same to you."

Red Wolf memorized that bit of advice as he and Piper left. As much as he wanted to minimize his time in this blasted Realm, they had to take their time. Be patient. Make all necessary preparations.

One did not kidnap the Iron Witch on a whim.

plant the rest

Steven's apartment was a shitty studio in the Midway that he shared with his girlfriend, who was out working a double at McDonald's. He pulled a Coke from the fridge, tapping his knuckles against the ultrasound photo they'd taped to the freezer. He scrolled through his phone, grimacing at his mother's text. *Your dad's heart meds are $220 this month.*

He checked his account, winced, and texted back, *I can venmo 50?*

Thank you, sweetie.

That handled, he called the number saved only as "Swan."

The detective's harsh voice answered: "This is Swanson."

"It's Steven, checking in. With some tea," he said, dropping on the couch with a sigh. It creaked dangerously but held him up. "Those fairies that Lance was so excited about? They showed up today."

The fairies had been a mystery to both Steven and the police for the last several weeks, ever since Lance had mentioned bringing them in for a deal. Unfortunately, his boss was smart enough not to tell anyone who those fairies were, what they wanted, or what they were bringing until the day of.

"And? What happened?" Swanson demanded.

"The jicks came with a suitcase full of marmair seeds. Enough for a whole damn farm. Lance handed them off for safekeeping, probably going to sell some and plant the rest." Where exactly the gang leader intended to plant those illegal seeds was a mystery. He'd probably recruit a few dozen people to do it for him in smaller plots, harder for the police to catch and no big loss if they did.

"And what did these fairies get in return?"

"Protection, I think? Guidance. Resources. They're in town for a while, not sure what for. But I overheard them talking and know a bit of Fae. They have wands."

"What kind?"

"No idea."

Swanson swore. Steven took a swig of pop. "Are you going to arrest them or what?"

"We might have enough on Lance to get a warrant—if we can find out where he stashed those seeds. It's the fairies that worry me. Keep an eye on them, as close as you can get."

Steven sighed and hung up. This was going to be a long few weeks.

the defector

An excerpt from *Round-Ears: A History of
Gialdon and Humans in the Fae Realm*

Exactly when and why the Violet Princess decided
to defect to the Gialdons' side is a matter of furious scholarly debate.

In the thousands of books, plays, movies, songs, and
shows that include her, many put forward the idea that
she fell in love with a mortal who died a tragic death, either before or during the Gialdonian War. Unfortunately
for the romantics, there is zero evidence of this.

Fairies—especially high-ranked fairies—did often take mortal lovers. Different cultures had different views of this, with Comhvi seeing it akin to bestiality even today. Ivae, on the other hand, saw such [inter-species] relations as shameful but inevitable, even helpful. While most mortal serfs were forced into military service, a significant minority were trained and used as sex slaves for the Fae elite. The kitrye who were a natural result of such unions were either invited into the lower tiers of Fae society (if they were immortal) or relegated to serf-dom (if they were mortal).

There is very little evidence that the Violet Princess indulged in this type of behavior. In fact, she forbade the use of sex slaves in her army as soon as she had the author-ity to do so—one of her most controversial moves, accord-ing to contemporary sources. This was largely unenforce-able, but it was widely known that anyone who indulged in [sex slaves] would never be promoted in the Violet Princess's army, no matter what strings they pulled. This is one of the earliest indications of her changing views.

Most scholars agree that her path to defection was likely a gradual process, brought on or at least exacerbated by her insistence of fighting on her soldiers' level. She would have seen their conditions, heard their stories, and empa-thized with them more deeply than others of her rank, even-tually realizing that the "necessary evil" of capturing mor-tals for Fae needs was only as "necessary" as Fae selfishness.

Still, when she did finally act, everyone was shocked

Pictured a Riadan wood carving depicting the two main characters from the classic Fae tragedy The Fairy and the Serf, where a Fae and human fall in love. When the characters' illicit relationship is discovered, the serf is sent to battle where he's killed, while the fairy is exiled from her homeland and spends the following centuries wandering the Realm, searching for her lover's bones..

yellow mud exodus

Red Wolf could not say for certain when Violet decided to betray her people, what pushed her to make that fatal decision. She never told him the exact moment. But if he had to hazard a guess, he'd probably say the Yellow Mud Exodus played a key role.

Fairies weren't as vigilant in tracking time as mortal races, but this was likely about five hundred years ago, when Violet was a Commander, a few decades away from her ultimate promotion to Chief Commander of all of Ivae's forces. At the time, Red Wolf had been one of her captains. They received the report of the latest mass mortal uprising right after his honeymoon.

"Is it too much to ask for a small reprieve to collect myself?" he grumbled, scanning the report a scribe had written for him.

"Yes. If it wasn't, it wouldn't be the military," retorted his wife, Oak, reading over his shoulder. The imposing woman had often said she had giants' blood, and Red Wolf was inclined to believe her. She towered over all other fairies and mortals, especially when she wore her dark green armor. While her whole family utilized trees for their public names, Oak's really did suit her, especially with her gold-green coloring. "Come on. Let's not keep the commander waiting."

The rebellion wasn't much of a rebellion. Several hundred mortals had stolen weapons and even some magical items, such as armor enchanted to withstand any blow. Thankfully, nothing as dangerous as an Elemental or druidic wand had gone missing.

Commander Violet quickly located the rebels' burgeoning supply lines and cut them, sending troops to guard all the places the rebels were likely to try to attack for basic necessities. It was standard procedure, and normally the rebels either risked it all for an attack that crushed them, or Violet starved them out.

These rebels did neither. Instead, they made for the nearest portal to Earth.

"What are they *thinking*?" Commander Violet grumbled, eyeing the reports stacked on her desk in her war tent. As she hadn't fought that day, she was in her usual royal regalia: a deep purple dress and several bits of gold jewelry dripping from her ears, neck, and wrists. "They can't be thinking to go back to Earth. Most of them have been eating Fae food their whole lives. They'll all starve to death within a week. They *know* this!"

"Vi, have you ever known mortals to think clearly when they're desperate?" Oak asked, leaning back in her seat. She and Violet had been friends long before Red Wolf had met either of them, and thus rarely used any of the princess's formal or royal titles in private. Not even Red Wolf could bring himself to be that informal, despite the fact that Violet had been the one to officiate their wedding last month.

The princess gave a deep sigh, then ordered their troops—most of them mortal, yes, but loyal to *her*—to move in on the forest hiding the new wild portal.

"Should we summon more musicians?" Red Wolf asked. Their army only had two, and while this rebellion force was cornered and foolish, the latest estimates put their numbers at well over a hundred.

"I think so," Oak agreed.

Violet's mouth thinned.

"You don't?"

"Mind rot has claimed more serfs than rebellions ever will," the princess said.

"Well, *these* mortals could probably stand relinquishing control of their minds for a little while, if they're not going to use them effectively."

Violet was clearly displeased, but ordered Red Wolf to summon the musicians anyway. One of them was a pale yellow fairy who went by Piper, though he wouldn't be counted among Red Wolf's friends for a while yet.

Portals between the Realms were heavily guarded. But as they were created by magic, there was an element of unpredictability. While many portals were stable (with later centuries even seeing the rise of artificially made and maintained portals), many others appeared and disappeared spontaneously, some lasting only a few hours while others decayed over the course of years. There was an entire branch of divination magic dedicated to predicting the creation and destruction of these wild portals, and a mortal serf by the name of Yellow Mud had gotten his hands on it.

Mud served as part of a minor fairy lord's bodyguard, and this lord dabbled in sorcery and divination. Apparently, Mud had been quietly preparing for a rebellion for a while, slowly gathering followers and stockpiling weapons, until he heard of the latest prediction of a wild portal.

Now, Violet, Red Wolf, Oak, and their army followed them into the woods where this portal was. Red Wolf was no student of magic and always had a hard time identifying it, but Violet spotted it easily and called a halt, pointing out the slight warping of air between two trees, like a heat mirage.

"Kitrye unit only," Violet ordered. "I only have thirty tokens."

As unpredictable as the physical destination was between portals, *time* was another factor. For the most part, time in the Fae Realm and mortal realm passed the same way. But everyone had heard at least one story of a portal's unpredictable magic displacing someone in time, sending them decades if not centuries forward or backward. It was best to be safe with enchanted tokens that served as anchors for the wearer, ensuring that they remained in their own time no matter where they ended up, and could return home without issue.

Violet's tokens—made and enchanted by her own hand, of course—were smooth pieces of wood just larger than Red Wolf's thumb, carved with magical runes. Red Wolf tucked his in his inside pocket, a task somewhat difficult because they were all wearing armor. Despite the fact that his gold-colored chainmail was enchanted to be light as a feather and tougher than diamond, it was still a lot of layers to get through before he found his pocket. Oak had the same problem, grumbling until her token was secured.

"Everyone gather extra food and water rations," Violet ordered. "Any we take back alive will likely need them. They were already starving when they crossed."

Red Wolf grimaced, but did as he was told. Frankly, he thought they should just let the humans die if they wanted to so badly. But perhaps Violet intended to make an example of them, or maybe she wanted to interrogate any survivors. Mud had managed to plan this little venture over the course of years; perhaps he had some allies that they'd missed.

In pairs, the thirty fairies and kitrye walked through the portal. The trees all looked the same, but Red Wolf could tell they were in a different Realm. A different taste in their air, subtle but there. And a slight salty smell. Were they near an ocean?

It was easy enough to find the escapees' trail, despite the fact that it was at least two days' old by Red Wolf's reckoning. Hiding the movements of over a hundred people was difficult, if not impossible, and it would take far more time for the elements to completely erase it.

Since the rebellious mortals had last been spotted in the Fae Realm yesterday, the havoc of time magic on the portal was already at play.

Red Wolf frowned. Mortals—and fairies—couldn't last long without food or water. And the Fae Realm wreaked havoc on mortal bodies. It was their greatest chain, the thing that prevented most uprisings before they started. It took far more than one meal or one sip of water, but eventually mortals would become dependent on Fae food, getting violently ill if they had so much as a bite of food from Earth, or any other Realm. He only knew a handful of mortals who had successfully managed to wean themselves off Fae food, and that was a process that took months if not years.

Had Mud and his followers packed enough? Or would they be too weak to fight back?

The fairies were silent as they made their way through the woods. Some, like Violet and Red Wolf, managed it through training. Others, such as Oak, relied on the enchantment in their boots to silence their steps.

The stench reached them first. One all the soldiers were familiar with. When a person died, their bowels released, and battlefields were ripe with the stench of blood, urine, and feces.

"Be on guard," Violet ordered, following the odor through the woods.

It didn't take long to find the bodies. Wolves, bears, and ravens had already been at them, tearing into flesh that covered the ground like a thick rug. Red Wolf could barely see the ground in the forest clearing, there were so many corpses and stray viscera.

"Was there a battle?" Oak asked, kicking one of the bodies with her boot, disturbing the trio of ravens that had been feasting on it.

Red Wolf and the kitrye spread out, trying to get an idea of what had happened. "I see several slit throats," he called.

"Me, too," one of the kitrye called. "But I don't see anyone *but* the runaways. I think they attacked each other."

Almost all the bodies held bloodied knives, spears, pitchforks, or axes, so that was definitely part of it. But Red Wolf took a closer look, and saw one's throat slit open in the more jagged way that suggested it was self-inflicted.

Those that died of obvious injuries were, somehow, better off than others. He spotted corpses that had no fatal wounds, but their arms were as skinny as twigs, their faces were gaunt, and when Red Wolf lifted one of their shirts he could count all the ribs. None of them were healthy; they all were horrendously skinny. But if was obvious that those who hadn't died of murder or suicide had gone the much slower route of starvation or, more likely, dehydration.

"I found a survivor!"

Red Wolf looked up as Violet jogged toward the kitrye that had called. The survivor was a man with straw-yellow hair and beard, leaning against a tree. He was splattered with blood, but not injured himself, and had the gaunt look of someone on the verge of death.

Violet stopped at his feet. "Yellow Mud."

"Princess," he croaked with chapped lips.

She pulled her canteen free from her belt. "Here. It's water..."

He shook his head, raising a knife to his neck. Red Wolf wondered if he even had the strength to use it, but the intent was clear. "We didn't come here to live."

Violet lowered the canteen and crouched next to him. "You staged an uprising, fought your way to a portal to Earth, only to die?"

He gave a crooked grin, dropping the hand with the knife. "Well, originally we planned on living. We were to get enough food and water to make it at least a month for each person, preferably more. Wean ourselves off the Fae magic and back onto Earth's. But you cut off our supplies and blocked our way."

"Then why not surrender? You may have suffered, but your people would have *lived*."

Violet's frustration was palpable, and Red Wolf could relate. One of a commanding officer's greatest responsibilities was the care and wellbeing of their troops, and a princess's first responsibility was the care and wellbeing of her people. That was the whole point of leadership.

Mud shook his head. "We considered. But we decided we weren't dying in Fae. We weren't dying in bondage."

Violet didn't say anything to that. Mud jerked his chin over to the corpses surrounding him. "Most didn't want to starve to death, so they took matters into their own hands. A few asked me to do it for them. The rest of us decided to enjoy what time in this Realm we had. Make peace with our gods." He huffed. "We tried to bury them, but didn't have the strength."

Red Wolf turned away, disgusted. They had *wanted* this? This death and carnage?

"And have you?" Violet asked, an odd note in her voice. "Made peace?"

Mud sighed, leaning further into the tree. "Yes."

Violet moved in a blur. One moment she was crouched by his feet, the next her sword was in his chest, piercing his heart.

"You should've let him die by his own hand," Oak said.

Violet pulled the sword free, cleaning the blade with a cloth. "It wasn't his own hand."

Red Wolf frowned, not understanding. These people had been well fed and cared for back in the Fae Realm. Plenty of other mortals had had the chance to join their foolish flight and had had the good sense not to do so. Who else could possibly be responsible?

"What shall we do with the bodies?" one of the kitrye asked.

"Leave them," Violet ordered.

On that, Red Wolf agreed. Let the corpses rot in the Realm they had blindly run to.

He largely forgot about the incident after returning to Fae. Oak also rarely mentioned it, and when she did it wasn't with any particular emotion, except perhaps frustration at the way mortal minds worked.

But Violet would become pensive and thoughtful anytime it was brought up. She'd always treated her mortal soldiers well and spent, in Red Wolf's opinion, too much time with them. But after Yellow Mud's Exodus, as the historians called it, she increased her care and outreach. She'd always put down mortal rebellions out of duty, but after that, when another uprising started that she had to end, she would wear a pinched expression when she thought no one was looking, one that became more haunted over time.

Red Wolf eventually realized that Yellow Mud's Exodus was the rock that had caused the avalanche. The handful of snow that had grown and grown on its tumble down the mountain, until it crushed everything in its path. But by then, it was far too late.

snapped down the middle

Violet settled on the couch with a sigh, ignoring the mayoral candidates bickering on screen. Changing Jennifer Charles's name had been exhausting, especially in today's age with the paper and digital footprints. She'd slept for at least three hours immediately after casting the spell and *still* felt drained. Turning them into a dragon would've been easier.

I must be out of practice, she grumbled to herself, lying back on the deep blue couch. It didn't help that she'd done the spell after a full shift. As much as she enjoyed her position, it was nice to come back home to her full bookshelves, purple and cream halls, and soft furniture. Blue was busy in the kitchen, the rich smell of tomato sauce and pasta indicating that dinner was almost ready.

She reached for her phone. As had become her habit since the internet was invented, she did a basic search on Gialdonian news.

Though the United States traded regularly with the Fae Realm, Gialdon was their only reliable ally. As Violet had feared, most of the Fae nations looked down on the mortal country even today, both out of anger for humiliating them in war, and because of the millennia of "we're better than you" rhetoric that had been spoon-fed to all Fae creatures—especially fairies—since they made contact with humanity.

But Gialdon was stubborn, just like its people. It survived, despite everyone else's attempts at strangling them—and, with the modern age, even managed to thrive.

New Senators elected...some good-looking policies in the works...oh, no, they refused to pass that farmers' pay act, that's going to cause problems...of course Ivae refuses to give them any All-Heal, even with all that extra income...oh, good, they're powering those new factories with solar and wind; perhaps this Realm can take the hint and follow suit...

She scrolled for a while, mostly pleased. No nation was free of sin, but Gialdon had managed to keep theirs manageable for the last 200 years, and it continued to be a safe haven for those of mortal blood—and even those without—in the Fae Realm.

"Anything juicy?" Blue asked, bringing her a bowl of spaghetti. Neither of them was a terrific cook, but modern food packaging certainly made it easier. And tastier.

Violet sat up, both of them sitting cross-legged on the couch, and happily dug in. "No assassinations, no wars, only a couple of sex scandals but everyone was a consenting adult..."

"Bo*ring*," he sing-songed, even as he smiled. His indigo hair clung to his skull after so long under a hat, and his t-shirt was so worn that Violet could barely guess the original design. "You ever think about going back?"

"A few times," she admitted. "But they haven't revoked the exile."

"All the people who exiled you are dead. Time heals all wounds, and all that jazz."

She shook her head. "Not enough time. And while Gialdon might allow me back on their soil, I can't imagine Ivae or any of the other immortal nations would be pleased with them. Much better to keep that hornets' nest unkicked. Besides, I am quite happy here. A visit would be nice, but it's not mandatory."

He shrugged. She set down her phone. "Why? Did you wish to return?"

"Eh..." He swallowed a mouthful of pasta and red sauce. "More out of curiosity than anything."

She finished her own mouthful, studying the boy that she had raised into a man. By Fae standards, he'd hadn't even been an adult for a decade. She'd done her best to keep him in touch with his Fae heritage, but he was very much a product of Earth.

It wasn't a bad thing. But still...

"You should," she encouraged. "*You* weren't banished, after all. I doubt the history books even make mention of you."

"Hey!"

Violet laughed as Blue kicked her leg, not nearly hard enough to send her off the couch.

"Nah," he said, slurping more spaghetti. He hunched over the bowl to reduce the speckles of red sauce that would land on the couch and carpet. "Someday, yeah, I'd like to pop in, take some tourist selfies, eat too much of the food. Tell the kids how much easier they have it and that, back in the day, we had to go to and from those battles uphill, in the snow, both ways..."

"We? What's this *we* nonsense? I was the one doing all the fighting," she teased.

"And I helped clean your armor—including the iron parts!—which was a battle itself," he argued. "Also, I stabbed that guy in the leg that one time."

"You grazed him."

"I was barely a century old!"

"I've seen more damage from papercuts."

"Ouch!"

She grinned, biting into her dinner.

"Seriously, though? No desire to go back?" he asked.

She shook her head. "My home is here now."

"Your family...?" he tried.

Another shake. "Even before the war, my blood relatives were...complicated."

"A piping hot mess?" he translated.

"Very much so."

He shrugged. "Fair enough. If they still haven't tried contacting you, then they can jump off a—"

A knock at the front door interrupted him.

They shared a confused look. Setting down her bowl, Violet answered the door.

"Caroline. Andy. What's wrong?" she asked, letting them in.

"'Evening, Miss Violet. Blue. Hope we weren't interruptin' anything," said Bernier Fire Chief Andrew "call me Andy" Moore, scraping the mud from his boots. His head had been gray and balding since he and his wife moved up from Mississippi. He usually covered it with a highlighter-yellow baseball cap, the logo of the town's volunteer fire department worn and beaten. Given the mud stains on the cargo pants, he'd just come back from a shift. Despite being chief of his fellow volunteers and his advanced age, he refused to stay behind a desk.

His wife Caroline followed him in. Her long, gray hair was kept back in a ponytail, and she always had a handmade scarf wrapped around her neck, no matter the weather. Tonight's was warm orange with a cream trim. Her skill with a crochet hook was matched by few Violet had ever met, which was why she ran Yarn Granny's Shop on Main Street, just half a block away from CaFae Latte.

"Coffee? Tea? Grape juice?" Blue offered, joining them with his half-eaten dinner in hand.

"Way too late for coffee, son," Andy said, even though the fairy had two centuries on him. "I'll take a Pepsi if you got it; otherwise, water."

"Iced tea, please," Caroline asked.

Violet led them into the kitchen, collecting her own dinner on the way. "Long shift?"

"Ugh. You've no idea," Andy grumbled. "Idiot got 'nto a car crash, tried to speed off 'n ended up hittin' 'nother car. 'Course he was drunk. And then, after we'd taped off the scene and had the police leadin' people around, 'nother idiot drives right through, clippin' one of my boys in the leg!"

"Is he all right?" Violet asked, leaning against the kitchen island.

"We think so. Took 'im to the hospital so he don't have to pay for an ambulance. Doctors're lookin' him over, but it don't look like he broke anything. He'll be back up in no time."

"I'm still makin' 'im and his family a casserole," Caroline declared. "One less thing for 'em to worry about."

"Can we get a casserole?" Blue asked hopefully, setting the drinks on the island in the center of the kitchen. "'Cause we've been stressed and worried, too. There's this pigeon that lives on top of the game store that I swear is out to get me..."

"Not today, baby," Caroline giggled.

"Rats."

"As much as we love your company, you two don't typically call on us this late," Violet said, nudging the conversation along. It was rude to eat in front of guests that had not been fed, even if it meant letting her dinner go cold. Blue had no reservations and slurped more spaghetti.

"Ah, yes. We came 'cause of this." Andy pulled a bracelet out of his cargo pants and set it on the island.

Violet took the medical alert bracelet. Andy's, declaring him allergic to peanuts and a couple of medications. She recognized it well. The old protective runes on the back were as sharp as the day she'd engraved them, but the bracelet had been snapped down the middle. Not the clasp, not any of the chains, the flat part with the engravings.

"Isn't that the one you enchanted?" Blue asked between bites.

"It is. It had another three years of life, unless I've completely lost track of time," she said.

"That's why were confused," Caroline said. "We thought to bring it to you right away."

Neither of them was angry, although Caroline's anxiety betrayed her with a tap of her clumsily-painted nails against her glass. (She and her grandchild must have had a "spa day" earlier.) Violet didn't blame her. Caroline was the one who had made the fairy deal in the first place, approaching Violet to ask for magical protection for her husband. "I love 'im 'n trust 'im 'n I know the chances of 'im gettin' killed are slim," she'd said, "but I'd sure sleep a lot better at night if I knew there was a little extra insurance."

Violet had agreed. If she'd had Andy's full name, she could have blessed his entire being. A bit of his hair, nails, or blood would have also been effective. Neither had been comfortable with those options, so she'd suggested a third alternative: enchanting a piece of jewelry. Preferably something metal, like her own bracelet or Blue's little black ring, as that had less chance of getting accidentally destroyed. Andy had offered his medical alert bracelet, since he never took it off.

"A charm like this breaking early means one of two things," she lectured. "Either someone purposefully destroyed it..."

Andy shook his head. "No, ma'am. It just fell right off."

"Then that means the magic was used up," she said. "I did intend for this to last seven years. But if something happened recently that required a large burst of luck, then that would've used it up immediately, rather than...rationing it out, for lack of a better term."

Andy winced. Caroline took a deep, steadying breath and gave him a stern look. "Andrew. How close did that speedin' car get to you?"

"...close," he admitted.

"And the bracelet fell off immediately after," Violet guessed.

He nodded. "Only reason I weren't standin' two feet to the left was 'cause the new girl had a question. Went over to talk to 'er, 'n then two seconds later..."

"Yikes," Blue said, as Caroline clutched her husband's free hand. "Did you get the guy's plate number? You can probably sue or something."

"Oh, don't worry 'bout that. Hendricks is already on it," Andy said with a smirk, regaining a bit of his swagger. "Well, I guess we can't complain 'bout 'broken goods,' seein' as it did exactly what it was supposed to."

"I would like to get another," Caroline said. "Same deal as last time?"

Violet considered. "Actually, I have a counter-offer."

the force of magic

Jennifer Charles arrived on their first day of work five minutes early, slightly sweaty in khakis and a jean jacket, with a
nonbinary pin in pride of place. Violet approved. She wanted
her new employee to feel safe in her domain.

The morning rush had been as chaotic as usual, leaving a
mess to clean up before lunch. So she cleaned the tables while
sending her ward to greet their new baker. Blue tossed an apron
at JC's face as soon as they stepped inside. They hadn't even put
it on before he smooshed a matching cap on their bushy brown
head. "We've got a broom closet where you can stash your jacket.
Or you can wear it; it looks cool."

"I'm always cold," JC explained, adjusting the new uniform.

Violet frowned over the table with a pesky coffee stain. JC
was skinny—a fact that she'd noted on their first meeting—but
seemed particularly pale today. "Are you feeling well? We can
postpone your first day."

They shook their head. "Just diabetic. Walmart insulin is
basically water."

Ah. "Well, the health insurance should kick in at the start
of next month. If they try to deny better insulin, let me know
and I'll sort it out."

"Don't healthcare CEOs keep their full names under lock
and key so fairies and witches can't curse them?"

"I have other ways." It'd take time, but it was perfectly doable.

Blue grinned. "Come on, I'll show you around. There's not
much." He patted a bowl of plastic and paper cards behind the
counter as they moved. "We got nametags that you can swap
out whenever."

He'd already been in them. Today his nametag read, *Call me Ishmael.* JC pointed to it. "No 'Luke, I am your father'?"

"That was last week. I've also done 'Bond, James Bond,' 'Isildur's Heir,' 'Harry Blackstone Copperfield Dresden'..."

"I only understood one of those." They hastily scribbled *JC* onto a tag and clipped it to their apron.

"You ever work in a café?" asked Blue.

"No, but I'm a quick learner."

"Not much to it. I know Boss wants you mostly as a baker but, when we get crushed, we'll want all hands on deck. I'll show you some basics..."

He showed them how to steam milk, get espresso, where all the different ingredients and flavors were stored, where to find the most important buttons on the register, and other essentials while Violet finished cleaning and restocking, bouncing between that and the handful of customers that trickled in over the next hour.

Behind her, Blue showed JC their new territory: the kitchen. There were two ovens, one stove, two refrigerators, a walk-in freezer, and a pantry.

"It's so shiny," JC breathed. The only reason Violet heard them at all from the other room was because of her sharp Fae hearing.

"We just renovated the place," Blue explained. "I tried baking something after the last guy quit. Ended up cleaning the oven for two hours after."

Violet bit back a shudder at the memory just as a couple of friendly faces walked in. "Andy, Caroline, good timing."

"'Afternoon, Miss Violet," Andy called.

"Where's Blue?" Caroline asked.

"He's training the newest employee," Violet said.

At the same time, in the kitchen, JC said, "I'll have to ask the boss what exactly she wants me to make, because I can whip up anything with what you've got."

"Cupcakes?" Blue asked hopefully.

"No. Cupcakes don't go with coffee. *Muffins* go with coffee."

"They're the same thing," he insisted, loud enough that Andy and Caroline could hear, their necks straining to catch a glimpse of the drama.

"They are not!" JC defended.

"Muffins are just bald cupcakes!"

"You take the heresy right out of this kitchen, young man!"

"No! Stop body-shaming the bald cupcakes!"

"Chil-dren," Violet called from the front.

Both JC and Blue poked out their heads. "Yes, ma'am?" JC called back.

"They started it," Blue said. JC punched him in the arm, looking annoyed when he didn't even flinch.

"If I could get a little help with the customers?" she said.

Blue brightened when he spotted their guests and tugged on JC's jacket. "This is an easy one."

"The usual, baby," Caroline said as Andy handed over their two travel mugs, both of them looking very amused.

"Dark roast coffee, no room for cream or sugar for him, and a medium roast with about an inch for cream for her," Blue instructed. JC got to work while he bagged a couple of donuts.

"You two in here often?" JC asked, filling the travel mugs, dented and scratched with use. Violet watched the exchange closely. Yes, JC was hired as baker and was expected to stay largely in the back, but they'd need to be able to speak with customers on a regular basis. And that type of skill took a long time to learn if it wasn't intuitive.

"Damn near every day," Andy said, tapping at the register's touchscreen that Violet had turned around. "Don't know if it's magic or just the good coffee beans."

"It might have to do with the fact that your wife owns the shop just down the street," Violet pointed out. "Did you get a new medical alert?"

"Yes, ma'am." Andy pulled a silver bracelet from his wrist and handed it to her.

Violet went to the sink, where she'd stored a metal engraving tool behind the jars of loose-leaf tea, charging in the outlet. The sound it made reminded her of the dentist.

JC finished with the drinks and handed them over. "Whaaaat's going on?"

"Just a little fairy deal," Caroline said slyly.

Andy huffed, but it was with a smile. "We moved up here from Mississippi 'bout four years ago. I was supposed to retire from my time in the military—spent forty years as a firefighter for the Air Force..."

"He made it three days before walkin' up to the fire department," his wife said dryly. "They took one look at 'im and made 'im their chief."

JC barked a laugh.

Andy grumbled something under his breath as Caroline continued: "I told 'im I was fine with it, but we were givin' him some extra protection. I know Andy ain't an idiot, and I pray for his safety every night and do believe in the might and power of our Lord. But it lets me sleep easier at night knowin' he's got a bit of extra protection. So we came right over 'n introduced ourselves like proper Southerners—I'd just bought the little store down the street and was gettin' ready to open my yarn shop, it's called Yarn Granny's if you're ever interested—and asked if the witch of the house'd be willin' to give us a fairy deal."

"As if you needed an excuse to bury 'em in yarn. You were gonna make 'em somethin' anyway," Andy accused.

"Of course I was! It gets cold up here! Their poor fairy ears must get frostbitten all the time!"

"What was the deal?" JC asked.

"She enchanted my medical alert bracelet, just like that," Andy said, motioning to Violet's drill work by the sink. "It was good for seven years, and for each year, Caroline had to whip somethin' up with her knittin' needles 'n crochet hooks."

"See that indigo scarf with the golden sheen she's wearin'?" Caroline said. "I made that. Also made a pair of gloves, a hat, and a shawl for Miss Violet, and Mister Blue got a thick winter scarf, a knit tie, and a hat designed like the Minnesota Vikings, horns 'n braids 'n everythin'. Some of my finest work if I do say so myself."

Violet finished the runes on the metal. The best way she could explain how magic worked was to liken reality to a river. The river flowed naturally in certain directions, depending on terrain and gravity. Magic altered that flow, more magic allowing for greater disruptions. But making those alterations required a combination of two things: the force of magic itself, and a "blueprint."

Fairies were inherently magical. It was a muscle that they could choose to exercise (or, in Blue's case, choose not to, the way most humans chose not to become astrophysicists). Pouring magic into the world was akin to pushing a boulder with those muscles. But as much as fairies liked to think they were unique and superior, the truth was every living being had at least a little magic within them, albeit some more than others: from humans to dragons and angels to demons. It was why, when it came to enchanting other people, the blueprint was so important. They needed access to the inner workings of a person's reality to alter it.

Fairies had traditionally preferred to use the subject's true name as their blueprint. Names had power, after all, their own form of magic. But sometimes that wasn't possible, and both Andy and Caroline weren't comfortable giving theirs up, even to a friend.

The second option was to use a piece of the subject's body: hair, blood, nails. Essentially, anything with their DNA. Whole dissertations had been written about the connection between magic and the science of genetics.

The third option—and by far the easiest—was to enchant a non-sentient object. Runes or words were carved or painted onto it, some sort of language dictating the shape of the magic (creating the tool that would shape the waters of reality), and then that object was given to a person. In Andy's case, Violet was creating a shield. Something that would block the harm that random reality could cause. But there were plenty of other spells for inanimate objects.

Reality shifted around the bracelet, the magic Violet had poured into it gently nudging it in the right direction. It often felt like a strange *pop* of air.

"So, you're getting a renewal?" JC guessed. "Another seven years for another seven pieces of clothing?"

"We switched it up this time," Caroline said proudly. "Seven years in exchange for seven of my recipes, includin' my sweet tea and lemon honeysuckle cake."

Violet returned with the bracelet. Andy was very pleased as he re-clasped it and his wife handed her a folder from her purse. "There they are, darlin'."

"Excellent." Violet skimmed through the papers. "Jennifer Charles is our new baker, so if they have any further questions, I'll refer them to you."

JC made grabby-hands at the folder. "Lemme see! I've gotta know what I'm working with."

Violet surrendered the recipes, JC gleefully going over them. "How unique do you want your stuff to be, Bob? Because I'm seeing a chocolate chip recipe that's almost identical to mine, except I add pistachios..."

"Now there's an interestin' twist," Caroline said, leaning forward on the counter. "Where'd you get that idea?"

"Instagram."

"I'm a Pinterest woman myself. You know I found one for chocolate orange loaf?"

"Chocolate *what*?"

Violet and Andy shared a look before going off to their own business, leaving the two to swap tips and tricks. Yes, Violet had definitely been right in following her instincts, hiring this one.

constellations of old paint

"Hey, JC. Just checking in—whoa."

JC scratched the back of their neck, getting flour in their bushy brown hair. "Yeah...I may have gone overboard."

Blue gaped at the three trays of muffins (holding a dozen each) cooling on the rack, two different trays of cookies, and a tray of dark chocolate coconut bars that were about to chill in the fridge. The smell was divine; the kitchen had been too clean and sterile when they'd come in, beautiful but not yet lived-in. Not that they were complaining. This kitchen was four times bigger than the halfway house's, with sleek, black appliances. They'd never worked with one of those before, only the battered white ones older than their parents with finicky gas stoves. They always had to sweet-talk the ovens into actually cooking anything.

"The muffins just came out of the oven, but the cookies should be cooled down enough to try. Everything's vegetarian—which you already know, because you don't even have eggs in the place..."

Eggs apparently didn't count as meat, since they weren't fertilized, so most vegetarians were fine with them. But some people counted it, and they were more expensive than the industrial-sized cans of applesauce JC had found in the pantry, which worked as a binding agent just as well. (Hell, JC could've used vinegar and baking soda, or flaxseed with water if they had to. But that didn't taste as good and messed with the texture. Applesauce and pumpkin puree were almost always the best substitutes for eggs in baking.)

Blue didn't need to be told twice. He scooped up one of the oatmeal chocolate chip cookies and took a big, bold bite. JC tried not to let their nervousness show as he chewed and swallowed.

"Holy shit," he said.

JC breathed out. "Yeah?"

"Holy *shit.*"

"Yeah."

"Do we have to put these in the display? I'm pretty sure you can just keep them in here…"

"Touch another and I'm whacking you with a spatula."

Blue pouted. JC put the cookies on a tray and took them out to Violet for final judgment. She was in the middle of adding "Southern Iced Tea" to the menu. Apparently, Caroline's secret ingredient was baking soda of all things, plus enough sugar to make JC's diabetes fritz just by looking at it. (They still helped themselves to a tiny plastic cup from Violet's first batch. Nice and smooth, not too syrupy, plenty of room for different flavors…it was well worth whatever magic Violet had traded for it.)

The factory-made cookies were in a clear, three-tiered display case on top of the counter. Within five minutes of Violet trying JC's batch, they were completely swapped out. They finished just as the door chimed, signaling another customer coming in and…

Damn, JC thought. *She cute.*

They had always liked their partners big and soft, like cuddly, squishy teddy bears, no matter the gender. This pear-shaped goddess was in a long-sleeved shirt with red-and-black plaid, making her even more cuddly-looking–the old, oversized shirt flecked with constellations of old paint. Her skin was warm brown, the lights giving it gold highlights. Dark locs (JC used to call them "dreadlocks" until someone had told them it was actually not a nice term) escaped from a high bun and curled into her round chin, her gloved fingers tapping a hasty pattern on the shoulder handle of her big black purse.

Why she was wearing gloves and long sleeves in summer, JC had no idea. But they weren't going to question it.

"Hey, Nicole," Blue greeted.

"Hi," she said. She tipped her head to JC. "You're new. I'm Nicole."

JC never understood the phrase "husky voice" until now: surprisingly deep and a bit rough. They liked it.

They gave their most charming smile. "Jennifer Charles. You caught me on my first day. Whether or not any of us will survive, who knows?"

Nicole gave a tiny, minute frown. JC realized she hadn't once made eye contact, and had instead focused on the nonbinary pin on their jean jacket.

Ah, shit. Why are the cute ones either taken or queerphobic bitches?

"Have you run into any trouble?" Nicole asked. "Sometimes customers are rude, but Aunt Violet's good about kicking them out. Or cursing them."

JC paused, absorbing that and re-configuring their assumptions before turning to Violet. "You curse homophobes?"

"I have to slip a cursed item on them, or somehow collect a body part or full name, but yes, sometimes," the fairy said breezily. "If you're going to be rude to my staff or customers, you can be silent for a few years."

"Someone told me to stop stimming one day. I told them no. They whacked my hand with a magazine. Aunt Violet tricked them into wearing a bracelet that cursed them with a year of sensory overload issues," Nicole added.

"Okay, I get sensory overload," JC said, feeling dumb for having to ask. "But what's stimming?"

Nicole moved her finger-tapping from her bag to her own thumb: pinky, ring, middle, pointer, middle, ring, pinky, ring, over and over again. "I'm autistic. Stimming is a physical way to regulate or express emotion, or deal with sensory overload."

"Ohhh." There were a few people who did that back in prison, especially those who couldn't get their meds—which was pretty much all of them. Some of them flapped their hands or tapped their legs or wiggled their fingers, and the guards always came down on them for "disruptive behavior." They were usually targets for anyone else looking for a fight, too, but most of them could throw a mean hook right back.

They turned back to Violet. "You only cursed them for a year?"

Violet gave a tiny smirk. "Magic takes energy. I try not to waste it."

"Fair point. A-ny-way, what can I get for you, beautiful?" JC internally cringed at themself, but Nicole let it slide.

Turned out, she just wanted a hot chocolate with nutmeg. And she frankly told JC that she got it every time she came in, which was almost every day, with whole milk and no whipped cream. Blue had JC prepare it, watching them as they carefully steamed the milk on their own for the first time. The hot cocoa itself wasn't Hershey's syrup like most places, but an in-house blend of sugar, cinnamon, a pinch of salt, and Ghirardelli cocoa—that was the good shit.

"Auntie, I saw something," Nicole said, digging through her purse.

"We all become billionaires?" Blue asked hopefully.

"No. Blood and danger."

"Aw, it's never billionaires."

JC frowned as they stirred the chocolate into the milk. Nicole pulled out a sketchbook and zipped through it, showing the pages to Violet (who was apparently her aunt?). "I don't know what it is. I keep seeing wolves, but I don't think it actually has anything to *do* with wolves. Or werewolves."

Violet hummed, flipping a page. JC finished with the drink and put it on the counter, using the excuse to look over Violet's shoulder.

Each page was filled with angry, rough sketches. They were like snapshots: a pair of chained hands, a small black book, a wolf with some sort of black bird on its shoulder...mostly wolves, actually. Lots of them.

Violet turned another page, and JC choked. They snatched the sketchbook, staring at a very good, very detailed pencil drawing of their own face and torso. Down to the jean jacket and flour in their hair.

They stared at the portrait, then at Nicole—who was calmly sipping her hot chocolate—then back at the portrait. "...okay. How? But also, why? But more importantly, *how?*"

"I'm a clairvoyant witch," Nicole said blandly. "I can see into the future. It's rarely clear; I only get fragments and images, sometimes literal, other times figurative. You've been popping up the last few days."

"...okay." They closed the sketchbook and gave it back. "It's...uh...really good."

"Thanks. I'm a freelance artist, and I also teach at the academy during the school season. Mostly, I make abstract portraits, like those two."

She pointed to two paintings hanging from the walls. One was a violent splash of bright purple, lavender, and gold that glowed against a black background. The colors looked like real liquid, which was impressive. The other was much lighter and oddly more light-hearted, with sky blue and gray-white playing over an indigo background.

Wait a minute...

"Oh, it's you two," JC realized, matching the colors with the two fairies' skin tones. "Those are really cool. And a lot less freaky than seeing my own face in the bag of a total stranger."

"Sorry," Nicole said. "But I know something bad is going to happen soon. I just don't know what."

Violet sighed, suddenly looking tired. "I suppose we have had quite a good streak of peace and quiet."

"Yeah, it's been what, fifty, sixty years since I got to stab someone?" Blue guessed, pouring himself a coffee. "I'm out of practice."

JC frowned. "When or why did you...you know what, I don't want to know."

"The '60s were a wild time."

"We appreciate the warning, Nicole. We'll stay on guard. Jennifer Charles, come here." Violet pointed out the hot chocolate button on the register. "And then be sure to hit the sale button before giving them the total. That'll calculate the tax."

"You got it, Bob."

Blue choked on his coffee. "Wait, *what* did you call her?"

JC shrugged. "The only real skill I picked up in prison was dishing out nicknames."

Nicole tipped her head. *Ah, shit, shouldn't have said the prison bit in front of her,* JC realized. But then Nicole asked, "I'm not good with expressions, people, or names, but shouldn't she get something a bit more...regal?"

"Nope," JC said cheerfully, relieved that the goddess in front of them wasn't freaked out by the prison comment. "I have no idea what an 'Ishmael' is, so I need to figure out something else for Blue."

"You haven't read *Moby Dick*?" he demanded.

"Ew. No. Why?"

"Don't," Nicole advised. "It's a 600-page novel that should've been 300, maximum. Also, it's full of racism."

"That...okay, yeah, you've got a point on the racism," Blue said, flagging a bit. "But everything else about it is incredible!"

Violet made a face. "I felt that I ought to have been compensated for my time after reading it."

He threw up his hands. "Whatever. I wanna be Cyrus. That 'Flowers' song slaps."

"I should name you 'Dork.'" JC picked up a pen, uncapped it, and tapped it to each of his shoulders like a knight. "But I shall dub thee Cyrus."

He whooped. Nicole and Violet shared a long-suffering look.

knock-off insulin

JC bit back a grin as Mrs. Jackson frowned at her tablet screen. Then her paperwork. The tablet again. Then, finally, at JC.

"What?" they asked innocently.

She tapped the paper. "This isn't your name."

"Isn't it?"

"It certainly wasn't last week."

"Weird. Does it match with the birth certificate and everything else?"

"Yes," she said at length. "That's what's so confusing."

"Well, then what is my legal name?"

"It certainly can't be Jennifer Charles. It was...your name was..." Her brow wrinkled. "I know it was *something*..."

JC bit their lip to keep from smiling.

Brandon scratched the top of his bald head. "JC..."

Mrs. Jackson sighed. "You made a deal with a fairy, didn't you?"

"Part of the employment plan," they cheered.

"This cannot be legal."

"Why not? All the paperwork's in order, isn't it? Nothing's fake or forged. And it's not like I'm screwing with my history. All the arrests and jailtime are just under my actual name."

Mrs. Jackson seemed to consider that for a moment. Brandon huffed. "Trying to get this before a judge would be both difficult and a waste of time. What's the point if literally no one on the planet remembers their deadname?"

She sighed and adjusted her glasses. "Fine, then, Mr. Sc–er, JC, how has your first week of employment gone?"

§

"Let's keep the fairy deals to a minimum in the future, all right?" Brandon said, after Mrs. Jackson had left.

JC nodded, heading into the kitchen to wash their hands. The dishes were stacking up, and so was the trash. "Yeah, I'm not rolling those dice twice."

Hands clean, they dug their glucose monitor out of their pocket, a cheap little thing bought second-hand that looked like an oversized Tamagotchi. They stuck a fresh testing strip into the top and pricked their finger, waiting for the clunky tech to calculate their blood sugar. It took a few seconds, and when it was done, they winced at the number. "I need insulin."

Brandon grunted and went to get it. JC's insulin was kept in a back corner of the fridge, but the needles were locked down tight in a safe in the office down the hall, a fact that Brandon had bitched about more than once, usually muttering, "I'm not trained in this shit," as he measured whatever dose of medicine he needed to give. He'd even submitted formal complaints about the lack of training a few times, but never got any answers. JC had had to walk him through how to do the insulin injection the first few times, since residents weren't allowed to handle any needles. He tossed JC the bag of alcohol wipes, clearly watching out of the corner of his eye as they wiped down their side. JC had never been desperate enough for booze to try to wring the alcohol out of the medical wipes, but they'd heard stories.

"By the way, it's your turn for dishes today," Brandon said, jabbing them in the side as they held up their shirt.

JC grimaced, and not just as the feeling of burning liquid spreading from the injection site after Brandon plunged the needle. They loved baking but hated cleaning up the mess after. "Who's on dust duty?"

"Alku."

"Awesome." Death staved off for another few hours, JC went into the basement. Half of the level was dedicated to storage, but the other had been cleared out years ago by a resident—now long gone, though JC didn't know if they were properly out or back in prison.

The space was an in-home gym, with a stack of weights, jump ropes, and one of those big exercise balls, all of it bought second-hand. No matter how many times the space got sprayed down with air freshener, there was always an underlying stench of sweat and cold stone.

Alku was right where JC had thought they'd be, using the twenty-pound weights. The goblin wasn't higher than JC's belly button, even with the horns curling out of his head, but he was built like a dark green tank. He went on early morning runs every chance he could—which was every day Elizabeth wasn't on the staff roster. That old spoilsport didn't think that was an acceptable "recreational activity" and denied it every time, telling him to exercise in the house.

"'Sup, kid," Alku greeted.

JC rolled their eyes. All the other residents were older than them, with Alku being in his forties. But nobody *treated* them like a kid, so they let it slide.

"Where are the five-pounders?" they asked, shedding their jean jacket. Might as well get some exercise done while they were down here.

Alku tipped his chin toward the rack, and JC got started, ignoring the slight nausea they always got from the knock-off insulin slithering through their system. Working out meant their diabetes was kept under better control, which meant fewer jabs. Also, they were tired of being a tiny twink. They deserved a himbo (thembo?) body, dammit, even if they'd never get taller than 5'6".

"Is your ex letting you see your son?" they asked.

He sighed. "Not this weekend. 'Something came up.'"

"Whaaat? Again?"

"I know. Shocking," he said with a humorless laugh.

JC shook their head, focusing on the weights. Alku had been in and out of prison for over a decade, for multiple counts of B&E, armed robbery, drug possession, drug selling, illegal possession of a weapon, pretty much everything short of rape and murder. He'd been in the halfway house for twice as long as JC, worked at a warehouse, and sent most of his paycheck to his ex-girlfriend and kid. In all those months, he had only been able to see his son twice.

"He's got a birthday party next month, though," he said. "His grandparents are coming, aunts and uncles, too, so she's not going to be able to keep me from that. Brandon's already approved it, too."

"Nice!"

"Yeah. I'm in charge of the cake. I'll have to get something at Walmart."

JC snorted, setting down the weights. "Screw that. What does the kid like?"

Alku paused. "What?"

"Chocolate? Vanilla? He a strawberry kid?"

"You want to bake my son's cake?"

They shrugged, heat creeping up their face. "Well, I was hoping to convince you to swap chores with me this week..."

"Brandon got you on dish duty?"

"Ugh. Yeah."

Alku laughed, slapping JC on the shoulder. "All right. We'll swap. We're not picky on cake flavors, just make enough for at least a dozen people. And see if you can make the frosting green; it's his favorite color."

"Done."

He smiled. "Thanks, JC. You're good people."

They shrugged, uncomfortable. "Just trying not to be a bad one."

§

Like most food service joints, CaFae Latte paid biweekly. Except for cash tips: those got paid out immediately after every shift, evenly split between the three of them. That kept JC from going hungry until their first actual paycheck, which they were shocked to see was in the quadruple digits, even after taxes. They double-checked the math to make sure it wasn't a mistake.

They had to wait until insurance kicked in to get a proper insulin pump so they wouldn't constantly stick themselves in the gut, but after paying their bills (all of them on time, even!) they were able to get *actual* insulin, not the knock-off crap.

And groceries! Getting as much fresh food as they wanted without having to worry about budgets or whether they were staying within SNAP's strict guidelines. With Violet's pay, they no longer qualified for it, anyway.

They wouldn't be able to do this every time. But it was their first proper paycheck, and they were going to treat themself, dammit.

They hauled their bags into the halfway house, ignoring couch potato Nick and his reality TV. Elizabeth, the other full-time staff besides Brandon, sat at the kitchen table, doing paperwork. She looked up as JC started putting away groceries, her short, gray hair an unforgiving silver in the light. "Where *were* you?"

"I went grocery shopping after NA. I texted you," they said, waving a plastic bag. NA had been rough, as per usual, but that was immediately fixed by their ability to get proper fresh ingredients rather than canned. And meat. And the fixings for homemade buttercream frosting—plus green food dye, of course—rather than buying the cheap pre-made stuff that was just sugar and chemicals. And mint—both the extract and the actual herb, for just a little extra kick, since they were making the cake chocolate. The kid wouldn't care, but the adults would appreciate it...

She narrowed her beady eyes. "You were gone for over two hours. It took you that long to get that little bit?"

"Yeah, the buses suck."

The house had a strict curfew, but it wasn't for another two hours. Even then, residents had to tell staff where they were going whenever they left. Unfortunately for them, bus schedules didn't give a crap, and JC usually had to let Elizabeth or Brandon know that their twenty-minute errand was now an hour.

She held out a hand. "Give me your phone."

JC groaned. "Really, Elizabeth?"

"You want me to write you up? Phone."

Sighing, they pulled their phone out of the pocket, unlocked it, and handed it over. She scrolled through while they finished putting away groceries. One of these days—probably after they left the halfway house—they were going get a collection of Dutch ovens. They'd always wanted at least one...

"Find anything?" JC prodded.

Elizabeth wrinkled face twisted. "Who's Cyrus?"

"One of my coworkers."

"And Bob?"

"My boss. She actually goes by Violet, I just call her Bob for shits and gigs."

"That's disrespectful."

"She's cool with it," they protested. Fairies collected nicknames like Pokémon, anyway.

Elizabeth returned the phone, going to the fridge and examining the groceries JC had just put away. "You got all that from SNAP?"

"No. First paycheck just came in. SNAP won't cover me anymore."

"You get paid this much for serving coffee?"

"And baking cookies," they retorted. "Nineteen bucks an hour, forty hours a week. Plus tips."

She glared at them. "There is no way anyone in their right mind is paying *you* that much."

JC shrugged, answering honestly, "No one was more surprised than me."

She poked a thin, gnarled finger at the bag of sugar on the counter. "You need sugar to make those marble drugs, don't you?"

They gritted their teeth. "And cakes. Alku's kid has a birthday."

"What's he paying you to do that?"

"Chore swap. You know I hate doing dishes," they said. "Besides, he's a good guy."

"He's a thief."

"Not for years," they snapped.

Elizabeth scoffed and left the kitchen, calling, "I'm searching your room."

JC sighed, but didn't argue, or even chase after her. Residents got searched all the time; it was part of the deal of living here. And privacy was a myth lost behind bars.

Pulling their brown hair back in a bun, they started baking.

the enslaver

An excerpt from *Round-Ears: A History of
Gialdon and Humans in the Fae Realm*

Humans are not native to the Fae Realm, and yet they've been there for thousands of years. Most of them unwillingly.

Fairies are, by and large, a proud race. In their writings they often call themselves, "the fair race," "the fair folk," "the greatest," "the best," "the joyous race," and, of course, "those above death." This immortality or separation from natural death was and remains the primary source of Fae superiority. The belief is that immortals are inherently better than mortals in all aspects of life because of this.

This led the Fae to have an abhorrence of death and anything to do with it. Fairies are, more often than not, vegetarian for this very reason; they want nothing to do with the killing of any creature. Extremists refuse to even eat root vegetables, not wanting to kill plants, either.

And yet, [fairy] nations often find themselves at war with each other and with other people in their Realm, most notably the giants (who are similarly immortal but whose culture has never reviled death), trolls, goblins, and dwarves.

In early history, the Fae defended themselves with non-lethal combat. The martial arts they developed could break bone and cause pain but would not be fatal. They also, of course, used magic, protecting their lands with illusions and glamours, as well as cursing their enemies with ill luck, poverty, ill health, no children, etc.

But then, sometime around 4000 BCE (though scholars debate the exact date), something happened. The Fae Realm made contact with the Mortal Realm.

When and how the first humans were enslaved into the Fae Realm is unknown. But at some point, likely over the course of several centuries, fairies started "recruiting" more and more humans, pressing them into military service and servitude.

Fae enslavement of humans worked in a fashion similar to Medieval and Russian serfdom, albeit not for working the land. The land is sacred to Fae, as it's the source of life. While wordsmithing [re: writing, poetry, singing, etc.] and magic are the highest and most revered pursuits in the Fae Realm, farming and agriculture are also very highly respected, and have always been considered well above the position of mortal serfs.

Mortal serfs are tied to the land, not a specific person or master. A person—Fae or otherwise—cannot legally own another being, but the land provides for us all.

It houses and feeds us. We are but guests, dependent on its bounty and temperament. Or so the Fae believe.

And from a human perspective, the Fae Realm itself is a trap. If one eats too much Fae food, the human body becomes dependent on it, rejecting food from other Realms. It takes weeks, if not months, of treatment to sever that Fae food dependency, the knowledge and resources of which only became more widely available in the last few decades.

Some serfs were forced into a life very similar to that of household slavery, almost exclusively in homes of the rich and powerful. They cleaned palaces and noble houses, took care of children, entertained their masters and, in many cases, were also used in sex slavery. Eventually, a whole new caste of serfs would be "bred" and trained for this purpose exclusively. However, brownies—a small, immortal cousin to fairies—had long served as household staff and were considered superior to mortals in that regard, even if they had to be paid.

Other mortals were pressed into entertainment work. While the Fae largely agreed that they were the superior musicians (and it's hard to argue when they would have literally centuries of experience), Fae have the hindrance of being unable to lie. This makes reading from scripts—even if they are playing a character—very difficult, if not impossible. Humans, on the other hand, have no physical block from lying or acting, and could play all manner of characters with little difficulty. Almost every actor in the Fae kingdoms before Gialdon was a human serf, serving at the will of the Fae Folk. Even today, most professional [actors] in that Realm are mortal.

But the most common form of service for mortals was military work. Anywhere from 80 to 90 percent of all serfs over the age of fifteen served at least once in active duty.

Fairies were and still are heavily discouraged from killing, that is true. Even if their target was a mortal, someone who was—given enough time—going to die anyway. But it quickly became apparent that if the fairy nations wanted to defend themselves or conquer other territories, then they would have to get used to the idea of *ordering* kills.

This idea of *directly* killing someone being abhorrent, but *ordering* it from a distance being fine, is still prevalent in the Fae Realm today. This also led to the military practice of mortals being in the fray while their immortal fairy officers watched, separate from the violence but still giving orders. In fact, many times, fairy officers from opposite sides of a battle would watch it together, on the same ridge or cliff, sometimes sharing the same war tent. These instances show just how much fairies hesitated to kill one of their own or even cause them [physical] harm.

The crowning exception to this rule, of course, is the Violet Princess.

Pictured *a musician making a mortal serf dance for Ivaenian royalty, possibly the Violet Princess herself. The disapproving mortals behind the dancer hint at the hatred and fear of this particular brand of magic.*

flash and smoke

"I have flash and smoke bombs, tasers, rifles, shotguns, handguns, and eleven mercenaries on my payroll," Michelle announced, motioning to her stockpile of weapons in a rented warehouse north of the Twin Cities.

Red Wolf looked over her armory. He had seen firearms used; Gialdon was especially fond of them these days. But he hadn't used them himself. They looked ugly, all clunky and metal. And, unlike the more dependable sword, they eventually ran out of ammunition. But his main complaint was: "They're rather loud."

"We'll be using suppressors; you and your people won't go deaf," she assured him, "or draw too much attention."

The no-nonsense mercenary had several tattoos snaking up her exposed arms, including one that Red Wolf recognized as the symbol of the Marines for the United States. Other than that, she was an unremarkable-looking woman: brown hair pulled back in a tail, suntanned skin, and red-tinted sunglasses. She'd brought one of her mercenaries with her, a short, lanky fellow with a distinct wine-colored birthmark beneath his left eye. He'd stayed behind in Michelle's car, reading from a thin device called a Kindle (which was somehow separate from phones and tablets?)

Gold and Crescent had come along for this bit of planning, meandering along the rows of weapons. Crescent had joined the Ivaenian military shortly after the Gialdonian War and had still been of low rank by the time Red Wolf decided to leave military life behind and pursue a more direct approach to his justice. Gold had served in a unit protecting the musician Piper, who had known Red Wolf for centuries.

All three had followed him here, along with Black Dove, Crow Moon, and Mouse, and he was eternally grateful for their faith in him.

Crescent's dark blue skin looked gray in the shadows, and his silver hair could be mistaken for an old mortal's. Gold was nicknamed after the metallic swirls across their pasty-white skin, and they were much more interested in the paper mug of coffee that Michelle and David had gotten for them in the café where they'd originally met an hour ago.

The two of them, plus Red Wolf himself and his four other fairies, brought Michelle and her people up to a total of nineteen.

"This is all yours?" Crescent asked, eyeing the weapons.

Michelle nodded. "Bits and bobs collected over the years. I have more stashes and safehouses around the world. It pays to be prepared."

"We'll not be killing unless absolutely necessary," Red Wolf said. "And no killing immortals."

"How about hurting them?" Michelle asked.

"That's fine. Even if it's permanent."

"Great. Do we have a time limit?"

"No. But the longer we're here, the greater risk of getting exposed by law enforcement."

"Obviously." Michelle tapped a finger against a box labeled *ammo*. "The more prep work and recon I do, the better our shot of success. Especially if the target is a fairy. You people have an annoying habit of picking up a lot of inconvenient skills. I've heard of magic that can mind-control humans. Anything for fairies?"

"Fairies are immune, or at least resistant to magical music," Red Wolf said carefully. "That won't work."

Gold glanced at him over their coffee, but didn't say anything. They'd all agreed not to mention Piper's abilities unless and until necessary.

Piper wasn't here for Violet. He was here in case Michelle and her people stepped out of line. And as Violet herself had told him, *Don't show your enemy your weapon until you intend to use it.*

"Well, if she's the type to go to bars or clubs, it'd be easy to spike her drink," Michelle mused. "Otherwise, we're going to have to get more obvious. Gimme a month to study her, and we'll come up with a plan."

"Excellent." Red Wolf handed her a small black suitcase. It'd been glamoured into a cell phone until he'd reached the motel.

She cracked it open, just enough to see the stacks of green, paper money. But rather than stash it in her safehouse, she closed it and took it with her. "This'll be handy for any extra supplies or bribes. Let's get to work!"

the current of chaos

CaFae Latte got the bulk of its customers in the morning, when people loaded up on caffeine and last-minute breakfast on their way to work. With such a small staff, and a few decades of trial and error, Violet had developed a "start early, leave early" mentality. They opened at six in the morning, closed by three. JC worked five days a week, with Wednesdays and Saturdays off.

That changed after their first month and a half at CaFae Latte.

"People still do car shows?" JC asked, pausing in mixing the muffin batter.

"They do here," Cyrus cheered, leaning against the opposite counter. "Bernier's one of the oldest cities in Minnesota, so there's a lot of historical stuff. Especially by the river. They block off the whole street and cram it full of cars built no later than the '70s. We've even got a Model T out there!"

"People come from as far as the Twin Cities to show off and look at vintage cars," Violet added over her inventory notes. "There's also a musical performance by the river."

"And the glorious, deep-fried miracle of carnival food."

JC shrugged. Yeah, if they ran a downtown business, they'd stay open for that, too. "So, it's gonna be a long one?"

"The show itself starts at five in the evening. We close when the music starts at seven. Open time is the same," Violet said apologetically. "But it's only every other Saturday, only in the summer, and you will get paid overtime."

"Tips are pretty good, too," Cyrus added. "Everyone's walking around in the heat, getting thirsty, hungry, wanting somewhere to sit down and chat with friends..."

"I don't know if I can compete with carnival food," JC teased.

He gave a dramatic sigh, placing a pale blue hand over his heart. "Few can. But alas, we must try."

§

JC had to be at the café an hour before open, and it usually took about thirty minutes to close, so their first car show shift was looking to be at least twelve hours. But they couldn't complain about that paycheck. And it's not like they were missing out on a thriving social life, so they spent the early morning as usual, got to take a luxuriously long break in the early afternoon, and then dedicated a couple of hours to making more baked goods for the evening rush.

And, boy, was there an evening rush! The vintage cars had barely been parked when the first wave hit, mostly families with young children who weren't going to the music show. When the car show got properly started, it seemed every Bernier resident and their mother came in: teenagers, old people, families, goblins, centaurs, cyclopses, even the odd troll, all of them wanting an iced tea or coffee and something to nibble on.

JC honestly didn't know what the fuss was about. They were just cars, most of them with parts too rare and expensive to conveniently fix. But hey, if it got people filling up the tip jar—which popped in and out of existence with every "thank you"—who were they to judge?

Violet took point on the register while JC and Cyrus made drinks and dished pastries, and JC was grateful they had most of the drinks memorized so they weren't slowing everything down. The three of them had a good groove going, and JC was in that headspace where they were just bobbing with the current of chaos, no real thoughts in their brain.

"I've got a large iced coffee for Jack and a medium roast for Michelle," they called, setting the drinks on the counter. "Next!"

A tattooed woman with red-tinted sunglasses took the beverages. "Are you always this busy?"

"God, I hope not. This is only my second month."

"Short staffed?"

"Fully staffed."

"And hiring," Violet called from the register.

Michelle chuckled and turned, knocking straight into a wall of plaid.

"Oh, shit!"

"That's okay," Nicole said, checking her shirt. Coffee dribbled down the front. "You didn't get much on me. Did you lose a lot?"

The woman checked her paper cup. "Nah. Sorry about that!" She wove through the crowd and left. Nicole frowned after her.

"You okay?" JC called, leaning over the counter to inspect the damage while Violet took the order of a group of teenagers: three humans and a goblin, all acne and memes.

"Yeah. Clairvoyance flared up. I think she's a soldier, but it's hard to tell through all the layers."

JC snagged a bunch of napkins and handed them over. They didn't have to be careful about skin-on-skin contact, since she still had the gloves, and golden rings sparkled in her locs like a hundred little suns. "My usual, please," Nicole said.

"It's eighty degrees out," JC argued, starting the hot chocolate anyway.

"And the air conditioning in here is on full blast."

"Fair point," they grumbled, checking the time. They'd close in about half an hour. The CaFae was still crammed, every table and most chairs occupied, the air full of chatter and the hiss of the espresso machine and the thick smell of coffee and tea, but the line was thinning as people left to get a good spot for the music show. A bunch of teenage girls had been giggling over it earlier: some new boy band from Hudson. "You staying for the music?"

Nicole's fingers were tap-tap-tapping away on the counter. "Maybe a little. It's usually a good idea to see what my students are obsessed with. You?"

"After today's shift? I think I'll go home and faceplant. Pretty sure this isn't going to be my brand of tunes, either."

"Me, neither. I like alternative folk. And sometimes Beyoncé."

"She's always the exception."

Nicole frowned, dark brow adorably wrinkled. "This is your first car show. Have you been stuck here all day?"

"I don't get paid to ogle cars," they said, popping the lid on her drink. "Bob, Nicole's here for her usual."

"On the screen," Violet called.

"Did you want to catch the first few songs with me?" Nicole asked, ignoring the fairy. Her finger-tapping was going faster. "I know it's not either of our scene, but it'll probably be like making fun of a bad movie."

JC perked up a little. "I do like making fun of bad movies..."

"Hey, the Eight Angels aren't bad!" the teen goblin protested, his skin literally as red as a tomato with black horns twisted down over his ears.

JC snorted. "They probably aren't that original, either. Are they ripping off Maroon 5 or My Chemical Romance?"

"Are *you* trying to rip off John Lennon without glasses?"

"Ohhhh, shots fired," Cyrus called while JC rolled their eyes. Jean jackets were a timeless classic, and they refused to be bullied out of them by someone younger than YouTube.

"You love John Lennon. You went to so many concerts," Violet accused. "Nicole, if I could get you to finish your purchase?"

While the witch handed over the cash, Violet said, "Jennifer Charles, we're slowing down enough that you can start on dishes. Once they're done, you can leave early if you like."

"Really?" they blurted.

"Don't be sloppy with it."

They glanced at Nicole. Going to their crowded halfway house—even with the temptation of faceplanting on a bed or couch—became a lot less appealing. Even with dish duty. "You okay waiting a bit?"

She smiled, curled around her hot chocolate. "Take your time. I've got a book."

§

The band wasn't terrible, but not terribly interesting, either. JC almost fell asleep on the grass, but kept their head in the game as the fifth break-up song started. "At what point do these guys just admit that they're bad boyfriends?"

"But then they wouldn't have any more song material," Nicole retorted, lying next to JC. Her shirt was still stained, but in the fading sunlight, JC could barely tell.

They laughed, and Nicole looked incredibly pleased and smug. The air smelled of fresh grass and river water and fried food, and they could've gotten drunk off it.

"Did you want to go? I think I have enough ammunition for my students when they try to tell me this is peak music," she said.

"Yeah, it's pretty dead." JC hauled themselves to their feet, then helped Nicole onto hers, careful to touch only what her gloves covered. The butter-soft leather licked their fingers. "You think we had better taste when we were teenagers?"

"I like to think so, but probably not."

Main Street was largely deserted, everyone congregating to the little stage by the river. The vintage cars drove away one by one, but there were still a few stragglers on the sidewalks, including that tattooed woman with the red sunglasses—what was her name? Mary? Margaret? Something with an M—with a guy too young to be her date but too old to be her son. Her eyes met JC through the red lenses, and they shared a friendly wave.

They checked the time on their old phone and swore. "I missed the bus."

"When's the next one?" Nicole asked.

"Two hours." Fuck. Lured away from common sense by a pretty face.

Sure, it was worth it. But parolees were often sent back to prison for missing curfew, even if they'd been acting perfectly legal. It broke the rules of parole.

The bus schedule was incorporated into JC's curfew, giving them a little breathing room. But even if they waited at the stop and caught the next one, they'd still be incredibly late. They texted Brandon: *missed the bus. help?*

"I didn't park too far. I can drive you home."

JC's head snapped up. "You sure? I'm all the way in St. Paul."

"I need to eat a proper meal, anyway, and I'm too lazy to cook this late." She raised her eyebrows. "Unless you'd rather spend the night at my place?"

JC's brain short-circuited. *Damn, this girl is forward.* "It kills a part of my soul to tell you that my halfway house has a really strict curfew."

As if on cue, their phone dinged with a text from Brandon: *Where are you?*

She tilted her head adorably. "Halfway house?"

They cringed, answering Brandon with a simple, *Bernier.* "Ah...yeah. Probably should have led with that..."

"Oh, right. You mentioned giving out nicknames in prison."

"Yeah...I only got out a few months ago. Served six years."

They waited for the judgment. The recoil. The polite *thanks, not interested.*

Nicole asked, "Does Aunt Violet know?"

"Yeah."

"Was it a sexual crime or domestic violence?"

"No. And I was high as a kite when it happened. I'm clean now. Got Sunday night NA meetings and everything." They pulled out their chip. It was a flashy new red one. Ninety days clean.

Nicole peeled off a glove with her teeth and took it with her bare fingers, which—fair. She held it for a long moment while JC's heartbeat thundered in their ears, the warm summer breeze toying with their hair.

Ding!

All right, I'll drive down and pick you up.

JC stole a glance up at Nicole before typing back: *don't think you have to. friend's offering to drive*

Does this friend live in St. Paul?

no shes local

Screw that. I'm paid back for my mileage, and we need a few things for the house, anyway.

Nicole gave the coin back, re-gloving. "You were really proud when you got that."

"Uh, yeah," they chuckled, weirdly embarrassed. The day before had been really shitty, stuck in a halfway house with Elizabeth refusing to let them see a movie with Alku and the anniversary of their stupid crime looming, and they'd wanted nothing more than to get high. They'd instead stress-baked, covering the halfway house's table and counters with brownies and cookies until they were tired enough to go to bed. Only Elizabeth had complained, and only because of the dishes. They'd brought most of the baked goods to the NA meeting—well, what their house-mates had left—completely forgetting that it was the three-month anniversary of them being clean until their sponsor had dropped the chip in their hands. They'd almost cried.

"Well, you're still cute," Nicole said, her husky, near-mono-tone voice yanking JC back into the present. "I trust Aunt Vio-let's judgment. You've been nothing but kind. And I keep getting those visions of danger and bloodshed and don't like the idea of you being by yourself, so I'll still drive you, unless you want to call someone or get an Uber."

Anyone else getting those "visions of danger and blood-shed" would have stayed as far away from JC as possible, prob-ably thinking they were the source of whatever nastiness was about to come. The fact that Nicole had the exact opposite reac-tion was really refreshing.

Nicole scrunched up her mouth. "Honestly, trying to pro-pose a first date right after an all-day shift was probably not my smartest move."

JC laughed. "Hey, it beats some of the dumb things I've tried...but, uh...we've got at least half an hour before my ride shows up?"

It was hard to read Nicole's face—it was as even as her voice. But it was very easy to read her intentions when she leaned over and kissed JC.

Her lips were thick and soft, and JC got the faintest hint of nutmeg from her hot chocolate.

When Nicole pulled back, JC instinctively chased after her, catching themselves before their forehead could bump into her wide nose. "Uh..."

They bluescreened for several seconds before rebooting. "So that's a yes?"

Nicole smirked. "Lucky us, I only live five minutes away."

dating criminals

J C was tugging their jean jacket back on when someone knocked on Nicole's front door.

It was a short trip—the two of them hadn't even made it to the bed. And Nicole had a very comfy couch, with fat cushions covered in soft leather. Honestly, now that JC wasn't distracted by *her*, the living room of her townhouse was warm and cozy: books spilling out of the cases in piles across the floor, soft lamp lights, an old fireplace in the wall. The television was crammed into the corner with literal dust on the remote, and through an open door down the hall JC could see a room with an easel, half-painted canvas, and part of a table covered in paints and brushes.

Another knock. JC glanced at Nicole, who was tugging on her sports bra. She'd kept the gloves on, which looked a little silly, but still cute. "We're not decent!" she called.

Another, more forceful knock. "Police! Open up."

They frowned at each other, then JC went to get it. "Coming!"

As soon as they opened the door, the police officer grabbed JC by the shirt and pushed them against the wall, shouting, "Let me see your hands. Let me see your hands!"

JC held up their hands. "Easy, easy. It's all good."

The officer was so close JC could smell the French fries on his breath and count the freckles on his cheeks, *Miller* stitched into his uniform.

"This seems disproportionate," Nicole said, strolling over in nothing but her pants and sports bra. "And I didn't give you permission to enter my house."

Miller glared at JC as he let them go. "You're harboring someone who's breaking their parole."

"I didn't break it, I missed the bus," JC argued. "I was waiting for my ride with a...friend? Girlfriend?" Too soon for that, right?

Nicole shrugged. "I'm open to a second date."

Boy, that and the adrenaline of being smooshed against a wall by an armed officer really made JC's head spin. They had to clear their throat before asking, "Where's Brandon? He said he'd get me."

"He's back in Saint Paul," Elizabeth said, pushing through the doorway with a second officer on her heels, a block-shaped woman with a severe ponytail and *Nelson* stitched into her uniform. "I'm not staying alone in a house full of dangerous criminals while one of them is causing problems."

JC's stomach sank. Brandon would've only given JC a warning. Elizabeth, on the other hand... "This is going on a report, isn't it?"

"Absolutely."

"Dammit."

"But it's my fault," Nicole argued. "I asked JC to watch the concert after work and we lost track of time."

Elizabeth's eyes narrowed in disapproval as she looked Nicole up and down, silver hair swishing with the movement. "Did they explain that they're a criminal?"

Her forehead furrowed. "They told me about it, yes."

"Do you know any details?"

"Why is my relationship any of your business? Who even are you?"

Miller held up his hand. "Ma'am, calm down."

JC gave him a bizarre look. Nicole hadn't even raised her voice.

"Elizabeth's one of the people who runs the halfway house," JC explained. "Elizabeth, this is Nicole."

Elizabeth hmphed before turning to JC. "You're allowed to leave town and stay out late for work, not pleasure. Did you even have a shift today?"

"Yeah, twelve hours," they retorted, and they could feel each and every one of them in their back.

"It's true. I asked them out at the café right before close," Nicole added. "You can ask the owner. I have her address in my phone—it's on the end table."

She stepped toward it, and both officers tensed. Nicole didn't seem to clock it.

"Are either of you armed?" Officer Nelson asked, hand on her gun.

"No," JC said, wondering if they'd be fast enough to push the officers away if they decided to get trigger-happy.

"No, I'm a pacifist." Nicole got a hold of her phone and scrolled through it. "If you're that nervous about being in my house, then leave."

"Ma'am, you don't need to give us attitude," Officer Miller scolded.

"She's not," JC replied testily. Honestly, Nicole was a god-damn *art teacher*. Teddy bears were more intimidating than her.

"Elizabeth, I've got thirty minutes until my curfew. If we leave now, we can make it," they said.

"I want to confirm that you were where you say you were," she said.

JC shrugged. "Fine. But then my breaking curfew is on you."

"It is *not*. You'll be getting a written warning at least. Your parole officer won't be happy."

"Fine. I'll text her now." They met Officer Nelson's eyes. "May I reach into my back pocket to get my phone?"

She nodded, finally taking her hand off her gun. JC dug out their phone, grimacing at the low battery warning, and shot off a quick text to Mrs. Jackson to let her know that Elizabeth was being a pill.

"Here." Nicole stood next to Elizabeth, showing her the screen. "Those are their phone numbers. They also live a few streets over if you want to talk to them in person."

"Believe me, I will," Elizabeth promised. "Officers, can you accompany us?"

"Sure," Officer Miller said. He put a hand on Nicole's arm. "And maybe avoid dating criminals, okay, sweetie? I know the dangerous stuff is exciting, but it can get you hurt. Or worse."

Nicole looked down at the hand touching her sweaty, black skin, then back up with a steely gaze. Her voice was perfectly flat when she said, "The ex-criminal isn't the one who punched their spouse in the gut for overcooking dinner."

Officer Miller jerked back, letting her go.

Elizabeth hadn't caught the exchange, too busy typing Violet's address into her phone. But Officer Nelson did, and her eyebrows rose.

JC crossed their arms, feeling smug. "Is now a bad time to mention she's clairvoyant?"

"That–" Officer Miller cleared his throat. "That's nothing but a scam."

Nicole turned to Officer Nelson. "I'd do an investigation into his home life, if I were you."

Officer Miller was already (finally) leaving the house. "Nelson, let's go meet with the fairies and settle this mess."

She frowned after him. Nicole took advantage of the officer's stupor to motion to JC's phone. "Let me give you my number."

JC handed it over. Elizabeth huffed in annoyance, brushing gray bangs out of her face. "Let's *go*. I'm going to end up with overtime with this nonsense."

Nicole returned JC's phone and kissed their cheek. "Be sure to text me. I didn't get the chance to show you my bedroom."

They choked. "Yes, ma'am."

Elizabeth looked at Nicole with thinly veiled disgust. JC hurried out of the house, because another second would've resulted in them saying something they'd regret. Officer Nelson closed the door behind her.

"Your car or Elizabeth's?" JC asked, only slightly teasing.

"Ours," Officer Nelson said. "For now."

all-team group chat

MICHELLE
Just got back
from Bernier.
Cafe is veeeery popular.
Will keep
everyone informed.

JACK
good coffee tho
prob why its so popular

ALEX
Really?
Michelle, take me for
scouting next time!
PETE
Honestly the fact that
the ex-con is the baker
makes so much sense
Have you ever gone to a
diner/cafe/restaurant
where the back of
house didn't have at
least ONE jailbird?
MICHELLE
No

                                            JACK
                                             no

ALEX
No
QUENTIN
Nope
ROGER
🐦🐦🐦
RACHEL
No
DAVID
Gotta be a
prerequisite, right?
OLSON
once, but the food
honestly wasn't that good
DAVID
Definitely a
prerequisite, then.
MICHELLE
I've recruited at
least one employee
from a kitchen.

                                            JACK
                                             0.0

QUENTIN
That tracks
PETE
Oh yea Timmy!
Hated that guy.

ALEX

☺

But he made THE
BEST burgers

PETE

Still hated him

                JACK

          why isnt he here
          could use him to
            get close?
      like make the cafe
    hire him or be friends
      with the baker?

PETE

Bailed on us a while ago.
Almost got M arrested.

MICHELLE

He and his wife are on
a permanent vacation.

                JACK

          oh THAT guy
     forgot we all use fake
        names for a sec
  really he went with timmy?

QUENTIN

Yup

Weird guy

PENNY

WOULD YOU PLEASE

STOP TEXTING
TOM, VIC AND I ARE
TRYING TO SLEEP
PETE
Together, or…?
QUENTIN
Aw, should've
invited me. ;)

                                    JACK
                    u can turn notifications
                                off ya know

PENNY
GO THE FUCK TO SLEEP
IT'S 11PM!!!
OLSON
Weak

fresh sweat

Cyrus laughed when Elizabeth knocked on his and Violet's door, JC and two police officers in tow. He was still laughing when Violet confirmed that yes, JC had worked at the café all day (with video proof from security cameras), yes, they had left the café with Nicole with plans to watch a bit of the concert, and yes, Nicole was a clairvoyant witch, why did you ask?

JC still got written up, their broken curfew on the record. Mrs. Jackson lectured them on the importance of playing by the rules, but added, "It's good that you're building these relationships. Your chances of recidivism go down—assuming you end your dates with enough time to return before curfew."

Brandon refrained from lecturing JC. Alku gave them a high-five. When they went back to work on Monday as the sun began to rise, Cyrus took one look at them and laughed again, the dick.

"Like you wouldn't have done the same thing," JC grumbled, tying on their apron. Honestly, they could've wound up back in handcuffs and they still would've called it a win.

"No, I wouldn't have," Cyrus said, pointing to his ace pride pin. "But I *have* broken parole because some jerk at the bar thought Isaac Asimov was the founder of science fiction, not Mary Shelley."

"...did you win?"

"Barely."

"What the hell were you on parole for?"

"I was in the Civil Rights movement, workers' rights, women's rights, queer rights, and obviously Fae rights..."

JC made a face. "Don't you ever get tired?"

"Why do you think I'm working food service? This is so much more relaxing."

Nicole showed up as she usually did that afternoon, fingers tapping away. But she was more jittery, more on-guard than the last time JC had seen her—and that had been with two police officers in her house.

She also wore jewelry beyond the loc rings, something JC hadn't seen from her. A few thin bangles decorated her wrists, she had a couple of necklaces, and more rings in her hair. It clashed a little with her long-sleeved, gray shirt, but still looked good.

"Hi," JC greeted, internally grimacing. *Seriously? First time you see her after hooking up, and that's the best you can do?*

"Hi," Nicole greeted. "Is Aunt Violet in? I've been getting more visions."

"Any new details?" Cyrus asked.

She shook her head. "I think whatever's going to happen will happen soon."

"I'll let her know," the fairy promised, then gave JC a very unsubtle look before going in the back, leaving JC at the front with Nicole. At least it was quiet, only one customer in the corner: a short, lanky man engrossed in a Kindle, a wine-colored birthmark under his left eye.

"So," they said, clearing their throat. "Hot chocolate?"

"Please."

JC got it on the register and whipped it up, trying to think of what to say. They didn't want Nicole to just be a one-night stand. They didn't know each other that well, but JC's day got so much better when the witch showed up. And she didn't give them any bullshit or mind games, which was an automatic plus.

"Hey, so, there's no car show this Saturday," JC said, handing over the drink. "And I have the day off. Did you...want to do something?"

Nicole did her finger-tap stim against the paper cup. "There's a dragon exhibit at the history museum I've been meaning to go to."

JC had never been a big fan of history. But Nicole could've suggested a full day of washing dishes and they would've said yes.

"Dragons sound really cool," they said. "You mind picking me up?"

"Sure."

When she left, JC fist-pumped like a kid. Cyrus patted them on the head. "Fucking finally. That's been driving me nuts since you two met."

JC was sure to get Brandon alone to ask for that time away from the halfway house, not Elizabeth. He smirked, saying, "Make sure you're back by curfew this time."

And, yeah. Fair.

§

Dating while on parole was tricky. In some cases, it was banned entirely, although that was usually for people convicted of things like sexual assault or abuse. JC had heard dozens of stories from ex-parolees that had found themselves back in prison for one reason or another. Most agreed that curfew was the biggest hurdle, because they couldn't spend the night at their SO's place, or take them back to their halfway house where privacy was nonexistent and non-relatives usually weren't allowed at all. That was often enough to break any fledgling relationship, as well as the general red flag of being a parolee in the first place. (If Nicole didn't have clairvoyance and divination straight-up proving to her that JC was leaving their old life in the dirt, they'd genuinely call her nuts.)

Another issue was parole officers and halfway house staff simply not allowing such relationships, or not allowing recreational activities for their parolees for whatever reason. Which was why JC was worried when they found out Elizabeth was on staff that Saturday, not Brandon.

Nicole was supposed to show up a little after one. JC spent the late morning and early afternoon trying to figure out what to wear, then stress-baking. Since everyone got muffins out of it, there weren't many complaints about them hogging the kitchen and dirtying dishes. Alku snatched a double-chocolate muffin bigger than his tiny green hand. "You that nervous for your date?"

"No. Why would I be?"

He rolled his eyes, peeling off the cup liner. "Fairies lie better than you do, kid."

"What's this about a date?" Elizabeth asked, coming into the kitchen.

JC glanced at the time on the stove. Less than fifteen minutes, unless Nicole was early. *Please be early.* "Brandon approved it. It should be on the calendar."

Mouth thinning into a line, Elizabeth pulled up the calendar on her phone that had all the residents' work schedules and approved time out of the house. "It just says you're going to the museum."

"Yeah, with Nicole. She's driving me. Brandon's got her name and number." He'd asked, JC had sent a text, and Nicole had approved.

"Is that the girl who was so rude to the police the other night?"

"She wasn't rude."

"Well, you can't go until the dishes are done."

"It's Nick's turn, and I already gave him extra muffins."

"Can you make cinnamon apple next time?" Nick called from the living room.

"Sure," JC called back, just as their phone chimed.

Here early, Nicole texted.

Thank fuck, they thought, pulling off the apron and checking that no flour got on their jean jacket or black, flowy skirt. "That's her. Gotta go. I'll be back by five."

"Good luck!" Alku said with his mouth full.

"Get that pussy," Nick added from his couch with a leer. As JC closed the door behind them, they belatedly realized they hadn't eaten lunch yet. *Ah, well. I'll get something later.*

Nicole drove a beat-up silver Ford that, when JC got into the passenger seat, smelled like fast food and old paint. A faded pink, crusty stain on the floor of the back seat was the most likely culprit.

"I thought the lid was on tight enough," Nicole said when she saw JC looking at it. "I had to swing by the store to get more. The school usually gives me enough supplies, but not that time."

"I thought schools *never* gave enough to teachers," JC said as Nicole started driving.

"Public schools don't. I work at the private art school."

"The art school...doesn't give you enough art supplies?"

Her lips twitched. "Not when two boys decide to steal some for some unflattering graffiti on the wall. They painted the principal as a pig."

JC snorted. That sounded like something they might've done in middle school.

"I was mostly annoyed at the lack of proper shading. I taught them better than that..."

They suddenly got the mental picture of Nicole disappointedly shaking her head as she filled out a grading rubric and stuck it on the wall next to the shitty graffiti, and laughed.

The museum was only about ten minutes away, traffic was light, and it was easy to prod Nicole for more stories about her students. Turned out, rich academy kids got into just as much trouble as ghetto brats, only they got to go to the principal's office, not get arrested by the SRO.

Once they got out of the car and started the walk through the parking lot to the museum itself, JC found a problem. Was it too soon to try to hold Nicole's hand? Sure, they'd already hooked up once, but that could be passed off as a casual thing. Established couples were the ones who held hands, and JC didn't think they were there yet. But if they didn't at least try, would that send the message that they didn't *want* to? What about Nicole's clairvoyance and sensitivity thing? Sure, she was wearing her light gloves and a thin, long-sleeved shirt (red looked really good on her, going with the mostly-gold jewelry that decorated her locs and wrists), but would that actually help or would she still get a dose of JC's anxiety? Fuck, they were already sweating—

"I remember when Aunt Violet first took me here," Nicole said. "My parents were doing a romantic getaway for the weekend, and Grandpa wanted to work overtime to save for a new car, so she had me all day, and we went here. There was a kids' program, I think, about rocks and volcanoes. We got to touch cold lava and obsidian."

"Cool," JC said. They'd never been the type of kid to go to museums outside of school field trips, so instead, they focused on the other part of the conversation: "Why do you call her Aunt? Are you guys actually related?"

They reached the front doors, the air conditioning almost blasting JC back into the summer heat. Nicole shook her head. "No, my grandfather was her first employee outside of Blue– Cyrus. And they all became friends. A lot of my earliest memories are drawing or doing homework in the corner of the café while waiting for Grandpa to finish his shift. My parents worked a lot, and if he and Grandma couldn't babysit me, Aunt Violet and Cyrus would. She was the first to realize I was clairvoyant and helped teach me how to control it, and some basic divination spells. Our magics are still pretty different, though, with her being a fairy and me not, so most of my magic was learned by the Stoughton Street Coven, which Aunt Violet helped create in the 1960s...or maybe it was the early '70s. Somewhere in there."

"You guys have a whole coven?" JC asked. The two of them creeped up the line to pay for their tickets. It was fairly long, almost ten people, with a lot more walking around the cavernous lobby, which had dragon flags *everywhere*, promoting the new exhibit. Most people were human–or at least appeared to be, it was hard to tell with vampires and werewolves–but there were a few dwarves and goblins running around, one of the three people at the front desk was a cyclops, and there were even a couple of fairies in line: a woman with ink-black skin and silver marbling going up her bald head, and another with gold swirls all over their pasty-white skin.

They grimaced at the prices displayed on the desk (twenty bucks a ticket), but they could actually do that. Hell, they could cover Nicole if she insisted they pay, since they were the...

Oh, wait. They *weren't* a man.

This is what happens when you don't realize you're nonbinary until you're in your twenties, and don't fully come out until you're twenty-eight, they realized. *Dating gets really confusing.*

"It's small," Nicole said. "We only have about half a dozen members. Our high priest is Michael; his wife's going to go into labor any day now."

"You didn't divine it?" JC teased.

"We're not *that* accurate."

They reached the front of the line. Before JC could speak, Nicole said, "Two tickets, please. I've got it."

"You sure?" JC asked.

"You can pay for food, if we get hungry. It doesn't have to be fancy, but I can't stand banana or melon. The texture's too weird."

The cyclops gave the two of them their tickets and maps, and they were off. JC didn't think they'd ever been to *this* museum, just the Children's Science Museum for that school field trip. But Nicole knew the place like it was her own home, pointing out the regular and permanent exhibits as they passed by: European history, Native American, a catch-all Asian exhibit that was apparently *way* too small...She barely had to look at the map to get to where they were going.

"Let me know if you want to see any of these others," she said.

"I'm not that big of a history nerd," JC admitted.

Nicole frowned. "Then why did you agree to come here?"

"Because dragons?" *And I'd probably jump off a cliff if you asked me to.*

"Ah." She nodded. JC breathed out a tiny sigh of relief at not completely derailing this out the gate.

The dragon exhibit was on the second floor, and JC made a face as they felt sweat slide down their back halfway up the stairs. They'd only been outside for a minute, but it *was* summer *and* today was a scorcher. Must have been some residue from that.

The first room centered a *massive* dragon skull that had JC gaping. "Is that *real*?"

Nicole checked the plaque, having to go around a couple of people also getting a closer look. The two fairies JC had noticed earlier were on the other side of the room, checking out some wall art. "A recreation. But it's to scale."

JC gaped at it. The skull itself was the size of a minibus, the type that comfortably held about eight people, but usually ended up hauling twelve or more in a shitty tour. "Some of those teeth are as big as me!"

Nicole hummed in agreement. "Dragons never stop growing, especially the aquatic ones that don't have wings, although that growth slows down a lot after puberty. This one was about eight centuries old when it died."

JC whistled.

"Aunt Violet and Cyrus know one who's about half that age, so probably two thirds this size," Nicole mused. "They live on Lake Superior."

"You ever meet them?"

She shook her head. "They prefer to keep to themselves."

They meandered through the exhibit, avoiding artifacts, jewelry, and art pieces that already had people clustered around them until there was room. JC mostly stuck with Nicole, not having much interest in the little snippets of information on the plaques. She didn't know everything, but the stuff she did know was a lot more and a lot more *interesting* than the slim paragraph the museum provided.

One of the cooler pieces was a medieval sword that had been carved from a real dragon's tooth. The carving was absolutely gorgeous, the guard and handle containing some of the most detailed and intricate designs JC had ever seen.

"Europeans have hunted dragons since antiquity," Nicole said sadly. "Some of them got away, going to Asia and parts of Africa where they were worshipped, and later the Americas, where they were at least left alone. Native tribes saw them as nature spirits."

"No riding them?" JC asked, leaning against the wall. They were feeling weirdly light-headed, but that was probably because they still hadn't figured out a way to ask for permission to hold Nicole's hand.

"Unfortunately, no. Part of the issue was food—dragons need to eat a lot of meat in their true form, and medieval shepherds had a lot of it out in the open. But I read somewhere that at least part of the hunting was motivated by queerphobia. Dragons are shapeshifters..."

That JC knew. Everyone knew. It was how dragons hid in plain sight: they turned into humans. Although there was one in California politics—Senator? House Rep? JC couldn't remember—who, while hanging out in human form, kept the tail, wings, and horns.

"...so they can change their external sex," Nicole continued. "Almost all of them are genderfluid, and a lot of scholars think that's a reason why there was so much hate."

"Wait, really?" JC asked. That wasn't anywhere in the museum—what the hell? Stupid plaques.

They knew that, in general, paras tended to be more open about gender and sexuality than humans. The first person they'd ever come out to as nonbinary bisexual was a part-demon named Erik, while he'd been serving time for robbery and B&E. He—and two other inmates, a dwarf and a goblin—were usually the ones picking fistfights in the yard with the Nazis and homophobes, so that probably should've been a clue that some of the para species would have completely different gender norms than the typical male/female split.

She nodded, doing that stim thing with her fingers. "You can tell me if I'm talking too much. I tend to infodump."

"No, this is fine. Way more interesting than—whoa." JC pushed off the wall and almost fell right back against it, head swimming.

"JC?" she asked, startled.

They held up a finger, one that shook just a little.

Sweaty, dizzy, shaky...

Fuck.

They pulled out their glucose monitor and jabbed their index finger, already knowing what they were going to see. Within seconds, *53* blinked up at them.

They frowned. "That number should be at least seventy..."

Nicole grabbed JC's shoulders and pulled them away from the wall, pushing them on one of the cushioned benches in the middle of the room. "What do you need? Sugar, right?"

"Yeah." They leaned their elbows against their legs, focusing on their breathing. "Orange juice is best. Gimme a minute and I can go get—"

"I can get it. There's a café downstairs. You should stay here; I don't want you hitting your head if you faint, and if your blood sugar gets below fifty, we'll have to call an ambulance."

"...how do you know that?"

"My grandmother had diabetes before she died. Stay put."

Before JC could argue that they just needed to rest or offer to pay her back, she was gone, jogging out of the exhibit that suddenly felt a lot bigger and emptier, despite at least five people still poking around the dragon stuff.

They sighed, crossing their arms in the hopes of warming their clammy hands. At least it wasn't cops busting in on them...

"You okay, man?"

They looked up, the source of the Southern (Texan?) accent being a tall, frankly *ridiculously* muscled black man with braids down his shoulders staring down at them. "You look like shit."

JC offered a wan smile. "On a date, too."

He sucked in air through his teeth. "Yikes."

"Yeah..."

"First date?"

"Second. Technically."

"Well, that's good. If things go wrong now, she's going in eyes wide open. Means it's got a better chance of lasting." He sat on the bench, giving JC about a foot of space. "But seriously, you do look terrible."

"Just diabetic," they admitted. "She's getting me some orange juice. I'll be good in a sec."

The man relaxed.

"What's diabetic?"

JC startled. They hadn't heard the pale, gold-marked fairy coming up on their other side. Between the open, curious expression and the khakis and polo shirt, they looked like one of those dorky kids JC used to beat up in high school.

"It's a type of disease," JC explained. "It's when your body can't regulate the sugar you eat, so if you're not careful, you can pass out and go into a coma."

The fairy's eyes widened. "Are all mortals afflicted with this?"

"Nah, just the unlucky ones."

"Gold, lay off," the Texan scolded. "Don't make them give a health lesson when they're trying not to hurl."

Gold stepped away sheepishly. "My apologies. Black Dove and I are new to the Mortal Realm and don't know many humans beyond Quentin."

JC waved them off, buoyed in part by sitting for a while (dammit, Nicole was right) and by not having to correct Quentin on his pronouns, probably thanks to the nonbinary pin on their jacket. They did *not* have the energy to get into those particular weeds. "It's all good. I'm just sorry Minnesota is your first impression. You should've aimed for California or New York. Maybe Florida."

"Don't touch Florida with a ten-foot pole," Quentin argued. "It's overrated. You'd know that if you've ever been."

Fair. JC had barely ever been out of the Cities, never mind the state. Still...

"Yeah, but they have to have better food," they said.

"Oh, definitely," Quentin agreed. "Your hot dish and lutefisk are the stuff of nightmares. But it's not worth it, in my opinion. The traffic alone is brutal."

Gold sputtered. "Food is the best part of the Mortal Realm! You're all so bizarre and creative..."

"Gold. You think a root beer float is the height of culinary creation."

"It is! It was *delicious!*"

Quentin ran a hand down his face. "That's it. You're not allowed to have any opinions on food until I can get you some barbecue and beer. *Proper* barbecue, the type that's been smoked for eleven hours."

JC had never had that, and now their mouth was watering.

Quentin looked around JC. "Dove? You okay?"

The ink-skinned, silver-marked fairy in an ivory dress was studying an old-timey painting of a knight shoving his sword through a dragon's head. She had both a weird intensity and faraway look on her face.

"Dove?"

She startled. "Huh?"

"Don't tell me fairies are also diabetic," JC muttered, running their fingers through their hair.

Black Dove scowled. "Of course not. Fairies don't get ill."

Quentin held up a placating hand. "You just looked a little lost there for a minute."

She huffed, glancing back at the painting. "I was...merely thinking of my son. He wanted to study dragons."

JC did not miss the past tense, or the sadness in Gold's gaze. "Well, that gives him bigger balls than me," JC said. "I'd rather stay *away* from the bus-sized tanks that can breathe fire."

Black Dove smirked, but it was still weighed by visible grief. "Good to see a mortal with sense."

They jerked a thumb at Quentin. "Does he not have any?"

"Nope," Quentin said. "I joined the army right out of high school."

They snorted. "Better than prison."

Quentin looked like he was going to say something else, but before he could, Nicole jogged back into the room, orange juice in hand and black purse swinging beneath her arm. "They only had one orange juice, so I also got you apple, grape, Coke, and sweet tea."

JC smiled, biting back a laugh. If they drank all of that, they'd wind up in a diabetic coma from the *opposite* end.

"Thanks, Nicole. I'll start with the OJ and go from there."

Quentin stood, surrendering the seat to Nicole. "We'll let you get back to your date. Glad to know you won't keel over."

JC waved in thanks, already guzzling the juice as the trio moved to the next room. It was gone in about fifteen seconds, and Nicole took the empty bottle to the trash.

"Sorry about this," they said as she rejoined them. Closer than Quentin, but still with an inch or two of space.

"It's fine," she replied, then frowned. "Well, it's not fine that you're sick, but I'm not mad about it."

They chuckled darkly. "First the cops, now this. I'm starting the think the universe doesn't want us to date."

"The universe can fuck off."

It was a good thing they had finished drinking, because otherwise they would've sprayed orange juice *everywhere*, and would've drawn more looks from museum guests than they already did with their cackling.

At Nicole's confused look, JC got their laughter under control enough to say, "I-I've never heard you swear, and you're a *teacher*! I feel like I just saw you commit a felony!"

Nicole snorted. "You've clearly never been in a teacher's lounge."

"Oh my god, do you actually bitch about students in there?"

"All. The. Time. My first week, I was complaining about a troublemaker rather viciously, and the principal walked in. I thought I would get fired, but it turned out that this student's parents were somehow *worse...*"

They stayed on that bench for the fifteen minutes it took the orange juice to hit JC's system. Then another fifteen when a quick blood sugar check placed their count at sixty-eight, not the seventy-plus they needed, making JC down the Coke.

"Are you ready to keep going?" Nicole asked.

JC carefully stood, relieved when they didn't get any dizziness or fresh sweat. "Yeah, I'm good. Keep those drinks handy, just in case."

"Sure." She stood, hesitated, then said, "I'm usually not comfortable holding hands, but we can link arms?"

There was no reason for that to make JC's face heat. They cleared their throat and offered their elbow with a teasing, "My lady."

Nicole slipped her arm in theirs, and they continued through the museum.

body language

J ack pretended to take a selfie in front of a replica of a baby
dragon's nest, keeping the camera on Jennifer Charles and
Nicole across the room.

Finding out about the date had been easy. David had overheard them during his recon mission earlier that week, and only
one museum in the Twin Cities currently had a dragon exhibit.

The tricky part was finding out the time, and that was where
Jack came in. Michelle hadn't just hired him for his aim; he'd
spent more time at his computer in the last month than he'd ever
spent behind a sniper rifle. But the digital security of the halfway
house and its staff was so paltry that his grandmother could've
hacked into it. He had the date's time within minutes of being
asked, something that filled him with both pride and dread.

He continued to follow the couple at a sedate pace, film-
ing them as Black Dove asked. Occasionally he saw her, as well
as Quentin and Gold as they meandered through the museum,
but as they'd already made direct contact, they couldn't get more
involved. Quentin had been *so close* to cracking into Jennifer
Charles, too. If Nicole had taken five more minutes, the other
mercenary probably would've had a natural opening to get the
baker's number or socials, and from there they could've exploited
that relationship for their own ends.

Jack was relieved it didn't work, though. He'd been keeping a close eye on the baker's finances, everyone knowing that
bribery would be the easiest way to get them to cooperate (and
also that hacking into a bank was *much* harder than a Google
calendar, not that anyone appreciated that). But ever since Violet started paying them, they had remained firmly in the black.

They'd probably be able to move into a decent apartment once their time in the halfway house was up, maybe even without a roommate.

Having said that, Red Wolf was willing to offer seven figures to Jennifer Charles if they would make this operation easier. He was happy to make a "betray your boss and never have to work again" kind of deal. Problem was, they didn't know if Jennifer Charles would be susceptible to that. Sure, they'd broken the law before, but even ex-cons had moral codes, and they needed to know the baker's before making their move.

Except they couldn't get close enough to have more than a five-minute conversation *in public* over the café's counter. The place was either too busy and crowded, or so empty that any grumblings about the owner would be easily heard by sharp fairy ears.

"Okay, fine," they'd thought. "We'll get them when they're not at work."

Except when Jennifer Charles *wasn't* at work, they were at the halfway house. No movies, no bars, no social life whatsoever. They occasionally went bicycling on their days off and ran errands, but those didn't have a routine. They also always changed up their bike routes, making it impossible to set up any kind of chance meeting.

The team had tried looking into the people of Jennifer Charles's life before their prison term: the gang they were in, the friends they'd made among the girls working the streets, even their family. Very little of that stuff existed online, so that had mostly been Michelle, Quentin, and Roger hitting the ground. Most of those gangster friends were dead or in jail; same with the prostitutes. Most of the Scott family hadn't had any contact with their jailbird in years, and a few more had cut contact shortly after release, which (given the Facebook posts around that time) Jack guessed had less to do with the drug and manslaughter charges and more to do with them coming out as queer.

They made it to the last room of the exhibit, Nicole going on about the portrait a dragon artist had made not with paint, but with controlled burns–although Jack initially thought it was a black-and-white photograph. He discreetly filmed them both, focusing more on Jennifer Charles: the awe and slight confusion playing across their face, the way they crossed their arms as they leaned in to take a closer look, the sheepish chuckle when they got *too* close and set off a quiet alarm. Black Dove had been adamant that he collect as much body language as possible.

After observing the rest of the pieces, the couple left, arm in arm. Jennifer Charles said something that made Nicole snort, but their backs were to Jack, so he stopped recording and texted Quentin instead: *they left the exhibit. dont think i can follow them thru the whole museum w/o them noticing*

Quentin responded immediately: *You're good. We'll meet you at the car. Want something from the café?*

Jack sent back a negative, stomach churning. He had to remind himself that if he deleted any of the footage, Michelle would chuck his corpse in the Mississippi.

§

Black Dove frowned over the footage as they drove back to base, she and Jack in the back seat with Quentin at the wheel and Gold experiencing the joy of fried food in the passenger seat. "You couldn't get any closer?" she asked, disappointment and disdain dripping from her voice.

"Not without being spotted," Jack said, pulling off the baseball cap that had helped hide his auburn curls. "I still don't get why we have to tail the baker this much. The more people we involve, the messier this gets."

"They may still be useful to us," Black Dove scolded.

"Yeah, and you know Michelle," Quentin added, his Texan drawl filling the car. "She doesn't like going into any situation without collecting as much information as possible."

"Smart," Gold said between bites. "'Specially going after the Iron Witch."

"Don't talk with your mouth full. Were you raised in a barn?"

"Yes!" the fairy cheered proudly. "I come from a long line of farmers."

"The hell made you join the army then?"

The cheer vanished. "Humans burned it down."

"No chance of rebuilding?" Quentin asked, sympathetic through the sudden awkwardness.

"Oh, it's been rebuilt," Gold said. "But while my parents, spouse, and siblings are willing to forget, I cannot."

"...fair enough."

After a lull in conversation—the only sounds being Gold's chewing and the surveillance video on low volume—Jack asked, "Why don't we just go after Violet in her house? Her ward has Dungeons and Dragons every Friday. Perfect time."

"Do you know *nothing* of magic?" Black Dove snapped. "We walked by her home the day we arrived. Even from the road, I could sense all the protective charms she placed on it. *Never* attack a fairy in their domain, especially a sorcerer. Your weapons will fail. Your armor will crack. Everything that could possibly go wrong, every bit of ill luck you could possibly run into, it will happen. And she'll barely have to lift a finger."

Jack made a face, both at the problem and disrespect.

"I assume the café is similarly guarded?" Quentin asked, always the calm voice of reason.

"Very much so," Black Dove confirmed.

"Phenomenal."

Black Dove re-started the video, concentrating on it. Jack hoped she got car-sick, but also didn't want her to puke on his phone.

Her form rippled, the ivory robes (which she'd glamoured into a sun dress while in the museum) turned into a jean jacket and skirt. Bushy brown hair grew from a bald head that lightened to slightly-sunburnt Caucasian, no silver marbling.

An exact copy of Jennifer Charles sat next to Jack. But the body language was all wrong, especially the facial expression. Jack couldn't quite place it, but the baker always appeared... warmer. Like a bonfire. Warm and comforting, sure, so long as it didn't snap and burn out of control. Black Dove was too cold and statuesque.

Until she replicated the slightly dreamy, amused look Jennifer Charles had made when Nicole had returned with half a fridge's worth of sugary drinks. Jack looked away, unnerved.

"Perhaps I can replace the baker at the café to keep a closer eye on Violet," Black Dove mused—in Jennifer Charles's voice, no less. "I wouldn't be able to attack her, but perhaps I could find and destroy the protective charms."

"You'd have to kill them," Jack argued.

"No, *you* would. Or one of your coworkers."

Jack's stomach churned. It wouldn't be his first kill. Hell, it wouldn't even be his most morally repugnant. But every day he worked for Michelle, every life he touched and ruined and destroyed, made him feel more and more like a mass of twisted thorns. He wondered how long it would take for them to strangle him.

Getting out was a death sentence. *No one* walked away from Michelle once they accepted a job. And even if he managed it, nowhere else was willing to hire a dishonorable discharge.

"Do you know anything about baking?" Quentin asked.

"How hard could it be?" Black Dove retorted, still with that damn voice.

"Hard. Especially if you're pretending to be a professional."

The sorceress *hmph*ed. "Perhaps we could stage a meeting outside of the café…"

"I'd pose as the witch, then," Gold said, licking their pale fingers. "The baker would have little reason to meet with Violet outside of their duties, but the witch is her apprentice, isn't she? Or at least used to be?"

"I'd need more footage," Black Dove said, glamour rippling over her again, this time replicating Nicole. She even started doing that finger-tapping stim. "Although replicating the girl's paltry magic is such an insult…"

Jack squeezed back into his seat and breathed through the sudden nausea. He really wasn't cut out for this line of work.

status

On Monday after work, JC finally got their hands on a prescription for a proper insulin pump. No more needles! Insurance refused to cover about half of their options, but not all of them, including the tubeless pumps: the ones that looked like white squares with tape that could stick almost anywhere, usually the back of the arm. JC went with tubeless because they just *knew* that tube would get tangled and caught on a million things while they worked. Even if they put it under their apron or clothes, it would find a way.

They considered another splurge, this time on clothes. But nothing was on sale, Violet's pay wouldn't let them be that reckless, and their storage space was limited. Still, they kept an eye out for deals on hiking or cargo pants, track pants, and skirts or dresses with pockets. *Actual* pockets, not those tiny bullshit ones that could barely hold a tube of chapstick.

Tuesday came, and they were back behind the counter.

"Anything else for you?" they asked.

The tattooed woman with the red-tinted sunglasses shook her head, taking the coffee and muffin. "Nah. Thanks."

The tip jar appeared on the light granite counter, right by the register. The woman snorted and dropped a few quarters in. "Most people just use a regular tip jar."

"It's a fairy thing," JC said with a shrug. "They're all about 'fair exchange.' Tips are extra, so they're not cool with it unless they feel they've 'earned' it with a 'thank you.' But even then, Violet's relaxed enough about it that she doesn't demand a tip every time someone accidentally says thanks. I think it's just a joke that I'm not smart enough to get."

The woman shook her head, eyes rolling behind her sunglasses. "So, you don't get any tips?"

"Sure I do. Just not as much. And I get good actual pay, so it's not like I need..." Movement out of the corner of their eye. From the kitchen.

They smiled at the customer. "Just a sec."

They left the counter, snagged a wooden spoon as they entered the kitchen, and whacked Cyrus's blue arm as he reached for the cookie dough in the fridge.

"Ow!"

"No touchy!" JC scolded.

Cyrus rubbed his arm, pouting. "I'm telling Boss."

"You do that. See who she chews out more."

"...I am *not* telling Boss."

The woman with the red sunglasses snorted and left. Another customer—sipping his coffee as he scrolled through his phone—watched JC and Cyrus through the entrance to the kitchen. "You know that's assault."

"Uh-oh, JC, back to jail," Cyrus crowed.

"Suuuure. And who's going to make those cookies? Or scones? Or brownies?" they challenged.

The man gave them a sharp look. With the way the sun hit his slouching form, he looked like he was made of melting bread dough. If he stood from his table, he'd be shaped like an oval. "How long have you been out?"

JC shrugged, crossing their arms. "A few months. Why?"

"What were you in for?"

"That's not really any of your business."

He reached into his pocket. "Since you're in my town, I think it is."

He dropped a police badge on the table.

JC met his gaze. "Get a warrant, then."

"I could arrest you now, you know. For assault."

They stiffened. If they hadn't broken curfew earlier that month, this would be easier to make go away. But as soon as a judge or prosecutor saw that they were having problems with their parole...

"Okay, no," Cyrus butted in. "Friends roughhouse each other all the time. And JC's literal job is to be a baker. Of course they're going to defend the cookie dough with their life! So just cool it, Hendricks."

Officer Hendricks looked between the two of them. "I suppose Violet's already aware of your status. And your girlfriend."

Right. Small town. News of the cops smashing into Nicole's house would've gotten around.

"Have you looked into that Miller guy?" JC asked.

He frowned. "It's not smart to accuse a police officer of something without evidence."

"The word of a clairvoyant is proof enough for us," Cyrus said, his tone surprisingly icy. "Especially that one. Now, is there anything else you need, Officer?"

He shook his head, reclaiming his badge. "No, I don't think so."

JC went back into the kitchen, glummer and grumpier than they'd been five minutes ago. Cyrus quickly joined them, wincing. "Sorry. I didn't mean to out you as a jailbird."

"It's fine. It was a good joke. Some people just have sticks up their asses," they said, checking on the dough Cyrus had tried to steal. It was firm enough to work with, so they started on the batch, rolling it out on the metal counter.

About half an hour later, when Cyrus had returned to the front, Violet joined them. Two of the trays had already come out of the oven, flooding the kitchen with the thick perfume of baked sweets that JC was quickly becoming numb to. She helped herself to one of the pistachio chocolate chip cookies while they were still goopy. JC glared, threateningly holding up the wooden spoon.

Violet gave them a very amused look, wiping the melted chocolate from her purple lips. "I had a conversation with Officer Hendricks. He's 'very concerned about hiring an ex-criminal. After all, they're more likely to break the law again.'"

She said his line in Hendricks's *exact* voice, a quirk of fairy magic–glamour–that made JC jump. "That is so creepy, please never do that again," they begged. "What did you say?"

She answered in her own voice, thankfully: "I asked him how he planned to lower the rate of recidivism if he treated all ex-convicts as if they would offend again. He did not deign to answer, and instead left. Rather rude of him, if you ask me."

They snickered. "Thanks, Bob."

"My pleasure. Although try to find other ways to dissuade Cyrus from sneaking bites. You can't guard the fridge twenty-four/seven."

genuine loyalty

"I don't think the baker's our way in," Michelle said, flipping through one of the many files spread out on the motel bed. Her red sunglasses were folded, hanging from her neckline, and her tank top exposed the scorpion tattoo creeping up her collarbone. "They're too loyal."

Red Wolf sat cross-legged on the hotel bed that had been his home for the last two months. He and his people had gotten more and more used to Earth life—the better to blend in—while he sent Michelle and her people to gather information on their target. Still, this place was stale and stuffy, while outside was far too loud, bruising his sharp, pointed ears with incessant car grumbles and mortal chatter. Worse, they didn't want the cleaning staff to find anything condemning, and Mouse had over-compensated for that by drenching their rooms with fruit-smelling air freshener that did not smell anything like real fruit.

"Can we blackmail them?" Red Wolf asked.

"No. They're not hiding anything, and as far as Jack can tell, they're estranged from their family, so no hostages for us to use."

He scanned Jennifer Charles's extensive record. The mercenary leader was right: this person was a social delinquent, and had the hope of stability only due to Violet's employment.

Genuine loyalty is far better than fear or mere bribery. The ideal soldier follows you because you are the only thing giving them a contented life. They need to understand that your wealth and well-being is their wealth and well-being. Your cause is their cause. Once they believe that, they'll fight for you as fiercely as they would their own survival.

That had been one of Violet's first lessons to him. In fact, that had been the whole reason Red Wolf had agreed to stay within her ranks, despite numerous opportunities to transfer: she had always taken care of her soldiers to the best of her ability, and had been especially generous to those who stayed loyal and true to her—until the end. It was comforting to know that she still employed such wisdom for herself, as that would make predicting her protections and counter-strategy much easier.

"How are we in tracing her assets?" Red Wolf asked Jack.

The young man grimaced, curled over his laptop like a gargoyle. He was the youngest of Michelle's workers, unable to legally rent a car. But he was excellent with a computer and, according to the other mortals, even better with a sniper rifle. He blew his auburn curls out of his face and said, "Not great. Everything digitally related to Violet Smith, a.k.a. Lavender Jones, a.k.a. Melora Johnson, is pretty standard. No unusual business expenses, no property taxes or mortgages outside of the Twin Cities area, no unusually massive expenses. I've calculated that she's got at least a few million dollars squared away, probably more in cash. Beyond that, I couldn't tell you. The Melora identity is bare bones, barely anything to her name, which means anything she's buying with that identity is probably cash-only. Untraceable."

"Most of the people she's friendly with are in Bernier, according to our observations," Michelle added. "And the biggest problems there are the Wulver and the witch coven."

"She's been in this Realm for two hundred years. I cannot believe those are her only allies," Red Wolf scolded. "Or her only identities."

"Well, they're the only ones that she's left a digital marker on," Jack retorted. "Anything else she has is dormant and/or off-grid."

Quentin, one of Michelle's other mercenaries with a few years on Jack, sighed: "We didn't find anything useful, either."

His frustration was palpable, as he'd been assigned dumpster duty: rifling through Violet's trash to see if anything turned up there. The dark-skinned mortal had not been happy about it, but Michelle's orders had been final. Unfortunately for him, if Violet did have physical contraband, she disposed of it much more discreetly. The man had complained for weeks about how difficult it'd been to get the stench of garbage out of his braids.

Michelle tossed her papers on the bed, by Red Wolf's left foot, and crossed her arms. "From what you've told us about this woman, things are probably going to get messy. That means law enforcement's going to come after us right away. We can't avoid it."

"Smoke and flash bombs, then?" Quentin suggested. "It'd give us a lot of cover if we've gotta do it publicly."

"She'll fight back," Red Wolf mused.

"Then we tase or drug her."

"She'll have good luck charms. You'll never hit."

Michelle held up a palm. "We'll get to that later. What I'm saying is, once we do have Violet, we can give the police a red herring. A different suspect to chase to give us some breathing room. You people can glamour to look like anything you want, right?"

"Within limits," he said, smiling. "Michelle, you are well worth your paycheck. And I think the baker *is* our way in, or at least our way close."

Jack's mouth thinned. "How long is that going to last, though? If they have an alibi..."

"You kill them before they can be arrested," Red Wolf interrupted. "Then you hide the body. The police will think they're on the run and won't learn the truth until it's too late."

"Easy enough," Quentin said. "They used to be a drug addict, right? Ran with gangs? Drive-by."

"That solves one problem. Now, for the issue of Violet..." There was no avoiding it. Red Wolf had put the musician off for as long as possible, but he wasn't seeing any other alternative for getting Violet into the van. "Get me Piper."

team 1 group chat

JACK
do jobs usually
take this long?

QUENTIN
Sometimes. Why?
ALEX
I've been on longer
Weirdest part is
the no-kill rule
That's kinda the opposite
of what we do?

JACK
getting hard to justify
my "road trip" to
my mom and sis

QUENTIN
Scared to miss curfew?
ROGER
What are you, 12?🌀🌀🌀

JACK
2?
i promised to help
them with $$
rent went up again

QUENTIN
It always does. Don't
worry, we'll be
closing in, soon.
DAVID
What does your mom
do for a living?

                                        JACK
                                cleaning lady
                          sis helps part-time
                             shes going to
                            college in fall
                           but mom wants to
                             be a gardener
                            landscaper too

ALEX
Did you want us to spot
you a couple hundred?
QUENTIN
You can also ask M
for an advance. She's
usually pretty good
about that stuff.

                                        JACK
                                        thx
                                 and maybe
                       depends on how much
                           longer we stay

MICHELLE
Unfortunately the half
up front RW gave me
has largely been going
into this operation
(food, hotel, equipment,
etc). So I can't give
anyone an advance.
We move on Friday.

marbles: the new cocaine

From a 2003 New York Times *article:*

"Marbles" is the street name given to drugs made from the marmair flower, a plant native to the Fae Realm and originally given to soldiers in battle, removing their fear and boosting confidence while making it easier to ignore pain. It gets its street name *marbles* from the appearance of the little candy-like balls–and possibly from the color effect of certain fairies' skin.

The marmair flowers are cooked into a syrup, mixed with sugar and several other chemicals to keep its shape and preserve it for long periods of time, and either eaten or smoked. Users describe its high as "being Superman: invincible and powerful. [We] can do anything."

Despite the feeling and rumors, marbles do not give its users magical powers and, in fact, have several debilitating side effects. In addition to the psychological and physical addiction (cooks and dealers often add nicotine to the drug for an even greater hook), marmair are Fae flowers. While some Fae ingredients can be purified and safely consumed (namely, meat from Fae animals–albeit sparingly), marmair is not one of them. While the magical ingredient is diluted with other, Earthly items, it still has many of the same side effects of any other Fae food: you eventually begin losing your ability to eat Earth food. Experts say that the true threat of marbles, especially with long-term use, is malnutrition and starvation.

thin red line

On Thursday, the bus dropped JC off a few blocks from the halfway house. It wasn't until shortly after they'd gotten on their bicycle that they realized they were being followed.

A black van had been behind the bus for the last ten minutes. And now, as they biked down the street and turned around the block, away from downtown St. Paul and toward the endless lines of quasi-suburban houses, the van continued behind them. Sure, it was a school zone with a low speed limit, but no one actually obeyed those signs unless the kids were actively running around. Why was it moving slow enough to keep pace with them?

They considered turning down a dirt road alley and giving them the slip, then decided that wasn't how they were going to spend their afternoon. They stopped in the middle of the block, near a bus stop, glaring at the black van as it drew closer and closer...

And drove right by them.

"Hm." JC watched it turn the corner, disappearing behind a cheap-looking bar. Maybe they were just being paranoid?

The bus stop had one of those quasi-shelters over the bench, the walls made of glass with Metro Transit's logo all over it. One of the men leaned against the wall, smoking, and paused. He did a double-take. "Scott?"

JC stiffened, then forced themselves to relax. "Hey, Rocket."

"Holy shit, dude!" Rocket dropped his cigarette and ruffled their bushy brown hair, like they were still a kid. "I haven't seen you since the trial!"

JC batted him away. "Yeah, it's been a while. How you doing?"

Rocket was a bit older than JC. Back when they were in their teens and twenties and denying their bisexuality, they'd thought he was the coolest thing ever, even a little hot, with the gold chain and rings, baseball hat, Air Jordans, muscled arms...

Now, he still dressed the same, except without the hat. The five o'clock shadow had some gray, and he'd grown a beer belly. He was still stupidly tall, though, towering over JC's petite frame.

"Doing good, doing good." Rocket's forehead wrinkled. "Shit, I must be more fried than I thought. I can't remember your first name."

They snickered. "Yeah, I'm queer and had a fairy wipe my dead name. Call me JC."

"You made a deal with a jick?"

"Dude." *Jick* was almost as bad as *nigger*.

"*And* you're gay?"

"Bisexual and nonbinary. Use they/them pronouns," they said.

Rocket snorted, shaking his head. "Whatever, man. You always were weird."

And that was why they'd always liked Rocket. He didn't understand much about the queer community—or Blacks, or Latinos, or Fae, or disabled people, or whatever—but he usually wasn't a dick about it. Not intentionally, anyway.

"How long you been out of prison?" he asked. "I thought you had at least a decade."

"Good behavior."

"Wh–*You*?"

JC punched his shoulder. Rocket laughed. "Come on, man. Let's get a drink."

They hesitated. Spending time with their old dealer was probably one of those things that they *shouldn't* do as a recovering addict.

But Rocket had been one of their best friends for a long time. Had pulled them out of gun fights and picked them up off the sidewalk and let them crash at his place to sober up and get away from their relatives more times than they could count. And they hadn't seen him in six years. Maybe he was out, or looking for a way out.

They followed him along the cracked sidewalk to that cheap bar, walking along their bike. "So, how's the wife?"

Rocket grimaced. "Which one? They're both my exes, now."

"Yikes. Sorry, man."

"Eh, some chicks just don't understand 'Ride or Die.' Remember Patty?"

"Ugh, she was the worst. How much did she steal from us?"

"Way too much. But goddamn, still the best pussy I've ever had."

Rocket led them to the small, hole-in-the-wall bar, dark and dingy. It was too early in the day for a rush, but there were a couple of dedicated drunks in one of the ripped-up booths in the back corner as the bartender fought a losing battle against the sticky countertop. JC wrinkled their nose; something in the air was sour.

"Couple of beers, please," Rocket said, settling into one of the stools.

"No, actually, make mine a diet coke," JC said before the barkeeper could turn away.

Rocket gaped. "You're not drinking?"

They considered pulling out the NA coin, but Rocket had never had much respect for being clean and sober. So instead, they said, "Diabetic. Gotta watch what goes in."

They pulled up their shirt and jean jacket, showing off the new insulin pump stuck right behind their bicep.

Rocket shook his head, pity on his face. "Ah, shit, man. Sorry about that."

"It happens. So, what've you been up to?"

"Same old, same old."

JC's stomach dropped as the barkeeper set their drinks down. "You're still dealing?"

"Pays the bills, doesn't it? Nobody's hiring these days. Except for me."

JC shook their head. "No thanks. I'm all set up."

Rocket frowned, his tone darkening. "You cooking for someone else?"

So much for avoiding the sober talk.

"No. I work at a café down in Bernier. I'm going clean." They pulled their chip out of the pocket and slid it across the counter.

He snorted. "Seriously, kid? You're the best cook in the Cities, and you're throwing it away?"

"Yup."

Rocket stared at them. JC slurped their diet coke through a straw. There was so much ice in the glass it didn't take long to empty it.

"You could make over a thousand bucks a batch," he said, keeping his voice low as the barkeeper cleaned his glasses.

"I'm done with that dumb kid stuff."

"Over a thousand a day is 'dumb kid stuff'?"

"Yup."

Rocket shook his head. "Whatever. Let me know when you change your mind. So, what's the craziest thing you saw in prison?"

JC relaxed, relieved that he was letting it go as they talked about some of the wackier characters they had met behind bars. Rocket laughed along with them, asking questions and paying for a refill.

JC's phone buzzed. Brandon had texted them. *Where are you?*

They winced. "Gimme a sec."

Rocket waved them off. JC quickly typed back, *sorry i met a friend. back soon.*

Curfew is 7 p.m.

Thanks to the punishing bus schedule—and their lack of car—they only had two hours. That was fine; with their bike, they could get there in ten minutes.

"Sorry about that," JC said, putting the phone away.

Rocket wiggled his greying eyebrows. "Girlfriend? Or, uh, boyfriend?"

"I wish. Staff at the halfway house. I swear, even when I try not to be a criminal, they still treat me as one. I do have a date on Sunday. There's this really sexy witch who's a regular and we're going to see a movie..."

JC took their diet coke, ready to dive into the details of Nicole: her straight-forward bluntness, her kindness, her tongue...

And froze.

"Ohhhh, do tell," Rocket prodded.

JC didn't answer.

"Hey, buddy? JC? Earth to cook."

They glared at him. "You know, marbles break down and melt pretty easily. But it has a really hard time dissolving and mixing with other liquids. When it is a liquid, it floats. Like oil."

They held up their glass, where a thin red line floated atop of their diet coke. It hadn't been there ten seconds ago.

Rocket looked like he would deny it for a couple of seconds, then clearly decided against it. He spread his hands. "I just thought you needed a reminder of what you were missing—"

JC punched him, cartilage crumbling beneath their knuckles.

Rocket yelped, clutching his bleeding nose and falling off his stool with a crash, deafening in the near-silent bar. "What the shit?"

"You spiked my fucking drink!"

"Chill out!"

"Don't fucking tell me to chill out, you piece of—"

A shotgun, pumped and loaded, cut them off. The barkeep held the gun, but pointed it toward the floor, not directly at them. Yet.

"Take it outside, gentlemen," he said.

"Fine," JC snapped, digging for their wallet and throwing a ten on the counter. "Leave me alone, Rocket. I see you again, I'll kill you."

"Pussy," he hollered at JC's back. "Fairy-fucking pussy!"

Six years ago, that would've been enough to make them turn right around and beat him until there was nothing but bruises, blood, and broken bones.

Now, JC flipped him off over their shoulder and left.

§

Brandon greeted JC with a plastic cup as soon as they walked in, still swearing and muttering under their breath. JC snatched the cup. "Actually, yeah. Can you put a rush on it?"

"Why?" Brandon asked mildly.

They told him what happened. Brandon straightened, Navy SEAL training putting him at a sharp, attentive parade rest. "Are you hurt?"

JC held up their hand, the knuckles bruised.

Brandon snorted. "How bad is *he* hurt?"

"He'll be fine."

Brandon took a penlight and checked JC's pupils just as Alku came in. "JC! Buddy! My kid loved the cake. And it was *so good*, we couldn't believe...what happened?"

"Old dealer tried to spike me," they grumbled, rage finally simmering a bit now that they were safe. "I'm fine. I think I caught it before I had anything."

"Better to be safe than sorry." Brandon turned off the light and motioned to the cup. "If it comes back positive, I'll be sure to let them know that you were unwilling."

JC grunted, snatching the cup.

"What on the earth made you think it was a good idea to meet with your old dealer?"

"We ran into each other. Total accident. And I thought..." They shook their head. "I don't know what I thought. That I owed it to him to help him get out? He was my friend, my first crush, and he never tried to pull that shit over me before."

That had made him one of the good ones—relatively speaking. JC could name more than one dealer who got their customers by literally forcing drugs down people's throats, or pinning them down for a needle. Rocket had never crossed that line before.

"People change," Brandon said quietly. "And not always for the better. Did you want to press charges?"

They gave a bitter laugh. "Yeah, sure. No evidence, an ex-criminal vs. another criminal, and *I* punched *him*, what exactly is that going to do besides get me in more trouble?"

"It starts a paper trail in case he comes at you again."

Alku shook his head. "Not worth it."

JC agreed, but said, "You can write whatever you want in your daily logs or whatever you do to keep your bosses happy, but I'd rather just forget about this."

Brandon didn't argue. JC did their business, washed their hands, and presented the covered cup to Brandon, who'd already called the lab geeks. Alku sat at the scratched and dented kitchen table, in one of the chairs specially designed for goblins in human spaces—basically an adult booster seat—tapping on his phone.

"I just asked around," he said as JC came into the kitchen. Someone had cleaned it recently, the smell of citrus lingering in the air. It did nothing to hide the bits of burnt food stuck to the stovetop burners, and there was something rotting in the fridge. "Your old gang the Bobcats lost their cook to a firefight a few months ago, and their usual supplier to an OD. They're still making marbles, but whoever they got to replace him isn't great. No wonder they want you back."

"Great. We have a regular Walter White," Brandon drawled.

"Who?" JC asked.

Alku laughed. "Didn't you see *Breaking Bad*?"

"Do the commercials count?"

He face-palmed.

"We'll rent it later. I'm sure you'll poke all sorts of holes in it," Brandon said. "Look, JC, I've seen this before. They're going to keep bugging you about this, trying to coax you back into that old life, maybe even try threatening you a bit. But after some time—a month at most—once they realize you're not coming back, they'll leave you alone. You'll be dead to them. You just have to stick it out until then, and leave them behind for good once they're gone."

"How bad is this going to get?" JC asked, mentally listing everywhere they could get a gun.

"Well, you have the advantage of being out of the game for six years. I don't think it'll get that bad. Try to avoid punching any more teeth in; we don't want you thrown back in for assault. Got it?"

JC nodded. Brandon's phone buzzed. He read the text. "All right, I've got someone coming to pick this up. We should have results in twenty-four hours. You work tomorrow?"

"Yeah."

"Maybe call in sick."

JC flared. "No way! Rocket, the Bobcats, they don't get to just barge back into my life and fuck things up! They definitely don't get to threaten my job."

Brandon held up his hands. "All right, fine."

Something crashed down the hall, followed by a, "Dammit, Nick! Clean your shit!"

"It is clean! Stop digging around my shaving kit!" Nick yelled from the living room.

"It is not!"

Brandon sighed, hauling himself out of the chair, beer belly brushing against the table. "I'd better defuse that. Everyone, stop shouting! Let's handle this like the adults we all pretend to be..."

He left, stopping briefly to drag Nick into the hall with him. JC shook their head. The house had thirty residents, one to four staff at any given time, and only two bathrooms.

They ran a hand down their face, exhausted. Alku tapped his phone against the table. It looked comically large in his little green goblin hands, almost like a tablet. "First time I tried getting out of the gang life, I was back on the street with my boys within a week. Needed the money. The second time, it was because everyone else was treating me like a criminal. I thought, 'If all they're going to give me is shit, I'll give it right back to them.'"

JC nodded. "Yeah. I was in and out of juvie since I was twelve. Then jail. Finally prison. It's a black fucking hole."

Alku hummed.

"What got you out for good?"

He huffed a laugh. "Can't say I really am out for good, can I? Not while I'm in here." He motioned to the house, the dingy kitchen and busted light bulb over the stove that hadn't been replaced in weeks, the arguing down the hall.

"But I didn't have a kid before," he said. "I do now. That's worth staying out for, even if all anyone else sees is a criminal."

JC bit their lip. "Well, I've got a Date No. 3 on Sunday, but I don't think she'll be on board that quick..."

Alku burst out laughing, almost drowning out the arguing. JC grinned.

The goblin shook his horned head and flipped through his phone. "I want to show you something...let me just...here."

He turned the phone around. JC took it and smiled.

The cake had been a challenge. Even though the halfway house had two fridges and freezers, that wasn't a whole lot of space for all the people who needed them. So, they'd made three small tiers and refrigerated them separately overnight, got up an hour early to make the green mint frosting, and assembled it, with a big yellow 3 on top and white trim, decorated with mint leaves for an extra bit of class. Alku had a red cooler he used to stash his own food (checked almost daily by Elizabeth), and that was where JC had put it before leaving for work.

The pictures Alku showed them had that cake *demolished*, half of it smeared across the face of a grinning three-year-old goblin, his tiny horns the size of peanuts.

"Well, I guess you all choked it down okay," they drawled, warmth unfurling in their chest.

"It was really good," Alku said. "I hope you're ready for my sister's birthday, because we're never getting store-bought again."

team 1 group chat

DAVID
Holy shit.
The fairies
brought All-Heal!

JACK
whoa really?

QUENTIN
Just a little
for emergencies
Like, 4 or 5 oz I think?
ALEX
Gotta be worth at
least $500k
QUENTIN
Good luck, RW's
guarding it.
ALEX
Crap
QUENTIN
And M would kill you
for robbing a client
ALEX
Oh yeah...
ROGER
What's All-Heal?
QUENTIN
Magic healing lotion.

DAVID

It's an enchanted
ointment designed to
cure all wounds. Some
stories say it can
even bring back the dead
under certain conditions.
Only fairies know how to
make it, so it can only be
bought from the Fae Realm.
Gialdon doesn't have much
of it, though. Most of
the fairy nations don't
sell to them, so we can't
get a lot of it here.

                              JACK
                    some hospitals have it
                    it costs a ton of $$$
                       even in military

ALEX

Yeah, my friend got hit
by a car and her heart
was literally stabbed
by a metal rod. They
used a tiny dollop of
All-Heal to fix it in
surgery. That plus the
surgery cost her $230k
ROGER

Before or after insurance?
ALEX

After. In network
and everything.

                                              JACK
                                              yikes

ALEX
No complications or
anything, though.
ROGER
You think it could
cure cancer?
ALEX
Maybe?
DAVID
No.
Sorry, Roger.

                                              JACK
                                              why not?

ROGER
Yeah, it's ALL-Heal.
It's in the name.
QUENTIN
Fairies made it
for fairies.
Fairies don't get sick.
DAVID
What Quentin said.
All-Heal was designed
for war/battle, for when
fairies get injured. It
didn't happen often, since
fairies usually stay away
from those fights and
historically made up their

armies out of humans.
They didn't really care if
humans got sick or hurt.

> JACK
>> wtf
>> thats messed up

DAVID
It is what it is.
Anyway, All-Heal can
be used to heal human
INJURIES, but every
time we try to use it
on disease, it's hit-
or-miss. The times it
does work require a LOT
more than even a bullet
wound. More than even a
billionaire could afford.
ROGER
Oh☹️
DAVID
Sorry.
ALEX
Your brother still
on chemo?
ROGER
Yeah
MICHELLE
Don't worry, we're getting
our target tomorrow.
Within a week, we'll all
get paid, and hospital
bills won't be an issue.

a gialdonian poem

Don't let the fairies sing
  Or play their flutes
  Their music is poison
  Worse than hemlock roots

When the fairies sing
  Their songs so sweet
  We cannot fight
  Or cry or weep

When the fairies sing
  Our lives aren't our own
  We are but mere puppets
  To their cruel throne

So don't you ever let the fairies sing
  Block out their music with wax and walls
  Best for you to be dead and buried
  Than to be their hollow doll

Gialdonian poem, dated roughly from the 18th century, published
in the Mortal Realm in 1952.
Original author unknown.

piper's song

"Good job today, both of you," Violet called as she locked the front door on Friday.

Jennifer Charles beamed, like they always did whenever Violet gave praise. They finished mopping the floor as Cyrus wiped the counter, wet rag squeaking against the white granite top.

"Cyrus" seemed to be a new favorite name for the boy. It happened every few decades, and Violet certainly couldn't judge. She had collected dozens, hundreds of names in her centuries of life, some more flattering than others. The more titles collected, the safer a fairy's *true* name. So she'd stick to Cyrus until he decided otherwise.

"Hey JC, you mind if I take the leftovers with me?" he asked. "I'm going to a DnD night."

"Nerd," they said. "Fine."

"Yus. Wanna come? We're doing a one-shot; it'd be easy to slot you in."

"Can't. Curfew."

"Ah."

Violet grimaced as she went over her checklist. Preventing ex-criminals from returning to crime was a conundrum plaguing almost every civilization across every realm, but one thing she had seen was that isolating them from the community usually set them up for failure. How anyone found it acceptable to drag two police officers into a full-blown investigation for missing a bus was beyond her. At least Jennifer Charles had taken it with good humor. (Although that may have had more to do with their evening with Nicole.)

"Perhaps you can join one of their digital groups," she suggested. "I know Cyrus is in at least three."

"Currently two, but yeah, the third one's going to start again in a few weeks," he offered.

"Those sessions run for what, three, four hours?" JC asked. "I can't hog the computer for that long. Ask me again when I can buy a laptop."

Cyrus shrugged, tossing his rag into the bucket, sending blue water and disinfectant splooshing onto the floor. "All right. I'm driving to the Cities; want me to give you a lift?"

"Would you? That'd be awesome—wait, what about Bob?"

"I live within walking distance," she assured them. "And it's a lovely afternoon."

Jennifer Charles frowned. "Hasn't Nicole been talking doom and gloom in her visions?"

"You trust the visions of a witch you've barely met?" she teased.

"Thaaaaat's a trap." They snapped their fingers. "But *you* trust those visions."

Violet smirked. "I do. And I'll be in public in the middle of the day. Those are less than ideal circumstances for an attack."

They shrugged. "Aight. Your funeral."

The three of them finished cleaning up. Violet always enjoyed quiet hours like this, after a day well spent. They turned out the lights, tossed their aprons in the dirty laundry, and locked the doors behind them. Jennifer Charles and Cyrus piled into the electric car with bags of leftover cookies, brownies, and muffins. "See you tonight, Boss!" Cyrus called as he drove off.

With it being the height of summer—and since CaFae Latte closed in the mid-afternoon—there was plenty of daylight and people. Violet took her time, meandering down Main Street. The Red Dahlia hosted most of its customers outside, everyone taking advantage of the sun and outdoor seating that had been hastily set up in the street's parking spots during the pandemic. The Mexican restaurant had since put up waist-high walls fashioned to look like weathered wooden fences—the kind often used to contain livestock. Business was just starting to pick up there, as well as the other restaurants down the street: Mrs. Sippy's was already spilling out college kids home for the summer, and she had to walk past a few bustling tables from Stefano's Grille. The former clogged their arteries with fries and burgers while the latter were overwhelmed with bowls of spaghetti and red sauce.

Caroline had taken a break from her yarn shop with her husband Andy—they each had an ice cream cone and were walking hand-in-hand, coming back from the river trail, the slight breeze from the water making the stifling summer heat a little more bearable. Their eyes met across the street, and the elderly woman smiled at her before turning back to whatever her husband was saying. A woman in a gray tank top leaned against the streetlight, giggling into a phone while her Doberman lay at her feet, watching Violet's approach.

Trapped in her purse, Violet's phone rang. She smiled at the ID. "Wulver. It's been a while."

"'Afternoon, lass!" the Scottish werewolf boomed. "Ye got a minute?"

"Several. I just closed."

"Beautiful. I just heard Toothie's comin' to town next week. Some 'o the mates were thinkin' a havin' a poker night. Ye'in?"

"That sounds absolutely lovely. You know how much I enjoy taking your money."

"Ah, yer not gettin' me this time, lass. I been practicin'!"

Violet chuckled, passing an antique store's window.

And noticed the black van in the reflection, parked across the street.

She'd seen it a handful of times over the last month. She had dismissed it at first, especially since it looked like the people using it were musicians, either passing through or preparing for tomorrow's car show.

But with Nicole's warnings ringing in her ears, something didn't feel right...

"Violet! Hey, wait up."

She paused. Turned around. Jennifer Charles jogged up to her, weaving around the half-dozen people on the sidewalk.

She narrowed her eyes. "Wulver, I'm going to have to call you back. There's a situation."

He picked up on her tone. "Ye safe, lass?"

"Don't know. I'm downtown, by the Red Dahlia. I'll call you in five." She hung up just as "Jennifer Charles" caught up to her.

"Glad I caught you. I forgot to ask something..." they said.

"Bob."

They tipped their head. "Huh?"

"Your glamour is excellent. You even got the voice right. But Jennifer Charles calls me Bob," she said. "Who are you?"

The being scowled, crossing their arms just like the baker when they were irate. "At least let me have a little fun with it. I spent almost two months working on this form."

It was time well-spent. The face, the bushy brown shoulder-length hair, the wear and tear of the jean jacket, all the details were right. Even the way they stood, walked, and cadence of their voice would have fooled almost any mortal and probably a few fairies, too.

And yet, there was a sense of not *quite* right, betraying itself to the expert eye.

"Glamour is not infallible," Violet lectured. "Perhaps to mortals it is. But I've used that magic for centuries."

She twitched her wrist, and the knife she'd glamoured into one of her bracelets reverted to its true form, dropping in her palm as she rested the tip against the other being's belly. They were so close together that nobody around them had noticed. Not yet, anyway.

The imposter gulped, but managed to keep a brave face. "Well. Just because *you* can see through the glamour doesn't mean all these witnesses can. Or the security cameras of the stores around you."

Violet frowned. "What are you trying to frame my baker for?"

"Easy, Violet," someone said behind her. "I'd like to avoid bloodshed if at all possible."

She glanced over her shoulder. He was glamoured as a human, one with a face she didn't know. That didn't matter. She recognized the voice.

She removed the knife, turning it back into a bracelet and approaching the new face with a smile that wasn't entirely fake. "Harvest Moon. I thought you hated this Realm."

"I go by Red Wolf now."

Nicole's premonitions, Violet thought. She pushed it aside.

She looked him up and down. He seemed to be in good health: eating every day and exercising. Her eyes caught on the three gold rings decorating his right hand. He had never liked jewelry, but they weren't glamoured. What *was* glamoured was the key chain dangling on the right of his belt and the cell phone case on his left. Weapons, most likely. "I'm glad to see you. You're looking well."

Red Wolf's eyebrows rose.

"You're surprised?" she asked.

"We didn't part on good terms."

"No, we did not. And I've always regretted that," she said. "You're still Chief Commander, I assume?"

"I resigned a while ago."

She blinked. "Really? That's...well, I suppose much can change in two hundred years, but I would have said that's not like you."

"I was less than impressed by Ivae's leadership," he said.

"I see..." she mused, taking the opportunity for another—far sharper—look at her surroundings. "Well, you have one fairy glamoured to look like my baker, a pair of them on the bench across the street posing as elderly sisters, a 'teenager' eating fries, and the woman pretending to talk on her phone has a dog who's been staring at me since I left the café. What exactly do you plan to do here?"

"Black Dove's job was to simply get you into the van. If she failed, they were backup," he said.

Black Dove must have been the sorcerer posed as Jennifer Charles, still standing and moving like them—down to the annoyed scowl.

At this point, Violet could admit it was more curiosity than fear that compelled her. Red Wolf was definitely armed, as were his compatriots. But so was Violet. She knew for a fact that Andy kept a revolver in his pocket anytime he went out in public, the current owner of the Red Dahlia kept a shotgun in his office (with both silver and regular slugs, both equally effective against fairies), and the police station itself was just up the street, barely a minute's stroll.

"There are several laws against kidnapping in this part of the Mortal Realm," she cautioned.

"Yes, there are. Just as there are laws against Fae music. Piper!"

The woman leaning against the streetlamp smirked as her phone glamoured back into its true form: a wooden flute.

Violet turned her bracelet back into a knife and threw it, aiming for the hand holding the flute.

A blur of color, and suddenly the dog was gone, replaced by a pink-skinned fairy who caught the knife mid-air. Almost as fast as a bullet.

Lightning boots, Violet realized, as the musician played a commanding, sonorous tune.

By the second note, all the mortals within twenty feet of Piper stopped walking, quite literally enchanted by the music. At the fourth note—with the sudden silence spreading the sound—fifty feet. Within seconds, the entire street was still and silent, except for Piper's playing. Even the cars had stopped, most windows open on account of the heat and those closed unable to fully protect their drivers from the sound.

The music washed over Violet, tingling in her ears and prodding at her mind, but fairies had always been immune to their own enchantments. The only people unaffected were herself, Red Wolf, Black Dove, and the other fairies she'd already spotted. All the humans were frozen in place, still and quiet beneath the song's notes.

"Piper doesn't get to play music like this very often," Red Wolf mused. "Not anymore. Ivae has too few serfs to justify hiring him, and the Gialdonians would sooner kill him."

"You wonder why?" she asked coldly.

"I do, actually. It'd be much easier on all of us if they just submitted the first time."

You haven't changed at all, she thought sadly. "Why are you here?"

"Justice." He nodded toward the black van. The side door opened from within, a tattooed mortal woman waiting for her with handcuffs ready and noise-blocking headphones over her ears.

Resignation pooled in her stomach. She'd always known someone would try to bury her with all the other corpses she'd put in the ground. It was inevitable.

And yet, she hesitated.

She could probably kill Red Wolf and/or Black Dove, right here and now. Their team likely already had some pre-established leadership, but it would still be a major blow. The lightning-boot wearer would be difficult, but not impossible to defeat.

But was it fair for her to kill him for thinking and acting the way *she* had for so long? Perhaps she could just wound the two of them and run...

Piper changed the tune in his music, sharper and more aggressive.

The result was immediate. A waitress slammed her tray on a patron's head. One of the enchanted drivers drove into a parked car, crumpling metal. Andy dropped his ice cream and wrapped his hands around Caroline's throat—

"Enough," Violet ordered, holding up her hands in surrender.

Piper slowed the music back down, keeping everyone frozen in position.

"Drop your weapons," Red Wolf said.

Violet removed the two earrings that became daggers and the two bracelets that turned into short swords, leaving them on the sidewalk. Black Dove—still as Jennifer Charles—patted her down, frowning at her last remaining golden bracelet. "This is enchanted."

"Yes. But it's not a weapon," she said.

"Remove it."

"No."

Police sirens wailed. Someone inside—or perhaps a deaf or hard-of-hearing person—must have realized what was happening and called it in. Those sirens were only at the fringe of hearing, but as soon as they got close enough it'd drown out Piper's song.

Red Wolf grabbed Violet's arm and pulled her to the van.

sleep standin' up

Officer Matt Hendricks pulled up in front of the Red Dahlia in the middle of utter chaos. At least two cars were crashed, several people were standing or even sitting on the pavement in stunned silence or weeping, and several more were screaming.

Andy—more visible than most with his higher-yellow cap and six-foot-three frame—was trying to calm the chaos, and had succeeded in creating a small semi-calm island on the sidewalk while his wife sat on a nearby bench, looking stunned. But everyone else was a sea of confusion: screaming, wailing, frantically on their phones.

What the hell happened?

Hendricks was the first on the scene by a few seconds. Half of the department had come out for this, earbuds in, as soon as they got the *multiple* calls of fairy music on Main Street. He didn't see any fairies at all, though. Not even Violet.

Officer Nelson went to check on the crashes, blond ponytail swishing back and forth as she jogged. Hendricks went for his megaphone. "Attention, everyone! Attention, *everyone!*"

It took a few tries for him to get at least the majority of people looking his way. Enough time for the other officers to spread out and try to find any major injuries or damage. A few people from inside various buildings came out—which made things more crowded—but it seemed they were less affected by…whatever had happened.

"Does anyone have any serious injuries?" he asked. "By which I mean broken bones, bleeding out, or anything else life-threatening?"

"Caroline got strangled!" Andy called, looking gutted. Hendricks had never seen the fire chief so scared and frazzled. It was terrifying.

One of the EMTs rushed to the elderly woman, and she managed to snap out of her daze enough to hold up a hand, probably muttering, "I'm fine, I'm fine."

"Car crashes were mostly fender benders. Nothing serious," Nelson reported. Despite the earbuds, he could still hear her. Cheap crap.

Hendricks nodded and went back to his mic: "We got a report of fairy music. Is the musician still here?"

Several people shook their heads. At least one called, "They've got Violet!"

Hendricks blinked. Nelson muttered, "Oh, shit," and went to confront whoever had hollered that.

"Okay, everyone, remain calm and stay where you are," he ordered. "We are going to start questioning everyone on what happened. Details are important, which is why we *cannot* rush this. We need to gather as much information as we can, then we can handle the musician."

He put the mic away and went straight to Andy. He was right, Caroline was fussing with the EMT in a hoarse voice, "It's barely a bruise. It don't hurt at all, darlin', go worry about the folks in the car crash..."

He pulled Andy aside, pulling out his earbuds. "What the hell happened?"

The older man took a deep, unsteady breath. His hands were shaking. "Someone started playin' the flute, and suddenly nobody could move. It was like I'd gone to sleep standin' up and was in a dream. Couldn't walk, couldn't talk, could only listen to that *damn* music."

Hendricks pulled his pen and pad out of his pants pocket, scribbling it down. Some of the younger officers took notes on their phones, and even Nelson preferred relying on audio recordings, but he'd never gotten the hang of that. "Okay. Then?"

"...the music changed. We were still sleepwalkin', still dreamin', but now..." He swallowed. "You ever been to war?"

Hendricks shook his head. "Can't say I have."

"When you're goin' out to fight, there's a clear message: us or them. If you wanna live, you gotta strike first and strike hard. That feelin', that order, it came from the music, and everybody started fightin'." He swallowed again, looking down. "I went for Caroline's throat."

Hendricks put down his pen and put a firm hand on the man's shoulder. "Andy, that was *not* you. Mind control magic is... there's a reason it's outlawed. It's not even as if you were drunk. You didn't *choose* to listen to it. They held you hostage, plain and simple. And Caroline, she's a tough cookie. Those EMTs are going to check her out, and you're going to take care of her, and she's going to get snippy at you for taking care of her, but not for what happened here, all right?"

Andy's eyes were glassy, but he nodded.

"All right. Then what happened?"

"The fight didn't last. They changed the music quick—thank God. But by then I'd turned, and I could see. There were a few people not affected by it. They looked human enough, but I'd bet my boots they were fairies usin' glamour. Them, and Violet. She was talkin' to 'em. I think she was talkin' 'em down. They made 'er drop 'er weapons. Then they took 'er to a black van 'n drove off soon as they heard you comin'."

Hostage is definitely the right word, Hendricks thought, writing down the details. He'd have to clarify with the others, but his guess was that these fairies had made Andy and the others fight to force Violet to go with them. "Was she injured?"

"No. At least, not that I could see. She was across the street." He pointed. A couple of other officers were already on it, sectioning off an area that probably held the dropped weapons.

"Can you describe who else you saw go into the van?" Hendricks asked. "Even if they were glamoured, they might try to use the same disguises."

Andy huffed a laugh. "Only recognized one: Violet's new baker, the one with the jean jacket. Jennifer Charles, I think they go by?"

Hendricks paused. "You're sure?"

"I'm in that café every damn day. It was them. Looked real chummy with the fairies, too. Didn't look affected by the music, neither, so I don't know if it was a glamour or if they had some sort of enchantment to protect 'em."

"Was Violet fooled by the glamour?"

"Couldn't tell yuh. Like I said, they were all the way across the street. Didn't even catch the license plate on the van, I was so rattled."

"Don't worry about it. Go to your wife."

They split, Andy to try to get his wife to submit to medical treatment, Hendricks to talk to more witnesses. They all said the same thing: flute-player controlled their minds, started a fight, took Violet with them on their way out. The captured fairy had apparently had multiple weapons that she'd left behind before being hauled away—two knives and two honest to God swords—and those closest to the confrontation said she only submitted to the capture when the piper made everyone hurt each other. Business owners readily surrendered security footage from their cameras, shaken by what they had seen. Nobody had died or gotten anything worse than cuts and bruises, the mini-brawl having been only a warning. The EMTs still checked everyone over. The restaurants freely gave out water, coffee, and hot chocolate. (Mrs. Sippy's also offered booze, but that was shut down by the police until after they'd spoken to the witnesses. Only then could they destroy their brain cells.)

The fact that there was no CaFae Latte coffee or comfort was wrong. Hendricks had never gotten along with Violet. Their last conversation had been about that new baker with a criminal record—and look who was caught on the cameras participating in the kidnapping?

But the satisfaction of being right soured. Violet was a pillar of her community; everyone knew that. When Hendricks was first stationed here a decade ago, a tornado had ripped through the neighboring town, stopping just on the edges of Bernier. CaFae Latte had not only run a fundraiser for those affected by the disaster, but had also hosted a food drive and resource center. Half of Bernier had turned out to help their neighbor. She'd helped campaign for and set up the car shows, regularly contributed to Bernier Family Service and the volunteer fire department, worked tightly with the Stoughton Street Coven, was *the spot* for teenagers to hang out so they wouldn't get in trouble...

Having something like *this* happen, and then have the lights of CaFae Latte remain dark and dormant, was like watching the sun rise from the west.

Hendricks must have asked "Did they say why or where they were taking her?" a hundred times. Nobody had an answer.

He met up with Nelson after half an hour of gathering statements. Someone had managed to get the plate number, but when she ran it, they came up empty. And not just empty of any police files or stolen vehicles; there was no file or car in existence that showed up connected to those plates.

"I'll put out an APB," she said.

"Soon as you're done, we're going to St. Paul."

"Why?"

"Because that's where our suspect lives."

"The baker?" Nelson asked. "How do you know that?"

Hendricks grimaced. "You remember when I told you about arguing with Violet? About her hiring an ex-con without any concerns or extra security?"

"Yeah, I imagine you'll be saying 'I told you so' pretty soon..."

"Well, there aren't a whole lot of people named 'Jennifer Charles' in the local system. Only one, actually. I squirreled away their info just in case something like this happened. They got out of prison just under four months ago and have been in a halfway house ever since. If we use sirens, we can get there in twenty."

Nelson grinned. "You're a paranoid genius, Matt, and I love it."

an iron sword

Violet swayed with the movement of the black van, watching impassively as the fairies tossed her cell phone and purse out the window, attached her handcuffs to a chain that attached to the bottom of the van (thankfully made of aluminum, not iron), then tried to remove her gold bracelet.

"It won't..." The human mercenary Michelle grunted, grabbing Violet's arm with one hand and the bracelet with the other and putting all of her formidable muscle into separating the two. Violet breathed through the pain of bruises forming on her lavender skin. "It won't come off."

Red Wolf had dropped the human glamour as soon as the doors closed behind him, revealing his familiar array of yellows, greens, and browns, a little red sneaking in there. Now, sitting on the opposite bench of Violet, he frowned and leaned forward, resting his elbows on his knees. "What does that do?"

"It's a protective charm," Violet said. "You're not getting it off."

Black Dove, who had finally dropped the Jennifer Charles glamour, smugly pulled a wand out of her ivory cloak.

Violet scoffed. "A druidic wand? How gauche."

"That is *rich* coming from you," she said.

"Effectiveness is far more important than style," Red Wolf said, quoting Violet's own words from centuries ago.

"Oh?" she asked. "*Is* it effective?"

Black Dove tapped Violet on her dark purple head.

The transformative magic washed over her like oil, her protective bracelet catching the light as it deflected the curse.

Black Dove frowned. She hit Violet again, and the same thing happened.

"Let me guess: the plan was to transform me into something less conspicuous and more manageable. Small enough to squeeze into that?" She motioned to the empty animal kennel by Red Wolf's seat. "Not a bad plan. I do hope you have a backup."

And it ought to be an effective backup. It was much easier to get a cat or dog through customs than a chained fairy.

"Take it off," Red Wolf said.

"No."

"Now."

"No."

He pulled the keys from his belt, and they transformed into an iron sword. "Take it off, or lose the hand."

Violet eyed the blade. "I put a curse on it. Anyone who takes it off without my permission dies within seven days. And you do not have my permission."

Red Wolf glared at her.

"I'm surprised you still have that," she said, motioning to his sword. It was short, ideal for close quarters combat, with a slight curve to it. Simple, but effective, and expensive. She had always been sure to equip her under-officers with the best materials.

"It's a good sword," was all he replied.

She bit back a smile. He'd pretended to be that stoic the day she'd given it to him, raising him to the rank of captain. The difference was, back then, he'd been fighting not to squeal and cheer in delight, especially in front of his crush, Oak. Now, he seemed to be actively reminding himself not to run her through.

Black Dove returned the wand to her cloak and yanked a couple of dark hairs from Violet's head. She winced at the sudden pain, but didn't protest. Honestly, she should have followed the example set by several sorcerers like Black Dove and kept her head clean-shaven.

Black Dove had a proper sorcerer's robes, with endless pockets full of magical ingredients. She pulled a small cat skull out of her pocket, wrapped Violet's long purple hair around it, and muttered an incantation, her voice echoing with magic.

Once again, the transformative magic wrapped around Violet like a bubble.

And once again, it slid right off her.

She smiled. "Good effort."

Black Dove struck her across the face, sending her reeling. Violet laughed, sitting back upright. "Sloppy technique! Though a backhand slap is better than a punch, I suppose. Less chance of you breaking a knuckle."

Black Dove wrung out her hand, glaring.

Michelle sighed. "Plan B, then?"

Red Wolf sheathed his sword and shuffled down his bench, getting something. Black Dove pulled another item from her robe: a leather bracelet.

"Unicorn pelt?" Violet asked as Black Dove wrapped it around her other wrist.

The sorceress grunted. "In case your little pet witch decides to try clairvoyance. It's also an anti-glamour charm."

Violet didn't get a good look at the runes etched into the inside of the cuff, but she didn't have to. When she tried to transform into a snake, reality refused to bend. That was going to be a problem. "And what's preventing me from taking it off?"

"I put a jailer's rune on it. Only the person who puts it on can take it off."

"Good."

At Black Dove's frown, she elaborated, "If I'd been kidnapped by amateurs, this would've been embarrassing."

There were, of course, ways around the jailer's rune. Most required quite a bit of Black Dove's blood. Failing that, Violet could try to break or destroy the cuff itself, but few things were as indestructible as unicorn pelts. Even werewolf claws and vampiric super-strength had a hard time piercing through it.

Violet did own a couple of swords with unicorn blood mixed into the metal, giving the blades a rainbow sheen. She'd gifted a couple of unicorn knives to Cyrus as well. Any of those would work here.

Unfortunately, one sword was in CaFae Latte, the other in her house, and Cyrus didn't even know she was in danger.

Michelle's phone rang. She answered it. "What's wrong, Pete?"

A human might have missed it, but Violet's pointed Fae ears caught every word on the other end despite the sounds of the moving, crowded van: "The baker didn't get on the bus. The other fairy's driving them home. Probably going to drop them off on the front porch."

"Are you following their car?"

"Obviously."

Michelle glanced at Red Wolf, who nodded. "Make it happen. We don't care how. And meet back at the Wolverines' place."

"Careful," Violet sing-songed, even as her insides turned to ice. "The more corpses you create, the more motivated the police will be to find you."

From the front passenger seat, Piper rolled his flute around his fingers and said, "I'd say they're already motivated."

"*And* the more difficult I will make this."

Black Dove chuckled darkly as Red Wolf said, "Are you certain about that?"

He dropped a pair of boots on her lap.

Even without seeing the magical rune on the soles, Violet would recognize them. They looked like ordinary ankle booties, only with metal soles, every piece of them expertly crafted by Fae artisans.

"I thought those were declared a war crime," she mused. "The King of Ivae even swore to remove them from his military and never order their use again."

"Take off the charm," Red Wolf said.

"So you're not operating under Grandfather's orders—or at the very least, he doesn't know about the shoes. Which would be just like him, giving you as much freedom as possible so that, when asked, he could give an honest answer of knowing very little and have an easier time disavowing you," she continued. "But he would still give you better equipment, and he and the rest of Ivae would think twice about meddling in the Mortal Realm. Even with their disdain for Michelle's people, they respect the iron. And the nuclear weaponry. So...you're not working with Ivae, are you?"

"No," he admitted. "Take off the charm, or put on the shoes."

"An unsanctioned mission, then."

He didn't answer.

"Turning into a hoard of dragons and plucking me from the street would've been faster. And more ethical." She pointedly directed that last one to Piper, who just grinned back at her.

"And be gunned down by mortal missiles?" Red Wolf asked. "No. Charm or shoes."

"So stubborn." She kicked off her sneakers and held up her right foot. Her cuffed hands wouldn't allow her to strap on the boots effectively.

Red Wolf put the boots on her, locking them in place. The runes on the inside of the leather ensured that they would stay locked on her feet until the person with the key—the magic ring around Red Wolf's left middle finger—undid them. The runes at the bottom, well...

She could feel the heat as soon as he let go of the boot, moving on to her left foot. She gritted her teeth, refusing to give them the satisfaction of watching her squirm. The heat wasn't that bad, yet. Not like she had stepped on a hot coal, just that she was inching too close to a fire pit.

Red Wolf finished with the boots and held up his hand, the one with the key ring. "Stay close to me, or you'll feel the burn. Understood?"

"I invented these," she retorted. "There's no need for a lecture."

hit or miss

"You want me to wait?" Cyrus asked, pulling into the Walgreens parking lot.

JC shook their head. "Nah, my place is only a couple blocks away. And there's only so much of your music I can take."

"Hey, Kelly Clarkson is a *classic*."

"Suuure."

"You know they have a drive-through, right?"

"Not for deodorant and conditioner."

"Point." He made a show of sniffing their general direction and gagging. "All right. See you tomorrow?"

They pushed his shoulder. "Asshole. Good luck with your geek night."

JC closed the passenger door behind them, ignoring the homeless man leaning against the tan bricks by the sliding door. Old, black, and way too skinny, he alternated between asking for cash and asking people to buy stuff for him. Everyone called him M&M. Nice guy; JC always felt bad when they turned him down, having to watch their own budget.

It took them all of ten minutes to get what they needed before they were out, tossing a bag of peanut M&M's to the beggar (his favorite). He sputtered out a thank you and "God bless you" that JC waved off as their feet hit the sidewalk. That morning, they'd been annoyed to find the chain of their bike busted; it would've taken too long to fix then and there, and they would've missed the bus. But now, with work behind them, they weren't as annoyed. Violet had been right: it was a really nice day. With a few more hours of daylight left, they could still see St. Paul's skyscrapers in the distance, silver shadows against the sky. Beautiful at a distance.

Less so on the ground. This block was clogged with fast food chains, dollar stores, and gas stations, with the occasional hair salon or tiny, shady bank. The trash bins were always overflowing, candy wrappers and plastic bags fluttering in the wind. The highway was just a few blocks down, and with evening rush hour about to start, the cracked streets were beginning to clutter with cars and people heading home.

They tried to avoid fast food on account of the diabetes. As bad as it was for non-diabetic people, it was worse for JC. Unfortunately, being perpetually broke didn't leave a whole lot of other options. Violet had given them breathing room, but they weren't out of the woods yet, and their choices were to either hope nobody had eaten their leftovers out of the fridge, scrounge up whatever ingredients they had on hand to make something (which, after an all-day shift of kitchen work, no thank you), or McNuggets.

Wait, do I have any of those ready-made dinners in the freezer? they thought, trying to remember if they'd already heated and eaten their stash of chicken pot pies...

"Hey!" M&M screamed. "GUN!"

JC's head jerked up and back. They saw the black truck, the window down, the barrel of an automatic handgun aimed at their back, and instinct took over.

They hit the ground, rolling to the nearest point of cover—trashcan—as bullets flew over their head and shattered the window of the barbershop behind them.

Who the hell did I piss off this time? they thought, glass showering down on the pavement as people screamed and hit the deck. Hopefully no one had been in the path of those bullets. A quick check confirmed that M&M had taken shelter behind one of the Walgreens' brick pillars and was nowhere in the shooter's path.

The thing about drive-bys is that the shooter always *drives by*. Hit or miss, target alive or dead, they leave the scene as quickly as possible.

So, when the truck shrieked to a halt, JC knew something was up.

They didn't have time to think it through, not with their attacker armed and themself with only a plastic bag of deodorant, conditioner, and tiny bottles of insulin. They abandoned the trash can and their bag, doubled back past the barbershop, and sprinted around the corner, into the alley.

Please don't be firing a Magnum or something equally powerful, they prayed. The dumpster was mostly empty–dammit, garbage day was recent. That meant fewer things inside to block the bullets.

Ah, fuck it. Beggars, choosers.

They slid around the dumpster's corner just as the shooter came into the alley and fired again.

JC pressed themselves between the dumpster and the wall, ignoring the rank smell of years of garbage being stashed here. Bullets pinged and ripped through metal...but didn't get through the other side to JC by the time the *BANGs* turned to *clicks*.

As soon as they heard that lovely sound, they abandoned their cover and kept going, ignoring the shooter grumbling as he reloaded, not even looking at him.

They turned the first corner, running along the mid-block vein between the two streets of businesses, then turned the next corner.

Trash bins.

They didn't hesitate, didn't think. The deep green trash and recycling bins stood against a little stone half-wall that they used to get up and over the lid, jumping in and splashing brown- gray trash water that reeked of vomit on their shoes. They crunched down into a ball and held their breath, counting the heartbeats thundering in their ears.

At eight beats, they heard the shuffle of footsteps round the corner. They stopped.

Another two beats. The footsteps came closer.

Closer...

Then a sudden dart, and he was past the trashcan.

He's checking behind the stone wall, JC realized, covering their mouth.

"...fuck," the shooter swore, before his footsteps carried him away.

§

JC waited in that stinking trashcan for a full five minutes before crawling out, and used the back alleys to reach the halfway house, pausing every time they had to cross a street to ensure the black truck wasn't there.

They didn't even bother looking at the police car in the driveway, just glad to be indoors and in relative safety.

"Mr. Scott!"

JC groaned, leaning back against the door. "Not now, Elizabeth. I'm not even late! Hell, I'm early!"

"Get in the kitchen! *Now!*"

"Yes, *Mother*," they grumbled. Couch potato Nick made a face as they passed, probably catching their absolutely *delightful* smell.

Standing around the kitchen table was Elizabeth and two police officers, both of whom JC recognized. They blinked. "The fuck are you doing out of Bernier?"

"There's been an incident," Officer Hendricks said, his dough-colored skin almost yellow in the harsh kitchen light. He frowned. "Why do you smell like a dumpster?"

"Because I had to hide in a dumpster from a guy trying to shoot me."

All three of them paused. "What?"

JC headed for the fridge, throat parched. "I don't even know. They tried a drive-by on my way out of Walgreens. Missed. But instead of driving by, they got out and tried to finish the job. Bobcats don't operate like that, and neither does the Brotherhood. Neither of them can get a car that nice, either. That truck was brand new. Probably rolled out of the factory this year."

By the time they'd turned back around, chugging down a bottle of water, Hendricks was scribbling in a notebook. "What type of truck?"

"Toyota. Black. Didn't get the plate."

"What about a description of the shooter?"

"Didn't see his face. Just heard his voice."

"How could you not see his face?" Officer Nelson demanded. Her blond ponytail was so tight, it was a wonder she still had hair.

"You know how in horror movies, the sucker about to be killed is always looking over their shoulder as they're running?" JC asked, glaring. "You do that in this situation, you end up dead."

They asked more questions: Where did this happen? What were you doing in the Walgreens? Where's your bag of purchases?

Elizabeth crossed her arms. "Do these people know where you live? We have thirty other residents to look after here! You're endangering all of us!"

"I don't even know who they are or what they want!" JC snapped back.

"You said that you got here early," Hendricks said, glancing between JC and Elizabeth. "How? Did you take the bus?"

"No, Cyrus offered to drive me home after work."

"And where were you at approximately 3:15 this afternoon?"

JC frowned, adrenaline dimmed enough to click that something was really not right here.

"Uh...I clocked out about ten to? Went right into Cyrus's car. I'd say we were probably just beyond the bridge, maybe halfway to Cottage Grove? Why are you here?"

"Don't ask questions," Elizabeth ordered.

"Fuck that, I live here."

Hendricks put his pad and pen away. "Jennifer Charles, I'm going to need you to come with us while we corroborate your story."

"Why, am I under arrest?"

"If you don't submit willingly to protective custody, then yes."

"For what?" they demanded.

"For kidnapping your boss, Violet Smith."

JC gaped at him. "...what."

the witch

An excerpt from *Round-Ears: A History of Gialdon and Humans in the Fae Realm*

The Violet Princess knew that the greatest weapon against human liberation was not military force, but magic. She herself had used it several times during the rebellions and revolts. Each province of Ivae had an archive that stored the name of every mortal brought to or born within its borders. When a mortal ran away or rebelled, their name was used to curse them, both as punishment and as an act of military strategy.

In the Violet Princess's early days as commander—about three centuries into her military career overall—a mortal rebellion in a northern province had not only resulted in the death of a handful of Fae families, but also the burning of their farmland and a small forest. As much as fairies abhor death, harming the land is the greatest sin of all, one of the few [if not only] crimes that will get even a fairy put to death.

In one of her more ruthless moments, after the Violet Princess managed to identify the six leaders of that particular rebellion, she pulled their names from the archives. Before ever meeting them face-to-face or commanding a single army, she cursed as many of the rebels as she could identify with "ill luck, ill health, [and] ill fortune." As for the six leaders, she extended that curse to include not only them, but everyone in their family "seven generations forward and back."

Within days, a plague struck the rebels, and an accidental fire burned their supplies. This made finding and arresting them much easier.

All the rebel leaders were executed shortly thereafter. The surviving records show that the siblings, parents, grandparents, and descendants for seven generations all died young, poor, and unhappy. The curse lasted almost two hundred years after the rebellion was put down, ending with the death of the seventh descendant of one of the leaders, who died of an unknown disease at the age of fifteen.

The Violet Princess defected centuries later, at the age of one thousand.

Pictured the Violet Princess searching for the names of the rebel leaders and cursing them and their families for seven generations. This wood carving is from the Wooden Palace of Ivae, and would have been displayed proudly in one of the main halls. After the Violet Princess's defection, all of her belongings, portraits, and carvings were taken down and stored away. Many were destroyed.

already decided

The first thing JC said in the Bernier Police Station was, "I want a lawyer."

"It'll go faster if you just talk to us," Hendricks replied.

"Tried that already. Now I want a lawyer."

Hendricks sighed and left the interrogation room. JC sat in the uncomfortable plastic chair, staring at the bland beige walls and one-way mirror, rubbing the ink on their fingers from when they'd been processed ten minutes ago. At least they'd let JC keep their insulin pump.

They waited.

And waited.

And waited.

Fucking cops with their fucking mind games, they thought with a sigh.

The cops had swung by the Walgreens. Nelson had gone in and stayed for a while, probably collecting video. St. Paul police had already secured the scene to investigate the shooting; no one had been hit, thankfully. One quick-thinking St. Paul cop had gotten the Walgreens staff to prepare a new batch of insulin for JC, since the amount left on the street was no longer safe to use, and had given it to Hendricks for JC to take so they wouldn't die. But now they were hungry. Trying to kill JC would be bad enough, but doing that before they'd had a chance to eat? Assholes.

Finally, the door opened, and in came...

"Mr. Scott," Mrs. Jackson said, striding in with her briefcase.

"JC. Your kid learn a new trick?" they asked. "Looks good."

Her hair had changed again, straight as a ruler rather than with the slight wavy curve, and dyed a deep crimson.

"Thank you," she said, sitting across from them and pulling out her tablet. "What happened?"

JC told her, ending with, "I still stink of dumpster, but they haven't let me shower yet. Or eat."

"It's good evidence," she replied. She made a couple notes on her tablet, then set it aside. "Now are you going to tell me what actually happened?"

They frowned. "Pardon?"

"The police have video evidence of you and your co-conspirators holding an entire street hostage with fairy music and then forcing your boss into a car. Make things easier on yourself and confess."

Fuck. Video evidence was a bitch and a half to deal with.

"There's nothing to confess! I didn't do anything wrong!" they insisted.

"Mr—JC," she said, and that caught their attention. She'd never said their real name unprompted before. "I know you think my job is to make your life more difficult, but it's actually to look out for you. To help you get back into society. If that fails, I have to make sure the prosecutor doesn't completely crucify you for your second go-around. That will be a lot easier if you're honest with me."

JC ran a hand down their face. "I have no idea who's on that video or why they look like me. But I really don't appreciate the fact that you've already decided I'm guilty."

"You're innocent until proven otherwise."

"Bullshit."

Mrs. Jackson's face pulled down in deep sympathy, and it made JC angrier. "You wouldn't be the first person to fall off this particular wagon. Most parolees wind up back in prison for one reason or another, no matter how hard they try."

"I must be special, since I didn't try to kidnap anyone, and yet here I am."

"You gave that fairy your name," she said, as if just realizing something.

"Ye-es..."

"Did she threaten you with it? Or curse you?"

JC shook their head. "No, the only time Bob—Boss, Violet, whatever—the only time she used any magic on me is when I asked her to change my name. That's it. That's all she's done. There's been no threatening or cursing or anything."

"You do know that the police can protect you—"

"By arresting me? Because that seems to be the vibe at the moment."

The door opened again, cutting off whatever Mrs. Jackson was going to say.

"Cyrus?" JC asked, sitting up straight.

"Motherfucker. They *did* arrest you!" the fairy grumbled, slamming the door shut behind him. He was still in the jeans, t-shirt, and backwards hat cluttered with pins he'd worn to work. All that was missing was the apron.

"Excuse me," Mrs. Jackson said sharply. "This a private discussion."

"And I'm their lawyer."

Both Mrs. Jackson and JC shared a confused look.

"Aren't you a barista at that café?" she asked, going through her tablet.

"That, too."

"No offense, Cyrus," JC said, "but don't you need a law degree, or something?"

"Sure do. Graduated from Harvard with a master's in law in 1974," he said, snatching the other chair and sitting at the table, uncomfortably close to Mrs. Jackson, who glared at him. "Tried to be an actual lawyer, too, but then I got bored and went back for a literary and English doctorate in '81. Did a Spanish one in '87. PhD in American history in '95, because why not? Did a pre-med bachelor's in '99, but never went for the full doctorate, and took the bar exam again in '02—drunk—just to prove to my buddy Patrick that I could. After that, college got too expensive. But I keep up with the laws and still have my license."

They stared at him, slowly grinning. "You nerd."

"Damn right." He glanced at Mrs. Jackson. "I'd like to speak with my client, please."

"What name is your license under?" she asked.

"Blue Johnson. State of Minnesota."

She didn't leave for several long minutes, tapping through her tablet until she apparently found what she was looking for. She huffed a sigh. "Unbelievable. Fine."

She gathered her things and stood, meeting JC's gaze again. "Think about what I said. I'll be back tomorrow."

As soon as the door closed behind her, Cyrus leaned forward. "What happened?"

They told him everything, from the shooting to the arrest. By the time they were done, they felt like a broken record, but that was police procedure for you.

Cyrus nodded. "That's what I thought. I think someone's using you as a smoke screen, and as long as *that's* happening, no one's going to be out looking for Boss. Not while you're such a convenient patsy. Would've worked better if you had died or disappeared, hence the drive- by."

"Wait, so..." They gaped at him. "It's not...I didn't do anything?"

He shook his head. "I doubt it. I think they chose you because you already have a record. If anything happens to me or Boss or really anyone in or near CaFae Latte, you're at the top of the suspect list."

"Son of a..." They didn't know if they should be relieved that they hadn't messed everything up, or insulted that some jerk was using them to pull this shit. "Any news on Bob?"

"Nothing. I think the cops are trying to run the plates, probably put an APB on the car. Since one of the suspects used magical music, they're not going to fuck around, which might actually help us."

Oh, Jesus. Fae music was no joke. One time, back in JC's days with the Bobcats, someone from a rival gang had gotten their hands on an enchanted harmonica. That would've been bad enough, except he'd had no idea how to properly play it, or which tunes and notes did different things. He'd tried to use it on some girls at a club to get them to go home with him, but instead of falling madly in love they had walked into traffic.

"That's the only reason Boss went with them," Cyrus continued. "If they'd just attacked *her*, she would've fought them off.

Probably collected their heads, too. But they had the whole street hostage. Nobody died, but it was close."

"Why go after her in the first place?" they asked.

"I have no idea," he admitted. "But the sooner we get you sprung, the sooner we can get the police to find out. If I asked for a truth potion—"

"Yes. Do it."

"Perfect. That'll make this go faster. Problem is, this is a small town. It's going to take a few hours to get one and it's already after five. You'll probably have to spend the night in lockup."

"But they got the video from Walgreens. They know I was there. I can't be in two places at once."

"You could have theoretically gotten there after kidnapping Boss if you broke the speed limit. Or gotten the fairy to glamour as you in the Walgreens while you were busy kidnapping Boss." He shrugged. "I don't know if they're trying to force you into protective custody or honestly convinced you were in on it. It's really hard to prove magical involvement. Which, lucky me, makes it easier to sow reasonable doubt if we end up in front of a jury."

JC snorted. "So long as they feed me and give me insulin, I'll be fine."

"I'll make sure they do."

"What happened on your end?"

He leaned back in his chair, one foot on the table and front chair legs swinging in the air. "Cops called me right when I got to DnD. I'm her next of kin, so this was probably half an hour after she went missing? They got the security footage and witness accounts pretty quick. I told them it wasn't you, you were with me the whole time, that someone must have shapeshifted or glamoured or something, but they weren't having it. Sorry."

JC shrugged. "It happens. I've been arrested just for smoking a cigarette outside a friend's house. Was over eighteen and everything, but I had a record and 'looked sketchy,' so..."

"That's depressing," Cyrus said. He stood. "I'll get you out of here. Promise. Don't do anything stupid until I do."

periwinkle

The wire and mic itched against Steven's chest, or maybe it was the lack of chest hair that was throwing him off. He kept scratching, and then feeling the wire, and then left it alone, then had to scratch again.

Detective Swanson had given him strict instructions while the police put the wire on. "Act natural. Just carry on as usual, and if you see the wands, say the code word. Code word is?"

"Periwinkle," Steven grumbled.

Now here he was, at the 9th Street bar with Lance and a few others, waiting for Red Wolf to show up with his prize. Everyone had a beer in hand. Steven was on his third, trying to calm his nerves by swallowing the watery acid. Lance had talked to the bartender—who knew better than to argue with them—and gotten the place cleared out with a closed sign early. The place was usually empty, anyway. The beer was shit and the food was worse. But today it felt even emptier. Hollow. Vast.

"They ran into a bit of trouble," Lance said, not looking up from his phone. "Apparently the jick has some sort of protection. They can't turn her into a cat, so they've gotta smuggle her across as-is."

"Can't they remove it?" Steven asked, adjusting his oversized coat. It was making him sweat more than usual. "The protection."

He shook his head. "They'd have done it if they could, wouldn't they?"

Point. And also: problem. Steven needed Lance arrested, yeah. But more than that, he needed the Bernier witch out of the picture. It'd have been much easier for her to "accidentally" die if she'd been in cat or dog form. As a human-sized fairy? That'd be harder.

She wasn't the only fairy in Bernier, but she was the only confirmed fairy sorcerer. Sure, Bernier also had a coven of witches running around, but Steven was positive that this fairy was the reason nobody was able to deal in that town. Once Lance was behind bars—and the fairy out of the picture—then Steven would be the first to move into prime territory while everyone else fought in the Cities. He'd be rich and running his own gang within a few months.

But only if she was gone.

Steven lowered his voice. "Boss, should we really be doing this? I mean, this jick sounds like serious trouble. If she slips the leash and decides to come after us..."

"Scared of a little fairy girl?"

"She ain't a little fairy girl, she's a witch. She's dangerous." He scratched again, making sure to aim for the little microphone under his shirt to muffle his muttered, "Maybe we should just have them transport a corpse."

Lance shook his head. "They want her alive. They're paying for her alive. We've got a few routes to the Fae Realm the cops haven't sniffed out yet. It'll be fine, Stevie."

He smacked Steven's shoulder.

That, and Steven's scratching, dislodged the mic, and it fell out of his shirt, swinging from the thin wire by his legs.

Steven jerked back, trying to recover, but it was too late. Lance had seen, and his face turned red with rage.

"Periwinkle!"

trying to scream

Red Wolf knew something had gone wrong when one of his three golden rings broke, slipping from his hand to the floor of the van, the two halves bouncing away from each other on the bumpy metal before settling.

He, Black Dove, Michelle, Piper, and even Violet all stared at it.

"Good luck charm?" Violet correctly guessed.

He handed the two ring halves to Black Dove, who barely brushed her fingers against it before giving a single sharp nod. A good luck charm wouldn't break by chance. It'd been used, reality twisting and turning to protect them from...something.

"Uh, Michelle!" Jack called from the driver's seat, separated from everyone in the back by a mesh screen. "We have a problem."

Michelle and Red Wolf moved up front, having to squeeze past the others in the tight space. Violet politely leaned back against the wall to let them through.

Jack turned up the volume of the police radio, its scratchy voice declaring, "...on the intersection of 9th and Bailey. Suspects have all been apprehended, but we have an officer down. Repeat, officer down at 9th and..."

Michelle swore. "That's the Wolverine clubhouse."

"The authorities raided it?" Red Wolf verified.

"Looks like."

"Did any escape?"

"I don't know, and I don't want to text or call them. Not if the cops have their phones. Jack, get us close. We'll see what we can see."

§

None of them liked what they saw.

Red Wolf left the van in the care of his (heavily glamoured) Fae guards as he and Michelle meandered closer to the police line, illusioning himself human and her as a short black man, as different as possible from her true form. The authorities had blocked off the entire street, steel and concrete buildings washed in blue and red light. The bar that Steven had often frequented swarmed with humans in blue uniforms, one of them loaded into an ambulance with a bleeding leg wound. Steven himself— as well as Lance and all of his associates—were sat on the ground, their wrists cuffed.

"Well, shit," Michelle said, hands on her hips. "This isn't good."

Red Wolf hummed in agreement.

"That's the gang's entire leadership right there," she said, jerking her chin at the line of captured criminals. "The cops will pressure them on where the entrance to the Fae Realm is. They crack down on that type of smuggling here."

"Is there any chance to beat them to the entrance?"

Michelle wavered her hand in a so-so gesture.

Jack jogged over to them, auburn curls flopping around his head. "Bad news. The motel's being raided. Cops are looking for 'a group of foreign fairies armed with wands.'"

Michelle's hand went from so-so to thumbs-down. "And there goes our chance at beating them to the entrance. One of them's already given us up."

Red Wolf frowned. He'd been very careful not to speak about Black Dove's wands to any mortals beyond Michelle. The one time he did, it was in the Fae tongue…

Steven. He was there when I first talked about them with Black Dove. He must know Fae.

What a foolish mistake.

Red Wolf considered for a moment, then had Michelle send a text to one of her mercenaries. They'd rented out five vehicles— including the van that Black Dove had enchanted to keep Violet trapped and hidden. He needed one of the others now.

As she did that, he moved behind the van and told Black Dove the plan. They waited for the car to arrive–driven by Quentin and transporting Gold and Crescent, as well as two more of Michelle's mercenaries. They parked, and all five left, walking away from the crime scene as Black Dove slipped into their vehicle. Reality rippled around the car.

When Red Wolf came out from behind the van, he'd glamoured himself into not just a mortal, but a mortal with a police officer's uniform. He moved past the little blue barrier and nobody protested. Not even when he came up to the line of captured criminals and hauled Steven to his feet by the scruff of his oversized jacket.

"Hey, watch it!" Steven snapped.

"What's going on?" one of the officers asked.

"The captain wishes to question this one," Red Wolf said, in the bored tone of an overworked underline praying for the end of their shift.

"Oh, he *wishes*, huh?" the officer snorted.

He silently cursed himself. He still hadn't acclimated to the dialect of these people.

But the officer waved him off. "Fine. Just make sure he gets there in one piece."

Red Wolf hauled Steven out of the boundary, to what looked to the naked eye like a very real police car.

"What are you doing, man?" Steven grumbled. "I did everything you guys said. It's not my fault your stupid mic dropped."

Red Wolf pushed him into the car, where Black Dove waited in the driver's seat.

Steven went rigid as Red Wolf followed him into the back seat, closing and locking the door behind him.

"I don't appreciate being betrayed," Red Wolf said, letting his glamour melt away.

The mortal's eyes widened. He gulped, looking down. "I didn't have a choice. Cops have enough on me to put me away for life. The only way I could get a good deal was by snitching on my boss, and then you came along."

"How much did you tell them?"

"Nothing, man."

"Dove."

She handed him a vial filled with a thick black liquid that had the faintest glimmer of gold in the light.

"Hold up..." Steven said.

Red Wolf shoved him against the back of the seat, an easy task with the mortal's hands locked behind his back, and forced the potion down his throat. Steven tried to wiggle out, but Red Wolf covered his mouth and pinched his nose, making him choose between swallowing and choking. He swallowed.

As soon as Red Wolf let him go, Steven screamed for help. The fairy rolled his eyes, letting him cry and shriek.

Nobody outside even turned to look, the civilians going about their day, mildly curious about the scene, and the police finishing their duties.

"Black Dove is quite talented in her enchantments," Red Wolf said as Steven finally quieted. "Nobody outside of this car is going to see or hear you."

Steven shook his head, eyes watering.

Judging that enough time had passed for the truth potion to take effect, Red Wolf tried again, "What did you tell them?"

"That you sold the marmair seeds," he blurted. "And that you have a wand. Nothing about your Bernier fairy."

"Why would you leave out such information?"

"Because if the witch is out of Bernier, and my boss is locked up, then I'd be able to take over the town. I'd get a head start on everyone, corner the market on drugs before anyone else even knew what's up."

Red Wolf raised his eyebrows. "That's almost clever."

Steven's face brightened, sudden hope infusing him with something close to madness. "Exactly! I didn't need you to get caught or nothing. I was hoping you wouldn't! That I could tell you right before the cops showed up so you'd get out before they closed in, taking Violet with you. Maybe we can keep doing business together after. Everyone wins—except Lance, but who cares?"

Red Wolf considered his next move carefully.

"We can't let him go," Black Dove said, her silver marbling dull and gray in the shade of the car. "If it weren't for that good luck charm, I think we would've been caught already, rather than stumbling in after the fact."

Steven's eyes widened. "I-I won't tell! I won't tell no one! I swear! And I'm on a truth serum, so you know it!"

"Yes, you do mean it," Red Wolf agreed. "Now. But when the authorities interrogate you? Demand answers because they were promised a greater prize? Or perhaps they'll pour their own truth potion down your throat. If there's one thing you mortals are good at it, it's stealing ideas from your betters."

Steven shook his head. "Please. Please don't kill me. My girl's pregnant, my dad needs heart meds..."

"Kill you?" Red Wolf scoffed. "Fairies don't kill. Death is abhorrent. Our immortality is one of the things that separates us from our lessers, so we don't indulge in it."

"Not unless you go by Violet," Black Dove grumbled. "I could turn him into an animal. A slug, maybe?"

Steven threw himself against the door, but the locks—and Black Dove's spells—held.

Red Wolf smiled. "I think we can be a little more creative, dear."

§

It took the police hours to realize that their prime witness had never been taken to any precinct captain, but the city-wide manhunt ended almost as soon as it began. The witness was dumped on the steps of one of the police stations. Alive.

The doctors who looked him over said there was nothing physically wrong with him. He barely had any bruises.

But he couldn't see.

He couldn't hear.

Doctors would later determine that he could not sense touch, either.

And he could not speak. Even when it was clear to everyone that he was trying to scream.

gotta have a code

The farther away Red Wolf walked, the more pain Violet felt. The heat at the soles of her feet gradually increased, uncomfortably so. Right now, the pain was on par with a particularly bad sunburn, and it would remain that way so long as she stayed off her feet. These boots were not designed to torture for the sake of torture. They were designed to keep particularly dangerous prisoners from escaping.

Of course, she hadn't stayed off her feet. As soon as Jack followed Michelle and Red Wolf out of the van, and then Black Dove left, too, she stood and looked around for anything that might be useful, hunched over by the chains connecting her to the floor, biting her lower lip as her mind screamed at her that she was stepping on hot coals. The pain pulsed up her feet and ankles until she sat back down, catching her breath. Piper hadn't noticed, too busy listening to the radio as she crept behind the metal mesh screen that divided them—and protected him from any harm she could do.

Another slim comfort was that the burns weren't real. Her feet were fine. It was all an illusion. A trick of the neurons.

It still hurt.

Violet watched, locked in the back of the van, as the mercenary leader Michelle climbed into the driver's seat with a sigh, the glamour washing off her. If Cyrus had been here, he'd have made a joke about leaving blackface in the '40s.

The fairy didn't try to scream for help, recognizing the thrum of magic running through the vehicle. A little probing had confirmed that the van was enchanted. No sound or sight would escape it.

As easy as the enchantment was to create, it was just as easy to break. That was why Violet had put the protective runes of her gold bracelet on the *inside*, so they couldn't be scratched out. While the others were busy outside the van, she had searched every inch that she could reach, even with the pain of the boots, hoping to find the silence and sight spells Black Dove had used so she could destroy them. But they hadn't been under the mat, or the benches lining the walls, or anywhere in the back that she could see. Which meant it was either at the front—separated from her by the screen—or (more likely) outside the van somewhere. Either beneath it or under the hood.

Someone knocked on Piper's window. Violet didn't recognize him, but saw that he was glamoured. "Red Wolf wants to talk."

Piper left and followed him out of Violet's hearing, leaving Michelle alone and tapping on her phone.

The fact that Red Wolf was willing to hire a mortal was somewhat surprising. He'd always preferred working with other immortals. But he was new to Earth, and thus required a guide. If Violet could severe their relationship, she'd be free, and Red Wolf could think about his folly.

"How much are they paying you?" she asked.

"Quiet," Michelle ordered.

"Half a million? More?"

The human snorted. "For capturing, escorting, and smuggling a person like you? Six million, split between me and my crew."

"Oh, good. You know your worth," Violet praised. "How about ten million to let me go?"

Michelle looked at her over the rim of her red sunglasses. "You run a coffeeshop, not Amazon."

"I run a café *now*. But I dabble in divination magic, which is quite handy when determining which stocks to buy and investments to make. I bought a few in Apple for less than a dollar apiece twenty years ago, as well Google, Facebook, and yes, Amazon, too. Oh, and DoorDash. Granted, I donate quite a bit of it. But the rest is divided among my various legal identities, stuffed into bank accounts, safety deposit boxes, safe houses, et cetera."

She let Michelle absorb that for a moment before asking, "How about fifteen million? Take me to any one of half a dozen addresses so I can get the paperwork, listen to me make the transfer over the phone, and then walk away."

Michelle tapped her finger against her phone. From this angle, Violet's couldn't make out much of her face through the mesh screen and curtain of dark hair. "Tempting...but I've never flubbed on a contract before, and I don't plan to start today."

"Ah, of course. You'd need enough to ensure you and your loved ones never work a day in their lives and have a little extra security on the side in case of retaliation," Violet said. "Twenty million, with half delivered upon my release and the rest within a month."

Michelle shook her head. "I've seen too many people make that mistake. They all either lose it somehow and have to go back to work in a field that will never hire them again, or they get a target on their back when all of their previous clients worry that they'll start blabbing for the right price. Hell, I've gone after people who've left me hanging out to dry because they took a target's money, almost getting me killed or arrested, too. I never back out of a contract once I take it, no matter how nasty it gets."

Violet chuckled. "You'll murder, kidnap, and steal, but not break a promise?"

"Girl's gotta have a code." Michelle's phone dinged with a notification, and she smiled.

Violet sighed, settling back in her seat. "I suppose I should be proud."

At Michelle's questioning sound, Violet explained, "I taught your employer everything he knows about war and combat. If he hired you, then he was definitely paying attention."

§

"Good news, I know someone who can find us another Fae portal," Michelle said as Black Dove, Red Wolf, Piper, and Jack rejoined her in the van. "Bad news: they're not available until morning."

Red Wolf scowled. "If it's a matter of money—"

"It's not. They're in the middle of a job. If they drop everything now, they'll wind up either in jail or a coffin by the end of the week."

Violet watched them as Jack started the van and drove, the fairies cramped in back with her. Red Wolf was on one side of her, Black Dove on the other. The most experienced soldier and the most experienced sorcerer.

Piper, seated across from her, tapped pale yellow fingers against his flute, wheat-colored marbling wrapped around the digits. "I can change that."

Violet wondered what pitch his scream would be if she cut off his fingers. Even before her defection, the nature of musicians' magic had sickened her, as had the musicians themselves. It took a very particular type of person to master the art of mind-control, and that person tended to find joy in breaking spirits.

They also tended to be cowards. As soon as they lost control of any given situation, they crumbled.

Jack gave him an uneasy look while Michelle shook her head. "They're a coven of witches. *If* your magic gets through their charms, then you'll have over a dozen pissed-off witches going for your head. Black Dove, can you glamour our vehicles? Especially the license plates."

"Already done," she said, clearly annoyed. "I'm no amateur."

"Just checking. All we have to do is find a spot to spend the night. I do have a safehouse in the suburbs, but it can't fit all of us."

"If we split up, it'll be harder for police to track us, anyway," Red Wolf decided. "We'll divide in teams. Mix Fae and mortal so no one is left floundering. We'll scatter across the Twin Cities. And then we meet your witches first thing in the morning."

Michelle nodded, typing up several texts. Violet cataloged everyone's responses to this new development. The fairies were a bit harder to read, but Black Dove's tapping foot betrayed her anxiety and frustration. Piper seemed more bored than anything. Jack's knuckles were white on the steering wheel—the least experienced and most nervous of the group.

Michelle's phone dinged, and she frowned. Cursed. "The baker's still alive."

Violet raised her eyebrows while Black Dove sputtered. "Your people didn't kill them? That's what you're for!"

"They slipped away from the drive-by. Pete sent Olson after them on foot, but couldn't find them. By the time they got to the halfway house, the cops had already grabbed them." She looked up. "Pete says he can probably get into the station. Finish the job."

Red Wolf obviously considered that for a moment, then shook his head. "That'll just raise more suspicion. The baker was a convenient smoke screen, but now it's more trouble than it's worth. Have your assassins pull back."

She sent a text. Violet mentally adjusted her previous assumptions of Jennifer Charles. Surviving a brush with two mercenaries was not a skill most people could claim.

"Jack, get off at the next exit," Michelle said. "I don't have much food at my place, so we're ordering pizza. Vegetarian and cheese good for you guys?"

the liberator

Excerpt from *Round-Ears: A History of
Gialdon and Humans in the Fae Realm*

The city of Srada was small and didn't have much of a strategic position in terms of defending [the Fae nation of] Ivae against foreign invaders, as it was deep in the heartland. Yet it was the first casualty of the Gialdonian War because of its archive, holding all the names of the human serfs in the province.

According to some sources, the Violet Princess sent a message to the Gialdon leaders explaining exactly what she was about to do. They did not believe her, and many feared that this was a trap. That she was trying to lure them closer to the city so she could arrest them. What the princess's thoughts were of this reaction is unknown, especially as it's never been confirmed that she did give them such warning. If she did, she probably was not surprised by the mistrust.

While we have several surviving sources from that day, many of them contradict each other. What everyone agrees on is that the Violet Princess came to the city during the week of a festival, when the scholars who worked at the archive would not be in the building, and burned it to the ground.

Because Srada, like most Fae cities, was made of wood and magically carved out of the forest itself, this presented a threat to the entire population. However, the Violet Princess used an Elemental Wand, specifically of fire, to control the burn, ensuring that it was only the archives that went down.

Several firefighters attempted to stop the burning, but the Princess ordered them to stand down. When the mayor—who was himself a minor royal cousin—demanded to know what she was doing, she reportedly answered, "We are built on centuries of horrors. This is the first step of rectifying that."

When the mayor attempted to use *his* Elemental Wand to conjure a storm, the Violet Princess knocked him out with a blow to the head.

The fire and commotion drew a crowd. Over half of Srada's population was mortal, and many realized the ramifications of what was happening almost immediately. A riot broke out. Many serfs attempted to flee. Their Fae keepers tried to keep them in line by [magical and military] force. Fights and brawls broke out across the city, sparking a turmoil that continued for four days, killing hundreds of Fae and mortals.

The Violet Princess was forced to flee. Either because they didn't realize that she was the one who started the fire, or as an act of attempted vengeance, part of the mob came after the (soon to be ex) Chief Commander with the clear intention of killing her.

The Violet Princess used her wand to create a temporary wall of flame between herself and the attackers. None of them were burned, but it startled them enough to stop them in their tracks, giving her a head start. When the flames vanished, they attempted to chase her down, but she disappeared in the crowd, likely through the use of glamour.

A combination of private and public records show that the Violet Princess—now the Traitor Princess—went to the Gialdon leaders in person, and fought on their side until the end of the war she had officially started.

Pictured the Burning of Srada, carved soon after the War of Human Liberation. The artist chose to depict the Violet Princess as shocked and saddened by the destruction she instigated, but many contemporary sources that actually spoke with the royal sorceress report that while she regretted the violence, she was not surprised by it, not did it stop her from continuing her defection.

the price of wisdom

Michelle's safehouse was a simple suburban home on the outskirts of St. Paul. Most important for the mercenaries, she had a connected garage, so nobody saw Violet get hauled out of the van, led through a sparse living room with plastic-covered furniture, and down into a basement.

The indigo-skinned Crescent chained her to a pillar firmly entrenched into the basement floor, Black Dove watching. She sneered, "Behave, and you might get to eat tonight."

"How magnanimous of you," Violet retorted, resigning herself to an empty stomach.

They left her, climbing back up the rickety wooden stairs. The basement was largely empty: cement floors, some storage against the walls, a washer and dryer, and maybe a bathroom beyond that door. None of which she could properly investigate. The chain was long enough that, though it wrapped behind her and the pillar, she still had her hands in front of her, but could not stretch her arm all the way without yanking on the other.

She *could*, however, lie flat on her back and brush the toe of her shoe against the table against the wall. More specifically, she could reach the rusty nail that had fallen to the floor, either dropping out of the table or forgotten from a previous project.

The bottom of her soles burned, the enchanted boots heating with Red Wolf a floor away. She breathed through the pain, using her foot to capture the nail and, after several minutes, roll it to her body so she could grab it.

She hissed when she finally got her fingers around it, pain blooming across her skin. Iron. Of course. It burned fairies as well as hot coals.

Gritting her teeth, she tried to undo the locks of her chains with the rusty end of the nail. Her fingers blistered and burned as she pushed against the metal, but to no avail.

The basement door opened. Violet tucked the nail in her pocket and sat, hiding her damaged hands under her legs as Jack came down with a plate and bottle of water. "I wasn't sure if you preferred veggie or cheese, so I got you one of each."

Violet smiled, taking the plate. "I appreciate that."

Jack nodded awkwardly, auburn curls flapping, and turned to go. She called, "You seem a little young to be a mercenary. If a man your age wants to shoot a gun, he typically just joins the army."

"I'm not supposed to talk to you," Jack grumbled, as if he were in his teens rather than his twenties. The slightly oversized T-shirt and jeans didn't help.

"Of course not. Few things are more terrifying to an officer than subordinates with critical thinking skills."

His face flushed. "It's not like that."

She gave him an unimpressed look. "Jack, I was in charge of armed forces for a long time. Exponentially longer than Michelle and twice as long as Red Wolf. Are you even allowed to ask questions or raise valid concerns?"

His worn sneakers shifted against the concrete floor. "Sure."

"And do they actually answer you, or just tell you to shut up and do your job?"

He glared at her.

"I suppose your age doesn't help," Violet mused, poking the pizza with her unburned pinky to test the heat. "You're barely out of high school, aren't you?"

He looked down.

"How did someone just starting their twenties end up here? Did the Army reject you?"

"No, I made it through Basic. Even got 34 out of 40 on my weapons course. Got to be a private and served half a tour. Then one night I got drunk. There was a fight. Court eventually ruled that it wasn't my fault, but I still got dishonorable discharge."

"I suppose food service wasn't an alternative?"

He scratched the back of his neck. "No one hires criminals. One of the officers watching the trial said he knew someone. My training scores and service record were really good, and he said it'd be a shame to see them go to waste over an accident. He introduced me to Michelle."

"And has she provided everything she promised?"

"Well, yeah. I'm getting paid way more than I did with the Army. Enough to send some extra home to my mom and sister. I just..."

Jack paused. Violet tipped her head. "You just..."

He shook his head. "I thought military life was what I wanted. And if this was the closest I was going to get, then fine."

"But kidnapping fairies and fighting for gold is not the glory you thought it would be," she suggested.

Jack huffed a sad laugh. "What did you fight for? When you were in charge."

"The subjugation of humanity," Violet admitted.

At his surprised look, she added, "And then when I realized how wrong that was, I fought for their freedom. It sounds trite, but it truly is never too late to turn it around. Or at the very least, end your harmful behavior so you stop hurting others. Perhaps you'll never be forgiven, but that's not the point. The point is making decisions that won't give you even worse insomnia."

He snorted, turning back to the stairs. "I know what you're trying to do."

"What am I trying to do?"

"Trying to get me to your side. It won't work."

"Why not?"

"I need the money," he said. "And anyone who crosses Michelle gets killed. You know what job we did before you? It was one of her old teammates who chickened out. Crisis of conscience, I guess. Went to Interpol and forced everyone to go underground to not get arrested. Once the dust settled, she had me track down that teammate. It took months. Two years after he betrayed her, we found him. She went into his house and put a bullet in his head—him *and* his wife. You do not betray Michelle."

"That's a fair counterargument," Violet admitted, poking the other slice of pizza. Still too hot. "How about ten million dollars and guaranteed protection from Michelle?"

He froze. "What?"

"I have that and more. Help me get free, and I will do everything in my power to keep you alive, unharmed, and give you ten million dollars—cash—over the course of a year, plus a protective charm immediately that will keep you safe and away from Michelle so long as you wear it. No one will be able to trace the money to any unlawful actions on your part, and I will not give any information about you to the police."

He stared at her, obviously thinking it over when the basement door opened.

He quickly looked away as Violet took a bite of pizza. Far too greasy and salty, but beggars couldn't be choosers, and she needed all the energy she could muster.

"Michelle's looking for you," Red Wolf said, coming down the stairs.

"Right. Of course," Jack stammered and hurried up the stairs without a backwards glance.

Red Wolf stood in front of Violet, well out of reach of her chain, arms crossed. "This would go much easier if you cooperated."

"You're alive, aren't you?" she said between bites. Unlike Jack, all of Red Wolf's clothing was from Fae: dark pants, dark shirt rolled up to the elbows, the boots that probably had a light enchantment for durability and stealth, even the cord pulling his dark hair back. Cyrus would tease him for his "edgy Legolas cosplay," but Red Wolf had always had limited style, even before their last war. It was a battle Violet had lost over and over again, and it'd only gotten worse after he'd married Oak, who'd cared even less about fashion than him. Violet had resigned herself to being the one to teach their children the basics of style.

He chuckled.

"What?" she asked.

"I was just thinking of this afternoon. I wasn't entirely certain that Piper's magic would be enough to convince you," he said, sitting on a crate. The single lightbulb in the basement was harsh against his green, gold, and brown skin. "I remember the Iron Witch who would curse whole bloodlines into extinction and slaughter entire battlefields. What happened to her?"

The pizza tasted sour. She forced herself to have another bite. "People change. We learn and grow. The price of wisdom is regret."

"For what came after?" he asked softly. "When you were spilling golden blood instead of red?"

"That, too," she admitted. "But not as much. *That* had to be done."

"No, it didn't."

She shook her head, wiping the grease from her fingers with a napkin. The last several conversations she'd had with him—before and after her defection—had gone like this. Time for a different approach. "How have you been, Red Wolf? What have you been up to for the last two centuries?"

He huffed. "Well, after the war, I had to help piece Ivae back together. With Gialdon established, several mortals still under our control tried to rebel, tried to kill their lords and flee. I guess they hadn't seen enough of the land burn. Then all of Ivae's enemies decided to take advantage of our weakened state. We survived, but it was close. Then I retired."

She raised her eyebrows. "You retired."

"I never had the patience for politics, and only rarely for royals."

They shared an old smile.

"How *are* the royals?" she asked.

His smile slipped. "You haven't asked in two hundred years?"

"Of course not. The last I saw them, I betrayed them, hurt them, and brought their nation to the brink of collapse. Contacting them would just bring about more pain."

"...they're all right," he said at length. "Your grandfather still rules. His heir is still a spoiled jackass. Your parents and sisters left court as soon as the Great Mortal Rebellion ended; they can't show their faces."

"Diamond?"

"Your cousin is still exiled and stripped of her titles, with no contact with the royal family as far as I'm aware. Only now, everyone thinks of you when they hear 'the Exiled Princess' rather than her."

Violet nodded. She had never been close with her blood family. But it was still a small relief to hear that they were alive, at least, if not thriving.

"What of your family?" she asked. "Does your father still sing?"

"He's started teaching others. Doesn't like performing anymore. Mother's also taken an apprentice, but they've a long way to go before they can sell their own hand-made lutes."

Under his mother's tutelage? That apprenticeship would last centuries before she deemed them worthy of even journeyman craftsmanship. Violet had seen less discipline and perfectionism in armies, and could count any number of commanders and politicians less intimidating than Red Wolf's mother. She had tried to recruit her into military or magical careers multiple times, but the craftwoman's passion was and always had been music. Not creating it herself, but listening to it and creating the instruments that made it possible. Unsurprisingly, it was the foundation of her relationship with her husband, who was an incredibly talented musician. (Regular music, not mind control.) It warmed Violet's heart to know they were not only still putting such art into the world, but also showing others how to do the same.

Now, if only their son would take their cue.

"What do you hope to accomplish here?" she asked, lifting her chains.

"Justice," he said. "Ivae let you go too easily. You don't get to make a mess of your country—your whole Realm—and walk away."

"Was my absence a detriment to Ivae or the Fae Realm?" she challenged.

"I'd say so, yes. Traitors deserve punishment."

"Exile isn't punishment enough?"

"No. In fact, I'd say it made it worse. Do you know how many traitors you inspired? Most of my duties as Chief Commander became investigating all the new leaks, trying to determine who was betraying Ivae's secrets to her enemies. Not just Gialdon or other fairies, but giants, dwarves, goblins. They see your treason, your murders, as heroic. If you'd gotten a just punishment, your copycats would've at least thought twice."

"There is no evidence that suggests harsher punishments deter criminal activity," Violet pointed out. "Not among mortals or immortals."

Red Wolf shrugged. "But they'd let me sleep better at night."

"So, it's selfishness," she sighed, more than a little disappointed.

He narrowed his eyes. "My followers would also sleep better, knowing you were brought to justice. Black Dove especially."

"Selfishness *and* an unwillingness to move beyond the past," Violet diagnosed. "I don't suppose a sincere apology would help?" It'd certainly helped her case with the Gialdonian revolutionaries.

"It would make us laugh," he said dryly.

She figured as such. Two hundred years of resentment wouldn't go away so easily.

"What exactly is the plan after you drag me back to the Fae Realm?" she asked. "Torture? Memory wipe? Servitude? Remove my senses of sight and hearing and release me into the wild?"

Red Wolf smirked, stretching dark green and yellow skin. "What would you have done to a traitor who caused so much destruction?"

He could've at least tried to lay a less obvious trap. "Depends on which part of my career you're talking about. When I fought for Gialdon, I simply killed them."

He shook his head, clearly disappointed. "How the mighty fall."

"I try to find other solutions these days. But you can't deny it was quite effective. And compared to whatever you have in store for me, merciful."

"What happened to 'Mercy is a tool that must be used carefully and sparingly'?" he asked.

Her face and spirits fell. "That was a mistaken belief that I will regret to the end of my days. And I sincerely hope you abandon it, too. Quickly."

"You'd rather I be cruel and merciless all the time?"

She gave him a flat look. "My current protégé is a third your age and already so much more original."

Red Wolf's humorous snort was a ghost of the great, big-belly laugh he used to give. He leaned forward, resting his elbows on his knees. "Here's the plan. We take you back to the Fae Realm, and lock you in a cage."

"How disappointingly uninspired." She finished the first slice of pizza and started on the second.

"With one of those televisions so you can see into the outside world," he continued. "So, you can see how we go to Gialdon and tear it apart brick by brick."

She narrowed her eyes, setting the grease-stained, paper plate down. "You have only half a dozen Fae followers."

"Gialdon has many enemies," he pointed out. "Even more than Ivae. I don't know how long it will take. Years. Decades. Perhaps even centuries. But by the time I'm done, Gialdon will be a distant memory. Its leaders will be dead, its people returned to their rightful place beneath their immortal masters. And everything that you have sacrificed, killed, and bled for will be gone, right before your eyes."

She absorbed that.

"...and yes, there will be the occasional torture," he added, leaning back. "You also have many enemies, and while I will enforce a no-death and no-cripple rule, I don't think that will cause too much of a fuss. I could charge a small fortune for just ten-minute sessions."

She did not disagree.

"No notes?" he asked.

"I'm trying to imagine what Lady Oak's reaction would have been to all of this," she said. "My guess is, not good—"

She expected it, but Red Wolf still moved shockingly quickly, punching her across the face with enough force to send her to the cement.

"Don't you dare say her name," he ordered.

Violet pulled herself up. "Before she was my enemy, she was my friend. For centuries. I dare say I knew her better than you ever did."

He moved to punch her again. She caught his fist, her chains rattling with the movement.

Red Wolf gritted his teeth, trying to remove his hand from hers. She did not let go.

"Your wife had several flaws, but vengeance was not one of them," she lectured, slipping the nail from her pocket, ignoring the fresh burn against her fingers. "If you had died instead of her, she'd have mourned you, cursed my name, and *moved on*."

"Well, I didn't die. She did. So, what she would have done doesn't matter," he growled, leaning closer.

"There's that selfishness," she scolded. She took the nail and brought it to his neck.

Red Wolf jerked back. She smiled at the burning kiss the nail gave his skin. Right over the jugular.

"The living take priority over the dead," she said, flicking the nail away. It bounced and rolled across the cement floor with a merry tinkle. "Which is why I hope you make the decisions that will let you live a long, happy life. Including, perhaps, a more thorough check of your prisoner's cell."

pale gold blood

Red Wolf glared at his reflection in the mirror. His skin was a marbled combination of browns, greens, and yellows with a touch of red, yet the little burn from that nail stuck out at him, darkening a bit of yellow that slithered up his neck.

"Damn you, Violet," he muttered, wetting the corner of a small towel to wipe away the droplets of pale gold blood. Michelle's safe house was small and sterile. Dead and primitive, using chopped wood and concrete rather than living trees. But it was dry and well-stocked, for a mortal. He couldn't find any all-heal in the first aid kit he'd found beneath the sink amid the plethora of bandages and pill bottles, but that was to be expected.

He shouldn't have gotten that close. He knew better than that.

Yet it was surprisingly difficult. Despite having spent their last several interactions trying to kill each other, it was so *easy* to slip back into the mentor-student mentality that had defined their relationship for centuries. Easy to pretend that Violet still cared about him, as a protégé, at least.

She'd cared about Oak as a protégé, too. He couldn't forget that.

Why didn't she kill me? he wondered, leaning closer to the mirror to ensure there were no tell-tale signs of poison. A nail wasn't an ideal weapon, but it could still be lethal. If she hadn't stopped when she had, he'd have bled out on the basement stairs.

Perhaps she realizes that that would only make things worse for herself, he thought. Just because Red Wolf died didn't mean that this mission would be over. They had a chain of command: Black Dove would take over for him, followed by Piper, then Crescent, Gold, Crow Moon, and finally Mouse. Most of them had served in the military for at least a century; they knew how to give and take orders.

Or perhaps she's trying to teach me something, he thought with a grumble. It seemed like a poor choice for a teaching moment. But she'd used that particular tone of voice when she gave a lesson, and this wouldn't even be the most dangerous situation she'd been in while lecturing him on tactics, or history, or leadership. Experience was the best teacher, after all, and she'd always preferred throwing her students in the deep end of the pond—with a safety line, of course.

That tone of voice was particularly irritating. It was the disappointment that annoyed him. As if she had any right to be disappointed in him, to call him selfish. *She* was the traitor. *She* was the one who brought her own country to the brink of collapse. *She* was the one drowning in oceans of fairy blood.

Satisfied that his burn wasn't anything more serious than his unruly captive making a point, he left the restroom.

Black Dove met him in the dark hall, opening the window. Combined with the night sky, her black skin molded into the darkness, the ivory robes and silver marbling popping. "I'll stay on the roof tonight, just in case."

"Good," he praised. "This isn't going as planned, and I apologize for that."

She shrugged. "It's the Iron Witch. She was never going to make this easy."

All fairies could glamour. Some changed their hair or faces so often they had to wear an identifying bit of clothing every day, like a scarf, hat, or gloves. For something non-biped, on the other hand, that required either extensive training or a druidic wand.

Black Dove did not need the wand. Her body shrank until she was a bat, and then she flew out the window and up onto the roof. Red Wolf closed the window, leaving it open a crack so she could easily get back in if needed. Despite himself, he grinned. Violet could glamour herself into an animal, but she'd never liked it, preferring instead to glamour others. That was one advantage Black Dove had over her.

In the living room, Piper, Crescent, and Michelle were finishing off the pizza as Jack sat on the couch with his boss, staring into space with his half-eaten meal on the coffee table. Everyone else's check-ins had streamed in over text messages around the same time the pizza had arrived. Michelle confirmed that all of her people were accounted for, staying in various hotels across the Twin Cities. Red Wolf had gotten an "all clear for the night" from Crow Moon, a selfie from the green-skinned Mouse with very poor lighting, and a much better picture from Gold of a mug of brown liquid and whipped cream, captioned, "IT'S LIQUID CHOCOLATE!" followed by a string of shocked and gleeful emojis.

(Alex, one of Michelle's mercenaries who was usually assigned to Gold, had apologized to Red Wolf a while ago for introducing Gold to emojis, as they used them constantly. But she'd been chuckling during her apology, so Red Wolf didn't think she was actually sorry. Mortals. Never honest.)

"We need to set a watch on Violet," Red Wolf said. "She almost killed me with a nail earlier."

Michelle raised her eyebrows. "Okay, then. Piper, is your flute any good on fairies?"

He snorted, wiping his dark yellow mouth with his napkin. "Obviously not. Fairies are resistant to such magic."

"Do you have any use outside of it, then?"

"Why would I bother?"

"I'm trying to see if you should be a part of the watch or not. I'm leaning toward not, since if she gets out, you're dead in seconds."

Glaring, Piper pulled out his flute and played a harsh note.

Both Michelle and Jack—the only humans in the room—slapped themselves.

"Seriously?" Jack snapped, jumping to his feet as Michelle reached for her gun.

"Ah-ah, careful dear," Piper said, lips around the head of his flute. "Wouldn't want you to aim that gun anywhere unfortunate, would you?"

"I *will* put a bullet in your skull," she promised, her voice cold.

"That's enough," Red Wolf ordered. "Piper, they're our contractors."

"We can replace them," he pointed out.

"Not that easily, we can't. No more music on them, not unless they turn on us."

Piper rolled his eyes, but removed the flute from his lips. "Fine."

Crescent took another bite of pizza, watching them as if they were a play.

Jack shook his head. "I'm not staying in the same room as him."

"Fine," Red Wolf said. "But you'd be just as helpless if Violet broke free."

The boy sputtered. Red Wolf ignored him. "Michelle, do you want first, second, or third watch?"

"First. I'm not getting to sleep anytime soon," she said, glaring at Piper.

"I'd like third," Crescent offered. "What are the chances of the law finding us and breaking in?"

"Slim, but not zero," Michelle admitted. "Jack and I can handle those so you don't have to get your hands dirty."

"I don't mind killing mortals."

Even Piper looked surprised at that. "Really?"

Crescent shrugged his wide shoulders. "Mortals attacked me and my family during the war. I fought back. I don't regret it."

Red Wolf had also shed a bit of red blood—purely in self-defense, of course. But he'd always regretted it after, if only because there were so many more elegant ways to handle it. The experience always made him feel slimy, like a swine bathed in mud. Yet Crescent finished his pizza as if it was nothing.

Red Wolf's phone trilled. He bit back a sigh. "Wake me in four hours," he said, leaving for the stairs and taking out the phone. "This is Red Wolf."

"You're late," the woman said, as if commenting on the clouds.

"We ran into a complication. One of your good luck charms prevented us from being captured today by local law enforcement, but that also means we have to wait to get back to the Fae Realm."

"How long?"

"Hopefully by tomorrow's end. But Violet is secured and not going anywhere."

"Good," she said. "I'm wiring you another few million dollars to make improvising easier."

He relaxed. "I appreciate that."

"Remember: she just has to be alive. She does not have to be in one piece."

michelle

JACK

pipers freaking me out

MICHELLE
I have one set of
noise-blocking headphones
Didn't have time
to get more

JACK

you didnt know??

MICHELLE
Not until yesterday
That was likely a
purposeful move
on RW's part
Clients like to pull
power moves like that

JACK

i really dont like this
all the fairies
are assholes
and I dont think
Violet deserves this

MICHELLE

Call her "the target"
It'll make it easier

                                    JACK

                        she doesnt deserve this
                          baker didn't deserve
                                    it either

MICHELLE

Then you're in the
wrong line of work
Finish this job and then
find a different career

all-team group chat

JACK
fyi pipers been trying
to mind-control me
and michelle

ALEX
WTF
PENNY
HELL NO
PETE
Phenomenal
ROGER
😠 😠 😠
QUENTIN
Great
DAVID
Why is he doing that?

JACK
dunno
i think hes just an ass

MICHELLE
I've already told him
and RW that if he pulls
it again, I'm putting
a bullet in his skull
If he's controlling ME,
you're all authorized

to do the same
ROGER
☺
🔫🔫🔫
PETE
I'll keep Team 1
away from Piper
RW can handle that
BS without us
MICHELLE
Jack and I will stay close

JACK
WHAT
NO

QUENTIN
Yeesh, M. He's just a kid
OLSON
He's 22. Adult
MICHELLE
Jack will do less
damage if controlled
I can overpower and
restrain him w/o killing
him more easily than
the rest of you
QUENTIN
Fair
PETE
Awwww, you DO care☺

JACK
NOT BETTER

RACHEL

Just take the hit

ALEX

Yeah, we'll make it
up to you later

Bernier Gazette Headline:

POLICE ARREST SUSPECT IN MAIN STREET MIND CONTROL CASE

At approximately 4:15 p.m. last night, Bernier Police arrested Jennifer Charles Scott for allegedly participating in the mass mind control that took place on Main Street earlier that day. Witnesses placed Scott at the scene of the crime talking to local café owner Violet Smith, who was seen leaving with approximately half a dozen other unidentified fairy suspects.

Scott was released from the Men's Correctional Facility in Oak Park Heights less than four months ago after serving a sentence for manslaughter, illegal possession of a firearm, and possession of narcotics. It is unclear whether Violet Smith knew about his background when she hired him at her establishment CaFae Latte two months ago.

Bernier police released a statement, saying that, "the investigation is ongoing," and that "our priority is making sure nothing like this happens again." When asked if Violet Smith had willingly gone with the other suspects or been taken against her will, police stated that they are "still investigating her role, but we are currently classifying this as a kidnapping."

Scott's lawyer Blue Johnson has publicly stated that, "This arrest is an insult and a sham... We will be demanding the use of a truth potion." He then implied that Scott's alleged accomplices were "obviously fairies very skilled in glamour."

Blue Johnson works with Violet Smith at CaFae Latte as a barista and was officially adopted as her son in 1967.

The Stoughton Street Coven has publicly offered their services in making and delivering a truth potion to Bernier Police Department for the purposes of questioning Scott, stating, "We are shocked and appalled by what happened on Main Street." The coven said that the potion should be ready first thing in the morning–by the time this article is released.

Pictured: Jennifer Charles Scott's mug shot

Devil's & Advocate

Independent News

(WEBSITE RUN BY WENDY HARRELL)

The *Bernier Gazette*'s article that dropped this morning regarding yesterday's mass mind control in my hometown of Bernier, MN, (read it here) left out several key details, as usual.

One: Jennifer Charles ("JC") is non-binary and uses they/them pronouns. Get it right.

Two: The full statement from their lawyer, Blue Johnson, is "This arrest is an insult and a sham. **My client has a clear alibi and wasn't even in town when the mind control occurred.** We will be demanding the use of a truth potion. As for the people who did kidnap Violet, they're obviously fairies very skilled in glamour."

The article points out that Johnson is Violet's adopted son and employee at CaFae Latte, but not that he has several law degrees, passed the bar exam, and is fully qualified as a criminal defense attorney. He has a long track record of representing himself, his adopted mother, and several others—usually Fae, and usually pro bono—since the 1970s. When I reached out to him to ask about the *Gazette* article and why he doesn't do lawyer   work full-time, he said, "It just doesn't 'spark joy' for me. Too much paperwork—which is *hell* on my dyslexia. But I'll do it when necessary. The *Gazette*'s slant does and doesn't surprise me. Normally they're way more anti-Fae, but I guess their queerphobia won out over their racism. My client's just too tempting a target."

The fact that fairies are involved is obvious. Although you don't need to be a fairy in order to play an enchanted flute, the vast majority of people in possession of those instruments across all Realms are Fae (according to the Violence Policy Center). Why none of this was in Bernier Police Department's statement is a mystery.

Three: Stoughton Street Coven also had a fuller statement: "We are shocked and appalled by what happened on Main Street. **Violet Smith is our dear friend and mentor, and we want her back home safe and sound as swiftly as possible. In addition to offering Bernier Police truth potions for use on *willing* suspects, we have also been attempting to use divination and clairvoyant magic to locate Violet. Unfortunately, all those efforts have been fruitless, which tells us someone has put a powerful block on her to prevent us from finding her."**

That's a pretty big piece of information to leave out, *Gazette*.

Most troubling of all, I believe, is not to do with the *Gazette*, but the police statement. They stated that "our priority is making sure nothing like this happens again," which is a very good stance to have, *after* finding the missing woman. The *Gazette* noted that witnesses placed Jennifer Charles (or at least, someone who looked like them) at the scene of the crime. They did not mention that several witnesses went on record saying that Violet unwillingly went with the suspects, one of whom ordered her to disarm herself before physically pulling her into the van.

This paints a rather clear picture, especially when one considers Violet's skill with martial arts and magic that she's displayed over the decades: the people on Main Street were not the true targets. They were the *hostages*.

While any mind control like what happened on Main Street yesterday should absolutely be prevented, it's clear that Bernier police are willing to sacrifice the primary victim of this crime—and the one still in direct danger—in the name of quick arrests and good PR.

hide the bruises

JC spent the night in lock-up. It was one of their nicer experiences behind bars: the mattress wasn't too thin or stained, there weren't a hundred other people making noise, and there was a halfway decent air conditioner keeping the summer heat off their skin. Food wasn't terrible. They even got a sink with soap, which they used on their jean jacket before letting it air-dry. Still no shower, though, so they woke up reeking of dumpster and day-old sweat.

In the morning, when Hendricks came with a tray of oatmeal, gas station fruit, and orange juice, he also brought Andy. "He's here to see if you need insulin," he explained.

JC shrugged. That was fine by them. But Andy seemed less than pleased. The usually jovial old man was stone-faced as he got the reading for the pump. Unsurprisingly, they needed insulin. Dawn Phenomenon was a weird one. Tubeless pumps like JC's required fresh pods, kind of like a Krueger, which they did not have on hand, so it was the ol' needles again.

As he wiped JC's side with an alcohol rub, he muttered, "You should've stayed right with Violet, then you would've been fine."

"I did."

"Then why'd I see you help a bunch of folks kidnap her?"

"That wasn't me," they stressed. "Our best guess is that the real kidnappers are using me as a smoke screen."

He grunted, disbelief dripping from the note. At least he gave JC the insulin before leaving. Hendricks watched him go, then said mildly, "That flute-player almost made him kill his wife. Got his hands around her throat and everything."

JC almost choked on their orange juice. "The yarn granny woman? Caroline?"

"Mm-hm. She's wearing a heavier scarf today to hide the bruises."

"Shit," they muttered. "No wonder he's pissed."

They'd only met Caroline as a customer. But she was a good woman, kind and generous, reminding them of their own grandmother. Those recipes she'd given over were simple and tasty, and she was always down to share some kitchen tricks with JC if there weren't any other customers clogging up the counter, like coating your hands in butter or oil to prevent sticky dough from clinging to your skin. She was quickly becoming JC's second-favorite customer, right behind Nicole.

"He just wants closure," Hendricks said. "The coven will be here with that truth potion in about an hour, assuming nothing goes wrong. Anything you say while on that will be put on record."

JC snorted. "And everything I've said before *hasn't* been on record?"

He shrugged. "Just saying. People tend to get lighter sentences if they confess willingly than if we have to drag it out like this."

JC groaned, pushing away their tray and half-eaten oatmeal. It was bland as hell, anyway. "Dude. You went to the Walgreens. You have the footage. I got shot at!"

"I know," he said. "I was thinking it over last night. And you know, there would've been time for you to help these people get Violet into their car and *then* go to the Cities. Not a lot, but enough. You're diabetic—maybe they drop you off so you can pick up your prescription and go home. But then something happens. Maybe they were always planning to double-cross you, or maybe there was an argument. Whatever it was, bullets start flying, and you have to make a run for it."

JC shook their head. "Just get that truth serum over here."

§

Cyrus showed up with a plastic bag, carefully avoiding the iron bars of the cell. Despite playing the role of lawyer, he was still in his usual casual wear: jeans, T-shirt, backwards cap with indigo bangs sticking out of it, way too many pins. The only change was a dark blazer over his t-shirt, which did nothing to upgrade his outfit. "I swung by your halfway house. Alku helped me get you a change of clothes and some toiletries. Hendricks is going to let you shower, brush your teeth, all that jazz. Coven should be here in about fifteen, so make it fast."

"Cyrus, you're my favorite," JC said, snatching the bag. They were so ready to not stink of garbage. And they could shave off the five o'clock shadow poking at their face! Gender dysphoria could take a fucking hike.

Sixteen minutes later, clean and feeling somewhat decent, JC and Cyrus were back in the barren, white-walled interrogation room with Hendricks, a still purple-haired Mrs. Jackson, and...

"Nicole?" JC gasped.

"Hi," she said, focusing on pulling a jar out of her massive purse. Same baggy long-sleeved shirt, same gold rings in her locs, same flat, husky voice that had no right to be as sexy as it was.

"*This* is Nicole?" Mrs. Jackson asked suspiciously. "Can we get someone more... impartial?"

JC silently agreed with her. They didn't want Nicole to see them like this, arrested and treated like a criminal. Especially one day before they were supposed to go on their third proper date. (Or was it their second? Did the music concert count?)

"It's a small town," Cyrus said. "There aren't a whole lot of options on such short notice."

"I did try to get Michael here, but his wife just went into labor," Nicole offered. "He's at the hospital."

"Oh, holy shit, finally!" Cyrus cheered, then cleared his throat and his expression. "Right. Good for him. Besides, Nicole's one of the Stoughton Street Coven's best witches."

"Yeah, except I can't find Aunt Violet," she grumbled. "I tried all night to get a lock on her. I even used some of the hair samples you gave me—*nothing*."

Hendricks stared at Cyrus. "You gave her your boss's hair?"

"We both trust Nicole implicitly," he replied. "Just like she trusts us. One of the main ingredients in truth serum is fairy blood."

He tugged up the sleeves of his suit jacket, showing off the SpongeBob SquarePants Band-Aid just under his elbow.

"You're not sick, are you?" JC muttered.

"Nope. Not a single blood-borne disease."

"It's boiled and added to a handful of other ingredients that make it safer for human consumption," Nicole added. "You're more at risk getting sick eating from Subway."

Good enough.

Hendricks set up a camera on a little tripod next to the table, surprisingly delicate with his pudgy fingers. Then he pulled out two paper cups. "All right. Nicole, you said that jar has enough serum for two people. I'm the control. JC and I each take a dose. Once I confirm that it's effective, I'll then start asking questions. Do we all understand?"

Everyone nodded.

Nicole handed over the glass jar, and Hendricks poured the liquid. It was thick and black, almost like tar, but had a sparkle of pale gold in the light.

JC sighed, taking their cup and toasting Hendricks. "Cheers." Down the hatch.

Just as sludgy and vile as the last time they'd done this. They gave a full-body shudder, and watched Hendricks slap a hand over his mouth to keep from gagging.

"How long does it take to work?" JC asked, wishing the cop had also brought some water. Coffee. Machine oil. Something.

"You've done this before. I've seen your file," Hendricks retorted.

"Then you would know I was high as a fucking kite the last time I did this. Memory's not the best, and street covens are usually hit or miss. No offense, Nicole."

He huffed. "Shouldn't be more than a few minutes." He pulled a green stress ball out of his pocket and set it on the table. "This ball is blue."

"Yup. Very blue," JC said. "And that truth potion tasted *fantastic*. We should sell it at the café."

"I'll be wanting a urine sample after this," Mrs. Jackson said, jotting a note in her tablet. "Just to double-check its efficacy."

They rolled their eyes. "Fine. Honestly, you people ask me that so much I'm starting to think you have a kink."

She glared at them. Cyrus snickered. "No, if she hadn't said that, I would've insisted. I remember there was one time they fed a cop and cooperating witness a fake serum, blaming a gruesome murder on a completely innocent person. He was in prison for twelve years before DNA evidence cleared him, and the witness admitted to the shenanigans."

"Bet the cop didn't get any consequences," JC said.

"Nope. He was already two transfers away from that mess."

Hendricks sighed. "You're one of those 'defund the police' people, aren't you?"

"Yes, I think that excess funds should go to community supports," Cyrus retorted.

"*What* excess funds?"

"It's definitely more of a big city thing," he admitted.

Nicole cleared her throat. "Have you started investigating Officer Miller yet?"

"The guy who threw me against the wall?" JC confirmed.

Cyrus blinked. "When did *this* happen?"

Hendricks grimaced. "Nelson talked to his wife. There isn't enough solid evidence to put a proper case against him, but she's filing for divorce and the chief is transferring Miller across the state, so he can't get to her as easily."

"Buuuuut he's not going to face any consequences," JC finished.

"I'd say divorce is a pretty big consequence," Hendricks argued. "The ball is bl–green. The ball is green. Can't say blue."

JC tried to say *The ball is flaming pink*, but what came out was, "The ball is green. And that truth serum tasted awful. Sorry, Nicole."

"I'm not good at cooking," she admitted, starting that finger-tapping stim against the table.

Hendricks pulled out his notepad. "Did you kidnap the fairy known as Violet?"

"No," JC said.

"Did you have anything to do with her getting in that van?"

"No."

"Then who is on the security footage?"

"I have no idea."

"Did you have any relationship or correspondence to the people in that van besides Violet?"

"Probably not. Like I said, I have no idea who they are."

He frowned. "What were you doing at 3:15pm yesterday afternoon?"

"I was in the car with Cyrus. He offered to drive me home so I wasn't hanging out at the bus stop for half an hour. We mostly listened to music–he's got a lot of variety, considering he named himself after Miley Cyrus. And too much Kelly Clarkson, in my opinion."

"She's a classic," Cyrus grumbled.

"He took me to the Walgreens, I got my prescription, and then some other guy in a truck took a shot at me. Not sure what time that was. 3:40? 3:45, maybe? Then I used the back ways to get back to the halfway house."

Hendricks scribbled in his pad. "Can you think of anyone who would want to hurt Violet? Or frame you?"

JC scratched the back of their neck, glancing at Nicole, who was watching with a curious, unreadable expression. "Well, the Brotherhood of Minneapolis is still pissed at me. They're a gang. Also, my old gang, the Bobcats, wants me to go back and cook for them. But they'd have to hire a fairy or coven to do that glamour thing, which usually costs about ten grand on the street. I'm not worth that. And Rocket only found out where I worked last week. That's enough time for a hit or a drive-by, but a kidnapping like this? No way."

"Who's Rocket?"

"My old drug dealer. He'd get the ingredients, and I'd use them to make marbles, taking ten percent as my cut while he sold the rest."

Surprisingly, they'd never been arrested for cooking. They and Rocket had been careful enough to keep that operation under wraps. Which was good, because that probably would've landed them in prison for life. And the statute of limitations was three years, so they were in the clear. Legally, anyway.

Hendricks wrote everything down. Mrs. Jackson tapped on her tablet. JC squirmed in their seat, not meeting anyone's eyes.

"Boss has plenty of enemies," Cyrus said, mercifully letting JC's past mistakes slide. "But almost all of them are in the Fae Realm."

"What kind of enemies?" Hendricks asked. "Personal, political..."

"Yes," he snarked. "She started a war there. How do you think Gialdon became a thing?"

Hendricks paused. Nicole sputtered. "That was *her*?"

Cyrus nodded. Mrs. Jackson started furiously typing on her tablet.

"She's in my history books!" the witch exclaimed.

"Yuuup. She doesn't like to talk about it."

Hendricks recovered first. "Why wait until now? Gialdon formed...what, two hundred years ago?"

"And I'm three hundred. Boss's family is royalty, and she betrayed them. Led a whole-ass war against them that killed one in twenty Ivanian fairies. That's going to make enemies. The immortal kind who don't care about time."

JC gaped. "She's royalty?!"

"Was," Cyrus corrected. "Originally, she was the Violet Princess. Now she's the Exiled Princess, when they're feeling polite. Traitor Princess when they're not. *Definitely* not in the line of succession anymore."

"That would make this a national security issue," Hendricks warned.

"Well, yeah, assuming the Ivanian government is in on it. Fifty-fifty whether they are or not. Boss always said everyone was better off pretending the other never existed. It's one of the reasons she left the Fae Realm entirely. She was only exiled from Ivae and Gialdon; she didn't have to come to Earth, but figured it was best for her to start over in a Realm where nobody had ever heard of her."

Hendricks shook his head. "People don't always think straight. If they did, I wouldn't have a job."

"Honestly...fair," JC admitted.

"Can you think of any other reason why someone would frame you, Mr. Scott?"

"JC. And no, not really."

"It's a rather effective smoke screen, don't you think?" Cyrus asked. "After all, you're wasting time with us rather than tracking down the real kidnappers. Any luck on finding the van?"

The officer shook his head, tucking the pad of paper away in his deep blue pocket. "No hits on the plate number or van description. It's like it never existed."

"If a fairy can glamour themselves to look exactly like JC, they can glamour a car," Nicole pointed out.

"Well, if they try to get back to the Fae Realm, they won't get past airport security."

JC burst out laughing, thinking of all the times their friends had gotten past airport security with bags of drugs and weapons.

He sighed. "Actually, forget I said that. Thank you for your time, JC. You're free to go."

facing a few demons

Mrs. Jackson wordlessly handed JC a plastic cup. When they came out of the bathroom, the sealed cup went into a Ziploc, and then into her briefcase. She sighed. "I'm sorry I didn't believe you."

JC paused in the skinny police station hallway. The walls were so close together that the bathroom door almost brushed against the other side of the hall. Police officers and admins could be seen in the rooms on either side, and if anyone tried to get past, it'd be a whole tango. They shifted their feet, unused to hearing this tone from their parole officer. "Why didn't you?"

She almost smiled. Somehow, it made it her look older than her forty-plus years. "When I first started, I had a parolee who served a decade for murder. He wasn't under the influence, like you had been. This had been premeditated. Lucky for him, he had a good attorney, so the sentence got cut from twenty years to ten. When he got out, I was convinced that he had changed. Everyone was. He seemed genuinely remorseful. He had a wife and two children that he had to live for. Talked his uncle into giving him a job at the warehouse...and then after about a year, his uncle was found dead. Warehouse broken into, money from the registers stolen. It looked like a robbery gone wrong, but my parolee's wife got suspicious and went through his things. Found the money in the floorboards."

"Sloppy," JC said. It would've been much better to put the cash in a plastic bag and bury it somewhere. The garden, if he had one. Or maybe the public park, if he could find a good place out of the way.

She shrugged, weirdly casual in her navy blue blazer and pencil skirt. "You get used to disappointment."

JC leaned against the wall and crossed their arms. Their jean jacket was still just a tiny bit damp from its bath in the jailhouse sink last night, uncomfortably tight around their arms and back with the movement.

They couldn't be angry at Mrs. Jackson. Not even when she had been actively not-listening to them. "Yeah, well. I don't blame you. I wouldn't have believed me, either."

She patted their arm. "Don't worry. They'll get this sorted out. You'll see. If nothing else, I'll have the labs run your sample to prove that the truth potion worked, and that'll remove any and all doubt about your involvement."

They snorted, watching her leave. They found Cyrus in the lobby with Nicole, Officer Hendricks nowhere in sight. Nicole was still stimming. "Can we go?"

"Yeah, this place is always so stuffy," Cyrus agreed. He put an arm around JC's shoulders and steered them outside...

Straight into a mob.

"What the—" they sputtered.

A wave of noise crashed over them. They didn't recognize anyone in the crowd, but all of their faces were twisted with fury. Some of them even had hastily-made posters with things like *Lock him up* and *Fairy Musicians Go Home*.

"That asshole mind-controlled us!"

"You work with tree-fuckers!"

"Get the fuck out of our town!"

Cyrus yanked JC back and slammed the door shut. "What the fuck, guys?"

"Ah, shit. Really?" Hendricks came back, scowling out the window. "Nelson, I thought you said the *Gazette* article was neutral!"

"It is!" the other officer protested. "But I'm pretty sure most of those people out there are the Main Street witnesses. Victims, even, of that flute-player."

"Can't you guys make a statement? You just cleared them," Cyrus argued.

"I'm on it," Hendricks grumbled, straightening his uniform. "But you should head out the back, just in case. Nelson, show 'em the way?"

She beckoned for the trio to follow her as Hendricks went to deal with the mob. JC's heart pounded in their chest. They'd been in some crazy situations in the past, but having an entire town hate them? For something they didn't even do? That was a first.

Nelson's swishing blond ponytail led them through the tight coils of the police station, to a back exit. Cyrus poked his capped indigo head out first, then nodded.

Nelson snatched JC's arm before they could follow him and Nicole out. "If you tricked that truth serum, we will find out. You and those jicks will pay for hurting our town."

She let them go. JC glared over their shoulder on their way out.

§

CaFae Latte was oddly empty. Obviously, JC had been here when it was empty before opening and after closing. Sometimes, they even beat Violet and Cyrus here and had the whole place to themselves.

But it was mid-morning. There should have been a rush. They should've had to swap out the pastry case at least once. Should've had to clean up some coffee spills while listening to Cyrus's poly*jam*orous playlist blasting over the speakers. Should be looking forward to a long lunch break and an evening rush with a car show.

With just the three of them sitting at a table, it didn't feel right. Even with the coffee and hot chocolate Cyrus had made so they had something to do with their hands while they stared at nothing.

"We're staying closed, then?" JC asked, crossing their arms.

Cyrus nodded, shedding his suit jacket. "Between you and me, we might be able to keep up. But..."

"Yeah."

He turned to Nicole. "You really can't find Boss?"

She shook her head. "I tried. Had multiple maps, all the ingredients, her hair...nothing."

JC shifted. "I hate to be that guy, but are we sure your magic isn't on the fritz?"

Cyrus chuckled. Nicole glared at them and dug through her purse, producing a map, a jar of bones, and a plain wooden wand with some purple hair tied to the end of it. "You said you were shot at yesterday? Give me some of your hair."

Confused, JC obeyed, pulling a few strands from their head. Nicole removed Violet's purple hair from the wand, carefully setting it aside, and tied JC's to it. Then she removed a leather watch from her wrist—old and somewhat masculine, but it suited her—and turned back the clock to 3:40.

She unwrapped one of the maps—it was of the Twin Cities. "St. Paul or Minneapolis?"

"I was in St. Paul, right by—"

"Uh-uh. No more details." She put down the watch and opened the jar of bones. "Coin-sith bones. They're fairy hunting dogs. Great trackers."

With that, she emptied the bones on the table. As they scattered, she held the wand over the map loosely between two fingers—brown hair pointed down—and closed her eyes.

Her hand moved as if jerked by an invisible force, to the southern edge of St. Paul's residential area. She opened her eyes and pointed to the bones. "These read 'violence' and 'escape.' Is this where it happened?"

JC leaned over, reading the street names right under the wand. They gasped. "Holy shit."

"Yeah..." Cyrus drawled. "Nicole's magic doesn't 'fritz.' When it comes to clairvoyance and divination, she's got clearer sight than anyone I've ever met—and most people Boss has met, too."

They blushed. "...sorry."

Nicole hissed a sigh, taking back her wristwatch and bones, and removed JC's hair from the wand. "Clearly I'm not *that* good, because every time I try to find Violet..." She wrapped the purple hair around the wand and tossed the bones again. JC couldn't tell the difference, but Nicole shook her head. "Nothing. I can't even tell if she's alive or dead."

"She's alive," Cyrus said. "If they wanted her dead, her corpse would've been left on the sidewalk."

"So why kidnap her?" JC asked. "A living person is a much bigger problem than a dead one."

"I don't know."

They went quiet as Nicole cleaned up the mess she'd made, carefully putting everything back in her purse. She pulled out her sketchbook. "Maybe there's something I saw earlier that can help us."

They crowded her shoulders as she started from the page of JC's portrait (still kind of freaky), then the chained hands, black book, pages of wolves and...crows? No, she'd written a note saying, "black dove." A forest, a beach, a dragon...

She flipped another page, and JC stopped her, their throat turning to sand. "That's Rocket."

Cyrus looked up. "Your old drug dealer? Why is he holding a key?" He pointed to the sketch where Rocket was, indeed, holding a key. Nicole had even managed to capture his smarmy smirk and the way the light reflected off his gold chain necklace.

"That's what I saw in my vision," Nicole answered. "Stuff like that is usually symbolic. He holds the key, literally. He knows something."

"What the fuck could he know? He's never even been to Bernier," JC said.

Cyrus tapped a pale blue finger against the sketchbook. "Any use giving this to the cops?"

They shook their head. "Rocket never talks to cops. He won't talk to you, and he probably won't talk to Nicole."

"Why not?" she asked with a frown.

"You're strangers. He won't trust you."

"...but he trusts *you*," Cyrus said at length.

JC gritted their teeth. "I really don't want to get more involved in this than I already am. Especially not where *this* asshole is concerned."

"I know. And I don't want you to, either," he placated. "But I'm not really seeing any other options. If the people who took

Boss are able to glamour to look like anyone, to make their cars look like anything, and everyone in town still blames you..."

JC got up and paced, their arms crossed. Nelson's words rang in their head. There *were* ways to beat a truth potion. Unless they got Violet back soon, no one was going to let JC continue to work in Bernier. They'd have to go back to an endless string of corporate ghosting–and that wouldn't pay rent or groceries. If they did stay in Bernier, it was only a matter of time before Violet's magic failed and dealers came in for the prime real estate.

Violet had taken one look at JC and given them a chance, a rope in the ocean. That was worth facing a few demons for, wasn't it?

"...fuck. Fine." They pulled out their phone and dialed, leaving the room for the back kitchen. They really didn't want to do this in front of everybody.

The first dials went to voicemail. Cursing, JC tried again.

Rocket picked up on the third call. "What?"

"Uh..." JC realized they had no idea what to say. They cleared their throat. "My Fae boss went missing. Any idea what happened to her?"

"And if I did know? Why should I care about that jick?"

Beyond the counter, Cyrus stuck his tongue out at the slur. Right. Fae hearing.

"Rocket, I am standing one room away from a pissed-off fairy and *shockingly* accurate clairvoyant, and we know you know something," JC snapped. "Maybe I should ask them where you've been keeping your stashes these days. I'd love a good bonfire right about now."

Rocket was quiet for so long that JC had to check to make sure he hadn't hung up.

"I might know something," he finally said. "But you've gotta do something for me."

"That's not how blackmail works."

"You don't know jack shit. Most of my stuff, you can't reach. Even with a witch. So, you want to know what I know about a Bernier fairy? You do what I say. Get to my house. I've got a job for you."

He hung up.

stabby when mistreated

Quentin's team came to Michelle's safehouse just before dawn to oversee Violet's transfer, in case she tried anything.

Michelle had divided her eleven people into two teams. Team Two was led by Pete–who, along with Olson, was still pissed about losing the baker. Pete and Olson had four others on their team, but Jack wasn't really familiar with them, because he was on Team One. Michelle led those people herself, usually. But for this job, since she stuck so close to Violet and Red Wolf, she relegated most of those duties to Quentin.

That meant it was Quentin, Roger, David, and Alex who came to the safehouse with breakfast burritos from Taco Bell. Alex grumbled about not being able to get Perkins, but they were on a schedule, which meant fast and filling, not slow and delicious.

They brought the other two fairies with them: Crow Moon, who had dark pink skin and those ridiculously fast shoes, and Mouse, who Jack didn't really know. The dark green fairy was short, though, and he and Crow Moon mostly kept to themselves, drifting over to Crescent, Piper, and Black Dove while they ate, Red Wolf and Michelle on guard duty in the basement. Gold was the only fairy absent, which was a shame. Quentin and Alex spent the most time with them, and according to those two, Gold was genuinely interested in how humans worked, even buying and wearing modern clothes instead of glamouring the Lord of the Rings/Renaissance Festival-core all the fairies had come here with. All the mercenaries had taken their turns suggesting their favorite foods, sports, TV shows–which might have been a mistake, since now Gold and Roger couldn't be in the same room for more than five minutes without arguing about *The Bachelor*.

Jack found himself nibbling at his food, stomach churning, and not just because of the Taco Bell. Violet's words swirled in his mind. She was giving him a way *out*, but with way more money than Michelle had ever offered. And the more time he spent around these fairies—especially Piper—the queasier he got.

"Earth to Jack!" Quentin ruffled his auburn curls.

Jack pushed him away. "Gah! What?"

"Did you hear anything about where we're going? We'd ask the fairies, but..." He rolled his eyes. The Fae weren't paying attention to them, as usual, absorbed in their own conversation in their own language on the couch across the room.

"Michelle's got some friends in Minneapolis who know where a Fae portal is," he said, forcing himself to take a bite of the rolled up grease and mystery meat that passed as a burrito. "That's all I got."

Quentin nodded, his braids swaying with the movement. Roger frowned, shoving the last of his burrito in his wide mouth. "Can't you find a portal? You're the computer guy."

"What are you, from the '90s?"

"'88."

Alex burst out laughing. The large Canadian woman had also barely touched her food, but that was mostly because this garbage barely counted as food. A meaner, dumber person would tell her that that was good, tell her that she could stand to lose a few pounds and maybe order a salad next time. That person would get an hour-long lecture on fatphobia and then a bullet. And then she'd carry the body away for disposal without any help—no matter how heavy it was—without complaint. She only complained when she had to help dispose of *other* people's victims.

"Fae portals are made with magic," Jack said. "And magic reacts *really* weird to tech. We've only just figured out how to scan for glamour, and even that just tells us glamour is being used, not what it's hiding."

"Well Black Dove's a sorceress," Roger said. "Can she make one?"

"I think she would if she could."

Roger leaned back to get a clearer view of the fairies, his bald head catching the overhead lights like a bowling ball. He shaved every morning, waking up early to do it and cleaning up the motel bathroom after he was done. He never said so, but Jack had seen his social media pictures, and he'd only started doing that when his brother went through chemotherapy and lost his hair that way.

"Hey guys! Can't Black Dove magic you back to the Fae Realm?" Roger asked.

Piper laughed. Crescent rolled his eyes, flicking gray hair away from his forehead. "I'm not even a sorcerer and I know that much."

"But she's got those wands, right? The ones that let her do cool stuff?"

"She has a druidic wand, allowing her to transform other people into animals without the use of their full name or body," the dark blue fairy corrected. "And she has an Elemental Wand, specifically water. That's to counter Violet's fire wand."

"Violet has a fire wand?" David asked. He was usually quiet, always having his nose in a mini-Kindle, even when he was going up into a sniper's nest. Jack would know; his first job with this group was second sniper, stationed at a building opposite of David's with a clear line of sight to him and their target. Jack had covered one exit while David covered the other, and Jack had watched as the short, lanky man spent the whole time reading— but still managed to see when the target left his exit and pulled the trigger. Sometimes he used makeup to hide the wine-colored birthmark under his left eye, but not today. "Why didn't she use it?"

"Obviously we caught her when she didn't have it on her."

"Aren't those things illegal?" Roger asked.

"All wands are illegal," Alex said, still poking at her burrito in disgust.

"Yeah, but a fire wand is really just a lightweight flame-thrower, which *is* legal to own," Quentin pointed out.

Roger lit up. "You can own a flamethrower? Legally?!"

"You have to register it," David said, going back to his Kindle. "But yes."

Jack frowned. "Why is a flamethrower legal but a fire wand not, if they do the exact same thing?"

"Wands are Fae," Quentin said, like that explained anything.

Alex made a face. "There's gotta be a better reason."

"Nope. Wands and most other enchanted items were outlawed back in the '60s, '70s, and '80s, mostly to discourage fairies from coming here, I think? Or maybe just as a 'fuck you.' It's like how weed was outlawed until white people started getting into it." He motioned to Mouse and Crow Moon. "Even your guys' stuff is illegal in most states."

Crow Moon shrugged her dark pink shoulders, bare in her plain, sleeveless dress. She crossed her enchanted boots. "Mortals hate what they can't understand."

"Or maybe they didn't like how you used them on humans," Jack grumbled.

It was too quiet for even the humans right next to him to hear, but all the fairies caught it. Piper laughed again. It grated on Jack's ears.

Crescent glared at him. "The one time we gave the mortals of the Fae Realm any modicum of freedom, they burned and bled everything in sight."

Jack ducked his head, face heating. Quentin drawled, his Dallas accent pushing through, "Ah, pretty sure that was because all humans in Fae had been kidnapped and enslaved. We tend to get stabby when mistreated."

"We treated them just fine! They had food, water, shelter, purpose..."

"And even after the war, they got violent," Crow Moon added. "Gialdon's been responsible for more wars than any of the fairy nations."

"That sounds like a vast oversimplification," Quentin said. "I'm not saying humans are perfect. Hell, I kill people for a living, just like these bozos."

He jerked a dark thumb at the other mercenaries, and Jack's insides squirmed. Sure, he'd pulled the trigger on a few people, but he'd never liked it, even in the military. He was always more comfortable with a computer than a gun.

He supposed that made him something of a coward.

"But if you try to force a bunch of people to serve you at all costs for however many generations, sooner or later it'll blow up in your face," Quentin finished.

Piper flipped his flute around his fingers. Jack dropped his burrito and plugged his ears. The pale yellow fairy smirked at him.

Someone cleared their throat. Everyone looked up at Michelle, coming in from the hall. "The prisoner's ready for transport."

the leader

Excerpt from *Round-Ears: A History of Gialdon and Humans in the Fae Realm*

As mentioned previously, the Violet Princess commanded an incredible amount of loyalty from her troops. After the events of Srada, that loyalty was put to the test.

Unsurprisingly, most of the human soldiers under her command immediately flocked to the Gialdon side. This may have been less because of their respect for their former Chief Commander and more for the simple desires for freedom and basic rights, coupled with the Violet Princess's promise of good wages from her own coffers. As she and the Gialdon forces destroyed more archives, thwarting Ivae's ability to curse and control their serf armies, more and more humans ran away from their Fae captors to join the war for freedom, or even just refused to fight for Ivae. This single act of fleeing was a devastating blow, as the population of Ivae's military dwindled to critical numbers.

[...]

Most of the humans who did not join Gialdon were household servants, mostly for the rich who could afford better security. Many Fae, in anticipation of their province's archives being lost, immediately collected blood and hair samples of all the serfs in their domain so they could still curse them in the event of their disobedience. This threat was enough to keep many mortals under their thumb. Other fairies wiped the memories of their serfs every time news of the rebellion reached them, preventing them from remembering that there was a war even going on, never mind plan an effective escape. [...]

There was also a sharp increase in the purchase and use of enchanted instruments, as well as hiring musicians who specialized in such magic. One of the primary methods of preventing human rebellions was that of mind-control music. Similar to Pied Pipers, this music could put mortals into a trance, making them work, sleep, even fight. Surviving accounts and even the [far less common] present-day victims describe the sensation as similar to sleepwalking, being in a dream-like state as they followed the fairy's orders with no will of their own.

But that required the music to continue the full length of days, with a rotation of musicians, something beyond the financial capabilities of all but the wealthiest of families. And the Fae were wary of "mind rot." When exposed to too much hypnotic magic for extended periods of time, it can cause brain damage to the subject. They are unable to make their own decisions, to start or stop work unless explicitly ordered. Indeed, many cannot rise from their bed without being ordered, or will continue to work even while asleep if not ordered to bed. In the worst cases, they lose all sense of identity and personality, barely able to remember their own name. This was a large reason why musical instruments were destroyed by Gialdon fighters and still treated with wariness today, with most mortal-controlled countries and Realms outlawing the instruments entirely.

Outside of magical coercion, most mortals' decision to go or not largely hinged on the ability of their family and loved ones to travel. Many of fighting age worried that their escape would result in the punishment of their parents, siblings, spouses, and/or children, and tried to take them with. These group escapes were far more likely to fail and resulted in mass generational curses.

Of course, some mortals chose to side with Ivae and the Fae of their own free will, hoping for greater status and favor. Or perhaps out of a sense of loyalty, or even love, as many of the mortals who made this decision had kitrye and Fae family.

Then there were the Violet Princess's Fae former under-officers.

Quite a few sided with their former Chief Commander. Despite the Violet Princess almost immediately being stripped of all official military and political power by her family as soon as her defection was made public, she still managed to talk several fairies onto her side.

Reasons for this varied. One went on record saying that they had also felt uncomfortable with Ivae's policy toward mortals, and wanted to make the choice that would ease their conscience. Another was outright bribed. Sunrise and Sunset, two of the most notorious sorcerers of the Gialdon war, spoke of a fiercer loyalty toward their teacher than their nation. Both had come from obscure families with little wealth, with Sunset not even being royal or noble. They felt—and perhaps their patron encouraged—that they had a debt to pay.

Two other fairies—known only to history as Pumpkin and Carver—had both fallen in love with a kitrye Gialdon guerilla fighter, Summer, about a century before the war started, and the throuple had a child. While Pumpkin had never been in the military, Carver had served as the Violet Princess's lieutenant for a couple centuries before deserting to be with Pumpkin and Summer, an act that had probably influenced the Violet Princess's own defection a hundred years later.

However, about two thirds of the Violet Princess's Fae officers stayed loyal to Ivae. The most notable of them were Lady Oak and Commander Harvest Moon.

Pictured the Violet Princess locating more records of serf names and destroying them. It's unclear whether or not this is supposed to depict Srada specifically.

stone oaks

They left Michelle's safehouse before dawn the next morning. Violet grumbled about how she was too old to be sleeping on concrete floors without a pillow as they chained her hands to the van, then drove into the heart of the city, where the buildings rose like skinny mountains all around them. The rest of the fairies and mercenaries, also in different cars, vans, and trucks, spread out over the Twin Cities to avoid detection, Red Wolf and Michelle keeping in text contact with all of them. Only Crescent's team stayed close, posted two spots behind their van to ensure Violet didn't escape.

Michelle's allies—the Stone Oaks Coven—operated out of a small building in the shadow of downtown Minneapolis. The neighborhood was a stretch of cracked concrete streets and stunted brick buildings, all crowded far too close together. Even in the rosy pre-dawn light, there were already cars rushing to and fro, a line wrapped around a nearby Caribou Coffee, and two men arguing in front of a building labeled "Food Market."

"What are the chances of these allies actually providing assistance?" Red Wolf asked.

"With the size of your pockets? Pretty good," Michelle replied, putting on her red-tinted sunglasses and a leather jacket, though the early morning was a smidge too warm for it. The ensemble did an adequate job of hiding both her face and tattoos.

The two of them climbed out and entered the coven's headquarters, a bell cheerfully ringing as they stepped inside. It was underwhelming to say the least. The shelves were stacked with crystals and amulets that Red Wolf would bet an entire kingdom didn't have even a drop of magic. A few animal skulls and teeth looked promising, but closer inspection revealed they were mortal animals, not magical, and thus largely useless in spellcraft. He was glad he'd left Black Dove in the van—she would've thrown a fit.

"Good morning!" yawned a woman behind the counter, drinking from a concernedly large mug of coffee. Red Wolf could smell it from across the room. "What can I do for you?"

"We're here to see Linda," Michelle said.

She set the mug down, glancing beyond Michelle's shoulders to Red Wolf. "And your friend?"

"Not a cop," she assured her. "Drop the glamour."

He did, grateful to let the uncomfortable "jeans" melt back into familiar linen.

"He's with me," Michelle added. "Not a product."

The woman shrugged. "Fine. But Linda's in the middle of something."

"Ah." Michelle glanced back at Red Wolf, studying him before coming to a decision. "We're in a rush."

"Fair enough." She pressed a button, and a high-pitched buzz vibrated through Red Wolf's pointed ears. "Door's open. She'll be downstairs."

Michelle led the way through a door marked "Employees Only." As soon as they were through, the buzzing stopped.

The stairs and walls were concrete, with metal railings. Red Wolf was sick and tired of seeing the stuff. "In the Fae Realm, our buildings are made of trees. Not chopped down, but grown and molded with magic," he muttered. "The house itself is alive. We are but guests within. This is walking through a corpse."

"Good for you," Michelle said. "We'd rather not split rent with squirrels. Now let me do the talking here."

"Might I remind you that you work for *me*?"

"Yes, I do. So let me do my job."

Red Wolf almost regretted leaving Piper in the car.

At the bottom of the stairs, Michelle opened a final door.

The smell of blood hit him first, not the thick copper of red mortals but the lighter, tangier smell of gold.

Red Wolf tensed, noting the stones, plants, and animal bones lining the shelves that came from the Fae Realm, a handful of draconic items, and even a few from the Abyss or "Demonic" Realm. The lights overhead were almost blinding, casting the woman standing with her back to the door in shadow until she turned around. Her apron was splattered with golden Fae blood, just a few shades darker than her silvering hair, pulled back in a bun.

On the table before her was the splayed, mutilated body of a fairy.

Red Wolf's face went hot with rage. "What is this?"

The mortal elder peeled off her gold-stained rubber gloves and adjusted her glasses. "A fairy. Obviously. One who had been causing problems for our friends. They needed a bit of help handling it last night, which I provided in exchange for the body."

"Harvesting the parts for yourself," he spat.

She held out her arms. "Why let it go to waste?"

"It doesn't concern you, Wolf," Michelle warned. "Linda and the others here, they only kill troublemakers."

"That doesn't matter," he argued.

Linda barked a laugh. "Sure, it does. This one was a human trafficker. Specialized in children. Took them from foster homes or off the streets and sold them to the highest bidder, again and again. No one's going to mourn him."

Oh, was he? Red Wolf wondered. Such crimes were horrendous, even when they happened to mortals. But mortals could lie to justify their horrors.

In any case...

"In my Realm, we don't soil our hands with blood," he said, "or dare to spill an immortal's, even if they are repugnant."

"Well, we're not in your Realm, are we?" the witch challenged. "At least I'm not punishing his children, grandchildren, and all other descendants for *his* crimes."

Michelle got between the two of them before it could escalate. "Linda, he's new. Red Wolf, *I'm* a killer. You hired me explicitly because of that. Deal with it. Now. We need a way to the Fae Realm. Secret, under-the-radar, and immediate. The fewer people who know about it, the better."

Linda glared at Red Wolf for another beat before focusing on Michelle. "I know a few. None of them are close."

"That's fine. We can drive."

"Information isn't cheap."

"Blackmail sure is," Red Wolf said. "I wonder how your local law enforcement will react to your brand of justice."

Linda scoffed. "This place is covered in good luck and protection charms. Any police who come here will be easily bribed, dumb enough to convince there's nothing going on, or too slow to catch us."

Frustrated, he left Michelle to haggle with the witch and ended up hovering over the dead fairy. All their organs had been removed, the blood drained into thick plastic bags hanging from a low rack. It seemed they'd interrupted Linda sawing through and harvesting the bones and teeth.

Not even on my worst enemy, he thought. He'd seen death before, of course. He was centuries old and a soldier. But he was a fairy. Immortal. And by definition, immortals were above death. They did not take a life with their own hands if they could help it. The closest they got was ordering mortals to kill, and never on another immortal unless every other option had been beyond exhausted. Death, murder, bloodshed, those were things only mortals did. Fairies were better than that.

Or at least, they should be.

In the years leading to her betrayal, Violet had questioned that more and more. Red Wolf, Oak, and the other military officers had learned how to use swords and knives only for self-defense, in case a mortal got too close. And that had saved their lives more than once.

Violet had gone further. She had learned those arts not to defend, but to attack. Had been in the middle of battles herself rather than watching from afar to give orders as needed. And she'd doubled down after Yellow Mud's Exodus.

If we're responsible for them losing their lives, then we should be risking our own.

Everyone had worried that she had lost her mind. Red Wolf had tried to talk her out of such nonsense multiple times, worried that she would get hurt, that she would die, that she would lose all social status among the other fairies. She didn't listen.

Didn't care. And worse, it had made her closer to the humans than her own kind. She sympathized with *them*, shed tears over *their* spilled blood, but hadn't cared about the *fairy* blood drawn over the war and anarchy she started.

He wasn't going to stoop to that level. And even if he did, death was too good for all the pain and suffering Violet had caused.

"Done," Michelle said. "Red Wolf, we need your paycheck."

"And I haven't told her anything," Linda added. "You only get the information after I see that money hit my bank account."

Damn impertinent mortal, he thought, writing the check with far too many zeros. Linda took it, pulled out her cell phone, and took a few pictures. After a minute, she nodded in satisfaction and tore the check into multiple pieces, dumping them in a blood-stained bucket. "Black Beach. A wild portal's just formed on the island there."

"That's on Lake Superior," Michelle pointed out.

"That's your only option if you want to avoid the airport. Without a frankly ridiculous amount of magic to artificially create bridges between the Realms, you're stuck with what occurs naturally. The closest wild spot with enough magic to create a portal on its own is Lake Superior, and it closes in about a week, according to our divinations."

Michelle sighed. "That's at least a three-and-a-half-hour drive, and it's the height of tourist season."

"I'd say the bigger problem is the dragon," Linda said, pulling something out of her pocket. "It lives in Superior National Forest and is *very* territorial, but you might be able to bribe them. Your second problem is this."

She handed Red Wolf a picture. He frowned at it. It was one of those digital arts, done on a computer and then printed. She'd even colored it, blue denim wrapped around pale skin under bushy brown hair.

"Violet's baker?" he scoffed. "Why are they an issue?"

Linda shrugged. "I don't know. I just know what I saw in the vision. They're what I like to call a 'nail of destiny.' Small, overlooked, but capable of building or collapsing major events.

I don't know exactly what they're going to do, but they're tied to your immediate future, and that's going to have some major consequences."

Which means I'm likely going to kill them, Red Wolf thought, giving the picture back. *Or perhaps they'll prove to be a useful tool like Michelle.*

He briefly considered having Michelle kill Linda to ensure secrecy. He had promised only money, after all, not protection.

But this was one of Michelle's allies, and he didn't want to alienate his subordinate more than necessary. And Linda did not have to give him those two warnings. That deserved something.

"Sounds like we have a long journey ahead of us," he said. "Let's not waste daylight."

unrepentant

Violet glanced out the front window, having to tip her head to the side to see beyond Jack's auburn curls, and said mildly, "I thought you didn't want to kill me."

Black Dove didn't turn, giving Violet only the view of the silver marbling creeping up her bald black head. "We don't."

"Then why are you bringing me to the most notorious paranormal body buyers and sellers on the black market?"

Black Dove blinked, then glared at Jack, who squirmed in the driver's seat. "Michelle works with them from time to time. I don't think she's done any of *those* jobs, but she sometimes uses their charms and spells to help with other stuff."

Violet glanced at Black Dove. "Interesting choice of allies."

"Shut up," the sorceress ordered, sulking in the passenger's seat. Piper was right outside, stretching his legs (and keeping all passers-by within easy hearing of his flute).

"I don't think I will," Violet mused, examining her aluminum cuffs and the long chain to the van's floor. With Red Wolf disappearing into the building, she had to remain off her feet to keep the enchanted boots from going red-hot with pain. They still ached with phantom fire, and talking helped distract her.

It also distracted her from the fact that she hadn't been able to shower last night after a full day's work. Or change out of her jeans and shirt. Or spare Caroline's mesh scarf from the dirt and grime.

"You've cuffed me, but haven't gagged me," she pointed out. "I suppose you were really relying on that druidic wand to work, hm?"

Black Dove pressed the back of her skull against her seat and sighed. "As much as I want you to suffer, killing you might just be worth it."

Surprisingly, Jack didn't immediately say anything. It was hard to tell, as Violet couldn't see their faces with their position and the wire mesh separating them, but she could've sworn his side-eye was a little uneasy.

"Why do you want me dead or suffering?" Violet asked. "Red Wolf, I can understand. He's always had a rebellious streak against authority and felt personally betrayed by my decisions—to say nothing of Lady Oak. But why are you following him instead of staying in the Fae Realm?"

"My son was at Srada."

"...ah." So much for turning this one into a potential ally.

Jack frowned between the two of them. "Uh...what's Srada?"

"A city in the Fae Realm, specifically the kingdom of Ivae," Violet lectured. "It was small, but extremely important for that part of the kingdom, as it held the true names of every human serf in the region. Every time a bound mortal defied the Fae in any way, it was only a matter of flipping through the records to find their names and that of their family, then curse them for their rebellion. Even if they were physically lost to us, hiding in woods or caves or cities, we could curse them with ill luck, ill health, even death. Thus, no rebellion could last for long."

Jack looked more and more uneasy as she spoke, his shoulders coming up to his ears. When he looked at Black Dove, she shrugged, unrepentant. "We needed them. They made up our armies, were our household servants, and they even made decent entertainers."

He wrinkled his face in disgust.

"I decided that fairies had washed their hands in enough mortal blood and suffering," Violet continued, agreeing with what he refused to say to the face of his employer. "The first thing I did was burn down the archives. It served a dual purpose: give the human serfs a proper chance at freedom, and also prove to the freedom fighters leading those efforts that I was serious about joining their side."

"And the riots that followed?" Black Dove demanded. "Was that part of your plan, too?"

Violet grimaced. "I knew violence would follow, but not to that extent."

"And you wonder why we kept the humans on such a short leash."

"I didn't wonder at all. I put down dozens of mortal rebellions before seeing the folly, and lost...I don't know how many troll, giant, dwarf, and fairy lives. And for what? So we could pretend to be better than them?"

"We *are* better than them," Black Dove insisted.

At Jack's frown, she added, "No offense, but we are."

Violet chuckled.

"So, as soon as the humans realized they were free, they rioted, right?" Jack asked. "Tear down the people who put them down for thousands of years and make sure they couldn't do it again?"

"Essentially, yes," Violet said. "I tried to control the violence in a healthier way, but they hadn't yet realized that I was the one who had freed them at Srada, so they tried to kill me, too."

"And you still joined them?" Black Dove gasped.

"It was a simple miscommunication on my part. I located the freedom fighter leaders as soon as I could afterwards, but by then, Srada had been razed to the ground, its fairy inhabitants either fled or dead."

"Animals," the sorcerer bit out.

"I'm sure many of them have felt your pain *acutely* over the last several centuries. Losing their own children and family to battles for wars that they didn't understand or want any part in..."

Black Dove pulled something out of the pocket of her ivory robes.

Seeing the motion, Jack frowned. "Wait—"

She shot through the mesh, at Violet.

Violet's whole body jerked as electricity ripped through her like a knife. She slipped off the bench to the floor, gritting her teeth as the pain washed over her.

The sorceress hummed in approval. "These tasers are lovely."

She hit the button again, sending more electrical pain until the back door opened.

Violet looked upside-down at Red Wolf, who frowned. "What's going on?"

"Oh, just a little quarrel about history," Violet grunted, yanking the taser wires out of her shoulder.

Red Wolf snatched the taser from a grumpy Black Dove. "Everyone, get ready. We have a long drive ahead of us."

concrete arteries

The car ride was largely silent on the way to the Cities. JC kept their eyes glued to the passenger window, trying not to drown in Cyrus and Nicole's silence, lightened only by Cyrus's "Chill Out" playlist. The state's concrete arteries cut through a landscape that alternated between farmland and towns.

At least Cyrus's car smelled nice. Despite some crumbs on the seat and wrappers on the floor, it was a mostly clean Toyota Prius with a cinnamon air freshener happily whirling in front of the vents.

About halfway there, the blue fairy frowned into the rear-view mirror.

"What?" JC asked.

"I think that cop car's following us."

They turned around. Beyond Nicole's ring-peppered locs was a police cruiser, at least five car lengths behind them.

"How long?" JC asked.

"Since the bridge," Cyrus said. The highway curved. He slowed down a bit to take the gentle turn. They all craned their necks, trying to get a good look at the cop car's side.

"Not a state trooper," JC said. Those cars were brown, at least in Minnesota. Their tail was a classic black-and-white.

"No, that's one of Bernier's."

"Is there reason they'd be going to the Cities other than to follow us?" Nicole asked.

"Nope." Cyrus made a face. "I guess JC's still a suspect."

"For fuck's sake," they grumbled. If they were going anywhere else, they'd have said to let the cop follow them. But since they were heading straight to a known drug dealer's house...

"Hold on," he said. "We're going to make this exit."

Nicole frowned as the exit came up. "Shouldn't you get into the right lane?"

"Sure. You guys are buckled in, right?"

At the very last second, Cyrus suddenly turned on his blinker and rushed into the exit lane, throwing JC into the door, their shoulder squished against the glass.

The cop tried to follow, but as another car was in the way, they ended up missing the exit.

"Nice work," Nicole complimented.

JC hiccuped, straightening. "Yeah, maybe next time don't leave my stomach behind."

"Wuss," Cyrus said.

"Couldn't you have glamoured us?"

"Do you *want* me to crash? The bigger the object, the larger and more exhausting the spell. Glamouring myself isn't that big of a deal. A whole-ass car? While driving it? Hope you don't mind napping in a ditch." He checked behind them again. "If I were him, I'd keep going until I passed a few exits, then stakeout under a bridge and link back with us when we return to 61. So, we're not going back on that highway."

"We had to take the 494 exit, anyway."

Nicole tipped her head, a couple stray locs swinging with the movement. "Why did Rocket spike your drink?"

JC shrugged. "When I came back clean, he lost a cook and a customer. Permanently. He's the one who got me hooked on it in the first place, so I guess he thought he could do it again."

Nicole frowned. "That doesn't sound like a friend."

Cyrus snorted. "That is the most mom response you could make."

"How did…" She paused. JC could see part of her round face through the side mirror as she visibly reconsidered. "You don't have to tell us. I'm just curious how someone can end up with 'friends' like that."

JC considered not answering. It was none of her business.

But Cyrus was driving them, helping them do this, and Nicole had wordlessly followed them into the car knowing where they were going. So maybe they owed it to them.

"I was a dumb kid in a poor family that thinks being queer is a personality flaw," they said. "The neighborhood I grew up in is dangerous. Gangs provide protection. Rocket was older, smarter, and—don't judge me—cute. I wanted to spend time with him, and the rest of his crowd. Fit in, be cool, pretend I belonged. And drugs, they're not just a way to make friends, they let me escape."

They jerked their chin at Cyrus. "You're a fairy, so marbles probably don't have much effect on you."

"Never tried marbles," he said. "I did try Fae weed, though, and it almost knocked me off my ass."

JC crossed their arms. "For me it's...it's like being teleported into another world. Not just that, but as a different person. Someone who *isn't* a screw-up. Someone that *everyone* would be proud to be friends with or related to. Earth drugs do a bit of that—cocaine, heroin, booze—but marbles did it best. I was fucking Superman when I was on those."

"Lots of marble addicts wind up dying of starvation," Cyrus commented. "Or problems caused by malnutrition."

"Yeah, 'cause the main ingredient is grown in the Fae Realm. You have to dilute it with stuff from Earth before you can take it. Usually sugar, water, a few chemicals. Some people mix it with tobacco and smoke it. And let me tell you, I was a damn good cook. Any way you wanted it, any flavor, I could deliver the best in the state. Probably the whole Midwest outside of Chicago," they said, a hollow pride ringing through their chest.

"When you first start, your appetite comes back almost as soon as you come down. Lots of high school girls take marbles to lose weight—you don't get hungry at all when you're on it—and the smart ones stop after a couple weeks," they said, remembering their last few months in high school before dropping out, selling marbles to those girls desperate for thinness and beauty in the parking lot, behind the gym lockers, under the bleachers...

"After a while, you don't get hungry until hours after coming down. Then it's days. You put reminders on your phone so you don't forget to eat even when you're sober. If it gets bad enough, you'll try to eat half a cup of soup after withdrawal and throw it all up. The hospital has to put a special saline in you so you can actually keep food down; it has some kind of para-berry juice, I think. *Great* for withdrawal. And you'd think, the first time that happens, you'd be smart enough to go sober for good. But that feeling, of being whole and good and confident, you can't resist that. You go back. And *keep* going back. Gets to the point where all the ER nurses know you by name and stop slipping rehab pamphlets into your bag."

Nicole was stimming on her knee. JC, who could hear the gentle *pat-pat-pat*, kept their gaze out the window.

"How'd you get sober? Since almost killing yourself didn't work," Cyrus asked, almost teasingly.

JC gave a dry chuckle. "If you survive the impact to rock bottom, the only other place to go is up. Mine was prison. Plenty of ways to get high in there, and plenty more ways to get yourself killed. But most of the guys behind bars do genuinely want to get better. They want to turn their lives around and go straight. And even when you know the odds aren't good...well, that kind of attitude rubs off on you. And I was so sick of it all. The malnutrition from the marbles and other magic shit gave me diabetes and a host of other problems. My family doesn't talk to me, my friends—well, either they were the ones who kept pushing me to get high, like Rocket, or I'd hurt them too much. I didn't have anything else for the drugs to take except my life, and that's when the survival instinct finally kicked into gear. I relapsed a few times in prison, but the halfway house keeps a tight lid on it, so it's a lot harder to get unless you actively seek it out. Since then, clean."

For now, the traitorous thought whispered in their head.

They pulled their four-month sobriety chip out of their pocket and played with it.

"On the plus side, losing everyone and everything made it easier to admit that I wasn't cishet," JC added, the coin darting in and out of their fingers. "Had to hide that little fact in prison. Best way to get raped or beat to death is to be a sissy. But as soon as I was out, I didn't have to hide it anymore."

"You're not het?" Cyrus asked.

"Bisexual."

"Eyyy! Biromantic ace!"

He held out his hand. Rolling their eyes, JC high-fived him.

"I never liked Superman," Nicole said. "I thought he was overrated."

"...okay?" JC said.

She grimaced. "I'm bad at this. I'm trying to say that...you said you felt like Superman. When you were high, and some other stuff about yourself that's really not nice. I'm *trying* to say that we like you as you are now. Or at least I do."

"Seconded," Cyrus added.

JC rolled their eyes. "Nicole, babe, you are a college-graduated artist, a witch, a scarily accurate clairvoyant, and teach at a fancy academy. I'm a 28-year-old high school dropout who doesn't even have a studio apartment and barely got a food service job."

"You've never teased me for covering myself even in summer," she said. "And you make really good hot chocolate and conversation. And you're honest. That's valuable. That's why I asked you out."

JC managed a thin smile. "Sweet of you to think that."

After a beat, Cyrus asked, "What, I don't get a list of good qualities?"

"Nope," they said.

"Aw, what?"

"You gotta be at least this cute." They jerked a thumb at Nicole. "Without cheating with glamour."

Nicole tipped her head in acknowledgement while Cyrus scoffed. "Well, fuck me, then."

"...I know, right? Fuck you."

Cyrus gave a mock gasp. JC grinned. Nicole giggled.

As they got off the highway and neared Rocket's neighborhood, Cyrus said, "Maybe Nicole was right. I can glamour myself as you, take your place for this meeting."

"Not happening," JC said.

"I can handle myself, you know. Been doing it for centuries."

"How old did you say you were?"

"Just over three hundred."

They frowned. "Isn't that fairy adulthood? Like, three centuries is our eighteen?"

"More like twenty, but yeah."

JC shared a look with Nicole, and knew right then and there that the two of them had never felt so young and yet simultaneously so old. "...yeah, no. I've got it."

§

Rocket lived in a beat-up house in a battered neighborhood along the eastern strip of Minneapolis, one of those streets that could almost be a suburb if it weren't so shitty. Trash littered every sidewalk, the basketball hoop rattled every time someone breathed on it, and the buildings were halfway through peeling off their makeup of cheap paint. JC had forgotten the exact address, but Rocket still had those ugly flamingoes peppering his dying grass. They were at least as old as his grandma.

As Nicole undid her seatbelt and reached for the door, JC sputtered. "Uh, what are you doing?"

"Going with you," she said.

"Nu-uh. Whatever he's going to ask me to do is going to be illegal. You..." They pointed to Cyrus. "...can't lie, and you..." Nicole. "...shouldn't have to. I'll go in there, alone, and you both get plausible deniability."

Nicole sank back in her seat, frowning.

"If you're not out in five minutes, I'm coming in," Cyrus said.

They unbuckled. "Ten."

"Fine."

"Wait." Nicole took off one of her gloves, revealing thick, dark fingers with at least two skinny rings each, and a small blue paint stain on her pointer finger. She removed one of the rings and gave it to JC. "For luck."

They didn't know if she had actually enchanted it, or if it was just a figure of speech. But they took it, and it fit on their middle finger. "Thanks. Not real gold, right?"

"No, it's from one of those cheap sets you get at Target."

Of course you shop at Target, they thought, leaving the car. *Walmart is so much cheaper.*

JC passed the creaking, rusting fence and climbed the two wooden steps of the peeling porch. The second one groaned, still needing to be replaced. JC knocked on the screen door, knowing that the doorbell was probably still busted.

It took a couple of tries, but eventually Rocket opened it. He grinned down at them. "I knew you'd come."

"How's the nose?" JC asked.

Whoop, there went the smile. The inside was so dark that it shadowed his face, but they were pretty sure there was a thick bruise on Rocket's nose.

JC cleared their throat. "So. What are we doing? I've got a deadline, and if you're gonna waste time, then I'm out of here."

Rocket held open the door. "Come inside...wait, who's in the car?"

"Friends of mine."

"Who?"

"Doesn't matter. They're not involved in this, and they're not *getting* involved."

Rocket stepped forward, crowding them so close they could count the chest hairs through his white V-neck. "You don't call the shots here, little man."

"Not a man," they said. "They. Are not. Involved."

JC slipped under Rocket's arm and went into the house, not giving him the chance to respond.

The house was a two-story, but small, with two bedrooms stacked above a living room and kitchen. Rocket liked to collect a lot of weird shit: anime posters with ripped edges, rusted and chipped figurines, old video games no one played anymore. The wallpaper was decaying, curling up at the edges. If he hadn't fixed that, then he probably hadn't fixed that one dead burner on his stove.

He came in behind JC and sat on one of the stuffed chairs, motioning to the couch on the other side of the dented coffee table. When JC perched on their seat, the couch coughed up stuffing from a tear near their leg.

They studied each other.

"I can't even remember the last time you punched me," Rocket said, playing with his golden chain. "Gotta be, what? A month before you were arrested? Two?"

"*You* punched *me*," they corrected. "I took too much of what I cooked. At least three thousand dollars' worth went into my gut."

Rocket laughed. "That's right. Those were the days. I think... yeah, didn't Luke also get into the fight? I don't think he even know which one of us he was actually fighting, he just saw fists flying and thought, 'I gotta get in on that.'"

"Ugh, that little bastard. Got me right in the balls."

"Yes, he did! Oh, man. He never fought fair."

"Can't blame him. He was so short, even for a kid."

"Careful you don't say that where he could hear you."

JC snickered, almost relaxing. When Luke had tagged along with the Bobcats, everyone had quickly learned that the best way to get him into a fight was to make any comment about his height. He could take literally any other insult: his crooked teeth, his mother, his stupidity, but height? That was off the table. (Or the main event, depending on the mood.)

"Where is he, anyway?" JC asked. "He's gotta be, what, 20 by now? Twenty-one? We can finally get him a legal beer."

Rocket's smile faded. "He's dead. Shot by Grizzlies."

JC wished they were surprised, but they'd heard this news a thousand times. The only thing that changed was the names. "When?"

"About...four years ago?"

So, when he was 16, maybe 17. "And you wonder why I wanted out?" JC asked.

"Didn't wonder at all. Nobody likes getting shot. Fewer people like being left behind."

They balked. "Rocket, if you want out, I'll help you get out. Just say the word. I don't have much money, but I know people. We can get you whatever you need..."

He shook his head. "There is no getting out. Not for me, and not for you."

They gritted their teeth. "I *am* out."

"You're here now."

"Because you're being an asshole and making me do a job for info. So, whatever it is you want me to do, just let me do it. And then you'll tell me what I need to know, and then I am gone."

Rocket's face blatantly said, *Yeah, right, we'll see how long that lasts.*

He went over to the China cabinet, full of dusty, chipped dishes, and removed the false back behind a stack of plates. After a bit of shuffling, he set a duffel bag on the table.

JC didn't have to unzip it. They knew what was inside.

They glared at him. "Really?"

"You know the drill. It needs to go to a distributor. New guy. Goes by Grillz. He's in Minneapolis."

JC crossed their arms. "I can't go there."

"Sure, you can."

"The Brotherhood's there."

"And?"

"And I killed one of them."

"Six years ago."

"It was Mark Austen," they said. "As in Peter Austen? Peter 'Bullsnake' Austen? Unless someone's managed to shoot *him*."

"...no, he's still kicking," Rocket admitted. "Made it up to lieutenant, too."

"Great. The second-in-command of one of the largest gangs in the Cities wants me dead for killing his brother."

"Don't go into his territory," Rocket said, like it was obvious. "The Brotherhood's in the south. You're going north. It's a big city; you'll be fine."

JC sighed, trying to think of a way out. They couldn't. "Where in the north?"

"I'll text you the address. Call me when you get there; they paid half up front and still owe the rest. Oh, and..." He unzipped the duffel. The marbles were divided into small bags, cocooned in foam and bubble wrap to keep them from clanking against each other and breaking. JC could barely make out the red balls through all the plastic, and oh, how they wanted them.

Rocket held up one of the Ziplocs. "Ten percent's yours. Just like old times."

"Rocket..." they growled.

"It's not as good as what you can make, obviously, but it's gotta be better than the shit you had in prison, right?"

They snatched the bag and threw it back in the duffel, zipping it back up like it was a live cobra. Rocket snickered.

"The *second* I tell you this is done, you call me. And we talk," JC snapped, standing. The duffel bag bit into their shoulder. "You understand?"

"On my honor."

You don't have any, JC thought, leaving the house with a bag of sins.

no good choices

J C didn't tell Cyrus or Nicole what was in the bag that they shoved in the trunk, just said to drive to northern Minneapolis. Their phone dinged with Rocket's text: an address.

They drove in silence. JC held their sobriety chip in their pocket with white knuckles, every minute a razor against their skin. Fuck, did they need a cigarette.

At least it wasn't rush hour, with it being almost noon on a Saturday. The summer sun was still high in the sky, reflecting off the Mississippi River as they crossed the bridge. JC glared at the water. "We should dump the duffel in there."

"Is there a way to do that and get the info we need?" Cyrus asked, his voice flatter than Nicole's.

JC hissed a sigh. "No."

"Pick your battles, then."

"I know what's going to happen to the people who take this, or who they sell it to."

"They're not your responsibility. Rocket would've sent another mule if we hadn't needed his help."

That was true. Rocket had dozens of JC's all over the Cities. It still twisted their guts with guilt.

"Also, pollution is bad," Nicole piped up. "You have to be really careful when disposing of magical ingredients, especially from the Fae Realm. If animals eat too much of it, they'll be unable to eat food from our world, so they scavenge for more Fae food, don't find it, and starve to death. The animals that eat their corpses often get secondhand cursed, eating enchanted flesh that makes them unable to eat mortal food, although it's usually not as severe and doesn't last as long. It still causes problems."

"...didn't know that," JC admitted, trying not to think of all the excess marmair–the stems, seeds, and leaves that didn't have nearly the potency of the flower itself–that they'd thrown out while cooking up marbles.

Minneapolis may have been Saint Paul's twin, but it had a distinctly different feel. The streets were wider and straighter, all grids and clean straight lines, while Saint Paul twisted and turned and had a case of older sibling syndrome. Minneapolis was also bigger, which made a lot of people think that *it* was the state capital.

They avoided the downtown area with all its skyscrapers and the stadium, instead going into a concrete neighborhood on the edge of the highway. One of those "not quite a suburb, but sure doesn't feel like a city" parts of the city, all busted houses, fast food chains, and graffitied businesses. And a bridge. A small bridge over a forgotten street, tucked away in the corner of the neighborhood at a dead-end street. The bridge wasn't for cars, but for trains. Given the state of the tracks, it probably hadn't been used in at least a decade.

Three figures clustered under it, one smoking a cigarette, the red embers glowing in the shadows.

Cyrus frowned. "You sure you don't want–"

"I'll be fine," JC interrupted. "Pop the trunk."

He did. JC grabbed the bag and marched over to the trio, pulling their phone and cigarette case out of their pocket. "Which one of you is Grillz?"

"Who's asking?" one of them demanded, the one with the cigarette. He was trying to grow a beard, but it came out in patches.

"I'm with Rocket. He told me to call him; you still owe half." They dropped the duffel by their feet and dialed.

The three teenagers watched them warily. JC had at least a decade on all of them–though right now it felt closer to a century. They had no doubt that all three were armed and ready to fill them with bullets. The smoker took another drag, never taking his eyes off JC. One of his friends had a nose ring and smattering of tattoos on his neck and arms, the other had shaved his head.

Rocket picked up on the third ring. "Hey, you still alive?"

"I'm here. Say hi, boys."

"Fuck you," the smoker said. "Check it."

Definitely the leader. Grillz.

Baldie took the bag and unzipped it, grabbing one of the Ziplocs. JC looked away as he pulled out the marbles, focusing on lighting their cigarette one-handed.

Grillz jerked his chin toward Cyrus's car. "That your bitch in the back seat?"

JC glared at him, letting smoke fill their lungs. "She's not a part of this."

"Just asking. Looks nice."

"She's almost thirty."

He grinned, showing off his golden grillz. JC was actually disappointed to see it; they could've come up with so many better nicknames. "So, she knows what she's doing."

"She's out of your league, kid."

The grin slipped off. "Why? Scared you ain't man enough for her?"

He flicked his fingers against JC's nonbinary pin. "Sissy."

JC grinned around their cigarette. "I sure hope so. She's a lesbian."

"Oooh, one of *those*."

They shook their head. "I can't believe I was that much of an asshole. Can we wrap this up?"

Grillz stepped closer, silently challenging JC. They didn't back down, taking another draw from their cigarette and strangling the urge to smack the boy upside the head. Respect was the greatest currency of the streets, more valuable than drugs, girls, or money. Respect got you jobs, let you avoid fights, let you *live*, and sometimes was the only thing you had left in the world.

But you had to give it to get it, and Grillz was not giving it.

Ugh. Why do I have to be the adult? JC thought.

"All good," Baldie announced, teeth stained red from the sugary marbles, bouncing a bit from the energy.

Still in JC's space, Grillz pulled out his phone, probably to Venmo Rocket.

"Make sure JC gets their cut," Rocket piped up from the phone. "Gotta pay the messenger."

"Don't bother," JC snapped. "I'm staying away from that shit."

"Then sell it."

Baldie threw a Ziploc at JC, forcing them to scramble to catch it without dropping either cigarette or phone.

"See you soon, JC," Rocket said, hanging up.

"Bastard," they muttered, putting away their phone and walking back to the car.

"Next time bring your girl with you," Grillz called. "I want a closer look."

They snorted. "Again, kid: lesbian."

"I can fix that."

Ugh. Douchebag.

They made it to the car. As soon as they were in, Cyrus sped away.

"What do we do with that?" he asked, motioning to the bag of marbles in JC's lap.

They studied the bag. Two dozen small, thumbnail-sized red balls stared back up at them. If they were careful, they could stay high for almost a week straight, flying on elation and confidence that they could only ever reach in their dreams.

"JC?" Cyrus prodded, hands shifting on the wheel. Ready to snatch the bag away.

JC tightened their grip, their palm slippery with sweat against the plastic. "Take us to the river."

The fairy did as he was told, pulling over when they were half-way across the bridge. A few cars honked at them, but they didn't care. JC climbed out, went to the railing, and threw the bag into the Mississippi. They could finally breathe when it sank out of sight.

Sure, it was bad for the environment. But anyone could dig that shit out of a dumpster. This way, there was no risk of them going back and finding it again.

They walked down the sidewalk, lighting another cigarette and trying not to puke. The smoke settled in their lungs, calming their jittery nerves. Cyrus slowly drove alongside them, hazards flashing. "You all right?"

"Fine," they said. "I just need some air."

He didn't protest, though he did sputter when Nicole scrambled out of the back seat without letting him fully stop.

JC held up their crumbled cigarette box. "Want one?"

She shook her head. "I don't smoke."

"Good."

"Why do you?"

"Been doing it since I was a kid," they admitted. "It's better than marbles. Kick one habit at a time, you know?"

She shrugged. "Not really. I've never been a part of...all this."

"Good. Let me know if the smoke's bothering you."

"My sensory issues were never about smell. Mostly just taste and touch."

They walked together, the sun bouncing off the Minneapolis skyscrapers.

"I'm sorry," she said. "I wish I'd seen someone else. Anyone else."

"Yeah, me too. Not your fault, though," they said. "Those kids are idiots. At least one of them will be dead in a year, the other two in cuffs. And they know that. And they don't care. And I know it, and I *do* care, but I gave them that shit anyway."

Nicole looked down at the sidewalk, ringed locs swinging in front of her face. "My parents volunteer a lot. They used to take me with them when I was a kid. Soup kitchens, homeless shelters, Bernier Family Service, that kind of thing. One day I asked them why there were so many poor people, why a lot of them did drugs or crime. Mom said that for some people, there are no good choices. Only bad and worse. I think this is one of those."

She was right. JC knew that. It still hurt.

They ran out of bridge, and Cyrus rolled down the window. "Hate to break it up, but we have a deadline."

JC finished their cigarette. They were about to toss it in the river, but Nicole's presence stopped them. They went down a few feet to stub it out and leave it on top of a trash lid before getting back in the car.

§

"Calling already?" Rocket asked, tinny voice filling the car on speaker phone. He didn't hide his surprise.

"I told you we were in a rush," JC said. "Now who took my boss?"

The three of them were parked at a McDonald's. Nicole had brought her maps, jar of bones, and wand with her, and stood in front of the open trunk. She'd thrown the bones a handful of times already, trying to find Violet. Given the thin frown on her wide face, it wasn't going well. Still magically blocked, then.

"All right, look," he said. "You remember Steven?"

"From the Wolverines?" JC asked, vaguely remembering a kid wearing oversized hoodies and too-tight tank tops back in the day.

"Yeah. He told me that they were working with a group of tree-fuckers. And they're loaded. Money, marmair, even some all-heal and magic weapons. They came in about two months ago, under the radar, and they planned to go back soon. They wanted to go yesterday and take someone with them. Some jick witch they need to teach a lesson."

JC and Cyrus shared a look.

"So, the Wolverines have them?" they clarified. Wolverines were the gang of west Minneapolis.

"Well, if they did, they don't now. They got busted yesterday."

"What?!"

"Steven snitched. Been snitching for a while, apparently. I heard he got cursed for it, but don't know the details. Cops are pissed; they wanted the fairies, too, but only got the Wolverines. So, whoever's got your boss, they're out in the wind."

JC tapped their fingers against the car door. "They came here under the radar, they'll leave under the radar. And if they could do it on their own, they wouldn't be asking for local help. Are any of our old gates still open?"

"No. Cops have been shutting them down and the magic's moved on. They'll have to go way out of the Cities, but that could be anywhere. Probably try to find a wild portal."

JC rested their head against the seat, trying to think. "If I were in a brand new city, and I needed to find a portal, how would I do that? Who would I ask...?"

"The jicks also hired some local muscle," Rocket offered. Every time he said that word, Cyrus grimaced. "You probably don't know Michelle, she didn't start coming around until you were locked up. She's a mercenary. But she works with the Stone Oaks."

JC straightened. "They'd know all about portals!"

"That's an underground coven, right?" Cyrus asked. "Not on the up-and-up like Stoughton Street?"

"They're the people to go to for magical ingredients, curses, illegal spells..." JC listed. "I never worked with them directly, but everyone's heard of them, and most gangs and mobs have worked with them at least once. Usually for body disposal, if it's a para. They'll put it to good use."

"They're also notorious for their secrets," Rocket added. "Good luck getting any information out of them, 'cause they don't talk about their clients. Not sellers, not buyers."

JC smirked. "We'll see about *that*."

the traitor

Excerpt from *Round-Ears: A History of Gialdon and Humans in the Fae Realm*

By destroying the archives and all written traces of the mortals' names, the Violet Princess turned a manageable mortal rebellion into a national crisis. Mortals enslaved as soldiers fled to join the Gialdons' cause in staggering numbers, despite the fairies' efforts to contain them with magic, threats, and bribes. The Gialdon leadership—most notably the future Chief Counselor Coral and future First Speaker Aster—secured an alliance with [the dwarven nation of] Skagron, supplying the rebellion with weapons, armor, and food, mostly purchased with coin from the Violet Princess's own coffers. Guerrilla fighters—some led by the Violet Princess, others by long-time Gialdon soldier and future Chief Commander Rat—struck more archives, and expanded their targets to include military storehouses and barracks. It was very obvious, very quickly, that this would not be another mere rebellion that could be broken within weeks. This was war, and the Gialdons were ready for it.

Still, the King of Ivae wanted to avoid the oncoming catastrophe. It was his granddaughter that was allowing these things to happen, after all. Perhaps he could get her to stop it.

The Violet Princess had had few friends before the war, most of them being fellow military commanders. The King sent the princess's two best and closest protégés to negotiate: Lady Oak and Commander Harvest Moon.

Lady Oak had joined the military a century after the Violet Princess, and had been her direct underofficer for over six hundred years. A daughter from a moderate but old noble house, Oak had earned her name by being "as strong and stubborn as an old oak tree." Modern historians and politicians also wax poetic about her enduring loyalty to her nation, but prior to this she had had plenty of her own disputes with the royal family. In one instance, the Diamond Princess—cousin to the Violet one—insulted Lady Oak during a festival, calling military commanders "little more than dogs on a leash," and that Lady Oak in particular "was a disappointment to her family and nation by playing with blades."

In response, Lady Oak commissioned the infamous song "Diamonds in Dung" from a band of Fae musicians. The princess was so insulted that she demanded all the Fae involved—the musicians and Lady Oak herself—be subjected to *iom cof'mihun*, where all memory and evidence of the subject be completely erased from the universe, leaving them to wander the Realms as little more than a living ghost. It is one of the harshest punishments any Fae nation can ever give, and also requires a coven's worth of sorcerers to accomplish.

The king refused. He ordered a fine to be paid that was steep, but well within Lady Oak's budget, and put her on a more dangerous and remote military expedition to the north, removing her from court for a few decades in the hopes that the situation would diffuse on its own. In a way, it did. The Diamond Princess was found to have committed treason and the murder of her father, an immortal Fae prince, in a case that was investigated and exposed by her cousin Violet. The Diamond Princess was exiled from Ivae and her allies during Oak's expedition.

A couple centuries later, Harvest Moon joined the military. His is a notable case, as, unlike most of the other military leadership of Ivae, he did not come from a noble or royal family. His was a family of musicians and artisans, and he attempted to learn to play multiple instruments before admitting defeat and changing careers, attempting agriculture. His farm was successful, but he quickly became restless. He won a scholarship that allowed him to attend a small, elite military school and joined the troops as a lieutenant when the Violet Princess was a captain.

Like Lady Oak, Harvest Moon also had his problems with authority. For Ivaenians, immortality and race are far more important than social status, but it does play a role. Harvest Moon received several fines and disciplinary actions for talking back to superiors, as he was unafraid to question them if he believed they were making a bad decision. According to some legends, during his first meeting with the Violet Princess, he questioned her strategy in the last mortal rebellion and asked why she hadn't used a different route. Any other captain would have immediately dismissed or at the very least reprimanded and punished him. The Violet Princess calmly explained her reasoning, then punished him with stable duty and transferred him as a lieutenant in her own army. She later remarked, "I want people who will question my logic as needed—albeit more respectfully."

One of the Violet Princess's greatest strengths was in recognizing young talent. She immediately took both Lady Oak and Harvest Moon as her personal protégés, raising their ranks right behind her. When she became commander, they became captains. When she became Chief Commander, they became commanders. Red Wolf specialized in stealth and infiltration, while Lady Oak preferred facing her enemies in an open field and even joined her mentor on the front lines before her promotion to commander, where she preferred watching from above to make better tactical decisions.

Unsurprisingly to all who knew them personally, Lady Oak and Harvest Moon eventually got married, with Harvest Moon signing the Fae version of a prenuptial agreement that kept him separated from the noblewoman's political and financial power. The Violet Princess was the one who ordained the marriage ceremony.

Centuries later, it was this married couple who went to talk their mentor out of co-leading a revolution.

There are precious few primary sources that could reveal what occurred in their meeting. No scribes were present to record what was said, and there were no witnesses. Not even guards, as both sides knew that neither would disrespect the other in such a way.

The choice of Lady Oak and Harvest Moon as representatives speaks of emotional blackmail, and this is likely what they attempted to use against the Violet Princess. She may have even reciprocated, trying to get her former protégés on her side through a sense of authority and platonic love. She almost certainly tried to use the moral argument, but both Lady Oak and Harvest Moon had a long and documented history of their disdain for mortals. Despite being responsible for thousands of them for centuries, they saw their enslaved charges as little more than tools. They followed their mentors' example in caring for them to the best of their ability, but only in the way one cares for a sword or hammer.

Whatever words were or were not spoken, Lady Oak and Harvest Moon returned to the capital empty-handed. Lady Oak, blunt as ever, was the one who reported to the king: "Your granddaughter has gone mad, Your Majesty. And she's not returning to sanity anytime soon."

Pictured the Violet Princess wearing a crown of leaves rather than of gold and jewels. After her defection, she rarely wore any kind of royal finery—though artists often continue to add them to differentiate her and denote her former status. This wood carving is likely referencing a popular (but likely fabricated) legend where, after she joined the freedom fighters, future Speaker Aster gave the Violet Princess a crown made of leaves to make up for the one of gold, to which she said that such a gift was more valuable than anything she'd ever touched. This piece was carved by a mortal artist and is displayed in the National History Museum in Gialdon's capital city.

environmental magic

Cyrus had a Bluetooth connection between his cell phone and his car, which meant Officer Hendricks's voice filled the entire vehicle as he asked, "You're sure?"

"Pretty sure," Cyrus said, having been the one to explain the whole Wolverines/mercenary/evil coven thing. "That's what the criminal expert's saying, anyway."

Someone on the other line snorted, and a woman—Nelson—retorted, "Criminals, sure. But experts?"

JC rolled their eyes. "You know you're on speaker, right?"

Silence.

"We'll let Minneapolis PD know and head up there ourselves," Hendricks said with a sigh. "But they've been trying to take that coven down for decades and haven't been successful. Either they never find any solid evidence, or it gets thrown out."

"They probably bribe some of the cops, too," JC pointed out. "They're rich enough to pull that off."

"That only happens in movies," Nelson argued.

"No, I've seen it happen. Not Stone Oaks specifically, but there are plenty of dirty cops in the Cities."

"Phenomenal," Hendricks grunted. "Where are you now?"

"Stuck in traffic," Cyrus grumbled, slowing his car down as the highway clogged up before them. At least he'd been able to tell Hendricks and Nelson about their lead without mentioning all the illegal drug dealing, so JC got to stay out of prison a little while longer.

"I *know* you're not going after the coven of very dangerous witches known for selling fairy body parts on the black market," Hendricks scolded. "Right?"

Cyrus winced. JC started making white-sound noises. "What was that...psshht...think we're losing you...psshht...through a tunnel..."

"You're not fooling–"

Cyrus hung up.

"So...we're not trusting the police with this?" Nicole guessed.

"Like JC said, they haven't been able to do jack shit," he said. "So, no, I don't think we are."

"Just checking." She frowned. "Why is there traffic? It's Saturday."

"There isn't any construction going on, is there?" JC asked. Granted, the roads were always under construction in Minnesota during the summer–and spring and fall, too–but they'd taken this route on the bus just a few days ago and it'd been clear.

"Not on this highway. I know there's a game happening at the stadium, but that's across town." Cyrus rolled down his window and stuck his head out, long, pointed ears twitching. He came back in. "Hard to tell with all the other noises, but I think there's been a crash. There's an ambulance coming."

"It's the Stone Oaks Coven," Nicole said.

"They don't even know about us," he protested. "Do they?"

"Probably not. Even if they did, they can't curse anyone from a distance without their full name or DNA. But they *can* protect *themselves*. There are several protective charms you can put on yourself and in your home. If anyone decides to come after you with the intent of causing harm or misfortune, magic can slow them down. It's environmental magic rather than targeted."

JC pressed the back of their head against their seat. "Great."

"Can you do something to counter it, oh learned and Buddhist witch?" Cyrus asked.

Nicole was Buddhist? JC was pretty sure they'd seen her eat meat at least once...

Nicole did that finger-tapping stim. "The most effective method would be to destroy their good luck charms. That's not a possibility, so..." She looked down at her maps, jar of bones, and wand.

"Nicole?" JC asked.

She didn't answer, instead tearing off her gloves and carefully untying Violet's hair from the wand. Then she took half a dozen rings off her own fingers and tied the hair through them. "I'm going to need some of your hair. Each of you."

"Uh..." JC undid their bun. "You got scissors?"

"No."

"Here." Cyrus pulled a pin out of his hat. The second it left the fabric, it transformed into a small throwing knife, barely the size of his palm.

JC took the knife, eyeing all the other pins he had on his hat, shirt, even his belt, and sliced about a dozen strands at the root on the left side of their head. "This enough?"

"Perfect." Nicole took the hair, removed more rings and even a bracelet from her hands, and tied them together with the hair. She took the knife from JC and removed one of her own locs, one with several little gold and silver rings already clamped around it, at the root.

Cyrus was a bit trickier, since his indigo hair was short. He solved that problem by pulling a vial of pale gold blood out of the glove compartment. Like you do. "Leftover from the truth potion."

Nicole took it and a larger, empty jar from her purse (JC didn't ask; you never question the mysteries of a woman's purse). She emptied the blood into the bigger jar, dropped a few of her loc rings into it, and shook it.

It was like a smaller version of what had happened when Violet changed their name: JC felt a tiny *pop* around them, like reality had shifted.

All the jewelry Nicole had just handled–the bloodied stuff in the jar, the rings and bracelet tied together by her and Violet and JC's hair–all broke, scattering across the seat and floor.

"What the–"

"They're good luck charms," Nicole interrupted, motioning to her jewelry as she cleaned up her mess. "All of them."

The traffic started to move, and within two minutes, they had a detour around the crash site, saving them at least half an hour.

"Damn, girl," JC praised. "If you did Uber or Lyft, you'd make a fortune in tips alone."

Nicole smiled with a shrug. "Thanks. Cyrus, here's your knife back."

teeth were stained red

Parking in Minneapolis was always hell, but especially when there was a Twins game happening.

"Baseball? Really?" JC demanded as Cyrus finally found a spot on the street. "The city's clogged because of the most boring sport known to humanity?"

"Don't you dare dis baseball! It's all about strategy and *not* getting a concussion, unlike certain *other* sports I could mention," Cyrus grumbled, paying the electronic parking meter. They only offered two hours max before you had to refill it. He paid with one hand, holding a bundle of cloth he'd gotten from the trunk with the other. A blanket?

"At least stuff *happens* in football," JC said. "And soccer. And basketball..."

"Please, soccer and basketball are for wusses. Football, too. If you're going to play a sport that'll give you brain damage, at least own it like the rugby players."

"What's rugby?"

Cyrus dropped his forehead against the parking meter. "The American education system has truly failed you on every level."

Nicole shook her head at both of them. "I don't know anything about sports. I watch campy movies and read books."

JC shared a look with Cyrus. "See, that's why she's the smart one."

He finished paying, and they started walking. The coven operated out of a store several blocks down (fucking Twins), and the summer sun beat down on them and the pavement as they passed multiple bars, clubs, churches, theaters, run-down apartment buildings, and more than one street corner where JC had loitered, sold drugs, or gotten into fights. They weren't usually in this part of town, though. Too close to enemy territory, and no one liked poking around the Coven, even if they weren't para.

"I managed to find something," Cyrus said, holding out the... blanket? Some sort of long cloth that he'd gotten from the trunk. JC honestly couldn't tell what color it was. One second it was dim green, the next it was concrete gray, the next dirt brown. "This is Boss's. She doesn't use it much, and it doesn't work nearly as well against fairies as it does against–"

They turned another corner and froze.

A half dozen gangsters–including a familiar trio–sat or leaned against the concrete stairs of a squat apartment building, barely a few feet away. And they spotted them at the exact same time.

For a moment, nobody moved.

A cigarette hung from Grillz's limp fingers as his eyes flashed in angry recognition. Baldie leaned against the railing with a new face, showing him something on his phone. Nose Ring and two others had been mid-argument when they realized something was up. The three must have come straight here after the deal, distributing it right on the streets and managing to avoid traffic. Just JC's luck.

Nicole broke the tension first, striding forward and past them. "Excuse us."

"Uh-uh. No way, baby," Grillz said, jumping to his feet. "Not after the bullshit your boy pulled earlier today."

"They're not a boy, and we're in a hurry."

JC and Cyrus hurried after her, not willing to let her handle this problem on her own. It wasn't even her problem in the first place!

Grillz cut her off, one of his friends hurrying to his side while the other four closed ranks around them. "That ain't how this works, sweetheart. I just wanted a look at you."

"Gentlemen, we all have better things to be doing with our time," Cyrus tried. But JC knew that wasn't going to work. Grillz' golden grillz and lower teeth were stained red, and there was more redness in his nostrils. Eating and snorting marbles. Most of his other friends–like Nose Ring–had similar marks.

Cyrus could've had a rocket launcher aimed at their thick skulls, and they'd still be foaming at the mouth for a fight.

"You don't know shit, jick," one of them jeered.

"Hey, I know you!" another called, pointed at JC. "Aren't you the guy who killed the Brotherhood lieutenant's brother?"

"No," JC tried to lie.

"Holy shit, yeah, he is!" Nose Ring cheered. "Bullsnake told everyone and shared the mug shot as soon as he got out. Can't believe I didn't recognize you..."

"Man, fuck the Brotherhood," Grillz drawled.

"I'm just saying, we could get some money for it. Bullsnake wants him dead or alive."

"In the middle of the day?" Cyrus pointed out, motioning to the street around him. It wasn't crowded, but there were more pedestrians across the street, cars driving by, and who knew who was watching through the dark windows. "Lots of witnesses. Come on, let's be smart about this."

"They won't care," Grillz sneered.

He was probably right. Nobody *would* care. But this whole thing was slowing them down when every minute counted.

"Look, you boys want to do this, fine," JC said, pulling Cyrus back. "But not here, and not now. We've got shit to do and a tight deadline to do it. Give me a time and place, and I'll meet you there. Fists, knives, guns, whatever. Call Bullsnake, too, if he wants in."

Grillz took a draw from his cigarette. JC prayed that he would take the comprise. Fifty-fifty odds were that he'd never show up, anyway. JC sure as hell wouldn't.

"You ran with the Bobcats, didn't you?" he said. "That's what Rocket says. And I never trust those pussies."

He blew smoke right into JC's face. He and everyone else had at least a few inches on them, and so he *loomed*. "Fuck Bullsnake. You have a debt to pay me. You're going to pay it."

"What debt?" JC asked.

"You disrespected me."

They shook their head. "No. You disrespected *her*..." They jabbed their thumb at Nicole. "...with your sexist, queerphobic bullshit. So technically, you're the one in debt."

"You need to stop running your mouth," he growled.

If it had been just Grillz, Nose Ring, and Baldie, then JC might've risked a fight. But being outnumbered two to one? And only Cyrus armed? (With a knife; useless against guns.)

"Cyrus. Nicole. Get to the coven. I'll meet you there," JC said. Getting beaten into the sidewalk sucked, but wasn't the worst.

"JC..." Cyrus warned.

"Now."

"Nu-uh," Grillz said, eyes lit with drugged insanity. "We're doing this with your bitch watching."

"Okay, seriously?" JC snapped. "I am giving you multiple outs. These two have nothing to do with our business."

"Sure, they do."

JC prayed to every deity they didn't believe in that they had never been this much of an asshole while high on marbles. They probably had been. Karma, bitch.

"I have another idea," Cyrus said, shaking out the blanket and wrapping it around himself. As soon as it hit his shoulders, the fairy disappeared entirely.

JC and all the gangsters swore, startled and confused. Grillz, Baldie, and one other yanked guns from their pants.

A knife whizzed through the air, flying and landing in Grillz's wrist. He screamed, dropping the gun as blood spurted out.

JC grabbed Nicole and ran behind the nearest bit of cover— the cars parked on the street—as the remaining idiots with guns swung them around. One of them fired, shattering the window by JC's head. The gangster shrieked as an invisible knife sliced through his leg and the gun was snatched from his hands.

The rest was a blur. Cyrus was impossible to track under his cloak. But he had the others either disarmed or running within five seconds. Two of them were too shocked and/or injured to run: Grillz stared at the knife in his wrist, and one of his buddies had gotten cut badly enough on the leg that he'd hit the cement. Everyone else vanished into the streets.

JC kept a hand on Nicole's arm, keeping them both down. The ring she'd given them fell from their finger, clinking on the pavement and breaking in half. They frowned.

"The—the shot to the car's window," Nicole said shakily. "I told you ... all my jewelry is good luck."

...holy shit. JC had never considered how good luck magic could deflect bullets.

Cyrus pulled off the cloak, kicking his opponents' guns away. He glamoured the large, bloody seven-inch knife in his hand back into a pin ("Talk Nerdy to Me"), returning it to his belt, then grabbed Grillz's hand. "Don't move."

"No, don't—gaaaah!"

Grillz cried and blubbered like a baby as Cyrus removed the slim throwing knife and cleaned it off on the gangster's shirt.

"Relax," the fairy scolded. "I didn't hit any major veins, arteries, or tendons. Get yourself to a hospital and you'll be fine, the both of you."

JC and Nicole came out from behind the car, surveying the damage. Grillz curled around his bloody wrist, and the guy with the cut-up leg was trying to drag himself down the sidewalk.

Note to self: do not pick a fight with a knife-wielding fairy, JC thought. "Holy shit, Cyrus. Did you get hit?"

He shook his head.

"Nicole, you okay?"

"Y-Yeah," she said, obviously shaken. JC winced. First gun fight was always the hardest.

Her finger trembled as she pointed to Cyrus. "That's Aunt Violet's invisibility cloak, right?"

"That it is," he cheered.

Grillz and his friend cowered away from the three of them. JC picked up the nearest handgun: a 9mm Glock. They checked the ammo, then stuck it in their own pants for safekeeping. "Boys. We good?"

Grillz sniffled. "We're good."

"Awesome." JC glanced at the shifting-color cloak in Cyrus's hands. "So, who's going invisible?"

a black book

Nicole's gloved hands were still shaking by the time they reached the coven. She looked across the street, at the unassuming shop with crystals and dreamcatchers in the windows, and walked away.

"Nicole?" JC asked, starting after her.

Cyrus clamped a hand on their shoulder and shook his head. He called after her, "We'll wait for you here."

She grunted in response, marching down the sidewalk and digging into her purse.

JC grimaced. "First time I got into a gunfight, I almost threw up."

"Yeah..." Cyrus sighed. "They're a lot less fun when you can't hit back."

"Shouldn't someone...I don't know. Talk to her?" That seemed like the healthy thing to do, anyway.

"High stress situations make her temporarily nonverbal," he said. "She's not going to do much talking at all until she's calmed herself down."

"...autism thing?" they guessed.

"It definitely doesn't help."

"Ah."

Honestly, JC's own nerves were getting to them, too, the residual adrenaline running static through their veins. They dug out their cigarettes. "You mind if I smoke?"

"Go for it."

"Want one?"

"Nah, it takes *way* more peer pressure before I do that."

"Can fairies even *get* cancer?" JC asked, sticking the cig in their mouth and lighting it.

Cyrus made a see-saw gesture with his hand. "Not naturally. It takes a *lot* to get to that point, and even then, I think most of those cases were kitrye, not full-blooded fairies. And while smoking might not kill us, it can still slow us down enough to be fatal in, say, a knife fight."

JC grunted, making sure to move downwind from Cyrus and blow the smoke away from him.

They were still waiting for Nicole when the cop car showed up. JC stiffened. Had someone called about the fight? The lights weren't on, but that didn't mean much...

The officer parked across the street, closed the door behind him with a yawn, and went into the Stone Oaks Coven's front door.

JC and Cyrus shared a look.

The cop was still there when Nicole finally arrived, having walked around the block. One of her gloves was off, which felt like Victorian levels of scandalous, and the naked hand was clutching a set of prayer beads. They weren't a Catholic rosary, but beyond that, JC couldn't identify them. Especially when Nicole shoved them in a little cloth bag that she buried back in her purse.

"What happened?" she asked, her voice rougher than usual as she tugged the glove back on. JC itched to offer some sort of comfort or support, but they didn't know what she needed, what would help or what would make things worse.

"Cop went in, hasn't come out," JC reported, taking another drag. "You think they're doing anything helpful?"

Cyrus shook his head as Nicole said, "I never trust police."

The cop left the coven's building, looking rather pleased with himself as he got in his car and drove away, no sirens or anything.

"Okay..." JC said. "I think I know how to play this. Nicole, are you...talking much?"

"No," she said.

"That's fine. I can do most of the talking. I just need you with me for credibility. You and I are the new witches on the block, looking to either join the coven or at least get in on their business. If we're lucky, we'll get them to tell us where they sent Violet. Otherwise, Cyrus is our invisible backup."

Nicole looked dubious, but Cyrus had a gleeful smile. She handed out more of her jewelry for luck (JC got a gold chain that actually went pretty well with the t-shirt and jean jacket) before Cyrus disappeared under the invisibility cloak.

"You haven't seen me die a horrible death in the near future, have you?" JC asked, only half-teasing.

Nicole shook her head, but followed it up with: "I'm not a goddess."

"Could've fooled me." JC offered their arm. "Would this help?"

Nicole studied the arm, then poked it. After a minute, she nodded, slipping her arm through the elbow. "You're calm."

"Yeah," they said awkwardly. "It's not my first rodeo."

On the block where JC had grown up, there'd been a witch who sold charms and curses, and also claimed to see into the future. She'd been arrested when JC was thirteen for fraud—turned out, Nicole had more magic in her pinky than that woman had had in her whole body. But before that, one of the biggest dares for all the kids on that street had been to steal something from the witch's store.

The Stone Oaks's front reminded JC of that fraud's store a lot. Lots of crystals and amulets, animal skulls and teeth, some cheap jewelry advertised as powerful charms, incense...

An older woman with silvering blond hair and glasses stood behind the counter, jotting something down in a black book. She looked up, closed the book, and said, "Good afternoon! I'm Linda. How can I help you?"

"Saw the cop car out front," JC mused, looking over some crystals. "You girls playing nice?"

"Never," she replied, eyeing Nicole, who had taken off her gloves and poked one of the crystals. "Careful, dear. That's powerful magic you're touching."

"No, it's not," she said, matter-of-factly. "Fake. The illegal stuff is in the back."

JC facepalmed.

Linda grinned. "Well, aren't you a clever little clairvoyant."

"One of the best," JC said, jumping on it. "That's actually why we're here. We're hoping for some...ingredients."

Linda leaned against her counter, looking way too smug. "Oh?"

JC really hoped that Nicole's face wasn't giving the game away, but they couldn't look away from Linda without appearing weak or fake. "'Course, if you have cops sniffing around, it's probably not the best time to be starting new deals..."

"Don't worry about Skinner. We've been friends for a very long time."

"So, you've got him in your pocket," JC said, not surprised. "What happens when the city sends someone else to come sniffing?"

"Then the person they send will either also end up in my pocket, or be too stupid to catch a cold. Luck magic is a powerful thing, if you have the right tools."

"Like fairy bones? We heard you might have some of those."

"You heard, did you?"

JC snorted, slipping out of Nicole's arm to join Linda at the counter. They leaned their arms against the dark wood. "Who else are we going to go to in this town for something like that? The gangs might be able to get what they need for marbles, but for the good shit? Everyone knows that's you."

Linda went to the other end of the counter, pulled out a couple of folders—having to set the small, weirdly familiar-looking black book aside to get it out of the way—and dropped a picture in front of JC and Nicole.

It was a digital sketch, a really good one. Of JC.

Their stomach sank, and they wondered if they'd have to use their new gun soon. They liked this situation a lot better when it was Nicole sketching them rather than murderers and corpse-harvesters.

"You want to tell me what you're actually here for?" Linda demanded.

Nicole came up from behind JC, put a bare finger on the sketch, then pushed it away. "That fairy kidnapped a friend of ours. We want her back."

"Too bad."

"You helped them."

"Call the cops. I'm sure they'll love a raise."

JC sighed. "If you squeal on them now, that's a breach of the deal you made with the kidnappers. Your reputation takes the hit. So how much for that?"

Linda laughed. "Far more than you can pay."

"Try me."

"Six hundred thousand. Cash."

JC balked. "Who the fuck is paying that much for a *café manager*?"

Linda shrugged. "Apparently her old life was a lot more exciting."

Right. Former princess.

"Where did they go?" JC asked.

"I didn't ask."

"Liar," Nicole accused.

JC put their hands on their waist, thinking of going for their gun and forcing the issue...

The little black book was gone.

"I wouldn't reach for that gun if I were you," Linda said, as if reading their mind. "Bullets have an unfortunate habit of ricocheting around here."

JC eyed her. She had a *lot* of jewelry on.

They wrapped a hand around Nicole's elbow–through the soft plaid shirt–and gently tugged her out the door, not saying anything until they were at least a block away.

"Bitch," Nicole grumbled, shoving her gloves back on. "Charlatan. *Evil* witch. Magic shouldn't be used for that."

"It's a lot easier to just go with the flow, whatever that is," JC said. "More profitable, too. You didn't see anything else from touching that picture?"

"No. Just the face of the fairy who held it for a little bit."

"Well, that's okay. I think she's missing something."

She frowned. "What?"

"Good question. Cyrus? What'd you swipe?"

He appeared next to them as he took off the invisibility cloak with a flourish, holding up the little black book. "No idea! But it's coded and the same one Nicole sketched from her visions, so that means it's probably important."

§

They stopped at a gas station so JC could get some orange juice, their insulin pump showing blood sugar numbers just a little too low for comfort. Of course, Cyrus pulled into Kwik Trip, the fanciest and most expensive gas station that was practically a grocery store. It had a few tables outside, too, and it was sunny enough that the three of them decided to try cracking Linda's book there, sodas and OJ in hand. The food and rest seemed to do Nicole some good, too. She was more relaxed and verbal—which seemed weirdly fast for a mental health issue. Maybe she'd done some sort of spell on herself?

She held the journal first, to see what she could get without her gloves. She frowned, flipping it over. "It's a ledger. She uses it to keep track of where her money is coming and going."

"I don't suppose you can crack the code that it's in, can you?" Cyrus asked, taking it back.

She shook her head.

JC frowned, looking over Cyrus's shoulder as he flipped through the pages. "What language is that? Arabic? Norse?"

"Fae. A lot of magic-users use our language for runes."

"You can't read Fae?"

"Course I can. But the translations don't make much sense." He wrote the first few lines on a napkin in messy handwriting, having to scratch out and re-start a few times while grumbling about dyslexia.

1256SM+1. Salon Day. P's treat. $200
1256SM+2. H's neighbor. $1500
1256SM+3. A whole chicken - given by neighbors.
1256SM+3. M & RW needed directions. Sold. $500k
1256SM+3. S - $500

"She said we needed at least six hundred thousand to bribe her for information," JC said, pointing to the second to last line where Linda got herself half a mil. "I'll bet that's from today. And S would stand for Officer Skinner, the kickback."

"What even are these dates?" Cyrus grumbled.

Nicole asked to see it, then snorted. "Lunar cycle. We're currently on cycle 1256. SM probably stands for Strawberry Moon. That ended three days ago."

JC gawked at her. "How do you *know* that?"

"Some spells can only be done at certain times, especially with certain phases of the moon." She pulled up an app on her phone, showing off all that information in a neat little graphic.

Cyrus gave a little impressed "Huh," before turning back to the book. "Okay. 'M & RW needed directions.' They were probably looking for a way to smuggle Boss out...M's popping up a lot, but I'm not seeing any RW's anywhere else."

"Rocket mentioned someone named Michelle," JC said. "A mercenary. RW is probably who hired her, especially if they're fairies and not from around here. Sometimes, when a gang or mafia expands its territory, it tries to hire the local syndicates rather than kill them. They know all the customers, all the best haunts, which cops are more likely to look the other way...if RW came to town just to take Bob, and if they were an outsider, then they'd want to hire local muscle. Especially if that local muscle has a connection to someone like Stone Oaks."

Nicole was halfway through her soda when her eyes suddenly bulged. "Oh! Oh, I'm an idiot!"

"Doubtful," JC said as she scrambled through her purse, pulling out her sketchbook of future secrets. She almost tore a few pages as she showed them page after page of wolves.

"I've been seeing this wolf everywhere for the last month," she said. "I almost always draw in pen or pencil—they're easier to carry. But every time the wolf's in my dreams or visions, it's *red*." She made it to the right page, showing off an angry, snarling wolf splattered with red watercolor.

"I'll bet Red Wolf is a fairy nickname," she concluded. "RW!"

"What type of name is Red Wolf?" JC asked. "All the fairies I know used celebrity names or just one word. The guy who sold us marmair went by Thorn. Another went by Beyoncé. I know a bunch of Jane and John Does, or John Smiths..."

"Those are modern *Earth* names," Cyrus interrupted. "Those of us who live here, who see Earth as home, we choose modern-sounding or even human names to fit in. But for those of us born and raised in the Fae Realm, the nicknames tend to be a lot more nature-driven. Or they'll be earned. The Violet Princess was Boss's original nickname, but by the time she was exiled, she'd *earned* the names Exiled Princess and Iron Witch. I usually went by Blue, obviously. Haven't really earned any of the more descriptive ones."

"Beyoncé's better," JC grumbled. "How did she get 'Iron Witch'?"

"I honestly don't remember," he admitted. "I think I heard someone say she had a 'heart of iron,' or maybe it was because her armor had iron in some parts so enemies had a hard time fighting her...I don't know. Not important."

"Did she ever mention anyone by the name of Red Wolf?" Nicole asked.

"If she did, I was too young to remember it." He brightened. "But Wulver might know."

"Wulver?" JC asked as Cyrus dug out his phone.

"Old friend of the boss. Runs the seafood place on the other side of Bernier. He was on the phone with her when she got grabbed." He dialed, helping himself to another slurp of soda as it rang.

"Lad!" a tinny Scottish voice cheered. "Ya hear any news?"

"Maybe," Cyrus said. "Did Boss ever mention anybody named Red Wolf to you?"

"Red Wolf, eh?" he clarified. "Sad to say I never heard of 'em."

"Really?" JC pressed.

"Who're you?"

"Friend of mine," Cyrus said. "Nicole's also here. They're helping."

"Ah," he said. "I may be old, but the fairy lass and I have only known each other for a little over a century, and we've only been friends since the '60s. That's not a lot of time to get to know someone. Well, not much time for an immortal, anyway."

"Are there werewolves in the Fae Realm?" Nicole asked. "Red *Wolf*..."

"Nay, lass, werewolves aren't fairy creatures. We came from *here*, not through any portals." From the other line, JC could make out the bustling chaos of a commercial kitchen. "Ye know who might know? Vlad."

Cyrus cringed. "Ugh. Shit. You're right, but *shit*."

"Who's Vlad?" JC asked.

"Boss's ex-boyfriend."

"And a real piece of shite," Wulver added. "I'll go with you."

"No way, big guy, they'll kill you on sight," Cyrus said.

"Oh, and they won't do the same with you?"

"They're more likely to talk to me, first."

Wulver sighed. "Aye, ye might be right..."

"That bad?" JC drawled.

"Vlad's part of a vampire clan, just on the edge of St. Paul," Cyrus explained. He gave a pained look at Nicole. "They only came up in the late '60s, early '70s. Before that, they were mostly in Louisiana, running a bunch of plantations since the Colonial Period. Fought for the Confederacy, too. He's in the same clan as Martha."

JC frowned, having no idea who Martha was, but figured that Confederate vampires and Black lesbian witches probably shouldn't be in the same room.

Nicole hummed. As usual, her husky voice was too monotone for JC to properly gauge her thoughts and feelings. "Are we going?"

"I think he's trying to say that if you go, they're going to be racist trash bags to you," JC replied. "And probably queerphobic trash bags to me, now that I think about it..."

"Martha chased my grandfather from his home. She tried to kill him and my grandmother," she said firmly, making JC do a double-take. "They don't get to do that anymore. Now let's *go*."

benny

Jennifer Charles was far from the only person to seek shelter in Bernier from a dangerous past. In the early 1960s, at the start of the Fae Migration and the thick of what scholars of Black American history would call the Great Migration, a young man named Benjamin—Benny—got on a train and went from Louisiana to Minneapolis as fast as he could. He barely had time to hug his mother goodbye and call ahead to his cousin.

After a thirty-hour train ride, Benny stumbled into his cousin Lewis's cramped apartment, bleary-eyed and sweat-stained. Lewis damn near dunked him in a bath before he passed out on the old, beaten couch.

"What brought you up north?" Lewis said the next day over a breakfast of eggs and toast. His wife Sandy had left early to run a couple of errands before work. "You didn't give me much detail over the phone."

Benny grimaced. "I was an idiot, Lu."

"More so than usual?"

"I led a strike against Mrs. Martha."

Lewis stilled, his fork halfway to his mouth. The rubbery egg slid off, landing on the plate with a *plop*. "You're joking."

Benny shook his head, appetite ruined. Shame, too. Lewis was one of the family's best cooks. "It was going good, too. Even got the newspapers sniffing around her drinking. Neighbors sold me out."

"And the rest of the family?"

"Had nothing to do with it, and the entire neighborhood knows."

"You sure about that?"

"You know Reggie's youngest boy, Willy? He overheard Mrs. Martha's men say they was coming for me. Me *alone*. That's why I practically flew up here."

Lewis nodded. "Well...hopefully that counts."

Benny tried not to drown in guilt. He and his family–his whole neighborhood–had been living and working on Mrs. Martha's cotton plantation since the days of slavery. Mrs. Martha had also been there at least that long, though it took a while for everyone *else* to figure that out. All the cotton pickers and their neighbors knew that Mrs. Martha didn't just hire and house them to tend her fields. If someone didn't pick enough that day, or broke one of Jim Crow's laws, or just got on her nerves, they'd be called to her big, white plantation house. If they were lucky, they'd come back, ashen, dizzy, and with some holes in their neck. Not many were lucky.

Benny was just the last in a long line of doomed fools who tried to fight back. He managed to get a bunch of the workers together, and they agreed to strike for both better wages and no more bloodletting. They all wore crosses around their necks, something that Mrs. Martha expressly forbade because it burned her skin when she touched it. That and silver, not that anyone could afford silver.

But the neighbors had gotten scared; they sold him out. If Willy hadn't been woken from his nap in the stables at just that moment, Benny would either be drained of blood in a ditch or hanging from a tree. He just hoped that his parents and sister had been spared Mrs. Martha's wrath. They'd tried to talk him out of the whole strike business multiple times–loudly and publicly. Hopefully, that'd save them.

"Well, we could always use more help in the restaurant," Lewis said, putting on a brave face. "There's hardly any good soul food up here, so the place is always packed."

Lewis and Sandy had their own restaurant right on the edge of the black neighborhood of Minneapolis. There were no "colored only" or "whites only" signs in this city, but there was still segregation. The rules were just invisible rather than blatant; in a way, that made them more dangerous. A white mob a few blocks over had burned down a house when a black family tried to move in just the week before Benny arrived.

Still, there were no vampires trying to kill him, and for that alone, Benny was grateful. He worked hard at the restaurant as a server, earning his keep as Lewis and Sandy let him stay in their tiny apartment. Rents were atrociously high, even though the apartments allowed to people like Benny were half the size and a fraction of the quality of those allowed to whites, so he couldn't even think of affording his own place. Especially when Fae folk started showing up in droves from a whole other realm of reality, trying to carve out what little piece of the neighborhood they could find for themselves. Benny found himself serving trolls, gnomes, goblins, dwarves, even a centaur once. He wasn't nearly as surprised as the northerners. If there were monsters like Mrs. Martha, then there were plenty of other odd things out there, and these people were friendly enough.

This carried on for over five years. JFK got shot. Benny's parents and sisters survived, one of those sisters even joining him in Minneapolis and finding a nice enough man to marry. Life was good.

Until Benny flipped through a newspaper one day during his break and stopped cold.

There, staring up at him from the page, was Mrs. Martha under the headline, *New Vampire Country Club Opening Near St. Paul.*

"She was supposed to stay in Louisiana," Benny panted, his heart crashing and his lungs refusing to work. He almost fell off one of the new stools Lewis had been proud enough to put in last year.

"Benny, hey ol' boy, come on." Lewis took the paper and set it on the counter. "Breathe for me."

"I can't stay here, Lu!"

"It's all right. She don't know you're here. We'll figure this out..."

"You need a fairy," someone said.

A dwarf had picked up the newspaper, eyes barely visible over his thick mustache and beard. "A powerful one."

Oh, not his. Her. Hard to tell with these folk. They *all* had beards.

"Like Nameless?" Benny panted. He'd seen that faceless fairy on the news, everyone watching her as intently as MLK as she publicly cursed the politicians into giving the Fae folk rights. They'd laughed it off, at first, until all those she named suddenly started getting sick or hit by cars. That scared a lot of the politicians straight, but others refused to budge, instead calling her a terrorist and offering a reward for any information that led to her arrest even as they got sick and poor. (This would last only another year, when the next election brought a new wave of officeholders more willing to sign the Fae Rights Act, as well as ensure and *enforce* the laws protecting their other, human citizens after Dr. King got shot. But that was months from now, and Benny didn't hold out hope for such a happy ending so soon.)

"Exactly," the she-dwarf said. She took a pen from Lewis's register and wrote something on the newspaper. "Go to this one. She's over in Bernier and goes by Violet. She'll help you. Might be a bit hard to find, though, what with the glamour."

"Fairies don't work for free," Lewis warned.

"No, but she's fair about it. *Actually* fair, not a gouger like some others. You want protection from anything, she'll deliver."

The she-dwarf had written a street address in the margins of the paper. After thinking it over and panicking a little more for a few days, Benny borrowed Lewis's car and drove to Bernier.

The town made him even more nervous. Almost everyone he saw was white, and giving him odd, suspicious looks. One man tried to get him to do some yard work for a dollar. "A whole dollar!"

"Sorry, sir, I need to find Miss Violet," Benny said. "The fairy?"

The man frowned. "That witch? She's just down the street."

He eventually found the house, a quaint little thing in a nice neighborhood, with a yard and flourishing flower garden. The walls were painted a deep blue with a white trim.

Palms sweating, he knocked on the door.

An apparently middle-aged woman answered, with lavender skin, long pointy ears with half a dozen piercings each, and black hair that looked almost purple in the sunlight. "Can I help you?"

He took off his hat. He'd always been a big man, both upwards and sideways. This fairy was almost eye-level with him, and had arms that could probably drag him across the floor without too much trouble. "Sorry, ma'am. I don't mean to be a bother, I'm just looking for a Miss Violet?"

"That'd be me. What's this about?"

He gulped. "You hear about the community club Mrs. Martha's starting near the Cities?"

Her eyes hardened. "Yes. From your accent, I assume you're also from Louisiana?"

"...from her plantation. I had to run. She..."

"Is a vampire. And not one of the kinder ones." Miss Violet stepped aside. "Come on in. Does she know you're here?"

He followed her inside. The entryway led to the kitchen and gave a view of the living room, stuffed with bookshelves, knickknacks, and a new Panasonic TV. Everything was deep blue, purple, or creamy white, almost like being underwater. "I don't think so, ma'am. I came up a few years ago. Didn't even know she was here 'til I read the paper."

"With the National Guard finally cracking down on the South, I'm not surprised she decided to move." She let him sit at her kitchen table, but didn't offer him anything to eat or drink. He didn't ask. "I *am* surprised she decided to move so close to *me*. The last time we spoke, I stabbed her."

Benny tried to hide his shock. Given Miss Violet's amused look, he failed. "Um...why?"

"That would take decades to answer. We've mostly been content to avoid each other, especially since the Civil War."

"The Civil..." He caught himself. "Sorry, ma'am, but I thought your folk only came here a few years ago?"

That wasn't his only point of confusion and dizziness. When he was a boy, he'd met a few people who'd been alive during the Civil War, but they'd all been wrinkled, gray, and dead within a decade. Miss Violet didn't look a day over thirty-five. Just how old *was* she?

"En masse, yes," she said. "But we've always visited or even immigrated to Earth since our Realms bumped into each other millennia ago. We typically hide our nature when we come here."

"Why? If I may ask, ma'am," he added hurriedly.

"You may. Most of the natural Fae-Earth portals lead to Europe, and its people have developed a hatred of us that is at least partially deserved. They've long attacked any person they even *remotely* believe is Fae with iron. Although more recent decades have led me to fear human governments far more than the populace. What do you think is the most likely outcome: me being strapped to a scientist's table, or forced to use my magic for the CIA?"

"Ah…both?" he guessed.

She nodded with a pleased smile, and he felt a jolt of warm accomplishment. "Luckily, there are now far too many of us, and I'm too well-entrenched in the paranormal community, for either outcome to happen easily. I would have preferred to stay secret, but cameras, international television, and now the uptick in Fae migrants have made that impossible, so my days of moving and hiding are well and truly gone."

"I've heard that most of the Fae folk are running from some kind of war," Benny said, finally settling in one of the tall chairs.

The fairy's face saddened. "Apparently there's a global war happening in the Fae Realm. It's been going on for years."

Benny winced. He was too young to remember the Second World War, but his father had fought in it, and his grandfathers had fought in *both*. The night terrors had plagued them for the rest of their lives, and there were parts of Europe *still* rebuilding. He thought of the photographs he'd seen of English people digging through the rubble of London. Didn't seem fair to make anyone go through that.

"In any event," Violet continued, "to return to your original question, my ward and I moved to Earth just over a hundred years ago. The portal led to Ireland, and just as we were getting settled, the famine hit. We followed all the emigrants to America, and we've been here ever since. Most of that time was spent in the West, traveling along the frontier so people wouldn't learn of our immortality. Except during the Civil War; I spent most of that time making Martha's clan's life miserable."

She smirked, and Benny almost snickered, feeling like a little boy listening to tales of teenagers pranking teachers.

"Now that the proverbial cat is out of the bag, we've decided to settle here. Permanently."

He nodded. "Well, aside from the winters, I'd say you made a good choice, ma'am."

She smiled. "What is it you're hoping to get from me today?"

"I..." He shook his head. "I just want to be safe. I challenged Mrs. Martha back on her planation. If she sees me, she'll kill me."

Miss Violet studied him, clearly thinking it over. Benny held his breath.

"You have a few options," she said. "Obviously, the first is to leave Minnesota and never come back, but you've already been uprooted once. Asking you to do it again is atrocious. The second option would be to purchase a charm of protection or luck, which will work as long as you're wearing it. The third is to give me your full name so I can charm you with protection and luck, permanently."

"How much is the second one?" Benny asked, unwilling to give his name to a fairy. Or any of the para-folk.

"That would depend. I assume you want that charm to be as powerful as possible?"

"A lifetime, if you can."

She snorted. "A human lifetime it is...can you do carpentry?"

He was thrown off by the sudden question and had to think on it. "I fixed my parents' furniture whenever it broke. And helped my pa with the roof when it leaked."

"Good enough. I've purchased a building on Main Street to turn into a café. Help me with the labor, and I'll give you the charm. You strike me as more of a watch person than a ring or necklace-wearer."

"Uh...I've never owned a watch, ma'am."

"It'll go well with your style. Now, are you staying in town?"

"I live with my cousin in Minneapolis."

She grimaced. "That's quite a drive. My ward is at Harvard. You can sleep in his room here until the project is done."

Benny almost choked. "Do...you have a husband?"

"No, there is no man of the house."

"Then won't the neighbors talk?"

She gave him a deadpan look. "I'm a purple fairy combat veteran and sorceress. They're *always* talking."

Miss Violet's boy had thankfully cleaned his room before going off to college. Benny did his best to keep it tidy in the two weeks he helped clean, renovate, and paint the downtown business, turning it into a proper coffee shop. The fairy was not at all afraid of getting her hands dirty alongside him, and she already knew everyone on the block. Half of them gave her a wide berth, but a few were friendly to her and, by extension, to Benny.

Bernier didn't have a colored neighborhood like Minneapolis did, but a handful of families had broken that invisible line, as he found out over a lunch break in the Mexican restaurant next to the café. The Latino owner had married a black woman, and their daughter Isabel served as a waitress. They all lived in the apartment above their restaurant.

"We got some grumbling when we moved here," Isabel admitted when he asked her about it over his taco lunch. She was unfairly pretty, almost exotic, and just a year younger than him. She spoke English with a northern accent and Spanish rolled off her tongue like melted butter. "Someone even threw a brick through the window when I was little. But that's it. Mostly they just try to charge us more money to buy things and pay as little as possible when buying from us."

"All of them?"

"Well, not everyone. Doña Violet's one of the good ones. You going to work for her when her place opens up?"

"Maybe," Benny mused. So far, she'd been a good boss, and Bernier was quieter than Minneapolis. More like home.

He gave her a winning smile. "The neighbors are certainly better here than in the Cities."

Isabel smiled back, collecting his plate. "The movie theater accepts everyone and always has good film. Cheap, too."

"...okay?"

"In case you wanted to ask a girl out."

Benny only had a few dollars in his pocket, but damn if he wasn't going to spend it on *that*. He and Isabel went on their first proper date two nights later, and he was sure to walk her back home after the movie. They passed by Miss Violet's café, the lights they had just installed giving it a warm glow. It was the talk of the town, and the sight filled Benny with pride and a bit of melancholy at the thought of leaving.

Main Street was well lit at night with its thick lamps, but there were still dark shadows across the wide empty streets that evening. Benny didn't mind. The emptiness went a long way to soothing him, since he wasn't passing a hundred strangers with unknown motives.

The empty streets also meant that he saw—and recognized—the woman walking toward them on the sidewalk almost immediately.

Benny tensed, and Isabel—holding his arm—noticed. "What?"

"We need to get inside. Now."

She didn't question it, hurrying them to the restaurant. As she dug the keys out of her purse, Benny turned away from the approaching woman, hoping she hadn't seen his face. *Walk away, walk away, walk away...*

"Benjamin."

Shit.

He cleared his throat and straightened, stepping between her and Isabel. "Mrs. Martha."

The woman grinned, the light glinting off her sharpened fangs. She still dressed like a Southerner, with an expensive pink pencil skirt and matching jacket. "Well, fancy that. I didn't expect to see you here."

Benny kept his eyes down, at her knees. You never looked a vampire in the eyes.

Isabel got the door open and braved a smile. "I am so sorry to interrupt, ma'am—"

"Then don't."

"But my father *desperately* needs to speak with Benny." She pulled him toward the door.

Martha moved quick as a snake, slamming the door shut and almost taking Isabel's fingers with it. The two skinny windows of the door cracked, and the humans jumped at suddenly having the predator in their personal space.

Benny took Isabel's arm and backed away. "We're not asking for trouble, Mrs. Martha. Please."

"Running away again?" She loomed closer. "Do you know how many others took your example? I couldn't get anyone in my fields after your little stunt. I've owned that plantation for *centuries*, and had to sell it at half its worth because suddenly everyone decides to leave!"

She punched the wall. Not the window next to it, the brick wall. The stone turned to dust under her knuckles.

Isabel squeaked, gripping the back of Benny's suit that he'd borrowed from Lewis, wrinkling it beyond repair.

Benny swallowed, dread curling its fingers around his guts. He wasn't getting out of this one.

"All right, all right," he said, holding up his hands. "Just...let Isabel get inside, Mrs. Martha. Please. I'll go with you, wherever you want, whatever you want. Isabel had nothing to do with it, has never even been to Louisiana."

"Ben," Isabel whispered.

"Let her go, and I go with you," he said.

"Good to see someone bringing Southern chivalry to this frozen wasteland," Mrs. Martha said, shaking the dust off her fist. The punch hadn't even cracked skin. "Look at me, Benjamin."

He kept his eyes on the sidewalk. Mrs. Martha's pointed shoes tapped in his line of sight, and she touched his chin. "Look at me. Or I gouge out your date's pretty brown eyes."

Benny swallowed and raised his head.

Immediately, he was washed away in a sense of surreal calm. Why had he been worried? Why was Isabel digging her fingers into his suit? It was just Mrs. Martha. No one was nicer or a better friend than Mrs. Martha...

"I came here to speak with someone important," she said, fangs elongating. "But I could do with a decent meal before—"

She cut off with a gasp, all the air punched out of her by a bloody blade sticking out of her gut.

Benny jumped, the hypnosis snapping as he scrambled back. Isabel cut off her own scream with her hand.

Miss Violet suddenly rippled into existence behind the vampire, a dark green cloak over her shoulders. "Really, Martha. I thought you'd know better than to act like that in a fairy's domain."

She withdrew out the sword—an actual *sword*—and let Mrs. Martha crumple to the sidewalk. Her cloak lazily breathed with the breeze, every ripple making it flicker. One minute, she was there, solid and real. The next, Benny could swear he saw right through her. He gripped Isabel's hand, disgusted with himself and the bleeding vampire. It didn't matter how many people she had hypnotized over the years, falling for it himself made him feel slimy.

Miss Violet knelt, keeping her sword—Benny would later learn the blade was pure silver—on full display. Mrs. Martha spat blood. "I came to *talk*," she hissed.

"No, you came to try to bribe and/or bully me on behalf of your clan into letting you kill and terrorize every mortal in and around the Twin Cities to support your 'country club,'" Miss Violet corrected. "I don't mind you setting up a new home. But you're going to have to properly and *legally* purchase your food from now on."

Mrs. Martha pushed herself up. She couldn't stand, but she was far more mobile than anyone with a hole in their gut had a right to be. "You want a war? With us?"

Benny had seen Miss Violet smile several times, warmly and secretly and amused and everything in between. This one was ice cold. "Do *you*?"

Mrs. Martha eyed her silver sword.

Miss Violet lifted the blade. Rivulets of blood slid down the metal, dripping onto the concrete. "The only reason I'm not driving this into that black, shriveled heart of yours is because I need you to send a message. Bernier is *my* domain. Spill blood on this land, and I will treat it as an act of war. If I hear of you killing or coercing anyone into feeding your clan, regardless of where they come from, I will remove the teeth of everyone who committed such foulness as a warning. Their second offense will cost them their heads. Our existence is no longer secret and your clan is obscenely rich, so you have no reason to keep your supply below-board."

Miss Violet dug through her magic cloak and pulled out a blood bag, the kind you get from hospitals or vets. She tossed it on the ground, next to Mrs. Martha's hand. "It's cattle, so you can stop bleeding on my sidewalk."

Mrs. Martha silently pulled the bag toward her, glaring at Miss Violet the whole time.

The fairy cleaned the dark red from her sword and sheathed it. "Isabel, I do believe your parents will be wondering where you are. Benjamin, I'd like to get home, soon."

"S-Si, Doña," Isabel stuttered. She stepped away from Benny, avoiding Mrs. Martha, and then paused. Came back. Kissed Benny on the cheek before running inside.

Which, Benny would recall later in life, almost made the whole ordeal worth it.

§

The next day, Benny made breakfast as usual in Miss Violet's house, because while the fairy was skilled in many (terrifying) things, she was a hopeless cook. It was a surreal experience. He'd done this dozens of times over the last couple of weeks. Yet something fundamental had changed.

Mrs. Martha was in the same state as him. Only a few towns away. And she knew exactly where he was.

Yet...she wouldn't come for him. He didn't have to look over his shoulder anymore.

He was free.

Miss Violet joined him at the table as he set up the plates, yawning with her thick purple hair a mess. She hadn't even changed out of her button-up pajamas. She placed a simple leather watch by his plate. "I will not order or advise you to stay. But I will say that if you leave Bernier, you should not *ever* take that off."

Benny carefully picked up the watch. The face was simple, edged with either copper or gold, and set in a basic black leather strip. "This is the charm?"

"I meant to have it ready tomorrow, when we were officially done with the café, but thought it prudent to rush it," she said sleepily. "That is a good luck and basic protection charm. If you're foolish enough to go directly to Martha's clan, it won't stop her from tearing you apart. But you'll never run into her by chance. And if you go to war, bullets and bombs will have a much harder time finding you. Additionally, you will never be hypnotized by a vampire or cursed by a witch so long as you wear it. Up to a hundred and five years."

Benny dropped into his chair. "What?"

"The longest-living human, to my knowledge, died at the age of a hundred and five. We agreed on one human lifetime."

He carefully put on the watch. It was heavy and comfortable around his left wrist. "Thank you, Miss Violet. I...honestly, I'm not sure I want to leave. I've come to really like this town."

"And the Mexican restaurant," she teased.

Benny's face heated. "It's a very good restaurant. Good food, good...staff..."

She laughed. "Well. If you want to keep affording your meals there, I am hiring full-time staff at my new café. Interested in working for human currency?"

§

Benny worked at CaFae Latte for almost fifty years, retiring just before he reached seventy in 2017. Miss Violet's ward—who was nicknamed Blue, for obvious reasons—eventually came home and joined him, and they all went from coworkers to friends in fairly short order (though Benny still called her *Miss* Violet when on the job). Both were present at Benny and Isabel's wedding and move-in party in 1971, their son's first birthday in '75, and his high school graduation in '92. (Benny did not know, but would not have been surprised that they attended his funeral in 2020, just as they had attended Isabel's a few years earlier. Damn Covid-19 got into his old lungs.)

At no point did Benny have to worry about how to feed and clothe his family, or about sending his son Charlie off to college.

He *did* worry about *where* he'd go to college. He trusted Violet's magic and mettle, but not Mrs. Martha or any of her vampire friends. As much as he hated to talk about it, to drudge up that pain and shame, he sat his son–then a teenager–down and told him exactly why he had left the South, why he so rarely left Bernier, and why Charlie ought to avoid the Twin Cities and Louisiana whenever possible.

Charlie chose South Dakota State University, which made Benny breathe a little easier. He still strapped that magic watch onto his boy's wrist. Violet noticed, but said nothing about it.

Charlie was gone for four years and ended up getting one of his classmates, Alice, pregnant.

The good news was Benny and Isabel (and Violet and Blue) had raised a responsible young man, and while the two didn't marry right away–not for five years–Charlie did look after Alice and their surprise child. Benny's granddaughter was born in South Dakota in 1994, and he took a month off to help look after her.

In 1995, Charlie brought the baby girl to Bernier for a proper visit, carrying her in one of those plastic carriers into CaFae Latte.

Blue glared at the baby. "I want you to know that I lost fifty bucks because of you. You *had* to be a girl."

Violet tugged on his pointy ear, making him shriek, and cooed at the little baby while Benny tried not to puff up like a peacock. His grandbaby was already stealing hearts.

"What are you calling her?" Violet asked.

Charlie gave a tired sigh. "Alice wanted to name her after her aunt Sharon, who was also named after her grandma, who also shares the name with an ungodly number of cousins, and is also my dad's aunt's name! That is too many Sharons."

"It lets us get creative with the nicknames," Benny defended.

Charlie rolled his eyes, reaching into the cradle and letting his daughter grip his finger. "We compromised. Sharon's one of her middle names, but her first name is Nicole."

bad blood

Nicole told the story of her grandfather while wrapping the old leather watch around JC's wrist. It felt oddly heavy, but maybe that was just because it was the most valuable thing they'd ever touched in their life.

"Shouldn't *you* be wearing this?" they asked, twisted around in the front seat so she could reach their wrist. "It's your grandpa's. And you shouldn't go into this without protection..."

"Are you a Nichiren Buddhist?" she asked, digging something out of her purse.

"I don't even know what that is."

"Then you need the watch." She wrapped the prayer beads JC had spotted earlier around her watch-less wrist, then hid them beneath her gloves and long sleeves.

Cyrus was behind the wheel, as usual. At this point, JC felt that the three of them lived in this car.

"Nicole should wear the invisibility cloak," he said. "It blocks vampires' sense of smell."

She frowned. "I don't want to hide from her."

"I know you don't. But do you really think they're going to talk to anyone with a skin tone darker than fish-belly white? Honestly, it might be better if you stay in the car. If this gets ugly, you're the first one they're going after. Especially if they find out about your connection to Benny."

She scowled. "Fine. I'll wear the cloak."

JC tapped the face of Nicole's watch, wondering if the strength and courage of her family would bleed through to them. "You don't happen to have silver bullets, do you? For a 9mm?"

Cyrus grimaced. "I don't use guns. They're hell on fairy ears."

"Well, I like staying alive. Pull over at a gun shop, will you?"

"Won't they card you, or something?"

"The state only requires registration for buying guns. Not bullets," JC said. "And lead's not going to work on vampires."

"Isn't it against the law for you to buy ammo? Or even to be holding on to that gun?"

"Well, yeah. But they're not going to check."

Nicole squirmed. "I don't like the thought of going into this with guns. Or anything outside of defensive magic."

"You want to walk into the den of the woman who tried to eat your grandpa *unarmed*?" JC demanded.

"I think if we go in wanting to fight, that's what we'll get. And I don't want a fight. I don't even want anything to do with her, and I hope we only have to deal with Vlad. We're after information, not blood."

Cyrus shook his head. "Nicole, I love the optimism, but the last time Boss and I had to deal with Vlad, the whole clan tried to kill us."

"Why?"

He tightened his grip on the steering wheel. "Lots of reasons: we were on opposite sides of the Civil War, we get along with Wulver and the werewolves while they hate anything to do with any kind of wolf, Vlad was an emotionally abusive boyfriend to Boss, they've been after my friend Patrick and his family for a while...there's a lot of bad blood."

"Vlad is Bob's ex?" JC clarified.

"Yeah. Not her best move. I can't tell if it was an emotional vulnerability thing, an allo thing, or both."

"Allo?"

"Not asexual or aromantic. I mean, I'm pretty sure she's aromantic, but she's definitely not ace, so that makes her allo," he explained. "That's okay. We love her despite her flaws."

"Maybe you can glamour yourself?" they asked. "The way Red Wolf's people did?"

"Vampire noses are too sharp for that. Some glamours can trick them, but mine's not nearly that good."

"...sorry, Nicole. I think we're going to need the silver bullets."

"So just fuck me going deaf, then," Cyrus grumbled, pulling one of the pins from his hat. It morphed into a small knife. JC wasn't close enough to be sure, but it looked like silver.

He handed it to Nicole, who didn't hide her distaste. "Just in case."

"You have more?" JC asked.

"Plenty."

He stopped by a gun store and range on the edge of the highway. God bless America: there was at least one in almost every Midwestern town. JC was in and out in five minutes. Even with Violet's generous pay, they didn't have enough for a magazine of pure silver bullets. They could only get a few magazines of silver-*coated* bullets, and hoped that was enough.

"You live near the vampire club house?" the cashier asked, ringing them up.

"Yeah," they lied, counting out their crumpled dollar bills. "You never know, right?"

"I hear that. Be careful out there."

"You, too."

They scooped up their goodies and left, loading the gun's magazine as Cyrus drove off.

§

"Should we have grabbed garlic?" JC asked as they drew closer to the club.

Cyrus laughed. "That doesn't actually work!"

"A crucifix, then."

"Are you Christian?"

"No, atheist."

"Then it won't work. Religious symbols only have power when you believe they do."

"Oh, I call hack!"

"Sunlight also won't hurt them," Nicole piped up. "Though they are sensitive to exposed sunlight more so than a human and tend to be nocturnal, they won't burst into flames."

"I knew that," JC grumbled.

"Did you?" Cyrus teased.

"...I thought they needed a lot of sunscreen to go out."

Nicole giggled. JC found themselves smiling, even if they did feel a bit like an idiot for going in blind. Everyone had heard of vampires, seen them on the news and in movies and whatnot. But JC had never had to work with them before. They never found one in the city ghettos or prison; they were usually too rich for either. If they did any drugs, it wasn't marbles, or any of the cheaper stuff JC's people used.

The country club was a blood red brick mansion behind a sprawling golf course, protected behind an iron gate, each spike as black as Death's robes. JC's mind boggled at all the space. Just...why? How could they fill it? Graveyards had less property than this.

Nicole wrapped herself up in the cloak, going completely invisible to JC's eyes. They asked Cyrus, "Can you still see her?"

"Eh..." He rocked his hand in a so-so gesture. "More like I see a ripple in the air. Kind of like heat waves? It's more obvious when she moves."

They were halted at the gate by a security guard with a clipboard. "Name?"

"We're not on there," Cyrus said.

"Then I'm going to have to ask you to turn around."

"Call Vlad before you do. Tell him it's about Violet, and that it's urgent."

The guard frowned, but pulled out his phone and stepped away. JC wondered if they were human or vampire; it was impossible to tell.

After a few minutes, the guard opened the gate for them. Cyrus flashed him a peace sign and drove them in, parking in the lot next to an honest-to-God Lamborghini.

It was hard not to feel like a grubby, dirt-stained trash bag as they entered the mansion. The butler—and how the hell did JC reach a point where they were talking to a *butler*? This was *definitely* the weirdest day of their life—led them to some sort of lobby or waiting room with bone white sofas, mahogany furniture, and portraits of probably long-dead people on the wall.

All this space, and the butler was the only person they'd seen so far. "Where is everyone? Golfing?" they asked. Did vampires golf?

"Yes. There's a tournament in Missouri," the butler explained. Because apparently, yeah, they did. "Would you like refreshments?"

"Nah," JC said, deciding they didn't want to know what a vampire club house considered *refreshments*. "We'll be out as soon as we're done with Vlad."

The butler left.

Cyrus strode up to one of the portraits. JC followed his gaze, studying the pale woman with black hair in a fluffy antebellum dress. "Is that the one who..."

"Boss put a hole in for trying to eat Nicole's pop-pop? Yup." His face darkened. "Benny was the first friend we made after we moved to Bernier. One of the first mortal friends we made who knew we were fairies right out the gate. Good guy, down-to-earth, mix of dorky and Southern charm. You'd have liked him. And she tortured and butchered his family for generations before he got out from under her, just because she could."

Footsteps alerted them to incoming company. JC patted Cyrus's shoulder, feeling him force himself to relax.

The woman herself came into the room, along with a man in a pinstripe suit. He looked more like a CEO than a bloodthirsty vampire—they both did. She'd swapped out the antebellum dress for a blouse and pencil skirt, and he had way too much gel in his black hair to keep it tall and slicked back. But he was, unfortunately, handsome. JC couldn't blame Violet for her choices there; they had gone down on their knees for less.

"Hey, kiddo," the man—Vlad—said with a smarmy smile. "Been a while. You remember Martha?"

"Hard to forget," Cyrus said, tipping his head to JC. "This is JC. They're with me."

"Charmed," Martha said, not offering her hand. JC maintained eye contact, refusing to take the social slight without at least a little challenge.

"I'm surprised to see you here," Vlad admitted, sitting on the couch. He motioned to the butler who had followed them.

"Jeff, can you get our guests some tea, please? Unless you want something stronger?"

"Nah, we're not sticking around for long," Cyrus promised, striking his usual casual tone as the butler left once again. "We just need to ask if you know anything about a fairy named Red Wolf."

"Wouldn't your mentor have those answers?"

"She's not available at the moment."

Vlad grinned, showing sharp canines. "Why not?"

JC crossed their arms. "What do you care?"

"Shush," he scolded, holding up a finger without even looking at them, keeping his eyes on Cyrus. "The adults are talking."

"Did something happen to our dear Violet?" Martha asked, prowling behind JC. She had a similar accent to Andy and Caroline, but unlike them, her voice didn't bring comfort. It made something in JC shudder. They pivoted so the vampire stayed in sight.

"She's out of town at the moment," Cyrus said with a shrug. "Left me in charge. But it looks like this Red Wolf character is going to cause problems while she's gone."

"Out of town," Vlad echoed, tasting the words. "Now that is an interesting phrase."

JC didn't like this. Any of this. Technically, the three of them outnumbered Vlad and Martha. But this was the vampires' home turf. Martha kept them surrounded, boxed in, and the hairs on the back of their neck stood straight as razors.

They had long ago learned to trust their gut, so they said, "Cyrus, these guys aren't going to give us anything."

A hand curled around their bicep, and they almost jumped out of their skin, stopping themself at the last second. The hand was invisible. Nicole, telling them to stay.

"You just got here," Vlad protested. "And if Red Wolf is sniffing you out, then you're all in trouble. Especially Violet."

JC tensed. Cyrus, curious, tipped his head. "What makes you say that?"

"He's a powerful fairy, that's what. Possibly more powerful than dear Violet, given his connections. Depending on what type of situation she's found herself in, I'm not sure I like her chances."

"Why would he care about her in the first place?" Cyrus asked.

"Oh, that." Vlad flicked some lint off his suit. "That's *ancient* history."

"We've got time."

"I'm not sure you do. How long as Violet been...'out of town'?"

"Not long," Cyrus said, with a lot more confidence than JC felt.

JC checked behind them, scoping out exits. Martha was still there, leaning against the wall by her portrait and watching the whole thing with an amused quirk of her lips. Just beyond her elbow was the hallway that led to the front door.

Martha's eyes caught theirs and she prowled forward. "You know, Vlad, darling, I think our guests are in a bit of a rush."

Vlad stood. "Oh, they definitely are. How rude of me."

Martha reached out, touching JC's chin. They jerked back, away from her and out of Nicole's invisible grip, snapping, "Personal bubble, lady."

Martha tsked. "So rude."

"If you're done being *creepy*," Cyrus drawled. "What do you two want?"

"Well, to be perfectly honest, kiddo, it's almost dinnertime," Vlad said. "And I'm *starving*."

JC reached for their gun.

Lightning-quick, Vlad grabbed their jaw, forcing their eyes to meet. "Don't."

Even with the magic of the watch, there was something off-putting and hypnotic about Vlad's gaze. Something piercing that made it very hard to look away.

Martha breathed down their neck, and JC was caught. Even if they did draw their pistol, they couldn't handle both vampires at the same time.

"You know that hypnotizing people without their consent is illegal, right?" Cyrus asked, annoyed.

"Then I suppose you have a choice to make, kiddo," Vlad drawled, dragging his nail across JC's neck. "If you want to know about Red Wolf, it's going to cost you one human snack."

silver blade

"You live in a mansion. You can't tell me you're starving," Cyrus said.

He hadn't gone for any of the pins on his hat, shirt, or belt, or said anything to indicate that JC wasn't actually hypnotized. They decided to play along, for now, keeping their eyes locked on Vlad's, who narrowed his.

"Your friend is quite stubborn," he said. "Not going down as easily as I'd hoped. But then again, that makes this more interesting. It's so much better straight from the vein—"

Crash!

One of the very expensive vases had flown across the room, smashing into the side of his head.

It didn't do any damage, barely made him step in surprise. But it caused a much-needed distraction.

JC drew their gun and fired directly behind them—twice. Martha shrieked as she went down, hands covering the fresh holes in her gut and blouse.

Before Vlad could retaliate, he gasped in shock and pain as Cyrus threw a pin-turned-knife into his back, bringing him to a knee.

Just as JC was thinking that, even with both vampires down, standing between the two of them probably wasn't the *smartest* thing, Martha grabbed their ankle and threw them across the room, like they were a pillow. Their back smashed into the wall, leaving a dent in the wood as their head pounded and something scraped against their arm.

Even through the pain, fresh bruises, and probably a broken rib or two, their only coherent thought was, *That bitch better not have broken my insulin pump.*

They clawed their way out of the wall, stumbling on their feet and shedding splinters everywhere, every move aching. Miraculously, they were unhurt enough to be functional, and their insulin pump hadn't been hit. Even more incredible, they were still holding the gun.

Then the golden chain around their neck–Nicole's good luck charm–broke and slipped away, puddling onto the floor. *Ah. Yeah. Got it.*

Martha was back on her feet, pulling the bullets out of her flesh. Stupid cheap silver coated pieces of shit had barely poked her, not doing nearly as much damage as JC had thought.

The vampire marched straight toward them as Cyrus and Vlad got into a knife fight, the vampire having yanked the blade out of his shoulder to block Cyrus's next hit.

JC fired twice more at Martha, their still-doubled vision meaning only one hit her. She stumbled back as the bullet hit her sternum, but shook it off and kept coming.

Until Nicole threw off the invisibility cloak and stabbed her in the back.

Martha gasped, freezing, teeth bared in shock and pain.

"I really don't want to do this," Nicole snapped, pulling the knife free and stepping away from Martha's reach. Her normal monotone was gone, washed away by her wrath. "We came only asking for information, and you try to kill my friends?!"

Cyrus shrieked.

Vlad had grabbed Cyrus's arm and twisted, hard and fast enough to *snap*.

Forearms were not supposed to bend in the middle.

JC stepped away from Martha and fired four of their remaining twelve rounds–they'd been counting–into Vlad's chest, knocking him away and allowing Cyrus to pull himself free from the vampire's super-strength grip. Their vision cleared up enough that every bullet hit.

Martha moved, going for Nicole. JC, barely having to pivot, put their remaining rounds into the vampire's stomach. As Martha fell back, JC expertly dropped the clip, reloaded, and fired again, this time aiming for Vlad as he started to get up. Ten rounds of silver-coated lead pummeled his chest and head, keeping him down. Cyrus collected himself off the floor, gritting his teeth, as Martha stalked Nicole. The witch retreated, backing closer to JC.

With Cyrus up, JC turned on the Southern belle. Martha slammed back into the floor when the last seven rounds of JC's Glock hit her in the head and neck.

Discard clip. Reload. Aim.

As Martha went down, Cyrus—with only one functional arm—stabbed Vlad three times with his silver knife: twice in the arm and once in the gut, before finally disarming him and pressing the silver knife to the vampire's throat.

JC sagged, gun still aimed at Martha even as everything throbbed.

Martha, still on the floor, glared up at Nicole. "Who are you?"

"Benny's granddaughter," she said. "He married the woman you threatened in Bernier that night. You should know they both lived long, happy, healthy lives."

Martha spat at Nicole's feet. "Nigger."

JC almost shot her again for that, but Nicole held up her hand. "Don't."

"You can't tell me she doesn't deserve it," JC argued, fuming at the insult and their bruised ribs and the attempted hypnosis and *eating*...

"I don't argue about 'deserved.' But killing her will cause us more problems than it will solve."

"She's right," Cyrus huffed, knife still at Vlad's throat. He spoke way too loudly, doing that thing with his jaw people do when they try to get their ears to stop ringing. "Everything before now was self-defense. They attacked first; we defended ourselves. Now? Unless they attack again, we're legally on the hook."

"You're in our home," Vlad pointed out, eyeing the silver hovering over his skin. "Who are the police going to believe?"

"Probably the fairy who can't lie, and the two mortals willing to take a truth potion." Heedless of his crooked arm, Cyrus pressed the silver blade deeper into Vlad's neck. As the vampire's pale skin started to blister, the fairy said lightly, "But. hey, try your luck."

JC fumed. Martha had murdered people, and she was just getting off the hook *again*? Violet should've killed her decades ago.

"Red Wolf," Cyrus prodded, easing up on the knife so it stopped burning the vampire. "Start talking."

Vlad sighed, one hand over the slash across his gut, the other held up in surrender. Hopefully he'd kept the receipt for that expensive suit. "I don't know much. He was a former lieutenant in Violet's armies, back when she was chief commander of...whatever her home country was."

"Ivae."

"Yeah, that's the one. They served together for a long time. Centuries. He was pretty much her protégé. An earlier, better version of you."

Cyrus didn't rise to the bait.

"Then she got all mopey about the mortals' being serfs and rebelled. Helped create Gialdon. Red Wolf stayed on the fairies' side. Even became their Chief Commander. He lost."

"That's it?" JC demanded, not taking their eyes off Martha. They already knew that!

"That's wrong," Nicole said. "Ivae's Chief Commander after Aunt Violet was Lady Oak, then a fairy named Harvest Moon."

"Same person, different name," Vlad replied, pressing his hand harder against the wound on his side. JC had seen humans walk off similar wounds after some stitches and sleep; he'd be fine. "Fairies collect them like stamps. Some even change their name every century or decade just to keep their enemies confused, or after a major life event. And losing a war and your wife? That's major."

"Wife?" JC asked. Nicole sucked in a breath.

Vlad snorted a laugh. "Yes, wife. Harvest Moon–Red Wolf, whatever you call him–his wife was Oak. She was killed during the war. Not just in any battle, either. Violet killed her herself."

...*shit*. JC and Nicole shared a dismayed look.

"How do you know this?" Nicole asked.

"He came here looking for her," he admitted. "About a year ago. Introduced himself as Red Wolf and asked about Violet. Where she was, what she was doing. After a few drinks and some talk, I realized that he was Harvest Moon. He confirmed it."

Martha started to gather herself to stand. JC waggled the Glock's barrel in warning. The vampire stayed down.

"What did you give him?" Cyrus demanded. "Beyond information?"

"Just that," Vlad said. "Well...and I introduced him to a few mortal mercenaries. Told him about a few crime syndicates who may or may not help him. Not my responsibility if he hired them or not."

So, Vlad introduced Red Wolf to Michelle, maybe even the Wolverines, and gave him the lay of the land so he could plan his kidnapping. JC was getting more pissed by the second.

"Is he still a part of Ivae's military?" Cyrus asked. Sweat trickled down his temple, but otherwise he gave no sign of what was probably the absolute agony of his broken arm.

Vlad shrugged, lopsided due to the wound in the back of his shoulder. "Hell if I know. But the fairies of the Fae Realm have largely stayed out of mortal business. At least, the governments have; I guess they didn't like the idea that mere humans could whip them that badly. And now with the nukes and bullets... well, better to just keep ignoring you until you eventually destroy yourselves. From what Violet told me, Red Wolf has always chomped at the bit. Always rebelling against authority. But even if he left, he still has friends in high places. You think vampires are fans of nepotism, you should look into your own roots, kiddo."

JC kept their eyes on Martha as Vlad talked. She glared back, not willing the risk the gun again.

"What's he going to do to Violet?" they asked. "Once they're back in the Fae Realm."

Vlad smirked. "Well, they definitely won't execute her. Fairies are 'above death.' Present company, excluded. But by the time they're done with her, she's going to wish they weren't."

Cyrus studied him for a minute, then returned his knife to pin form. "Let's go."

the murderer

An excerpt from *Round-Ears: A History of
Gialdon and Humans in the Fae Realm*

Most of the War of Gialdonian Independence
was fought with guerrilla tactics for a wide
variety of reasons. For one, the Gialdons did
not have the numerical advantage, even as they got new
recruits near-daily. Secondly, they—much like their Fae
enslavers—hesitated to use lethal force. They wanted to
free the mortals forced to fight for Ivae, not kill them on
the field. And thirdly, despite having the Iron Witch and
a handful of other sorcerers on their payroll, they still had

a severe magical disadvantage. Ivae utilized hundreds of enchanted objects, ranging from enchanted armor to objects of invisibility and disguise; magical [and rare] transportation that allowed them to traverse hundreds of miles in hours, if not minutes; and of course, druidic wands. The Gialdons only had a handful of such objects, and only one wand: the Violet Princess's Elemental Fire Wand.

What few major battles were fought were largely done by other nations. In addition to the dwarves, Aster and Coral managed to get [the fairy nation of] Riada and [the giants of] Famhyr fighting Ivae as well, largely in retaliation for previous wars that Ivae had won. The fact that both of those nations also enslaved mortals—Riada for military work, Famhyr for eating—ruffled some feathers, but beggars cannot be choosers.

It wasn't until the Battle of Oak Hill that the Violet Princess was once again in a "proper" battlefield, and it didn't go at all the way most thought it would.

Lady Oak, who had been promoted to Chief Commander in the wake of her mentor's betrayal, sent her husband Harvest Moon to meddle with the Gialdons' supply lines. While he did that, she received news that the Violet Princess had been spotted near Oak Hill (then named Leighi Hill), likely trying to convince the Benevolent Patron to defect to her side.

A noblewoman in charge of the province, the [fairy commonly known as the] Benevolent Patron had been neutral since the start of the civil war. The agricultural province was small, so its wealth and prestige came largely from its university for magical studies, specializing in healing magic, and the Patron took pride in funding both the university and its most talented students. Graduates tended to the injured on both sides, mortal and immortal. As their food stores and supplies began to run low, both sides had been hoping to secure the Patron's allegiance, as she was more than wealthy enough to fix such a problem, at least for a few months.

Lady Oak took her army of 50,000 mortals—kept in line with dozens of musicians playing enchanted instruments—and marched them to Leighi Hill. They outnumbered the Violet Princess's contingent at least two to one. The hill overlooked a vast plain that the Patron's family had been using for agriculture for thousands of years, meaning there was nowhere for the Gialdons to hide and ambush them.

The battle should have been an Ivaenian victory, although perhaps a long and drawn-out one. But it was over almost as soon as it began.

The Violet Princess was easy to spot in her silver and iron armor and purple skin, right at the front of the field as usual. Lady Oak, her under-officers, and scribes took position on top of Leighi Hill so they could see the field. The scribes reported that the Fae officers were surprised that they didn't see the Gialdon leaders do the same in another area, largely going into the fray rather than staying above it. Lady Oak retorted, "They're mortals. They don't know how to do anything properly except die."

Lady Oak's first order was to attempt to mind-control the Violet Princess's troops the way she did her own: with magic music. But despite all thirty of her musicians playing at once, the lines of 20,000 Gialdon soldiers did not budge. Later reports revealed that Commander Rat had ordered them to stuff their ears full of wax, which was why so many of them relied on flags instead of horns for this battle, as well as all others in the future.

Again, Lady Oak was not surprised. "Of course, she wouldn't make this easy on us. Order a charge. Try to envelop them."

"We'll try to take the Violet Princess alive," one of her lieutenants said.

"Don't," she ordered. "She chose to live by mortals, she'll die with them."

As the Ivaenian force charged and the Gialdons fired their bows, one of Lady Oak's Fae lieutenants noticed something out of the corner of his eye. At first, he thought it was just the wind playing with the grass. Or perhaps an odd ripple of heat on the summer day. By the time he realized what it truly was, it was far too late.

When the Ivaenian forces reached the Gialdons, the initial clash was the usual chaos of battle. One of the Ivaenian soldiers got close enough to the Violet Princess to slash at her arm. It didn't break the armor, but it *did* break the bracelet around her wrist.

The bracelet had been enchanted with a glamour. When it fell, the "Violet Princess" turned out to be Commander Rat.

Lady Oak did not have any time to adjust her strategy, however, as the "wind" or "odd heat ripple" that had been creeping closer up the hill turned out to be an invisibility cloak. The Violet Princess discarded it as soon as she was close enough to attack, and used her Fire Wand to incinerate all the military officers. Only the scribes were spared.

From their accounts:

There was a flash of fire, a sudden inferno that consumed all in its path. It was too quick even for anyone to scream. Within three heartbeats, the fire died. All that was left of Chief Commander Oak and her under-officers were charred corpses in blackened armor.

The Iron Witch lowered her wand and told us, "Nobody gets to force others to shed blood against their will. Not anymore. If the fairies of Ivae wish to keep fighting this war, they can fight it themselves."

The Violet Princess then went down the hill, to where the musicians had been too occupied coordinating their military music to even notice what had happened behind them, and killed them with the same method, destroying their instruments as she did.

When the last note faded, the entire battlefield stopped. Those mortal soldiers who had managed to endure the weeks of magical mind control broke into tears and hysterics.

◇
◇
◇

◇
◇
◇

Many more simply stood there, waiting for orders that would never come.

> **Pictured** the Battle of Oak Hill, the armies led by Lady Oak and Commander Rat.

revolt and rebellion

Red Wolf stood by his decision to bring multiple fairies on this mission, as well as hiring local mercenaries to assist. But the problem with that was transporting them, which required several vehicles. They had considered a bus, but that was putting all the eggs in a single basket. Having multiple vehicles ensured that if one broke down or crashed, it wouldn't jeopardize the entire mission.

The downside of this method was gas. Someone in their caravan had run out, and now everyone needed to stop if they all wanted to stay together.

They didn't crowd the same gas station, of course. That would draw too much attention. Instead, they found a street with multiple stations and fast-food joints, taking the opportunity to get food and use the restroom while they could, leaving Violet chained to the floor of the van and under guard.

"Are we getting her anything?" Jack asked, motioning to the captive.

Red Wolf leaned against the van, studying his former mentor. He didn't have to worry about anyone seeing or hearing her, even with the doors wide open. Black Dove's spells ensured that no one would know.

The last twenty-four hours had clearly taken their toll on the Traitor Princess, though Red Wolf had seen her push through far worse. Her work clothes were wrinkled, stained with the sweat and drinks from her new vocation. Her near-black hair, still in its ponytail, hadn't seen a brush and sported several tangles.

And she still gave him that same look, the one that annoyed him when she'd been his mentor and was even worse now.

The one that said, *I'm trying to teach you something important, and you're purposefully refusing to grasp it.*

"What did you feed your prisoners during the Great Mortal Rebellion?" he asked.

"Whatever we could, when we *had* prisoners," Violet answered. "Earlier in my career, when I was a lieutenant, I didn't pay attention to my POWs. Even neglected and mistreated them, or handed them off to subordinates who would be cruel and merciless. And that came back to haunt me, as my adversaries would fight to the death, to the last one standing, because they would rather die than be given such a fate. Once I started treating my prisoners better, I got more peaceful surrenders and fewer problems, no matter who I was fighting."

Red Wolf grunted. He hadn't been there for her early days, but when he *had* joined her ranks, she'd been giving her prisoners at least minimal comforts. He'd always thought it was to flaunt her wealth and title as princess, to have the resources and time to care for prisoners, even in war.

It was tempting to starve her, but he'd be damned if he let her be the better general.

"We'll get her a salad," he decided. "Piper, you're on guard. If she moves, there are plenty of mortals around. Use your flute."

The musician grinned, sharp and Fae even when disguised as a mortal. Michelle rolled her eyes while Jack shifted his feet. "Is that necessary?" the boy asked. "I mean, we've already got APBs on our asses. That type of magic is taken *really* seriously."

"I'm aware," Red Wolf said, irritated at the mortal for questioning him. "Which is why Piper will only use it as a last resort."

The boy squirmed, looking at Michelle. She shook her head. "I don't like it, either. Give me a bullet over that mind magic any day. But it'll keep her in line." She jerked a thumb to Violet.

"Yes, threatening civilians does work for a time," Violet said, twisting her aluminum chains around her fingers. It had been a mercy, not to get iron shackles, that Red Wolf was starting to regret. "I wonder what he'll order *you* to do with that flute, seeing as you two are 'just mortals.'"

Red Wolf slammed the doors in her face.

Michelle lowered her voice: "You brought a fairy musician with you knowing you were going to hire mortal mercenaries, but did nothing to protect those mercenaries from his magic?"

"Given Vlad's high recommendation of you, I didn't think you'd need them," Red Wolf gritted out. It wasn't a lie. Vlad had stressed how loyal Michelle was to her employers, thus making it less likely for Piper to need to directly control her.

"If you had told me in advance, then I would've been able to get the equipment. You didn't. You didn't even tell me what he could do until two days ago," she retorted, glaring at him through her red-tinted lenses. "If you want me to do my job properly, I need these details."

"You were told only what you needed to know," he said.

"Or did you not want us to have the ability to resist your man's magic?"

Oh, how Red Wolf wished he could lie, just this once.

Piper whistled. "Busted..."

Michelle nodded, shoving her shoulder into him as she walked past. "I never back out of a contract, Red Wolf. No matter how bad it gets. But there are no promises for after."

Jack scrambled to keep up with her. Red Wolf and Piper shared a look.

"Are we killing them after we get to the portal?" Piper asked, slipping his thumbs in his belt loops. He and Gold had both picked up a fondness for jeans, although Red Wolf was pretty sure Piper's were just a glamour. Gold, on the other hand, had spent a full day with Michelle's mercenaries purchasing clothes a few weeks ago, arguing that it saved them energy in the long run. They always got a little enthusiastic every time they got to visit a new country or Realm, no matter how serious the work was.

"...maybe," Red Wolf said.

"It's on a lake. Easy enough to get them to drown themselves. Or perhaps Crescent can manage it. He's never shied away from dirty work."

That didn't mean he enjoyed it. And Red Wolf would hate to order any of his followers to do something he wouldn't do himself.

"We'll see how they behave," he decided. "Watch the van."
He followed the mortals to the restaurant.

"...doesn't feel right," Jack whispered. Red Wolf slowed his
pace, his sharp ears picking up the boy's hushed conversation
with his employer. "If they don't respect us, why are we working
for them?"

"Because they've already paid us," Michelle replied lowly.

"So? We can give the money back and leave."

"That's a surefire way to start a shoot-out. We know too
much. We see it through."

"Violet didn't even do anything wrong!" he hissed.

Red Wolf bit back a curse. *Have you been talking to these
people, Violet?*

"She started a war, didn't she?" Michelle replied.

"Yeah, but she kind of had to. They were enslaving humans.
That's like her fighting for the Union, and we're working for the
guy who led the Confederacy."

"If you feel that bad about it, you can donate your share of
the money to charity," she said. "But we've already accepted their
payment. We've already got their target, and we're just a couple
hours away from being rid of her and them. Chin up and bear it."

Jack sulked as they finally got in line to make their order
for meals that would be more grease than food. Red Wolf considered him, then Michelle. Was it worth it, ordering her to kill
Jack now as a precaution...

His phone rang.

Rolling his eyes, he answered it. "We'll be in the Fae Realm
in three, perhaps four hours."

"Good," said the voice on the other end. "Just checking in.
Any fresh, nasty surprises today?"

"Besides the black market of Fae body parts being sold to
mortals?" he grumbled in Fae, getting a few odd looks. He'd
made sure to glamour himself with a plain, forgettable, human
face. "No, not for us."

"Keep me posted." She hung up.

"What's that look?" Michelle asked, as Red Wolf finished
his call and joined them in line. This building reeked of grease

and oil, and while the walls, booths, and tables were meant to look like wood, a single touch confirmed that they were plastic. At least it wasn't concrete.

"My...benefactor, I suppose you could say," he admitted. "She's wondering why we're behind schedule.

"Is she still going to pay you? And by you, I mean me?"

"Yes. Fairies don't break their word."

"Not on purpose, anyway," Michelle muttered, stretching her arms and back. Quite a few things popped, making Red Wolf grateful that his kind didn't age beyond maturity. He couldn't imagine a life so short, with half of it spent in a deteriorating body, rotting from within.

He hesitated. "I...apologize for Piper. I've been burned by mortals too many times to not have such security measures in place."

She gave him a measured look, then nodded. "Honestly, same. It's not the flute, or musician. You do what you've gotta do. It's the dishonesty that irritates me. And don't say fairies don't lie—you just can't say falsehoods. You can still lie by omission or half-truths."

"Very true," he admitted. He frowned, looking around. "Where's Jack?"

"Said he wasn't hungry, or feeling too well. Cited car sickness, but I think he's just got to deal with the music problem," she said. "No offense, but I cannot wait for this job to be over and I'm out of this state. Give me a warm beach, some mimosas, and a trashy romance novel."

Red Wolf blinked. "Is that all I needed to pay you with?"

"A *big* beach. With a five-star resort or private lodge."

"Ah." Red Wolf leaned against the side of the plastic-coated wall, enjoying the moment of peace, even in a chaotic, greasy place.

"What about you?" Michelle asked. "Once you're done with..." She jerked a tattooed thumb to the outside.

He should've been annoyed at the question. After all, it was none of her business.

But Michelle had proven to be a valuable resource, and Violet had always taught him to give one's subordinates at least a little respect. Disrespect was the first step toward revolt and rebellion—and he'd already committed such an act against her.

Funny enough, he didn't want to order her killed.

The question itself gave him pause. He'd spent so long pursuing this. After cleaning up the mess Violet had left in her wake, Red Wolf had spent decades begging the Ivaenian royal family to let him get justice. For the nation. For the Realm. For all the bodies he'd had to bury. But they'd refused. Perhaps it was because Violet was herself a royal and they didn't want to set a precedent, or there was still an inkling of love and familial obligation. Maybe they didn't want to expend the resources after losing so much to the human rebellions and wars. Maybe they feared retaliation from the mortal societies of Earth with which she had managed to ingratiate herself – especially since they were so much more technologically advanced than Gialdon, which had already humiliated them.

Whatever the reason, Violet had been allowed to live free from the consequences of the destruction she had wrought. And Red Wolf couldn't stand it. So, he'd resigned from his post, gathered his best and most devoted followers, and set out to get justice himself.

"I'm not sure," he admitted. "But I have quite a bit more time to figure that out."

Michelle shrugged in agreement.

"Well, I will be throwing a celebration," Black Dove announced, joining them with an armful of cheap, processed, mortal food. She was in her usual mortal disguise of a dark-skinned woman in a summer dress. "A big one, lasting at least a week with far too much food and alcohol."

"Hell, yeah," Michelle cheered.

Gold was right behind the sorceress, pale, slim hands wrapped around one of those coffee drinks, Alex on one side and Pete on the other. Given his failure at eliminating the baker the other day, he and Olson should've been flogged, cursed, or otherwise punished for the failure. But he'd left that decision up to Michelle, who had instead lowered his share of the money.

Alex grinned around the straw in her soda and admitted, "Boss, I think we created a monster."

"Can we grow these coffee plants back home?" Gold asked, vibrating between sips. "I see why Violet became a merchant of this stuff."

Red Wolf shook his head, smiling. Gold's simple joy was somehow infectious, and Alex—with her own love of food—had brought out more than Red Wolf usually saw.

No, he wouldn't be ordering any of these mortals' deaths. Not unless they truly gave him no other choice.

Michelle's phone rang. She answered it. "Linda? What's going on?"

"You have a problem," Linda said, quietly enough that Red Wolf had to strain his hearing. He straightened, immediately concerned.

"I have several problems. Can you give me the details on this one?" Michelle asked.

"That jean-jacket person is chasing you, with friends. And they stole my goddamn ledger."

Michelle hissed. "Ouch. Hope you've got it coded."

"Of course it's coded. The cops showed up and cleared out our headquarters, but we got away with luck charms to spare. We'll be fine as long as we lay low for a while. You and your friends, on the other hand, are in trouble if you don't handle that guy—and their clairvoyant friend, too. I managed to divine a place for you: Moose Lake Hospital. They'll be there soon. If you can get my ledger back, we'll call it even."

Michelle glanced up at Red Wolf, whom she knew could hear the call, even though it wasn't on speaker. He nodded.

"Consider it done," she promised, hanging up. "I think we can send at least half of my people to handle this. Preferably with a glamour to confuse any witnesses."

"I agree," Red Wolf said. "Send six to seven of your best to handle this problem. Black Dove will give you artifacts that will glamour you while you wear them. Discard them after it's done."

"Pete," Michelle ordered. "Your team's on this one. Call me when it's done, we'll meet up later. If you can actually hit your mark, you'll get your original cut."

Pete's grin was full of menace. "Oh, they're not getting away a second time."

ten million dollars

Violet waited patiently in the van, hearing Piper's shuffled footsteps and whistling just outside. Just because no one could hear within, didn't mean she couldn't hear without.

He stopped. "Back so soon?"

"I'll play guard. Go get yourself some food."

Violet raised her eyebrows. That was Jack.

"Sure you can handle her, boy?"

"She's chained to the floor of an enchanted van. I'll be fine," Jack replied. "Go before I change my mind."

"Touchy." Footsteps signaled Piper leaving.

Jack got in the front, separated from Violet by the mesh wire, and closed the door so not even fairy ears could hear them. He ran his hands through his auburn curls.

"Theoretically," he said, his breath shaky, "if you had an ally, how would you escape?"

Violet smiled. "Theoretically? I'd need Red Wolf's key for these." She lifted a foot, the sole prickling with heat in his absence. "As well as an opportunity—some sort of distraction, something that puts fewer guards on us. Alternatively, you could just call the police."

"And get arrested, too?" he demanded.

"A fair point. But I do want you to text someone. Theoretically, of course. They're not affiliated with law enforcement."

He hesitated, hand already going for his phone. "I still want that ten million dollars and protection charm. One that covers me and my family for the rest of our lives."

"If you help me escape, then you'll have both as soon as I can deliver them."

He gulped, knuckles white around his phone. "Okay. What about the wand?"

"Ah, yes, Black Dove might transform a few people into animals better suited to following us–"

"No, not that one. I mean the water wand," he said.

She paused. "Black Dove has an Elemental Water Wand?"

"That's what they said. Apparently, you have a fire wand, or something?"

"Not on me," she muttered, recalculating. "Ideally, we would disarm her during the escape, but I'd argue that Piper is the much bigger threat."

"Yeah...can't argue with that." He pulled out his phone. "Who am I texting?"

ivory swords

A few years after Martin Luther King Jr.'s "I Have a Dream" speech, Violet visited Lake Superior for the first time. There were endless state parks to choose from, a line of them going up the great lake's snout to Superior National Forest. She visited all of them, having to fight park rangers and tourists because she didn't glamour herself as a white woman.

The Northern states liked to believe they were morally better than their Southern neighbors, and perhaps they had fewer laws that were as blatantly racist as the Jim Crow codes. But they still believed in racial segregation and had no qualms about throwing rocks at a purple-skinned fairy. (Not that any of them hit their target.)

By the time she reached Silver Bay, the ranger was waiting for her, leaning against the wooden sign by the trail that cut through the trees. At least there was no one else here. Perks of doing this in the middle of a weekday.

"Park's closed," he said as she climbed out of her car. Clunky thing—she'd only recently learned how to handle it and got her license.

"That's not what your hours say," she replied, heading for the trail that led to the beach.

"Let me rephrase," he said, holding up a hand. "Park's closed to colored folks. Human or otherwise. If I let you in, tourism rates plummet, and then we'll be getting layoffs. You understand."

She made a show of looking around while gauging the threat before her. He was fit, in his early thirties, with at least one handgun visible on his waist. She wore only a yellow sun dress and sandals (and a few enchanted but glamoured pieces of jewelry), wanting to meet her real audience as a non-threat.

This ranger was no threat to her. But she indulged him, saying, "I don't see a 'whites only' sign."

"Doesn't matter," he insisted. "I've heard of you. Everyone's been complaining about the purple jick scaring off all the tourists."

Violet narrowed her eyes. "I really don't like that word. And why is my existence so terrifying when you have a dragon living on the lake, long before these parks ever existed?"

"We'll be shooting that dragon down soon enough. Until then, you need to leave."

She walked past him.

"Hey!" He grabbed her arm.

Within the space of a heartbeat, she twisted, pivoted, snatched his wrist and shoulder, and brought him to the ground. He coughed, dirt and leaves pushed away with his breath.

"For a nation supposedly built on immigrants and individual freedom, you do an excellent job of acting like a totalitarian regime," she commented. "It's disappointing, truly."

"Lady, you've just signed your death warrant," he snapped, trying to wiggle free.

"If you're going to use a proper address, it should be Your Highness, or Princess. I also accept Commander, although that's a little outdated." She let him go and stood, brushing off her dress. "I won't be long."

As soon as she turned her back, she heard the distinctive sound of a gun being pulled from its holster, right before two shots rang out.

The bullets hit the trees in front of her. Two of the pearls of her necklace slipped off, transforming back into their true form—beads carved from a Fae tree and enchanted with good luck—as they hit the ground.

She looked over her shoulder with a raised eyebrow. "Only a coward strikes someone in the back."

Still on the ground, he fired again. And missed. And another "pearl" slipped free.

Huffing a sigh, Violet marched back to him, ignoring his fourth and fifth shots. She knelt before him, took his wrist, and guided the gun to her forehead. His hand trembled, the hot barrel of the gun bouncing between her eyebrows.

"Go on," she said. "Try again."

He yanked on the trigger.

Click.

She smiled and pulled the jammed gun from his limp fingers. Hissing in pain (so much iron, *why*?), she glamoured the weapon, its form elongating and slimming down into a nine-inch needle. Luckily, the revolver had enough wood in the handle that she could give the needle a wooden end that wouldn't burn her fingers. She stuck it in her hair bun. "You'll get this back when you've earned it."

She left him pale and shaking on the forest floor as she left for the beach. The air was thick with the smell of fresh water and green, growing things. The sandy beach narrowed into a thin strip that cut through the water, leading to a tiny island that was nothing but red-rock cliffs topped with trees.

This was several years before Black Beach earned its name from the taconite tailings that were dumped into the lake by local miners. Such relentless contamination would cause a long, grueling legal battle between taconite miners and the fishermen who resented the pollution obscuring visibility in the water–to say nothing of the mermaids who lived in it. In the end, the fishermen won, and the tail-dumping was outlawed in 1980. After a little more time, all that black ore washed ashore, creating Black Beach. But we're getting ahead of ourselves.

Even with the cloudy water and lack of black sand, Silver Bay was a gorgeous location, and Violet was treated to a sight of endless water she rarely expected so far from the ocean.

Until a dragon flew overhead and landed on the sand next to her, the wind beneath its wings so strong it almost knocked over the nearby trees.

She smiled. "There you are."

Smoke hissed out from the dragon's teeth. It was surprisingly small, barely the length of a school bus, with gray scales that turned black on the wings, tail, and horns. A relatively young dragon, then. No older than four centuries.

"So, *you're* who all the rangers have been complaining about," they said, their voice a growl deeper than thunder.

Violet's smile turned into a beam. "And you're the one who's been making the murderers of shapeshifters and mermaids *mysteriously* disappear."

Lake Superior was deep enough to house a thriving merfolk community, and the forest was large and wild enough for various other shapeshifters and spirits to make their homes there.

Unfortunately, many humans tried hunting them for sport, or to kidnap the women for a classic animal bride. Such spirits always fought back, of course, and many would-be hunters never left the forest alive. But many more did.

However, in recent decades, there'd been an uptick in wildfires, with interlopers disappearing and presumed killed by such surprisingly contained disasters. More than one had been burned alive in his own home, the cause of his housefire inconclusive.

Mortal insurance investigators and firefighters hadn't yet learned how to track a dragon's trail.

"What are you doing in my territory?" the dragon demanded.

"Introducing myself," Violet said with a slight bow. "I've recently moved to the state, specifically Bernier, just south of the Twin Cities. I believe your territory does not extend quite that far, but I still wanted to properly meet my new neighbor. I've already met your sister Amyth and her spouse in Duluth. She makes *excellent* matzoh ball soup. Best I've had in decades."

The dragon gradually lowered their wings, and while tension remained in their shoulders, they straightened away from Violet, no longer overtly threatening. "That's...all you wanted?"

Violet shrugged. "I thought it wise to determine some ground rules now before anything becomes an issue later. Especially since I suspect many more Fae will be coming here, trying to escape the chaos of their original home."

The Fae Realm was rarely quiet. But with the advent of national and international television on Earth confirming the existence of fairies and Gialdon getting its hands on Earth weapons, it'd gotten even more explosive, the Fae countries deciding to once again try to destroy Gialdon and its allies before it became too powerful. Such a war would prove not only futile–as Gialdon emerged victorious a few years after CaFae Latte's grand opening–but extraordinarily destructive as more and more Fae nations got pulled into the fighting, and more and more people lost their lives and livelihoods.

Many of them–especially those of mortal descent, like dwarves and goblins and kitrye– decided to flee altogether to the only other Realm they could easily get to: Earth. And while some were acclimating to human cities, others were drawn to the wilder parts of the world, so much more like home.

The dragon shifted their wings. "Some of them are already here. Mostly part-fairies. So long as they don't bother the merfolk or skinchangers, they can do whatever they want."

Violet brightened. "Ah, yes. I heard you were their protector."

They shrugged, a somewhat sheepish look for such a mighty creature. "Someone's gotta look after them. And a dragon's gotta make a living."

Violet pounced on the opening. "What do you charge?"

"No more than a couple bucks a month. Except for the bookseller; she gives me a free book. Those who can't afford that owe me favors–something I'm sure a fairy is familiar with."

Violet tucked that information away for later. "Refugees aren't known for having many *bucks* to spare. I'd like to cover their payment for...shall we say, two months per head? To give them time to orient themselves."

The dragon tilted its horned, scaly head, coming closer. Tendrils of smoke came out of their nostrils, each the size of Violet's fist. "You got enough cash in that dress for that?"

"I was thinking a more magical trade. The state rangers want to shoot you out of the sky. How many times have the police tried to arrest you, or worse?"

The dragon bared its teeth, showing impressive rows of ivory swords. "Free meals are always welcome."

Violet chuckled. "I'm sure. But when they find your lair, they'll likely destroy it and everything within. *If* they find it."

The dragon considered her. "You're suggesting some glamour magic on my home?"

"I can bespell it any number of ways. One is that only you and anyone you invite can get there. Another is to have only those who have been there before be able to find it. Or perhaps only those who share blood ties with you?"

The dragon thought it over. "The first one. In exchange for covering any Fae settling here for their first two months. After that, they're treated just like everyone else."

"Done."

The dragon morphed. Its large scaly body shrank into a human's, though they kept the horns, wings, and tail. Black scales turned into pale skin and ebony hair that slithered around their shoulders. Even in human form, they were intimidatingly tall. Over six feet, not including the horns. A Star of David, large and carved in Nordic Viking style, hung from their neck.

"You got a nickname beyond 'Trespasser'?" they asked with a playful smirk.

"Violet. You?"

"Rethu."

rethu

JACK
violets calling an sos

RETHU
Who tf is this?

JACK
jack
a fairy called red
wolf hired my crew
to kidnap violet
he wants to take
her to fae
via wild portal
its on ur turf
black beach
opened recently i think?

RETHU
How many?

JACK
12 humans 7 fae

RETHU
Is Violet hurt?

                                          JACK

                                           no
                           she has magic boots
                       they hurt her if she runs
                        she says "do not kill"

RETHU

: (

                                          JACK

                         "bloodshed got us into
                           this mess. its unwise
                         to use it to get out."
                            "and i don't want
                            anyone else pulled
                             into my problems"
                       also I think she and RW
                          used to be friends?
                       idk I just don't want
                              you to kill ME
                                      or her
                            she's paying me
                                       a lot

RETHU

Fiiiine.
ETA?

                                          JACK

                               2.5 hr
                   but we might escape before
                         she says "if they
                           get there w/o me,

let them thru"
"if they get there WITH
me, then plz help"

quentin, roger, david, alex

                                    JACK
                        have you guys ever felt
                             bad about a job?
                            like killed someone
                             u wish you didn't

ALEX
JFC what's with you?
QUENTIN
First job's always
the hardest.

                                    JACK
                                   3rd job
                                      dick

QUENTIN
You didn't have a problem
with those other 2?
JACK
1st guy was a mob boss
2nd almost got m killed
didnt feel bad about
that until later
DAVID
I've been reading a lot
of stuff on the target
during her Fae Realm days.
A looooot of stuff.

I don't feel bad
about this. At all.
QUENTIN
Geek
ALEX
Nerd

JACK
but she changed
ACTUALLY changed

DAVID
So?
Just because SHE changed
doesn't mean anything
else did. She's way
worse than any
of us could ever
hope to be.

JACK
so is rw

QUENTIN
No, I've worked for worse.
"Worse" would've had
us using condoms in
the van w/target
ROGER
😵 😵 😵
DAVID
Yikes.
ALEX

Quentin!

QUENTIN

I didn't join that shit!
Just saying, there are
worse. We might as
well take their money
and make it quick.

messy

JC was pretty sure Nicole was doing some sort of spell, mumbling a mantra over and over again in the back seat as they sped away from the vampire manor, breaking a few speed limits on the way. JC didn't stop until they were at least two towns over and needed to gas up.

They pulled into a station. "Let's see the arm."

"It's not a bad break," Cyrus hissed, curled into the passenger seat.

Bull*shit*. He practically had a second elbow. And he'd shed about a bucket's worth of sweat since leaving the vampires' sight.

He swallowed, taking a steadying breath. "Nicole? You with us?"

She stopped her chanting. "Hm?"

"There's all-heal in the trunk. Grab it."

She got out. JC popped the trunk, intrigued. They'd heard of all-heal. Even helped smuggle it a few times. The biggest containers they'd seen were four-ounce jars worth almost seven figures.

The mason jar Nicole produced was *way* bigger. About a quart.

"Jesus fuck, how long has *that* been there?" they demanded.

"A while," Cyrus grunted, taking the jar. "Boss doesn't know how to make the stuff, but she has friends who do. Okay, this part's gonna suck."

"Why? Don't you just slather it on?"

"If I do that now, it'll heal wrong."

When JC realized what he needed to do, they really wished they didn't. "Seriously, dude. Hospital."

"That'll take too long. And I've done this before. I just need something to bite down on."

Swearing, JC shed their jean jacket, ignoring the painful twinge of their ribs. After a couple of folds, they shoved the denim into Cyrus's mouth.

JC asked, "Do you need–"

Crack!

They cringed away. Nicole jerked back, covering her mouth. Cyrus's scream was muffled through the jacket, but...well, the arm did look less fucked up. And no one outside the car had heard him.

After about a minute of heavy breathing, JC carefully pulled their jacket free of his teeth. "You good?"

"Yeah," he panted. "You can start slathering now. Shouldn't take more than a half-dollar coin."

"I have never seen one of those in my life."

"For fuck's sake, modern currency changes way too fast."

Nicole cleared her throat and made a circle with her thumbs and pointer fingers, about two inches in diameter. JC scooped out a rough amount and lightly, carefully rubbed it into Cyrus's arm, muttering apologies when he hissed in pain.

His pale blue, white-marbled skin absorbed the ointment faster than lotion. When it was gone, Cyrus tested his fingers, then twisted his wrist. After a wince, he scooped a bit more himself and rubbed it into the belly of his forearm.

Another test: wiggle fingers, rotate wrist, shake the whole arm. He pulled a pin from his hat that turned into a knife and flicked it around his fingers before nodding and sheathing the weapon. "Thanks."

"Yup. Cool. You're welcome. *Never fucking do that again.*"

Nicole nodded.

"Yeah, but..." He picked up a broken necklace from his lap. One of the ones Nicole had given them. JC hadn't noticed it fall from his neck. "I knew I'd get lucky."

She scowled, snatching the necklace. Cyrus closed the jar of all-heal and asked, "What about you two? Are you okay?"

Another nod.

"Ow," JC admitted, rolling their shoulder. "I bruised a couple of ribs and I definitely need some sugar."

"Do you have a concussion?" Cyrus asked, handing them the jar.

"I don't think so." They ran their fingers through their hair, shaking out a handful of wooden splinters, wincing as one of them jabbed their thumb. "No fewer brain cells than usual."

"I'll get you some OJ and Advil," he promised. He glanced back up at Nicole. "First knife fight's always the hardest. You did pretty good."

She managed a weak smile.

Cyrus left, disappearing into the gas station. JC spread some of the magic lotion over their ribs, relieved when they could take a full breath without fingers of pain scratching beneath their skin. The more superficial bruises vanished before their eyes, too. They got out to put the jar back in the trunk, then took the opportunity to shake the splinters and debris from their hair and clothes before leaning against the car with a sigh. Back when they'd been a teenager, they could get into drug-fueled brawls, take a dozen hits, and barely feel the bruises. Now, they needed a nap.

There were a handful of other cars and people in the station. Like true Midwesterners, they all ignored each other.

After retreating to the back seat, Nicole rolled her prayer beads in her hands, almost hiding the fact that they were shaking. JC expected her to resume her muttering, but she didn't.

"You, uh...going nonverbal?" they asked.

She nodded.

"Okay...want me to shut up?"

She considered, then shrugged.

"Okay." JC blew a raspberry, thinking, inhaling the smell of car exhaust and cow manure. They honestly had no idea which town they were in, but they were far enough from the Cities to be back in farmers' territory.

Cyrus was taking a while. They craned their neck and saw that there was a bit of a line for the register.

Eventually, Nicole started muttering again. It was the same words over and over, but JC couldn't tell what they were. They didn't think it was English.

"Is that a witch's spell?" they asked.

She shook her head. "Buddhist. Mantra. *Nam-Myoho-Renge-Kyo*."

"...huh." Good, she was verbal again. "Wait, I thought Buddhists were vegetarian."

"Some are. Nichiren Buddhists? Not required. Why I chose them. Partly."

"Ah." They cleared their throat. "Cyrus is right. You did really good."

"You got hurt. Both of you."

They shrugged. "Yeah, but that was more our fault than yours. We all got out alive. That means we did it right. Oh..."

They carefully peeled off the watch, which had also been relatively undamaged. There was a small scratch on the face, which JC pointed out and apologized for. Nicole shrugged, strapping it back on her own wrist. "That means it did its job. That and the necklace I gave you. I think if you hadn't been wearing both, you would've broken something a lot more important than your ribs."

She removed three more necklaces from her neck and handed them to JC, who gratefully took them.

"You don't happen to know any spells or charms that deal with diabetes, do you?" they asked, only partially teasing, more relaxed now that Nicole was back to using full sentences.

"I know a few spells and potion recipes that would bring general good luck and health," she offered, her voice stabilizing back to its regular flat monotone as her mind shifted away from the day's fresh trauma. She still gripped the prayer beads like a lifeline. "Maybe they would help you find a good doctor or treatment. But a specific cure for a disease? No. Getting rid of it with magic would require either a very powerful object–like a golden apple–or a trade of some kind with a being that can actually bend and twist reality rather than nudge it along like I can."

"You think Bob might be able to pull it off?"

"I think she'd have offered if she could. And besides, fairies don't really do healing magic. They have no need, being immortal and immune to disease."

"Cheaters," JC grumbled.

"Demons might be able to make such a trade," Nicole mused. "Or djinn. But their deals tend to be Faustian."

"Use dumb words, please. I'm not as smart as you."

"Sure, you are. You're just smart about different things," she said. "A Faustian bargain is a bad or short-sighted deal. Sell your soul for a life of pleasure, only to have an afterlife of torment. That type of thing."

JC snorted. *I guess I am smart about that.*

Nicole held up her beads. "I enchanted these. Physical health is tricky to magically manage, but mental health is easier. This helps me with my sensory issues and lets me recover from non-verbal episodes much faster. Stress can make everything too much. Prayer helps. Prayer with a magical artifact that takes the edge off helps even more. Did you need it?"

They shook their head. "No, thanks. That wasn't my first fight."

"And you've been to prison."

JC didn't know if Nicole's blunt, straight-forward approach to things was attractive or infuriating.

"Yeah, well, I was a shitty person before. Still kind of am, apparently," they said. It'd only been a day since Violet went missing, and already they'd made a drug deal, tried to bargain with an evil coven, and almost killed someone.

I guess people don't really change, they thought darkly.

"I don't think so," Nicole said, twirling her beads around her bare fingers, her gloves tossed haphazardly on the seat next to her. "If you hadn't been there, Cyrus and I could've gotten hurt, if not died. I don't think we would've gotten this far without your knowledge. And you've always been kind to me. That's why I asked you out and invited you into my home."

They studied the rust on the truck parked in front of them. "That's...pretty new. A few years ago, I was a lot closer to the kid Cyrus had to stab today."

"But you're not anymore," she stressed. "That's the important thing."

JC wasn't so sure about that. They liked to think that the past was the past, but that was a lie. No matter how deep they buried it, it crawled out and dragged them down.

Cyrus returned with orange juice, water, coffee, and several snacks ranging from healthy pistachios to double chocolate Pop-Tarts. He gassed up while JC guzzled the OJ and Nicole nibbled on some beef jerky.

"Okay. This Red Wolf/Harvest Moon guy wants to drag Bob back to the Fae Realm to...I guess torture her? For killing his girl?" JC summarized, once Cyrus had dropped back into the driver's seat. "I don't know any portals. All the ones I used to use are either gone or blocked up by police."

The airport, of course, was an option. But it would be much harder for Red Wolf to smuggle Violet through instead of a non-living thing like weapons or drugs. Since he'd shelled out half a million to the Stone Oaks for directions, he probably wasn't taking that option. JC sure wouldn't.

"He's probably using a wild portal," Cyrus suggested. "Those aren't as regulated."

"Risky, though," JC said, thinking of the handful of people they knew personally who'd gone through one of those and never came back.

Still, if someone was desperate enough...

"Nicole, can you divine something?" they asked.

"Violet's still blocked," she argued.

"So don't focus on her," Cyrus said. "Focus on us. What's *our* future?"

Nicole tapped her fingers for a moment before digging out her sketchbook, a tissue-filled jar, and a set of headphones. She dumped out the jar and peeled away the tissue, revealing some kind of cat skull, then opened her sketchbook to a blank page and said, "I need some hair again."

JC handed her a few strands, which she tied to the cat skull's eyes. "*Cat si*, or Fae cat," she explained. "Good for seeing the future."

She put on the headphones, put her free hand on the skull, and closed her eyes.

For a few seconds, nothing happened. JC glanced at Cyrus, but he pressed a finger to his lips.

Suddenly, Nicole started sketching. Trees. Rocks. Cliffs. A beach, with a narrow point leading to a rocky, tree-topped island.

What looked like a bat flew in the sky, way in the distance, and the sand was covered in fire and wolves.

JC was more impressed by the fact that she was doing this with her eyes closed.

Nicole tugged off her headphones and frowned at her drawing. "Not my best. The sand is supposed to be black. I don't know why, but that's what I saw."

"That's Black Beach!" Cyrus cheered. "Up on Lake Superior."

JC sputtered. "That's at least a two-hour drive!"

"Three and a half, to get to the park," Nicole corrected, tapping on her phone. "That's if traffic's good."

"Ooh, road trip," Cyrus said, before sobering. "I can drop one or both of you off at the nearest bus stop. Or get an Uber. This is going to get messy. You've both done enough."

JC and Nicole shared a look. JC wasn't afraid of "messy." That was their whole life. And those jerks had tried to shoot them; they didn't get to get away with that.

But Nicole was an art teacher. She'd never been involved in this type of thing before and probably shouldn't be now.

"Honestly, backing out would probably be the smart thing to do," they said.

She squeezed the prayer beads in her fist. "They don't get to kidnap my aunt and torture her because she chose to do the right thing. Because they choose to keep doing the *wrong* thing. I'm staying."

Well. You can't argue with that. And that blunt, straight-forward approach to things? *Sexy as hell*, they decided.

JC smirked and turned back to Cyrus. "The lady has spoken. Let's roll."

unknown number

Hey Hendricks it's Cyrus
Blue
Violet Smith's ward

                Hi. Found something?

Nicole's got a vision
We think Boss is being
taken to Black Beach

                Going that far up,
                I'm gonna need more
                than just visions.

FFS
Fine
We'll contact you
in a few hours

                You're not going there
                yourself, are you?
                ARE YOU?
                DON'T YOU DARE!

Move your ass then

one little fairy

Muttering swears, Officer Hendricks had to look up the police departments in and around Black Beach and Silver Bay. Like all rural precincts, it was a large area with only a smattering of people. He called all of them, letting them know the situation—and added Duluth to the list, too, because chances were good the suspects would pass through there. Fish and game wardens, too, because why not?

He wished he was doing this at his little desk down in Bernier, but he and Nelson had wound up in the Twin Cities, trying to go after that coven that Cyrus and Jennifer Charles had mentioned. The Minneapolis Police Department had been thrilled to finally have a reason to get a warrant that'd let them bust down the door to the Stone Oaks Coven.

But they'd been delayed by two flat tires, a civilian car crash, and the plague of all Minnesota roads in summer: construction.

By the time they'd gotten to the coven's base of operations, it was empty. They'd found the basement—which CSI was going through inch by inch—but nothing obviously illegal. No blood. No weapons. And the paper records had either been taken or destroyed. Hendricks pitied the poor department captain.

Speaking of, as soon as the local captain had heard that one of Hendricks and Nelson's suspects was a fairy musician, he'd all but thrown them the mutual aid paperwork so they could borrow the department's proper protective charms against such magic. Hendricks had been filling it all out, squirreled away in a corner of the large, tiled room crammed full of too-small desks, bustling officers, ringing phones, and piles of paperwork tall enough to rival the Rockies.

Then, Cyrus had texted.

"Black Beach?" Nelson argued as soon as he told her. "That's a three-hour drive, at least!"

"It's the only lead we have so far," he said. "The captain here is loaning us some equipment: enchanted earbuds. They also have enchanted earrings if that's more your speed. Typically used in undercover, but they're just as effective in stopping mind-control music."

Nelson ran a hand down her square face. "All this trouble for one little fairy. I swear if it turns out she was actually working with them..."

"I sincerely doubt she was," he drawled.

"You don't know that." She snatched a few of the files and sat with him at the corner desk. Every precinct ran on paperwork, and when they did decide to share resources or personnel, it was only made possible through far too many forms.

They were about halfway through when someone politely cleared their throat. Striped blue button-down, beaten up leather jacket, crew cut. "I'm Detective Swanson. Saint Paul police. Heard you two were hunting fairies?"

"Just the one who mind-controlled our town," Nelson said cheerfully.

"And kidnapped Violet," Hendricks added.

"Was it a group of seven fairies?" Swanson asked.

"At least seven *people*. We haven't yet confirmed that they're all fairies..."

Swanson pulled up a plastic chair, joining them at their table. "Pretty sure that's the group I've been trying to pin down for the last couple of months. They sold a ton of marmair seeds—the stuff that makes marbles?—to one of the local gangs, and one of our cooperating witnesses heard that they had a couple of wands."

Hendricks straightened. Enchanted instruments were bad enough, but they were packing *wands*, too? Those had been outlawed since the '70s, no exceptions.

"Can we talk to this witness?" Hendricks asked.

Swanson shook his head, mouth thinning into a tense line. "The fairies got to him before we did. Far as the doctors can tell, he's been cursed. Can't hear, can't speak, can't see, can't touch."

Nelson swore.

"Can you tell me about your case?" he asked.

Hendricks filled him in while Nelson finished up the paperwork. By the time he was done, Swanson frowned. "This whole thing was just to kidnap a single fairy? And *not* sell her to Stone Oaks for parts?"

"She really pissed off the Fae Realm," Nelson muttered.

"Are we sure she's not working with them? You said she's a sorcerer—maybe she helped them get or enchant their weapons and then they turned on her?"

"That's what I've been saying!"

"We have no evidence for that," Hendricks pointed out. "Why do you keep thinking she's a suspect?"

"She's a fairy," Nelson said, as if that explained anything.

"It's what they do," Swanson added. "The immortality goes right to their heads. Gives them a superiority complex like you would not believe. I get so many cases of curses, cursed artifacts, hexes, marmair, all traced back to them. If a fairy is involved in a case, they're probably at least partially responsible."

"Well, right now, all evidence suggests that Violet is unwilling, and I'd like to get her back before something happens to her," Hendricks stressed. "You're welcome to come with..."

"Oh, I will."

paul bunyan

Excerpt from *Fact & Fiction: A Study of American Folklore*

The myth of Paul Bunyan is a staple in Midwestern lore, with plenty of possible sources. Two of the most common theories are Fae in origin. One suggests that he was at least part giant, and possibly skilled in magical glamours as well. The other is that he was a regular human who somehow got his hands on an enchanted shirt, often called a "strongman shirt." This Fae item is enchanted to give the wearer the strength of anywhere from ten to a hundred men, depending on the skill and power of the sorcerer enchanting it.

snake lake

The stops at the gas station and restaurant created a slight delay and shuffle. Piper ended up in a different car. Black Dove had to enchant several objects for Pete's team before they could go take care of their pursuers, so she ended up staying behind while Red Wolf, Michelle, and Jack went forward in Violet's van, with a couple of other cars to act as escorts. She'd catch up with them shortly.

"If your baker had done us the courtesy of dying yesterday, your pet witch wouldn't be in danger," Red Wolf grumbled.

"It's poor taste to blame the victim," Violet scolded. She couldn't deny that she was a bit nervous. If Nicole and Jennifer Charles were trying to track her down, then Cyrus was almost certainly helping them. She was worried for Nicole, although she knew the young witch to be capable. And while she could admit that Jennifer Charles had surprised her with their previous escape, a dozen armed professionals would still be dangerous, even for Cyrus, who'd mastered his knife skills over the course of two centuries.

Don't worry about what you cannot control, she reminded herself. She would just have to trust in their skills while she got out of her own mess.

Because that mission against Jennifer Charles meant fewer guards and less backup on *her*.

Jack had told her that Red Wolf kept their van in the middle of the convoy: there was always at least one vehicle in front and one behind. The biggest issue was Black Dove's water wand. But as she was lagging behind, they had a five-minute window, one that dwindled the longer they drove. Considering they were on Route 35 heading north to Duluth, they should be right around...

"Yeesh, *another* lake?" Jack grumbled. "How many does this state need?"

Elm City, according to the signal the young mercenary had just given. The van rocked and bumped a bit as they reached the long bridge arcing over Snake Lake. As its name implied, it was long and winding. Any longer and it would be mistaken for a river.

The older roads went around the lake. But when the highway was built, the state had elected to build a bridge to go straight over the most narrow point of the water.

Violet smiled. "It's the land of ten thousand lakes, although two hundred thousand is a little more accurate," she lectured.

"Seriously?"

"This state has more shoreline than California and Oregon combined. If you include rivers and streams."

Jack gaped at her over his shoulder (*not* a signal or part of a script), then at Michelle in the passenger seat. "Okay, I know fairies can't lie, but can we fact-check that?"

The elder mercenary rolled her eyes as she pulled out her phone.

Red Wolf was the only person in the back with Violet, sitting on the bench across from hers, keeping one sword against his left leg for easy access. His ring–the key to her boots– winked at her from his right hand, while his two remaining good luck charms stayed on his left.

"Why here?" he asked, swaying with the vehicle's movement. "Why not this nation's capital? You could've had the entire country bowing to your whims within a few decades."

"I've had my fill of politics and bloodshed," she replied. "Haven't you?"

"Politics? Yes. But I'll be seeing a lot more blood before I'm done."

She sighed. "That's disappointing."

"I'll be damned," Michelle muttered at her phone. "She's right–"

The van gave that tell-tale bump and lurch, signaling the end of the bridge.

Violet shot up and kicked Red Wolf in the throat. He gasped, wheezing in pain as she grabbed his right arm—stopping him from drawing his sword—and brought him to the floor of the van, sitting on his back with his arm twisted behind him, her chain halfway wrapped around them.

"Hey!" Michelle barked. "Stop the car!"

Jack hit the brakes, almost sending Violet off her quarry. She rocked with the movement, focusing on keeping control of Red Wolf's arm behind his back, ignoring his grunts of pain.

"What's your plan?" he gritted out. "You can't unchain yourself."

"You let me worry about the plan," she said. Her wrists were chained too close together for her to both secure her prisoner and take the ring for her boots, especially as he clenched his hands into fists. She jabbed her thumb into his wrist, hitting a nerve that made the whole arm spasm and fist break, then used her teeth to pull the ring free from his finger, doing the reverse to put it on her own.

Enchanted boots were now neutralized.

Michelle and Jack rushed out of the van. There was shouting, and then cars honking and tires sliding, as well as the sound of gas hissing out of cannisters and a flash bomb.

Red Wolf glared up at her. "What did you do?"

"Relax. This is the version of the escape plan that *avoids* killing your people. Except perhaps Piper."

The lock for the back door unlatched. Violet jumped off Red Wolf, onto the bench, her hands awkwardly pulled to the side by the chain as the door opened.

Red Wolf sat up, going for his sword—

Jack tasered him.

The fairy jerked. Violet scooped up the sword and—trusting the smiths she had hired all those centuries ago to prioritize durability—bashed it against the lock on the floor of the van as Jack tasered Red Wolf again. "Hurry up!"

With a final hit, Violet's chain broke.

"I'm reclaiming your sword until you've earned it again," she said, hopping away from Red Wolf as he tried to swipe at her—failing, again, with another tase from Jack.

When she jumped out of the van, she saw a world of smoke and chaos. Cars honked. People shouted and screamed. Someone fired a gun, the shots muffled with a suppresser. She closed the van doors behind her, locking Red Wolf in. "How many smoke bombs did you use?"

"One flash, three smoke. I've got one more of each–"

Violet yanked Jack behind the van as Michelle appeared from the smoke, firing her pistol and hitting only air and metal. The gunshots were mere whispers, even to Violet's ears. Suppressors.

"Can you swim?" she asked.

"Yes!"

"Give us cover, then we go to the left. Three, two, one, go!"

He tossed his final flash bomb as the two of them sprinted across the concrete. Violet kept her eyes closed as the flash went off, but couldn't dampen the sound. Her pointed ears went completely deaf as she opened her eyes to find she and Jack were at the grass and dirt that sloped down to the water.

The bridge was too high to safely jump, but they could use it for cover as they climbed down as quickly and recklessly as they dared, Violet somewhat hobbled by her chains. Michelle had the keys, and getting them would have required a one-on-one fight that Jack had been adamant he would lose and Violet didn't have time to win.

Movement caught the corner of Violet's eye. Michelle had followed them, aiming her gun.

"Jack!" she warned.

The boy jerked to the side as Michelle fired. A line of blood trailed down his arm as he lobbed his last gas bomb, giving them a literal smoke screen as the two of them dove into the water.

recruit

"They're going west," Michelle barked, her voice tinny in Red Wolf's phone as Piper let him out of the van. "They've swum out of handgun range."

"How far behind is Black Dove?" he asked, checking himself for weapons. He'd lost one sword, but he had another, plus the taser he'd confiscated from Black Dove.

"Less than four minutes," Piper said.

"Hey! What's going on?" one of the mortals demanded, coming out of his car. The bridge was clogged with vehicles and people, confused and scared by the smoke and weaponry. Red Wolf counted at least three people on their phones, likely calling the authorities. The lake and road on either side of the bridge was crowded with forest, easy to hide and get lost in. Violet had chosen an excellent point of escape.

He had half a dozen fairies. That wouldn't be enough to take down Violet and escape from law enforcement. They'd lost the element of stealth, anyway.

"Piper, recruit some searchers," Red Wolf ordered.

fighting a defensive war

While its overall shape was long and winding, Snake Lake had something of an hourglass figure: thin at the point of the bridge, thick and unwieldy on either side of it. That was likely altered on purpose by humans, and Violet used it to her advantage, pushing herself and Jack to swim south and west, staying in the water as long as possible and reaching the fat, safer part of the lake very quickly. Well, safer until Black Dove arrived with her Elemental Wand.

Once her pointed ears finally stopping ringing, she picked up the distinct sound of flute music.

"That's Piper," she snapped, pausing and covering Jack's ears–almost smacking him and herself with the sword. "Stay under as long as possible, understand?"

He nodded, going under before she was done talking. Good to know he was just as keen on avoiding mind control as she was.

It slowed their progress, as Jack would stay under as he swam, but still had to breathe. When he did, he'd stop swimming, plug his ears, and dart up for a quick gulp of air before plunging back down, splashing hard and violently to further deafen himself. Violet kept a sharp eye over her shoulder, to the bridge of fading smoke and music as they got farther and farther away.

As they swam, Violet found herself in a conundrum. Houses poked out of the trees closest to her and Jack. Houses where she could easily find a phone and alert the authorities, who had magical charms that would protect them from Piper's enchantment.

Except there was no guarantee that Red Wolf and his people would walk away alive from that encounter. More to the point, houses meant people. Civilians. Who were unprepared and could easily find themselves under Piper's control as soon as Violet was tracked there. Or shot full of mercenary bullets.

The other option was to ignore the houses and keep going until they came across wilder forest, with fewer people, fewer chances of civilian casualties, and also fewer opportunities to call for help.

Except, the only reason she was hearing flute music at all was because Piper was already pushing his control onto the mortals on the bridge. That could not be allowed to happen. She had to stop it—now.

Violet pushed herself and Jack past the initial houses, until they hit a thicker stretch of trees. The flute music was distant to her pointed ears, which meant Jack couldn't hear it at all. She pulled him out of the water and onto the shore.

A falcon flew overhead. Violet narrowed her eyes at it, pulling Jack under cover of the trees. "How many bullets do you have?"

"Uh..." He pulled out his handgun and patted his pockets. "...shit. My spares must've fallen out. I've only got six rounds."

"Fine." She tugged on the enchanted leather cuff that Black Dove had put on her. She wouldn't be able to glamour herself with it on.

"Let me get that." Jack pulled a knife from his belt and slipped the blade under the leather.

It didn't budge.

He frowned, yanking. Any other bracelet would have been shredded to ribbons, but his efforts only bruised Violet's lavender wrist.

"It's unicorn pelt," she said, pulling her hand away. "You can't cut it with anything less than a blade forged in unicorn blood. Or one of their horns."

"Seriously? Fuck."

She eyed the falcon circling overhead, and pulled a few strands of hair from Jack's auburn head.

"Ow! What the hell?" he demanded.

The bird swooped down, meeting them at the shore, and glamoured into Black Dove.

Jack pulled his pistol and fired.

The bullet missed. One of the silver beads on Black Dove's ivory robes fell off.

"Save your bullets," Violet ordered, leaning her sword against her shoulder as she studied the other sorcerer. "You know the best thing about fighting a defensive war? You don't have to win. You just have to prove to the aggressor that it's too much trouble to keep attacking."

Black Dove scoffed. "Are you saying I have the disadvantage?"

"A 200-year disadvantage, yes."

"You have only a sword." Black Dove pulled a wand from her robe. "I have so much more."

It wasn't the druidic wand.

She waved it over her head, and the water from Snake Lake jumped at her command. Gallons and gallons of it flowed into the air, creating its own river that snaked around Violet and Jack before constricting.

"You'll have to push through that," Violet said, pressing Jack's hair to the leather cuff.

He sputtered. "Are you nuts? I'm not that strong! We're dead."

"Not yet. Just trust me."

She closed her eyes, reaching for the flow of reality—or rather, the flow of *Jack's* reality, accessible to her through the hair she'd taken. She let the hair held in her fingers guide her to her subject, and then melded it with the reality—or blueprint—offered by the leather cuff.

Her voice echoed and reverberated with magic, though only Jack could truly hear her: "You are a unicorn."

Jack yelped, then whinnied as his body grew and morphed. Auburn curls turned into auburn fur that covered his entire body, a few darker spots dotting his elongated face and flank like freckles. A horn sprouted from his head, thick, curved, and sharper than any blade. Within seconds, Jack the human was gone, replaced by Jack the unicorn.

"Your horn and teeth are venomous," she said, "or you could simply trample her."

Jack whinnied and burst through the wall of water.

Black Dove yelped. The water cage dropped, and where the sorceress had stood, a falcon darted away, flying around Violet—

She swiped at the bird with her sheathed sword, like a baseball bat. Something crunched, Black Dove shrieked and tumbled to the ground, wing crooked. If and when she transformed back into a bipedal fairy, that broken wing would become a broken arm.

Jack charged.

Black Dove turned into a snake—her injury moving from a limb to probably some ribs, or perhaps the tail—and slithered out of the way, biting at Jack as he trampled by. The fangs hit, but couldn't pierce through the impenetrable unicorn fur. She'd have to be a unicorn herself to do that, and if she did, she'd have a broken leg.

So, instead, she turned into a walleye and dove into the water.

Jack snorted, stamping his hoof. Violet held up her chained hands. "Help me with this."

Very carefully, wary of the venom in his horn, Jack snapped her chains, baring her wrists. Then the anti-glamor cuff.

Sure, the jailer's rune prevented everyone but Black Dove from *removing* the cuff, but not from breaking it.

She rubbed her free wrists, silently celebrating the victory before transforming Jack back into a human.

He staggered a bit, his weight distribution off. "Oh, that was *weird*."

She patted his back, internally congratulating herself for mastering the spell in a way that also glamoured the target's clothes as well as their bodies. "You did remarkably well. Most people vomit or pass out their first time."

"I can't imagine why," he hiccupped. "They've got all-heal."

Which meant Black Dove would be back to fighting form in minutes.

Violet nodded, tying the sword to her belt. She sat on the muddy, squishy ground and, with the jailor ring, removed those damn boots. And her socks, because one felt less foolish outside in bare feet than in just socks. "Do you have a way to disappear from the law and your former employers?"

"We're splitting up?" he demanded. "How will I get my protection charm?"

"You know where I live and work. Go."

Grumbling, Jack obeyed, sprinting into the forest. Violet stood, toes wiggling in the mud.

Glamouring oneself into an animal was more exhausting than glamouring someone else, the physical strain of the transformation combined with the magical energy required to make it happen in the first place. But it was doable and, on a technical level, easier than transforming someone else. Violet reached into that core of herself and twisted it, expanded it...

Feathers sprouted from her arms that twisted and bent. Her legs shrank and formed talons. And an eagle flew off the ground.

The transformation made her so dizzy she almost fell out of the sky. She had to blink spots out of her eyes.

I am far too out of practice, she thought, grateful she'd chosen an eagle instead of a dragon, which would have probably made her pass out without proper preparation. She wobbled in the air against the dizziness. No more glamours after this; she'd be limited to only the tools in her hands.

sheathed sword

From the sky, Violet could see the situation clearly: Piper had amassed every mortal on the bridge—at least fifty souls—to get out of the cars and head south. He would either use them to search for Violet or use them as hostages in case she didn't reveal herself. There were at least twenty children in the lot, their eyes as glazed as their parents' as they followed the music's commands.

Near the back of the mob were Red Wolf and four other fairies: Crescent, Gold, pink-skinned Crow Moon with the lightning boots, and the final fairy of Red Wolf's regiment, Mouse. The dark green fairy had obviously earned the name for his stature; he couldn't be more than five-foot-two. Violet eyed him warily. They hadn't interacted with each other, and she hadn't heard about any of his strengths or weaknesses. He was an unknown, and that made him dangerous.

She flew over them all, getting a good look at the battlefield. She positioned herself over Piper, in the dead center of the mob, dove down, and glamoured herself back into her normal form.

The musician had no time to look up before she bashed the heel of her sword into his head. Piper dropped, and the music abruptly stopped.

The effect was immediate. The mortals all startled, shaken out of the trance. At least two of the children began crying and screaming. Several adults whirled right around toward Red Wolf and his posse, furious.

Once she was certain that she wouldn't fall over despite two heavy glamours in as many minutes, Violet scooped up the wooden flute and held it up. "Really, Red Wolf. I'd have thought the war you lost would have taught you that this is not a reliable source of labor."

Red Wolf...did not answer.

She frowned at the man—the group of fairies who were suddenly so still and...off.

Glamoured.

Movement.

One of the humans—or rather, someone glamoured to look like a human—shot a taser at her side, sending pain and electricity ripping through her, bringing her down.

Chaos exploded. Some humans ran—especially those with children. Others joined in the fight, even without knowing who they fought. The one who tasered Violet went to pull the sword from her hands, only to get tackled to the pavement.

Violet yanked the taser wires out of her side, grimacing at the pinch of pain, and hauled herself to her knees. The bridge was a mass of bodies, and with everyone moving and fighting, it was impossible to tell who was glamoured and who wasn't.

Someone grabbed her shoulder and hauled her up, then tried to punch her in the face. She grabbed the fist and rolled him off her. Piper's flute was still on the ground, dropped when she was tasered.

She snatched it, hesitated only a brief moment, and blew into it.

Everyone on the bridge froze, the magic halting their movements until Violet stopped playing.

She sheepishly removed the flute from her lips. "My apologies, but this is just going to get more innocent people hurt. So: all mortals please leave the bridge so I can deal with the fairies who have been trying to kidnap me for the last twenty-four hours."

For a moment, no one moved.

Violet threateningly put the flute closer to her lips—as if she could make them move—and that got them going. More than one muttered "fucking jick" to her on their way out.

In the distance, police sirens sang, growing closer and closer.

Violet shoved the flute in her pocket and went over to Piper. Still unconscious. She stood over him as the mob moved away from the bridge, watching them all to catch any little tells of glamour. The ones glamoured to look like Red Wolf and the other fairies mercifully got their enchantments melted away as they left. Only five "mortals" remained on the bridge, and they quickly dropped their unnecessary illusions.

"Considering the time restraints, that was a very good trick," Violet said, flipping the sheathed sword around like a baton.

"Make this easier on yourself and come with us," Red Wolf said. His cell phone transformed into its true form: another sword.

"No. I've already attempted diplomacy multiple times. You leave me no choice but to escalate. Non-lethally, of course."

"You're outnumbered."

"Not for long. The local police may not have my restraint," she warned. "Many of them tend to escalate situations until they're needlessly harmful or fatal—and their steel is just as fatal to us as iron."

He smiled. "You're severely out of practice with your glamour. Otherwise, you'd already be gone."

Violet frowned, and only then registered a slight, growing roaring.

Down the river, water grew and grew into a massive wave, with Black Dove balanced on top of it.

All-heal worked quickly. Her arm didn't look broken at all.

Then the wave and its sorceress surged forward at tremendous speed, carrying her to the bridge.

Violet braced herself, but it wasn't enough. As soon as Black Dove was deposited on the concrete, she sent a powerful stream of water smashing into the elder sorceress, sending her down the bridge and into Red Wolf's clutches.

Gold swung his baton, trying to knock Violet out. She blocked with her sword, blinking water from her eyes as she kicked them in the leg and jumped to her feet.

Crescent took a swing with his own sheathed sword. Violet blocked, pivoted, and tripped him up. Mouse and Crow Moon rushed her, and she darted away, running up the nearest car's trunk and roof—

Only to get slammed by a wall of water again, bringing her painfully back down to the pavement.

Violet shook the water from her face and eyes, re-categorizing the threats. Black Dove needed to be out of the picture if she were to stay free.

Mouse met her as she ran down the length of cars, using them as cover to get closer to her target. No weapons, the little fairy came at her with fists. She deflected the blow with the sheathed sword, sending it into the car.

His fist crumpled the metal.

A quick glance at his silver shirt made her guess, "Strongman enchantment?"

He grinned and went to grab her.

She darted away. So long as he was wearing that enchanted shirt, he'd have the strength of a hundred men.

Whoever they have funding this little campaign has quite *a bit of wealth, magic, or both*, she thought, sprinting down the length of cars to get away from the strongman.

He picked up one of the cars like it was kindling and threw it at her.

She hit the ground, cringing as the car smashed into the roofs of the two vehicles on either side of her. Glass rained down on her hair and chest.

"Don't kill her!" Red Wolf snapped.

"I didn't! I just trapped her."

Mouse came up from behind. Violet had to crawl to get away, glass cutting her arms and hands on the gravel as she went. But that wasn't the enchanted item she was worried about.

Between one blink and the next, the pink-skinned Crow Moon appeared before her, with her distinctly Fae boots. "Hello," she said with a grin.

"I hate lightning boots," Violet admitted.

Crow Moon kicked her in the face, sending her head snapping backwards and bloodying her nose. It happened far too fast to block or dodge.

Flat on her back, Violet wiped the golden blood from her face. Crow Moon leaned down and reached for her.

Violet waited for her to get close before snatching her hand, twisting, and bringing her down to the ground, just like with

Red Wolf. "The funny thing about lightning boots is they only work if you're on your feet."

Crow Moon tried to throw her off, but Violet smashed her head into the ground once, twice, three times until she was out. Concussed, possibly with a cracked skull, but not dead.

The car next to her moved, Mouse hauling it aside. "Found her!"

Violet rolled away, forced to go on the sidewalk between the cars and the bridge rail—a narrow path that Black Dove took full advantage of, blasting her with more water and sending her careening back several feet, almost back into the lake.

By now the police sirens were deafening. She almost didn't hear Red Wolf holler, "Get her to the damn van!"

Violet hauled herself to her feet, only for Mouse to finally grab her from behind, reeling her in a bear hug. Her arms were pinned, sword useless. Dragging her was easy. "Grab Crow! She's out!"

Crescent and Gold—finally having picked their way through the jungle of vehicles—went to the unconscious Crow Moon while Mouse ran, unimpeded by Violet's weight as he sprinted for the van. She waited a handful of seconds, getting used to the rhythm of his body, before slamming the heel of her muddy foot into his knee.

Mouse staggered, almost dropping her. She braced herself with one heel on the ground and slammed the other into the arch of his foot—breaking one of the bones—and then into his knee again. He gasped in pain, but still didn't let go.

Strong and *stubborn*, she thought, both annoyed and impressed. She slammed her heel into his knee a third time, breaking it and making it bend the wrong way. *That* finally made him drop her.

She gave him another roundhouse kick for good measure, sending him into the ground with a fresh bruise on his cheek, before running the opposite direction, ignoring Crescent and Gold dragging Crow Moon between them. Red Wolf and Black Dove had gone for Piper.

No, Violet thought viciously. *That one stays.*

Red Wolf sensed her coming first and dropped the musician. As Black Dove straightened, going for her wand, Violet threw the sheathed sword. It hit her square in the forehead, sending her stumbling back, dazed.

Red Wolf met her with his sheathed sword. She snatched his wrist and tried to kick, only for him to grab her leg and toss her behind him. She rolled with the movement, pavement licking the skin off her back and arms, before popping back up closer to Black Dove than Red Wolf. She hit the sorceress on the side of the head to keep her dazed and down before returning to her former student, trying to send a palm strike to his neck.

He blocked, grabbed her arm, and tried to twist her as she had done him. She moved with him and kicked his shin. He grunted in pain, letting go of her arm but staying in a defensive position. Some corner of her mind was very pleased, remembering times where they had used these moves on each other while sparring and training. He'd kept up with them.

"Go home, Red Wolf," she ordered. "And leave Piper. He's the price you pay for the pain you've brought."

"And what about *my* pain?" he demanded.

"See a therapist about it."

He swung again.

BANG!

They both jolted. One of the car door windows shattered from the bullet.

A thin drop of pale gold blood went down Red Wolf's arm as one of his good luck rings slipped off his finger. It broke in two when it bounced on the pavement.

Violet glanced at the police cars blocking off the bridge, at least one officer out and pointing his gun at them. She smirked at Red Wolf. "I told you."

She turned her back on him and held up her hands, even going down on her knees. Red Wolf and Black Dove shared a frustrated look as more police poured out of their vehicles, ordering them to put their hands in the air.

Black Dove turned into a duck and flew off while Red Wolf sprinted for the van. Violet watched the police give chase, forced to do so on foot with all the abandoned cars blocking the bridge. They quickly lost sight of their suspects.

When one of the police officers came up to her, she motioned to the unconscious Piper. "There's your musician."

"Sure," one of them said, pulling out a pair of cuffs. "You're under arrest."

the ghost

Excerpt from *Round-Ears: A History of
Gialdon and Humans in the Fae Realm*

After the shocking death of Lady Oak, rage against
the Violet Princess skyrocketed. She was officially disowned and removed from the royal line
of succession. Cries for her to be subjected to *iom cof'mihun* and even execution were heard from all over the kingdom. Even [the fairy nation of] Nudach, which had been
considering officially joining the war on the side of Gialdon against their long-time enemy Ivae, instead stepped
back. The official reason given was that they could not ally

363

with anyone who could so casually kill so many immortals. (They still offered aid in the form of weapons, magic, and food, but all those deals were private and largely secret.)

The King of Ivae sent out a decree stating that any mortal who could bring the Iron Witch to him—dead or alive— would be granted their freedom, and any immortal would be granted a place in his royal court. Multiple assassins, professional and amateur, went on the hunt for the Violet Princess.

She mailed their severed heads back to the Ivaenian court.

The Battle of Leighi Hill (officially re-named Oak Hill almost immediately after the battle) had not just been a random act of cruelty or heat-of-the-moment murder. It had a significant place in the larger strategy of the war. The Violet Princess's actions so shocked and enraged Ivae that Gialdon and the mortals were considered far less important. When given the choice between stopping the Gialdons from resupplying or chasing after the last sighting of the Rogue Princess (as she had collected a new title), almost everyone chose the latter, giving Gialdon more opportunities to strengthen itself. She made it easy for her hunters, as in addition to getting into deadly fights multiple times a week with would-be assassins, she also continued to use her Fire Wand to burn the homes of Ivaenian officials, storerooms that Gialdon couldn't get to, monuments of Ivaenian heroes, and more—though thanks to her skill and control over the flames, she never hurt a civilian unless they attacked her first.

Tracing her path from Oak Hill to the end of the war is extraordinarily easy, far more so than trying to trace her precise or even general location before the battle, and that was on purpose. She hadn't grown sloppy. It was a diversion. And it worked.

Commander Rat recruited the surviving mortals from Oak Hill into his own army, a force that grew by the day. Sorcerers such as Sunrise and Sunset did their best to undo the damage done to those suffering under the aftereffects of mind control and were largely successful, incidentally starting a whole new field of mind medicine that Sunset has continued to grow and explore ever since, earning the new name of Mind Healer. Indigo, a notorious mortal thief and kitrye who joined Gialdon soon after the Violet Princess, led raids on multiple rich Ivaenian homes, stealing their most valuable possessions and freeing any mortals they had. Coral and Aster smoothed over the ruffled feathers from their foreign allies, claiming that the Violet Princess had gone against Gialdon's orders. (This was a misdirection, as it had been planned by both her and Commander Rat days if not weeks beforehand. While it damaged their reputations among foreign nations in the long-term, it kept [the fairy nation of] Riada in the war long enough to ensure Gialdons' survival. [The giants of] Famhyr had no complaints about Oak Hill and didn't need any soothing.)

By the time Ivae's forces had finally managed to pin the Violet Princess against the Red River, it was too late. Commander Rat led his enlarged and formidable army after them, pinning them to the river. The Violet Princess burned or collapsed every bridge she could reach, forcing the Ivaenians to attempt to move upstream, to one of the few remaining bridges that would allow them to cross, but it was a two-week march even in peacetime.

The Violet Princess became the Violet Ghost, using her invisibility cloak and glamour to sneak behind enemy lines. First, she destroyed any magical items that would lead to a hasty escape: boats glamoured into smaller, more easily transportable objects, cloaks of flight, and water-dresses (essentially the Fae equivalent of snorkeling equipment). As this was a land force, there were few of these, most of them in the possession of the officers and elite. The Violet Princess destroyed as many as she could find, isolating the force. Then she started killing officers and military musicians, as well as set fire to supply tents so they ran out of food.

In what became known as the Nine Days' Campaign, where five battles were fought between the Ivaenians and Gialdons, the Violet Ghost carried out eleven assassinations, most of them at group meals and meetings. Many Ivaenian officers abandoned their soldiers, using their own magic and enchanted artifacts the Ghost hadn't found to make a hasty escape.

Although Harvest Moon—who had succeeded his slain wife as Chief Commander—wanted to keep fighting, his soldiers, officers, and supplies had been badly depleted. Harvest Moon was abandoned by his under-officers, who went to Commander Rat under a flag of truce and declared their surrender. Chief Commander Harvest Moon was forced to flee, as he believed (probably correctly) that Commander Rat's mortal forces would kill him if he refused to cooperate.

The Nine Days' Campaign was the last major battle of the Gialdonian War of Independence. Aster and Coral—now elected Speaker and Chief Counselor in the first ever Gialdonian Senate—were sent to the King of Ivae to negotiate. The peace treaty was drafted over the next week and signed within the month. Among its terms, Ivae recognized Gialdon as a sovereign nation and would never again enslave its people.

Senators Aster and Coral tried to make Ivae no longer enslave any mortal ever again, but the Silver King refused to put that in the treaty. "You are a sovereign nation now. But you are not *my* sovereign nation. And any of my mortals who flee to your territory ought to be returned to their rightful land."

"Their rightful land is Earth," Speaker Aster retorted. "Since that is not possible, they will be free for as long as they are on free soil, regardless of their origins."

After quite a bit of back and forth, Speaker Aster's words made their way into the treaty, and it was eventually signed.

Pictured *the Silver King is presented with the heads of assassins sent to kill his granddaughter, the Violet Princess.*

buy yourself some mercy

The officer hauled Violet off the bridge, to the line of police vehicles, and leaned her against the door of his car. He made a face at the golden blood on his hands, smeared from the cuts on her arms, and wiped it off on his pants. He was a big, blocky man, with crew-cut blond hair and *Rogers* stitched into his uniform. Violet memorized it and his badge number.

Hands newly cleaned, Rogers patted her down, pausing at the flute in her back pocket. "What's this?"

"I took it from Piper, the unconscious fairy," Violet explained as Rogers examined the little flute. "He was using it to mind-control the people on the bridge."

"I'm sure he was," Rogers said, voice dripping with disdain. "You used this?"

If she wasn't already in handcuffs, Violet would have told him the truth. Every detail. But she *was* in handcuffs, and he clearly was not interested in anything she had to say.

So, she replied with, "I'm not answering any other questions until I get a lawyer."

"It'll go easier and faster if you just tell me."

"You should've thought of that before you arrested me." She tipped her head. "What have you arrested me *for*, anyway? You haven't said."

"Right now? Possession and use of illegal Fae instruments. That can land you in prison for life, so I recommend you start talking."

"Summon my lawyer, then," Violet said, leaning more heavily against the car as the bridge was taped off and witnesses rounded up. "His legal name is Blue Johnson, although these days he goes by Cyrus. I can tell you his phone number."

He was never going to let her hear the end of this, but that was fine.

Rogers had the flute bagged as evidence as police continued to swarm the scene. An ambulance arrived, the EMTs jumping out and being led to Piper, rousing to consciousness on the bridge. Violet couldn't see much through the cars, but she could hear bits of conversation: "head injury," "probable concussion," "arresting you..."

Rogers flagged down one of the EMTs to see to Violet's arms, a Somali woman with a hijab who winced in sympathy as she got a closer look. "Well...this'll take some tweezers."

"Make sure you bag up whatever you pull," Rogers said. "You knocked that other fairy out, didn't you? Did you two have a fight over the flute?"

Violet ignored him. She rolled her shoulders before the EMT got started, the cuffs digging into her wrists, slick with lake water and her own blood. They were tighter than what Red Wolf had used.

Another police car joined the madness just as Piper was cuffed to a gurney and rolled toward the ambulance, three people piling out. One was in plain clothes, a detective's badge hanging from around his neck over his pale blue button-down. The other two were officers: a square-chinned woman with a severe ponytail, and an oval-shaped man with skin the color of bread dough, whose eyes quickly found hers.

"Violet!" Hendricks called, hurrying to the police vehicle that she leaned against.

She gave the trio an amused smile that quickly turned into a wince as the EMT pulled out a piece of glass. "Officers Hendricks, Nelson. You're far from home."

"So are you. Hey, why is she cuffed?" he asked Officer Rogers.

"She's a suspect," he answered. "Report was that a fairy was using music to puppet everyone. She even had the flute in her pocket."

"What?" Nelson demanded, glaring at Violet.

"I took it from Piper," she corrected. "Something that I've already told Officer Rogers. I only used it once: to get everyone to stop fighting each other in a mob."

"So, you used mind-control music," Nelson bit out. "That's illegal."

"Do you have any other injuries?" Hendricks asked.

"Scrapes and bruises," Violet said.

"Good. We'll be taking her, then."

Rogers shook his head. "Not possible. That's my suspect—"

"She was kidnapped. That makes her the victim."

"*Was* she?" Nelson asked. "Violet, *were* you kidnapped?"

"Yes," she said. "When I refused to go along with Red Wolf, he had Piper use his magic to take control of every mortal on Main Street. If I continued to refuse, he'd make them kill each other. They pulled the same stunt just now, until I managed to get the flute away from Piper."

She grunted.

"Lots of witnesses say you knocked him out after turning into a bird to get over his head," Rogers said. "If you could do that the whole time, how'd you get kidnapped in the first place?"

"For starters, they had hostages. If I resisted, Piper would control any mortals around him and make them hurt each other, so I had to be careful. Secondly, glamour—and any other magic—is like a muscle. It's only as strong as you practice it." She grimaced. "And I am, unfortunately, embarrassingly out of practice. Thirdly, they placed a cursed object on me almost immediately. It's down by the riverbank with the fire-sole boots, and it prevented me from utilizing that kind of magic on myself. And finally, I'd hoped I could talk my captors into letting me go and dealing with their inner turmoil in a healthier manner. Obviously, that didn't work."

Nelson lit up. "You know the people who did this?"

"Their leader, yes."

Hendricks grabbed his pad and pen from his pockets so fast he almost dropped them. "All right. Start from the top."

She talked for a long time. By the time she was finished, her arms were bandaged, Rogers had uncuffed her, the EMT had her bundled in a towel with a bottle of water, and most of the other witnesses had been questioned as well. It was well after five o'clock, but the summer sun wouldn't set for another few hours.

"I didn't know you could play a fairy flute," Hendricks said as she rounded out her statement.

She gave a self-deprecating smile. "Only the note for 'cease and desist.' Beyond that, I'm rather hopeless at music."

The officers all tried to hide their relief, but Hendricks failed rather miserably. "So, with the exception of Piper, all the other suspects are still at large?"

"Yes. And Michelle sent some of her people to 'handle' Nicole and Jennifer Charles, who are most likely with Cyrus."

He hissed a sigh. "I told those idiots not to go after you..."

Violet raised an eyebrow. "How did you know to come north, Officer? Did 'those idiots' perhaps give you a tip?"

He paused. Glared at her. "Not the point."

"Mm-hm. The good news is that the order to send so many of the mortal mercenaries away gave me an opening to escape."

"What about this Jack kid? Where did you say you sent him?"

"Nowhere in particular."

When she didn't say anything else, Hendricks pressed, "Finding him will really help us get the people who took you."

"I don't know where he went." And she had purposefully given him his orders to flee without a clear destination so she could say that. "But he was rather low in the hierarchy and wouldn't know much, unlike Piper."

"Well, let's hope you didn't scramble his brains with that hit you gave him," Hendricks muttered.

"Swanson's going to want to know more about those wands that Black Dove's carrying," Nelson said. "Where is he, anyway...?"

"Questioning Piper, I believe," Violet said, pointing at the other ambulance, where their detective—Swanson—had wandered off.

One of the officers' radios cackled to life. "Officer Hendricks, do you read?"

He stepped away from Violet to take the call. Far enough that a human wouldn't be able to hear, still too close to a fairy. "Hendricks here."

"Sir, we just got a call that two Bernier residents and one of our persons of interest has been arrested in Moose Lake. They were involved in a shoot-out in a hospital. Multiple casualties."

Violet kept her eyes on Nelson as she eavesdropped. What had those three been doing in a hospital?

Hendricks gaped at the radio. "Would those arrests include a fairy, a witch, and an ex-con from St. Paul?"

"Yessir. Locals are trying to figure out if they were victim or perpetrator. There are a lot of bodies to sort through."

That wasn't good.

"All right, well, I found our kidnapped fairy, but most of her suspects are still at large," he said. "We're only half an hour out from Moose Lake, so we'll go check it out."

"10-4."

He went back to Violet. She didn't let him speak before accusing, "You didn't ask if they were injured."

"If they were dead or taken to the hospital, they would've told me," he assured her. "The quicker we get moving, the quicker we can sort this out."

Not as quickly as I can.

Violet handed her blanket to a passing EMT and went to the other ambulance, blatantly ignoring Hendricks, who hurried after her.

Swanson was grilling Piper from where he was cuffed to the gurney, just outside the ambulance doors, but the fairy said nothing.

"Red Wolf has a cell phone," Violet interrupted. "I need the number."

"Hey, I'm interviewing this suspect," Swanson snapped. "And you're still in custody—"

"On what charge? Officer Rogers's claims have already been disproven."

"I need her," Hendricks added. "Something else just came up."

"And Red Wolf may want some way to contact us to negotiate your release," she said to Piper. "Of course, he *did* leave you behind after using you as bait, so perhaps not."

Piper rubbed the bump on his pale yellow head. He spoke in Fae: "I didn't realize that was his plan until it happened, that sneaky little..."

"The police will lie to you, but I won't and can't," she continued, sticking to English and ignoring the outraged looks from

Swanson and Hendricks. "They will be far more lenient with you if you cooperate with them. The easier you make it for us to ensure Red Wolf doesn't endanger more civilian lives, the easier you make it for yourself."

Piper glanced at the officers. Hendricks kept his face blank, while Swanson and Nelson did nothing to hide their fury.

She lowered her voice. "You mind-controlled dozens of their people. Twice. We both know how mortals retaliate against that."

The musician blanched, no doubt thinking of the burned cities and mutilated fairy bodies produced by the Gialdonian War.

"Buy yourself some mercy and give me a phone number," she said.

Piper swallowed and gave her a number. Hendricks jotted it down, and Violet ensured it was the right one, Piper saying, "That is the number to Red Wolf's cell phone. Yes, he should have it with him."

"Good," Violet said. "Tell the police nothing, except 'I demand an attorney.' Mortal law is a complicated mess, but that lawyer will make your life easier—if you listen to them."

"That's not necessary," Swanson argued.

She motioned to the detective. "See? Liar."

"Right," Piper squeaked. "Good to know."

Violet rejoined Hendricks. "May I borrow your phone on the way to Moose Lake?"

"Only if you put it on speakerphone and let me record," he said, leading her to his vehicle. "You ever consider becoming a cop or detective?"

She almost laughed. "I spent enough time enforcing immoral laws in the Fae Realm. I don't need to do that here."

fresh holes

"Can we hit a hospital?" JC asked, checking their blood sugar and wringing out their pricked finger. "I need insulin."

"Will they just give it to you?" Nicole asked.

"Yeah, but it's expensive." They glared at the high numbers. "I should've grabbed some when they arrested me..."

"Yeah, how dare you not think you'd be spending hours in a car chasing after fairy kidnappers after being shot at and arrested," Cyrus teased.

JC yawned, glancing at the time. Almost five. They remembered when they spent all night with their gang and friends, sometimes getting high, sometimes just causing trouble, got home around dawn, slept for an hour, and then popped up fresh as a daisy for work. Now a single night in lock-up and a couple of firefights made them want to take a nap. And they weren't even thirty!

A small hit of marbles would keep me from falling asleep, they thought, watching Nicole stretch in the mirror. They shook their head to drive out the intrusive thought.

They found a hospital three exits later, the road cutting through the thick trees. At first, JC worried that maybe it was too small, even if it did have an ER. It was the only building on the street not made of wood or designed to look like a rustic cabin, instead using big, smooth bricks. The sign above the door was still a bit dinged up and read *Moose Lake Hospital.*

"You guys can stay in the car," JC said. "I should be in and out."

"If you're sure," Cyrus said, leaning back in the seat. Nicole had already pulled out a book from her purse.

Inside was just like any other hospital waiting room: bland walls, uncomfortable chairs, magazines older than JC. The waiting room was small, with the receptionists' desk big enough for three people, quietly guarding the hallway to the labs and patient rooms. Two receptionists worked the front desk: one battling a mountain of paperwork, the other sucking down a water bottle. The drinker looked up at them. "Hello. How can we help you?"

"I'm diabetic, I'm on a road trip, and I'm running low on insulin," JC said, pulling halfway out of their jacket and rolling up the t-shirt sleeve to reveal the cordless pump.

"Ah. Are you experiencing any symptoms?" she asked, clicking away at her computer.

"Not yet." They handed over their insurance and ID.

She frowned at it. "Why is there an X for your gender?"

And here we go, JC thought, circus music filling their head. "I'm non-binary."

"I need to know if you're male or female."

"You should be able to just pull up my previous prescriptions. The pump does all the work for me."

"I still need to know."

JC huffed, annoyed. "My doctor might need to know what's in my pants, but you don't."

She gave them a nasty look, then went back to clicking at her computer. "It's going to be a while."

They raised a skeptical eyebrow at the small waiting room, which only had two guys in the wood and cloth chairs–neither of them visibly sick or injured. "Really."

"Small town. Not a whole lot of doctors on staff. I'll print out your paperwork for you to fill."

"Great," they said, false joy dripping from their voice.

Clipboard in hand, they scoped out a spot on the other side of the waiting room from the two guys. Joy of joys, they got to fill out their long history of drug abuse: marbles, cocaine, crack, a bit of alcoholism, yes, they smoked (and would love a cigarette right about now, maybe blow it right in that nasty receptionist's face)–

"You in a rush?"

They looked up. One of the two men had spoken to them, leg crossed over his knee and leaning his chin on his hand. T-shirt, bright orange hunter's vest, jeans, beer belly. Since the guy next to him also had a hunter's vest, JC would bet they hadn't had the best time out in the wilderness today.

"Sort of. Road trip," JC said, only half a lie. "I just forgot to pack more insulin."

He snorted. "Seems kind of silly. Don't you need that to live?"

"Well, yeah, but this is the first trip I've taken since getting diagnosed." They'd gotten their diagnosis a year or two before leaving prison. The guards had been in charge of giving them insulin—when they felt like it. If JC got into a fight that day, or talked back, or even looked at them funny, the prison hospital suddenly didn't have any room or time for them today. Check back tomorrow.

"Where you heading? North?"

"Yeah...checking out Lake Superior. Never been." That, at least, was true. They'd barely stepped out of the Twin Cities their whole life, usually only leaving to visit relatives they'd only heard of once or twice, mostly through Facebook posts. They went back to their paperwork, but decided to be polite and ask, "What are you in for?"

"Waiting for you."

They looked up just as he pulled a hidden pistol from his waist and fired.

The bullet went into the plaster behind them, and one of Nicole's charms slipped off JC's fingers.

The receptionist screamed. JC threw their clipboard at the shooter. The pen followed as his friend pulled a shotgun out of nowhere, and JC sprinted for the door.

A shotgun blast shattered the wood by JC's head as they crashed through the door, bursting outside to find Cyrus darting out of his car. Three more people armed with guns emerged from the parking lot. One of them aimed at JC.

They hit the deck as they fired. The shot went overhead.

"Olson!" someone cried behind them.

JC looked over their shoulder to see the shotgun-handler fall, bullet in his chest, blood sprayed across the floor and chairs.

His friend immediately went to his side, then glared outside. "You moron!"

"Sor–" The killer's apology was cut off by Cyrus's knife flying into the back of his head. He dropped.

JC pulled their gun out of their pants and fired into the building. Their shots hit, the remaining "hunter" going down with a couple of fresh holes in his chest.

Hoo, boy. Haven't done that in a while, JC thought. It was different with the vampires, who had only been bruised. Actually killing someone? That hadn't happened in seven years.

They army-crawled closer to the corpses, retreating to the cover of the building. They sat beside the door as Cyrus deftly dodged bullets, going for cover behind a car that quickly got shattered windows, glass spraying everywhere.

One of the remaining two shooters–a woman–ignored him, going instead for Cyrus's car.

Nicole, JC realized. They aimed, but the shooter was out of range.

"Hey!" they shouted, standing, leaning out the door and trying to get her attention.

It didn't work. She fired at the witch, shattering the back window.

JC couldn't see anything through the spray of glass and metal, but they thought they saw the car door open on the other side.

JC dropped their pistol and snatched Olson's shotgun, pulling it from his limp fingers. There was one more slug in the double-barrel.

Cyrus was playing cat-and-mouse with his shooter, who had a rifle and seemingly endless stream of bullets. He ducked and wove through the maze of cars, getting closer and closer.

Nicole was nowhere to be found, and her shooter was getting closer to the trunk of Cyrus's Toyota. Sure, the witch's charms could make bullets miss, but if you were only five feet away, even that wouldn't do any good.

JC pumped the shotgun, aimed, and fired.

If they'd been ten, twenty feet closer, they might have been able to take the shooter's whole leg. As it was, the slug only shattered her knee, sending her spilling onto the pavement with a cry.

JC reclaimed their pistol, dropping the shotgun—no time to dig for bullets from the other corpse—and ran to check on Nicole. Cyrus's shooter finally ran out of ammo, and the fairy darted out from the front of a car and threw two daggers in quick succession. Shooter went down.

The woman with the leg injury saw JC coming and raised her rifle, bracing the butt of it against the pavement. JC's handgun rose, tracking—

Thwack!

The shooter jerked as if struck, bracing her elbow against the ground. Her rifle was yanked out of her hands, as if by a ghost—

Nicole pulled the hood off the invisibility cloak, locs falling out of their ponytail. She tore off her glove with her teeth and touched the woman's head.

"Are you all right?" JC asked Nicole, keeping their gun trained on the woman.

Cyrus answered instead. "*No.*" The fairy glared at the broken windows of his car. "I just paid it off last month."

"Ha. Sucker."

"They're from Red Wolf," Nicole said, pulling away from the woman who glared at her. "Mercenaries. All of them are glamoured. There should be six of them."

JC frowned. "I only count five: two in there, three out—"

A car revved and careened toward them, tearing through the parking lot. The three of them barely dove out of the way as it smashed into Cyrus's car, grinding the shooter Nicole had touched under its wheels. The mercenary didn't even have time to scream; blood and bone splattered against the pavement as the metal of Cyrus's car crumpled, and every remaining window broke.

"Seriously!?" Cyrus cried.

JC was by the rear of the attacking car—an SUV, big enough for six—while Nicole was closest to the driver. The driver who stuck a gun out the window and fired at her.

The witch jumped as three shots went her way, but none of them hit. Good luck charms fell from her hair, neck, and fingers like golden tears.

The final mercenary—a woman—fired again, swearing, and more charms fell. JC scrambled to their feet, picking their way around the wreckage to get a good angle.

Nicole marched toward the mercenary, barely blinking as the shooter fired again, and again, and again, each shot going wide, until Nicole was barely ten feet from her.

Click.

The gun jammed.

Nicole reached into the car. The mercenary snatched her arm and slammed her head against the door.

"Hey!" JC barked, almost there. Blood gushed from Nicole's nose.

But the mercenary didn't try to finish the job. As JC pulled Nicole away, the mercenary slammed on the gas and sped off, tearing into the street and making for the highway.

Cyrus joined them. Nicole clutched her bleeding nose. "She goes by Rachel," she said, sprinkling blood with every word. "Glamoured. She's been too far from Violet for me to know anything else with so little contact."

"It's fine. You're *nuts*," JC said, hysterical laughter threatening to bubble out.

They looked around at the carnage: Cyrus's busted car, three corpses outside and two inside, and at least four busted cars. "We, uh...we should probably call someone."

imply or mislead

All the hospital staff had survived, the two receptionists taking cover behind the desk and calling the cops. While they waited for the sirens, JC came back in, stepping carefully over the bodies and blood pools and said, "Insulin, please. I'd rather not slip into a diabetic coma while being questioned."

The receptionist took them in the back to see the doctor immediately, who refilled the plastic pod of their pump with shaking hands. Newbie. JC knew multiple doctors, nurses, and pharmacists who'd been held at gunpoint in the Cities for their drugs. They barely took a fifteen-minute smoke break before going back on shift.

At least the staff didn't ask for JC's billing info, so at least they got some free healthcare out of this.

Cyrus and Nicole met them in the parking lot, the witch's bloody nose stuffed with tissues and enchanted prayer beads firmly in ungloved hands.

"We've got a problem," Cyrus said.

"No shit," they retorted.

"Your gun, JC. As soon as the cops see you with it, it won't matter that you were defending yourself. You're on parole."

"...*fuck*." They glanced at the hospital. Small town, sure. But they still had security cameras in the lobby and outside. "Think the cameras missed that?"

Nicole perked up. Cyrus shook his head. "Not likely."

"Damn," they grumbled, choking back their fear. Missing curfew because of a crappy bus schedule and cute girl was one thing. With an unregistered weapon, they were absolutely going back to prison. And while they'd come to terms with being bisexual and nonbinary while behind bars, they sure as hell hadn't advertised it. They could try to go back in the closet, but chances were good that Rocket and his friends would spread the word.

Being the "sissy" in a men's prison meant constant beatings at best. And JC was not one to hope for the best.

"I might be able to talk them out of sending you back to prison," Cyrus continued, partially pulling JC out of their spiral. "Unusual circumstances and all. But..."

"Won't work. One month into my halfway house, one of the guys I shared a room with went back to prison for two grams of coke. Illegal carry? I'm done."

Fuck. Fuckity fuckity fucking–

"JC, give me some hair," Nicole ordered, her voice coming out clogged. "Cyrus, come up with a lie."

He sputtered. "I can't lie!"

"But JC and I can, and you can imply or mislead. The only proof is the cameras, right?"

"Yeah..." JC said, tugging a couple of strands from their brown head. They didn't think the receptionists had seen them pull out their handgun.

"So that's all I need to fix."

"You can use magic to fuck with security cameras?" they asked, handing over the hairs.

"I can use it to manipulate luck. And if that can make bullets miss, it can keep you out of jail," she said. She pulled a few rings from her fingers–she was running out of bling–and tied them together with JC's hair. She covered the new charm with both hands. "Jennifer Charles will remain free."

Reality gently popped.

When she opened her hands, all the rings were broken amid the coils of brown hair. She tossed them into the black void of her purse.

"Tell them you got the gun from one of the mercenaries," Cyrus said. "It was probably unregistered, anyway."

"Ammo, too?" JC asked.

"Yeah. They were wearing gloves, so it makes sense for their fingerprints to not be on it."

Four police cars raged into the parking lot, almost running over one of the shooters' corpses. JC sighed. "This'll be fun."

§

The police separated JC, Cyrus, and Nicole for questioning, keeping them in different hospital rooms. They'd given Cyrus's version of events, JC immediately surrendering the gun. More officers explored the area while at least two went to look over the security footage. A few others took pictures. Corpses were covered in tarps. The parking lot was completely taped off, and JC hoped that nobody in Moose Lake needed this hospital for the rest of the day. Or maybe the week.

They hid their anxiety by checking their insulin pump, despite having just filled it. They would've vastly preferred being outdoors so they could smoke, but that was an active crime scene, and smoking *inside* a hospital just seemed like a dick move. Everyone's doors were open, and the hallways were small and narrow. Behind the officer questioning them, they could see Nicole in the room across the hall, tapping her fingers against her prayer beads and gently rocking back and forth.

Adrenalin's still fucking with her head, JC thought with a sympathetic wince. Hopefully one of those good luck charms would be enough to let her dodge the trauma.

"Can I see your ID?" the officer asked, a woman who'd introduced herself as O'Brian and had taken JC's statement with no outward judgment. Most Minnesotans had some Scandinavian ancestry, but this woman looked like she'd stepped right off the Viking ship, swapping her helmet for police blues.

Knowing what was coming, JC handed it over. O'Brian took out her cell phone, probably sending JC's name in a text to whoever was in the cop car with the computer full of criminal records. Then she handed it back.

One of the cops that had gone into the back room for the security feed knocked on the open door, looking frustrated. "Virus got into the system. The last ten minutes are completely wiped."

JC hid their relief with a cough. *Nicole, you beautiful bitch.*

O'Brian's phone dinged. She pulled it out and raised her eyebrows.

JC snorted. "Would it help if I said I'm clean now?"

"Maybe."

They showed her their sobriety chip. She handed it back. "What are you doing so far from St. Paul, anyway?"

"Road trip," they said. "We want to see the forest, up by Superior."

"Hm." She shared a look with her colleagues. "The other witness still saying it happened differently?"

"Yup," he said.

JC frowned. "Other witness?"

"The one outside."

"Outside..." They bit back a swear. "You mean the one who tried to run us over and bloodied Nicole's nose?" They thought she would've gotten as far away from the crime scene as possible, not stick around.

"According to her, you guys started firing, not the hunters, and she tried to stop you," O'Brian said.

"That's the ballsiest lie I've ever heard. You see how many guns those guys had?"

"Do you know why these people are after you?" she asked.

JC hesitated, then decided on truth. "Nicole's clairvoyant. She got her hands on a couple of them, and said that they're working with the people who kidnapped my boss, a fairy named Violet Smith. I guess they thought she wasn't enough?"

That caught her attention. "The one taken with a fairy flute?"

JC shrugged. "I guess. I wasn't there, but that's what I heard."

"You're saying your attackers work with a fairy musician."

"According to Nicole's clairvoyance, which hasn't been wrong yet."

"And that they, for whatever reason, decided to track you down in the middle of bumfuck Minnesota to kill..." She checked her notes. "A baker."

They held up their arms, helpless. "I have no idea, lady."

Well, that wasn't quite true. They were trying to rescue Violet, and these guys probably came to stop them. The question was, how did they know the three of them were going to be here at this exact time–

The answer hit them as soon as they thought of the question: if JC and Cyrus had a witch, why not the bad guys? Hell, the Stone Oaks Coven had seen them coming from over a mile away, and they probably weren't too happy with them, since Cyrus had stolen their little black book.

"Hm," O'Brian said. "Well, the fact is, there's no video proof on who started the fight. I think you're a lot more involved in this jick flute–"

"Whoa."

"–business than you're letting on. And all three of you have records while our fourth witness doesn't."

"All..." They looked back at Nicole through the door. "All three of us?"

"Until we can figure out who's telling the truth, all four of you are under arrest," O'Brian said. "Put your hands behind your back. You have the right to remain silent..."

cardboard shields

Officer O'Brian squeezed all three of them into the back of her car and drove to the Moose Lake police station. JC was squished in the middle, with Nicole on their left and Cyrus on their right. Being in the middle wasn't necessarily fun, but while Cyrus was trying to fold himself so he wasn't brushing up against JC as much, Nicole pressed her leg and arm against JC's. They sure as hell didn't complain.

O'Brian had asked them if they had any more weapons on them, so Cyrus had had to surrender all of his knives-turned-pins. Dozens of them filled police evidence bags; they'd actually had to call the station for more. All but his "too ace for this shit" and the little coffee pot on a stack of books had proven to be knives. Nicole hadn't mentioned her good luck charms, probably because they weren't technically weapons, so those stayed on.

Another cop car drove behind them, holding the woman who'd bloodied Nicole's nose. The mercenary who apparently went by Rachel. At least Nicole's nose had stopped bleeding, though her face was still stained with dried blood.

"...okay, I get Cyrus," JC said, watching the street lights go by outside. "He's annoying and frankly way too good with...cutlery."

They had to be careful with what they said. O'Brian was undoubtedly listening, and she probably had some sort of camera or recorder in the car. (At least, cops were *supposed* to have those.)

"I am not annoying," Cyrus protested. "Also, most of my arrests were for Fae Rights Movement stuff, back in the '50s and '60s. I haven't been in cuffs since...the '90s? Yeah...pro tip, don't try to drink a werewolf pack under the table. You'll get into some gnarly shit."

JC snorted. "Learned that the hard way, but, yeah, that makes sense...what's with your face?"

Cyrus was wrinkling and twisting his mouth and nose. "My nose itches."

They winced in sympathy. It never failed: as soon as those cuffs went on, you got an itch where you couldn't reach.

"Wanna use my jacket?" they asked, offering their shoulder.

"You mind?"

"Nah, go for it." They let Cyrus rub his blue nose on their jean jacket as they turned to Nicole. "What I don't get is what did *you* get arrested for? They said you already had a record."

She crossed her legs, casual and comfortable despite the arms chained behind her back. "George Floyd protests."

"...ah." They could see that. She'd probably made a really beautiful sign, too, either of Floyd's face or a splash of swirling color behind a BLM slogan.

Much as they respected that, JC had never been in a protest. They didn't see the point. Those pretty signs were only as good as cardboard shields against bullets and legislation.

"How many times have you been arrested?" she asked.

"I've lost count," they admitted. "They just love seeing me in handcuffs."

Nicole looked them up and down. "Well, they do look very good on you."

JC's brain stalled as their face went hot enough to cook an egg. Cyrus finished his scratching with a groan. "Gross. No more talking. Especially with the cops in earshot. At least until the lawyer shows up."

They frowned, brain going back online. "Cyrus, *you're* our lawyer."

"Not when I'm arrested, too!" he scolded. "A lawyer needs to be able to run around, do research, gather paperwork and argue in front of judges, all that jazz. I love your faith in me, but I can't be in two places at once. Luckily, I know a few people who can represent us. But they're probably not going to get here until tomorrow morning, at least."

"What about Aunt Violet?" Nicole asked.

He shook his head. "We're just going to have to trust that she can handle herself."

§

Moose Lake's police station was even smaller than Bernier's. JC had been in houses bigger than this. And it was made of old crumbling brick that looked one stray sneeze away from collapsing on everyone.

The three of them were led out of the car and into the building by O'Brian and a couple other officers who came to help. O'Brian's partner pulled up next to her in the lot and pulled Rachel out, also with her hands cuffed behind her back. She was a redhead, with crow's feet and wiry arms.

They went through the usual: fingerprinting, mug shots, getting the first and last names. The cops asked for their middle names–they always did–but they all refused to give it. If the mercenary's true name was Rachel, JC would eat their jacket.

All of them were relieved of cell phones and other electronics, including JC's insulin pump.

"Hey, whoa, that's a diabetic device," Cyrus argued.

"We'll measure your blood sugar and administer the insulin as needed," O'Brian said, sounding bored.

"Doesn't matter. Leave the device."

"Shut up." She took the pump. Even Rachel made a face at that.

JC wasn't surprised. They knew several diabetics who had almost gone into comas and some who had even died while in custody, even though police weren't supposed to deny them medical devices, medicines, *food*...

Cyrus shrugged. "Welp, that's gonna be a fun lawsuit. JC, I accept check, cash, and/or snacks."

"Sold," they said, instinctively moving to cross their arms, but couldn't. The cuffs were still on. Still, they tried to hide their fear while asking, "Can't you just truth serum us?"

"We don't have any in stock," O'Brian said, not looking up from her paperwork. "It'll have to wait until tomorrow, maybe later. Probably later, since tomorrow's Sunday..."

They gave a frustrated sigh.

Another cop showed up carrying a box. He muttered something to O'Brian that made Cyrus glare at them.

"How the hell did you get your hands on an invisibility cloak?" O'Brian asked.

"You searched my car?" he countered.

"Yeah."

"Without a warrant?"

"You were involved in a shooting and tied to a fairy flute. That's reason enough. How'd you get the cloak?"

"It's my adopted mother's. Should be registered under Violet Smith. Don't tear it."

"These things are barely legal."

"It's not a wand or enchanted instrument. So long as it's registered, it's fine."

"But she was the one wearing it, not you," Rachel argued, motioning to Nicole.

"Yes, I put it on when your friends started shooting at us," Nicole replied, her monotone voice flatter than usual.

As O'Brian wrote in her stack of papers, JC met Cyrus's eyes and silently asked, *All-heal?*

Hidden, he mouthed back.

That much all-heal? Yeah, JC would put that in a secret compartment, too. Or maybe it was like the tip jar, invisible except under specific circumstances.

O'Brian finished one bit of paperwork and moved on to the next. She flipped through JC's wallet. "Why is there an X for your gender?"

"I'm nonbinary," JC gritted out. "They/them pronouns."

She rolled her eyes. "You're going to be a snowflake about this, aren't you? You went to a men's prison, right?"

"That's what it says on my paperwork."

"Then you're in the men's cell."

Cyrus raised a hand. Well, both of them, since he was also still handcuffed. "If you're separating us strictly based on penises and vaginas, you should know that fairies are not-so-technically unisex."

Nicole nodded while JC sputtered. "What?"

"Yeah. Every fairy can get pregnant *and* impregnate others—barring any medical issues."

"Like sea slugs," Nicole offered.

"Exactly!" he cheered.

"Sea slugs can do that?" Rachel asked. JC shrugged in response, completely out of their depth.

O'Brian blinked. "That makes no sense."

"Why not?" Cyrus replied. "We're not human, so why would we reproduce like you?"

"Should I have been using other pronouns?" JC asked.

He waved off their concern. "Nah. We're pretty sure that fairies adopted some of the human ideas of gender when we bumped into your Realm however many thousands of years ago. It's basically a fashion trend that never went out of style. Of course, different cultures within the Fae Realm have different ideas about it, having anywhere from one to dozens of recognized genders..."

"Okay, the snowflakes get to be in the men's cell together," O'Brian interrupted. "The lady gets her own cell."

JC relaxed. "Sounds good, as long as you keep her" - they motioned toward Nicole - "away from the woman who tried to kill us, all right?"

"Yeah, that works," Cyrus agreed.

"*You* tried to kill *me*," Rachel insisted. JC snorted. They had to hand it to her, she was dedicated to the bit.

The redhead was pulled into one interrogation room, and the three of them in another. They were uncuffed. O'Brian promised someone would be with them shortly, and then left them alone.

JC rubbed their thin wrists. Cyrus claimed one of the chairs and leaned back so the first two legs were in the air. Nicole took the other, finger-tapping on the table and rocking back and forth. O'Brian had also taken her prayer beads, saying that because the beads were all different colors, they were a security risk. "It's how gang members identify each other," she said. Which, as an ex-gang member themself, JC knew was total bullshit.

"You're still wearing my good luck charms, so you shouldn't die," she said. "Not soon, anyway."

JC touched the remaining chain necklace. They breathed a little easier. "...right. Thanks."

She nodded. "Those cuffs have been on a lot of people."

"Obviously."

"The last one to wear them was a drunk driver. He kept trying to flirt with O'Brian. Badly."

At JC and Cyrus's looks, she shrugged. "My gloves slipped, so the metal hit my skin a couple of times."

"Did you at least get some good one-liners?" JC asked, grateful to latch onto the lighter topic.

"He kept saying that she looked just like his first wife, but 'even hotter.' It was hard to read her face, but I don't think she was interested."

They snickered, shaking their head. "Man, even I know not to compare girls to previous dates. Bad form."

"He was drunk," Cyrus pointed out.

"That's no excuse. I could flirt so much better while drunk and high off my ass when I was a teenager. Hell, just off the top of my head: 'Nicole is magically good-looking.' 'She's enchanting.' 'She makes Glinda greener than the Wicked Witch of the West with envy'..."

"Okay, the first two sucked, but that's a good one," he admitted. "Now, stop talking. They're probably listening."

"Yeah, yeah..." JC sat on the opposite chair.

The silence was annoying, but not awkward. The evening dragged, the adrenaline faded, they started yawning and Nicole eventually stopped stimming, though JC couldn't say how long it took.

Just as JC was wondering if the cops had forgotten about them and was ready to stake out a spot on the floor, O'Brian came back into the room with a couple of other cops, who stayed by the door. She had three thick folders in hand. "Wow. You three... hell of a rap sheet."

"We're not talking until we get a lawyer," Cyrus said.

"That's fine. I'll just talk." O'Brian sat at the table and opened the first folder. "Let's see...Nicole Walker. Disorderly conduct."

What a weird way to describe peaceful protest, JC thought.

"Don't know why you're hanging out with these people," O'Brian mused, opening the second folder. "Mr. Blue Johnson. You couldn't have come up with something more original?"

He shrugged.

"Drunk and disorderly, lots of disorderly conduct, a few assault charges…but really, that pales in comparison to you, Mr. Scott. Which is saying something, considering the age gap."

JC's stomach sank as O'Brian opened the final folder. "You just got out. Served six years of a fifteen-year sentence for illegal possession of a firearm, drug possession, and of course, voluntary manslaughter. Though, let's be real, that was actually a murder."

JC glared at her. Out of the corner of their eye, they saw Nicole glance between them and the file. Their stomach sank further.

"So…" O'Brian left the file open as she put it on the table, revealing the paperwork and one of the crime scene photos: a body bleeding on the sidewalk from two chest wounds and a head shot. "Considering that you were holding a handgun that was not registered to anyone—in blatant violation of your parole—"

"I got it from one of the bodies," they argued.

"—why don't you tell us what actually happened?"

"We did."

"Lawyer," Cyrus added. "Now."

"That's going to take time. This will go much faster if you just start talking."

None of them spoke.

"You said you were going on a road trip," she tried. "Why aren't there any suitcases or packed bags in your car?"

They were quiet.

"What about Violet Smith? You said she was missing."

JC and Nicole both turned to Cyrus, willing to follow his lead.

"Call Officer Hendricks in Bernier," he said. "Last I checked, he was the one heading that investigation."

"Investigation into what? What happened?"

"We maintain our right to remain silent, and for an attorney."

O'Brian tapped a fingernail against JC's file, next to the photo of the bloodied corpse.

Someone knocked on the door and poked their head in. "O'Brian. We got a call. I think you'll want to hear it."

She stood, the metal chair shrieking against the floor. "Get them in lockup. We'll deal with them in the morning."

an honorable fairy

Michelle drove the van recklessly out of Elm City, then slowed to something less likely to draw attention once they reached the endless stretches of farmland and forest. Red Wolf was in the passenger seat, glaring at the scenery. The forests were thicker in the north, almost tricking him into believing he was already home. Black Dove tended to everyone's injuries in the crowded back, going through half of their limited supply of all-heal. She'd already used a bit on her arm, which had been broken by Violet. She'd gotten it down to a hairline fracture before arriving on the bridge, and now it was fully healed.

Michelle's phone pinged. She glanced at it, then pulled over. "Fuck. Fuck!"

"Please tell me it's good news," Red Wolf groaned, knowing it wasn't.

"Pete's whole team just got fucking slaughtered!"

"The ones we sent after the baker?" Black Dove confirmed.

She gritted her teeth. "Rachel just texted me: 'Targets alive. Team dead. Police here. At Moose Lake, probably about to get arrested.'"

Another cheerful *ding*. Michelle huffed, visibly calming herself down. "'Gonna try to put blame on targets, get them arrested, too.'"

Red Wolf leaned back against his seat. It was a nice sentiment, but with Violet free it was only a matter of time before that trio was released, as well.

"What do we do now?" Gold asked, squished and folded between the other fairies.

Crow Moon sighed, wiping the pale gold blood from her pink forehead. "I hate to say it, but we might have to retreat back to Fae."

Black Dove glared at her. "Don't even say that!"

"We've lost Piper! That was our best leverage."

Red Wolf bit back the guilt that rose up. He'd known Violet would go after Piper. But he'd had every reason to believe they'd be able to contain her *and* recover him. Piper should be complaining to him about the headache while Black Dove put all-heal on his injury, and Red Wolf would swear to make it up to him—and he would.

Now, though, he didn't know if he'd ever see his friend again. And it was his fault.

"She got help from one of the mortals," Crow Moon pointed out. "That won't happen again."

"We sure about that?" Mouse asked, jerking his chin toward Michelle.

"Jack won't get away with this," Michelle promised, voice eerily calm. "As soon as my business with you is done, I'm hunting him down. His mother and sister, too."

Crescent scoffed, gray hair lashing with his movement. "We're supposed to believe that?"

"Dove, you got a truth potion?"

The dark sorceress studied her. "No, but it doesn't matter. What good are you and your people if you can't even handle a single mortal baker?"

"Are you forgetting the *im*mortal fairy that was probably with them? How about the witch? They're all clearly more dangerous than we thought."

Red Wolf's phone rang.

He expected to see the usual number from the Fae Realm, but paused when he didn't recognize it.

All of his contacts were the people on his team or those he'd hired. He hadn't given the number to anyone else, not even companies that Michelle had warned could and would "spam him into oblivion."

He answered it. "Hello?"

"How is your retreat going?" Violet asked.

He glared at the phone as he switched it to speaker. There was no reason to try to keep it private, not in a car full of fairies. "I never took you for a coward, Commander. An honorable fairy would have met their fate without flinching."

"There is no justice in your vision, Red Wolf. There may be some if you turn yourself in, as you worked with Piper to traumatize the people of this Realm. But I'm willing to let that slide, as none of them died or got truly hurt."

"How generous."

"Go home," she pushed.

"Not without you in chains."

There was a long beat of silence on the other end. It sounded like she was driving, or at least in a car. Red Wolf's van was even quieter, everyone listening.

"Do you remember when you first came under my command?" she asked. "I asked you what you wanted to do with your life. What were your ambitions, your vision for your future. Do you remember what you said to me?"

Red Wolf swallowed, her words bringing him back. He didn't know if his younger years were truly a simpler, happier time, or if he just hadn't run into the world's cruelty yet. "'I am a poor musician born to great ones. There's not much room for ambition.'"

"And then?"

He paused, struggling to remember. It had been centuries ago. Before Oak, before Gialdon, before two hundred years of grief and rage and frustration. He did recall that she'd been very amused by his statement, being the youngest child of a youngest child herself, with no hope of ever getting the crown and little chance of glory, ambition a useless and dangerous sentiment for her.

He hadn't expected to bond with the formidable, intimidating Violet Princess, someone so high above his station and already making a name for herself. But they'd found so much in common and gotten along so well...

"You said, 'A good home, some friends and family, and the satisfaction of making my corner of the Realm a little better and brighter," Violet said. "I don't think that 'ambition,' that dream, has changed much. Not in all of our centuries working together or our time apart. I always thought that was a gorgeous dream, something that more people should indulge in."

"That was a long time ago," he said stiffly.

"Not too long. All this effort into capturing me and destroying Gialdon—is that actually going to make you happy? Are you any closer to a good home? Is Ivae any better now than when you started this quest?"

"It will be!"

"How? How is my suffering a benefit for anyone other than you?" she snapped.

Red Wolf opened his mouth to answer, but no words came.

She huffed, audibly getting herself under control. "The portal you plan to take? It's clear. Its guardian will let you and your posse through with minimal bribery. Money works, but rare books or *Magic: The Gathering* cards are better."

"And Piper?" he asked.

"Piper has a debt to owe this society. But don't worry—Minnesota does not execute its criminals. At worst, he'll serve a few decades in prison and likely do a bit of menial labor."

Decades was nothing to fairy. But to serve *mortals*? How humiliating.

Still, a tiny thread of tension unwound in Red Wolf's chest. He could eventually return for Piper.

"The rest of you largely only hurt *me*," she continued. "Your plan to kill my ward, baker, and witch failed. Because of that, I'm willing to look the other way, *if* you leave this Realm immediately. Don't come back until you give up this idea of vengeance."

She hung up, leaving Red Wolf to stare at the road. The eyes of everyone on his team weighed against his skin: Black Dove and Crescent's fury, Crow Moon's caution, Gold and Mouse's despair, Michelle's determination.

"I know how to get her back," he declared.

team 2 group chat

QUENTIN
WHAT THE FUCK JACK?
ALEX
Michelle, if you need help
tracking him down after
this, I'll do it 50% off
QUENTIN
I'LL GO 100%
SERIOUSLY WHAT THE FUCK
ROGER
I know we're not FRIENDS
friends, but jeez
Also David can't talk
b/c he's driving, but he
says even if we weren't
friends it's at least
a professional
courtesy to not stab
people in the back
ALEX
She probably paid him off.
QUENTIN
WHAT WERE YOU THINKING

JACK
cant talk
driving
gonna ditch my phone too
and I think she was
holding back
seriously guys. bail.

break their bones and souls

Violet returned Hendricks's phone. "I appreciate you letting me handle that."

"Sure," he said, tucking it away in the drink holder. They had to slow down as traffic clogged the road. With Route 35 out of commission, the streets had gotten more crowded. And it was made worse with construction; apparently, Elm City needed to redo its roads. Swanson followed them in his own car at a snail's pace. Nelson took the passenger seat while Violet lounged in the back, toes wiggling against the felt floor. Even as old as she was, it was odd to have no shoes while traveling in public like this. Or wearing days-old clothes and tangled hair stained with blood and mud. It wasn't a rare occurrence in her life, but she preferred the opportunity to put effort into her appearance, or to at least be clean.

"You're really okay with letting him go?" Nelson asked.

"Yes."

Hendricks glanced at her in the rear-view mirror. "Look, I know the last day has been rough, and truly terrifying. But you don't have to worry—"

"It's not fear," she interrupted, recognizing the speech to inspire her to triumph over her own reservations. "It's...well, at the moment it's primarily fatigue. But I meant what I said. Vengeance is inherently selfish and only causes more suffering. I've learned that the hard way."

"It's not vengeance, it's justice," Nelson argued, a few strands of blonde hair escaping her ponytail as she turned to Violet. "I just don't see how you're okay with letting people like that go."

"I *was* a person like that," she said. "And I created others in my image, Red Wolf among them."

Both cops stared at her.

"There is a big difference between punishment and justice," she lectured. "Punishment can be a useful tool in deterrence and even restoration. I imagine you'll be using that against Piper—although whether that'll actually instill any respect for mortal life and autonomy in him is...questionable at best. But at some point, you're just punishing people for the sake of punishing them. Usually it's for show, to convince others and yourself that you love the law. You love it so much that you're willing to destroy others, to break their bones and souls when all they needed was a slap and a nod in the right direction."

Hendricks shook his head. "The law is the law. If you don't want the punishment, don't break it."

She gave him an unimpressed look. "Look me in the eye and tell me that your prisons effectively redeem people."

"It's not about redemption."

"Then what's the point? Those people are going to re-enter society eventually. Do you want them to be better or worse?"

"So, it's *our* fault that they break the law?" Nelson laughed. "If it's about money, they just need to get better jobs. If it's anger issues, therapy."

Hendricks nodded in agreement. "Actions have consequences, society has rules, and that's that."

Violet shook her head, leaning against her seat and closing her eyes. It had been a long day, and she had no interest in making it longer.

better late than never

O'Brian came back to the interrogation room and wordlessly led them to their cells. Nicole got her own down the hall while Cyrus and JC squeezed into one together. It wasn't designed for an overnight stay. No cots or bunk beds, just benches, a urinal, and cement floors. JC settled on one of the benches, grateful that their short size made it more comfortable, unlike Cyrus, whose legs dangled over the end until he decided to give up and move to the floor. At least they were each given a pillow and blanket, though JC doubted either had been washed in the last year.

It was almost seven. Lawyer offices would be closed, or at least not taking calls. They'd be stuck here for the night.

"So much for rescuing Bob," JC grumbled.

"We've just got to hope that Boss can handle herself," Cyrus said. "I mean...the Lake Superior Fae portal *is* guarded by a dragon."

They remembered the size of that skull in the museum and swallowed. "A nice dragon?"

"Sort of. I've only met Rethu a handful of times. We've got a group chat with my friend Patrick—he's a werewolf—where we all give book recs. But Boss wouldn't want them to get involved unless and until she's ready to scorch the earth. Wouldn't want anyone dragged into any of her problems at all, if she can help it. She kind of sucks at asking for help."

JC made a face. "I can't see Bob 'scorching earth.'"

He laughed. "I can, and I *have*. It's not pretty."

They grunted. They supposed everyone had a dark side, but Violet had struck them as smarter than that. In all the weeks they'd worked for her—in American food service, no less—they'd never seen her lose her temper or get anything worse than mildly frustrated.

"We don't really care, you know," he continued. "About your record."

JC winced. They hadn't heard a sound from Nicole since they were separated, but they were still worried: both about her being alone in a cell, and about her reaction to their record.

"That was when you were a different person," he continued. "You don't do that anymore. And Boss would argue that she's done way worse, and she'd be right."

"Doesn't mean I'm proud of it," they grumbled.

"Good." Cyrus discarded his hat, running his fingers through short, indigo hair. "I remember when a person like you could move to a different city across the country, change their name easy enough, and start completely fresh, for better and worse. It's a lot harder to do that these days. Second chances are almost impossible."

JC put their hands behind their head, staring at the concrete ceiling. "More like seventeenth chance. I could've stopped a hundred times before I did."

He shrugged. "Better late than never."

"Tell that to Markus."

"Who?"

"The guy I killed. Landed me in prison."

"Ah." He glanced up at JC. "Are you going to do it again?"

"What?" they snapped. "No! I was high off my ass. And self-defense doesn't count."

"Would killing you or even keeping you behind bars beyond what you've already spent do anyone any bit of good?"

"I mean...probably not? But I'm a little biased."

He held up his pale blue hands. "There you go. You did a shitty thing, yeah. But you served your time, you got clean, and you're not a danger to the community anymore. So, what's the point of punishing you any further?"

"I'm sure plenty of people would say I deserve it," they grumbled.

Cyrus snorted. "It's not about what anyone deserves. It's about fixing what's broken to the best of your ability *and* preventing similar problems from happening in the future. *That's* justice. Punishment is only useful when it gets that result. Any further, and it's just to make other people feel better about themselves, and that just causes more trauma and more problems."

JC gave an indulgent smile. "Sounds like a lot of smart-people talk. And a lot of work."

"Yup. It's a lot easier to just find a bad guy to throw behind bars."

The guy was such a goofball most of the time that it actually surprised JC to hear him talk like this. "What the hell are you doing pouring coffee if you know so much?" they asked. "You're a lawyer with a million degrees."

Cyrus snorted. "I'm barely three hundred. If I were human, I'd be about eighteen, maybe nineteen. And it's not like I have a deadline to figure out what I want to do with my life. Unless and until I'm killed, I will live for a very, very long time. I'm just...I don't know. Trying to play it by ear, I guess? Enjoy my life, explore my options, spend time with friends and family. Maybe go back to the Fae Realm and get in touch with my roots—but I'd probably wind up back here. All my friends are here."

JC hummed. "Bet that's a lot easier to do when your adopted mom isn't being kidnapped, huh?"

"So much easier!" he laughed. "I could do a whole Power-Point presentation on why kidnapping is such a drain on *my* time and present it to Red Wolf as part of his punishment."

"The judge might have to give him a choice. A decade in prison, or sit through your 'Kidnapping Is Wrong' class."

"With a test at the end, so he can't sleep through it," Cyrus added.

"And people say justice reform is too complicated."

§

JC dozed until the cell door clanked open. Three officers came in: a woman and two men, a blond and a brunet. They looked like regular ol' cops, but Cyrus went rigid.

"We're here to transport you two," the woman said.

"Hell of a glamour you've got," Cyrus replied.

She shrugged.

"Officer O'Brian!" Cyrus called. "You've got an unlawful transport happening here!"

"Shut up," the brunette "officer" hissed, pulling out a pair of handcuffs.

JC jumped to their feet. "Don't you need some sort of warrant? Cops run on coffee and paperwork, you know."

"What the hell is happening now?" O'Brian demanded, a beaten-up book in hand as she marched down the hall. "You know I take these graveyard shifts so I don't have to deal with any drama? And why the *hell* are you going into a cell with weapons? The chief doesn't mind us breaking protocol in the building at large, but it's common sense to lock that shit up before going in an occupied cell!"

She pointed to the guns on the belts of the three "cops."

"We just need to move these two," the blond said, an authority in his voice that made JC want to straighten their back. "We won't be long."

"They're glamoured," Cyrus insisted. "Look up their badge numbers."

"I'm more interested in a warrant," O'Brian said, holding out a hand. "Lemme see the paperwork."

For a second, nobody moved.

The blond rushed O'Brian, slamming her into the bars. She slumped onto the floor, out cold.

JC went after the brunet, punching him in the neck as he tried to draw the gun—which turned in a sword as soon as it left the holster. Cyrus pulled a paperclip out of his pocket that turned into a knife, and he met the blade of the woman, who swiped at him with her own sword. "JC, get out! Call for help!"

They went for the door, only to be blocked by the blond. Another gun turned into another sword—were fairies fucking allergic to firearms?

(Oh, wait. Iron. Yeah, they probably were...)

JC snagged Cyrus's pillow from the floor.

"Really?" the fairy drawled.

Behind them, Cyrus was busy with the other two, the brunet moving a bit slow with his neck bruised. Cyrus blocked the woman's sword, snatched her wrist, and spun her into the cell's iron bars.

She screamed when her face hit the iron bars, skin sizzling as Cyrus kept pushing her head against it. Her friend tried to help, calling, "Gold!" but Cyrus blocked his sword with his knife.

JC threw the pillow at the blond blocking their way. They cut it in half with the sword while JC went for O'Brian. Specifically, O'Brian's gun.

I am so getting arrested again, they thought, taking aim and firing.

The brunet attacking Cyrus howled in pain, going down with a fresh hole in his leg.

The woman finally managed to free herself from Cyrus and the iron bars, staggering back with two nasty golden burns down her face that cut right through the glamour. The blond disarmed Cyrus with a flick of his wrist and got between him and the woman.

JC aimed the gun at them. "Cyrus, let's get Nicole and–"

"Put down the gun!"

...fuck.

Coming from the hall was another trio of fairies glamoured to be police officers, along with "Rachel," who had a gun against Nicole's temple and a swelling black eye.

"I tried to fight back, but I'm not good against four," Nicole grumbled.

Cyrus sighed, lowering his knife. "Yeah...same."

JC still had the gun, but held up both hands.

"How many of them are we taking?" Rachel asked.

"All of them," the blond said–clearly the one in charge. "We can kill one of the mortals she cares so much about to prove our resolve."

O'Brian groaned, shifting.

They all looked at each other.

"How many witnesses do you want?" Rachel asked.

"None."

Rachel pointed her gun down at O'Brian.

Nicole elbowed her in the gut. Rachel wheezed, loosening her grip enough for the witch to tear herself free and sprint down the hall, only to get immediately tackled by one of the fairies—they moved inhumanely fast, almost like a bullet.

JC seized their chance, shooting Rachel in the chest and aiming for the one next to her—

A slice of blinding hot pain in their leg brought them down. They gasped, dropping to a knee as the blond glared down at them over his bloodied sword.

JC moved to aim their gun at that stabby asshole, only for him to use the flat of his blade to smack it away, nicking their fingers and sending the pistol spinning across the floor, out of the cell.

Cyrus also tried to fight back, but had two fairies locking his arms behind his back with no way to wiggle free.

JC pressed their hands against the cut on their leg, blood blooming across the khakis and dripping down their leg. It'd probably need stitches.

"Wha—what's going on?" O'Brian slurred, sitting up.

The blond stomped on her chest, keeping her down. "Is Rachel dead?"

"Mm-hm," one of the fairies grumbled, checking for a pulse. "Are *you* killing the officer?"

"We're not barbarians. Black Dove?"

One of the fake officers came over and yanked a couple of hairs from O'Brian's head, ignoring her protests.

She muttered something in the Fae language, her voice echoing, and then there was that pop of reality, and—

O'Brian gasped, struggling against the fairy's boot. "I can't—what did you do? I can't see!"

"And when Black Dove is finished, you won't be able to hear, speak, or feel, either," the leader said.

"Red Wolf, don't," Cyrus said, uncharacteristically serious. "Cursing officers will just send more people after you, and then you'll never reach Black Beach."

The fairies ignored him as Black Dove finished her spell, and O'Brian continued to struggle even as she went silent. JC gulped. *Jesus, just slit her throat and be done with it.*

Red Wolf kicked her back down, ignoring her blind groping. He met the eyes of Cyrus, Nicole, and JC. "Any of you cause any more problems, and you'll get worse. Understood?"

All three of them nodded.

reality altered course

Hendricks pulled into the Moose Lake Police Station after a nearly 45-minute drive, which was half again as long as it needed to be, thanks to traffic and construction. Violet had spent most of the time dozing until he parked. She yawned, stretched her back, and stepped outside, the warm summer air cocooning her after so long exposed to air conditioning. Gravel clung to her bare feet, scratching at her soles. Swanson followed close behind.

The contentment died as soon as she stepped inside, the familiar stench of blood stopping her cold.

"Be on alert," she ordered.

The three officers frowned, looking at the empty welcome desk and dark, narrow halls. "Yeah...Hello? This is Officer Hendricks from Bernier. Anyone home?"

"We're here for those hospital suspects," Nelson added, hand on her gun.

She went left while Hendricks went right, muttering, "Violet, stay with Swanson."

She crept behind Detective Swanson, straining her ears. There was some shuffling and scraping around the corner, which she quietly alerted him to with a tap on his shoulder.

They both crept forward, the detective insisting on taking point, hand on his gun but not drawing it yet.

The hallway led to one of the wider cells—probably used to house multiple inmates of the same gender—and a room with a body. Crimson blood had pooled on and around her unmoving chest, her eyes open to the ceiling.

Swanson swore and went to check for signs of life while Violet went further, finding the source of the noise within the cell.

It was an officer, *O'Brian* stitched into her shirt as she crawled around, bumping into things like the bench and urinal and cell bars, seemingly not even noticing the blood from a cut on her forehead–

Oh.

"Your fellow officer is cursed," Violet called. "No sight, sound, or speech. Probably no touch, either."

Swanson swore again. "Can you fix it?"

"Yes, but I'll need her DNA. It'll be easier if she's calm."

"No touch, huh? Not sure that's possible..."

"Give me your badge."

He surrendered the little gold shield. Violet took it, knelt before the woman, and put it in front of her face. She bumped into it, but paused, no doubt picking up the smell of leather and metal. Violet carefully put it partially in her mouth, letting her explore the world as infants do, the only way available left to her.

O'Brian's unfocused eyes widened and she banged her fist against the floor until Violet stopped her.

"Excellent, she knows you're here." Violet gave the badge back, ignoring Swanson as he cleaned it and radioed for help. Violet put one hand on top of O'Brian's head and the other in front of the woman's face, right under her nose. She couldn't imagine she smelled particularly pleasant, but it would help keep the officer calm.

She closed her eyes, reaching for the flow of reality, focusing on her subject, to where that flow had been disrupted, warped and twisted.

"You are not deaf," Violet ordered, her words echoing through reality, time, and space.

Behind her, Swanson almost dropped his radio, and Nelson and Hendricks came in.

The wrinkle within reality was fresh, put in place only minutes earlier. It was easy enough to iron it out with nothing but her will and magic. O'Brian gasped.

"You are not blind," she continued, waiting for that wrinkle to smooth out before moving on: "You are not mute. You *can* feel."

Reality altered course.

O'Brian's eyes focused on her, and she burst into tears. Violet pulled her into a hug.

"You're all right, you're all right. Your comrades are calling for help, but you're safe now."

Swanson left them alone, going through the rest of the station while Violet soothed the distressed mortal. O'Brian's sobs turned to sniffles, and she visibly pulled herself together. "We've gotta–they were dressed like police."

"You've got cameras?" Hendricks asked.

"Yeah, but no sound. Pieces of shit. The fake police took the suspects–all three of them."

Violet's stomach plummeted. "Were their legal names Blue Johnson, Nicole Walker, and Jennifer Charles Scott?"

"You *know* them?"

"Did you get the fake officers' names?" Hendricks asked.

"Johnson called one of them Red Wolf. And said something about going to Black Beach right before that bitch cursed me."

Good boy, Violet thought, *leaving clues like that for the witness.*

"Who's this?" he asked, motioning to the body.

"ID says Rachel Hanson."

"I will bet seven figures that's a fake identity," Violet said, standing. "Did you confiscate anything from the captives? Particularly any magic items?"

O'Brian got on shaky feet. "Look, I appreciate what you did, but I can't just–"

"Those magic items would be registered in my name: Violet Smith. They are my property. Do you really want to deal with that legal battle right now?"

The officer obviously considered that, then left. Swanson puttered in the office, presumably getting security footage. Violet looked over Rachel, trying to find signs of glamour or magic. She had them, very subtly wrapped over her skin, thin threads of reality tied at her necklace.

"This one's wearing enchanted jewelry," she announced as O'Brian came back. "The necklace is an anchor for transformative magic. Remove it, and you'll find her true face.

Ah! My invisibility cloak." She took the cloak, looking it over for damage. A bit of blood speckled the ever-changing fabric, but everything else seemed to be in order.

"These people look pretty human," Swanson called from the office.

Violet joined him. She frowned at the black-and-white screens. "There's too much distortion. I can't tell."

"Why did they even take those three in the first place?" O'Brian demanded.

In answer, Hendricks's phone rang. He glanced at the number and hissed, handing it to Violet. "Pretty sure it's for you."

why should i stop

Michelle zip-tied all three prisoners in the back of the van that Crescent drove. Gold had been taken to one of the other mercenaries' vehicles that followed the van, along with Crow Moon and Mouse, to tend to their iron burns. Every whimper of pain had increased Red Wolf's fury.

He and Black Dove checked the prisoners over for weapons and magical items. The young witch was covered in good luck charms, not that they had done her much good here. Luck could only take you so far, especially when it was mortal magic. She had clearly shared those items with her companions, as Red Wolf had to pull a necklace off the glaring baker and the young fairy.

The young fairy—"Call me Cyrus, if you care."—also had a magic ring on his right pinky. And it would not come off.

Red Wolf gave a tired sigh, sitting on the van's bench between Michelle and Black Dove. Everyone's knees knocked against each other. "What does it do?"

"Protection spell," Cyrus said. "No curses or enchantments. Boss made it herself and tops it off every few years."

"Try to transform him."

Black Dove took out her druidic wand and tapped Cyrus on the head.

It had no effect.

Neither of the mortals had such protection, which meant Cyrus was far more valuable to Violet. He was also the greater threat, and Red Wolf wasn't about to repeat his last mistake. This boy was being transformed into something non-threatening and getting locked up in a kennel like the pet he was.

"Why shouldn't I just chop it off?" he asked.

The mortal witch straightened. "He could go into shock, it can get infected and lead to serious illness or even death…"

"You'd be leaving a shit-ton of DNA evidence all over your van," the baker pointed out.

"Aaaaand you'd be cursed," Cyrus finished. "Anyone who manages to get it off without my permission dies within a week. Usually less."

"Seriously?" the baker asked, shocked. "How would they die?"

He shrugged. "Whatever way's easiest. Illness, accident, a fight…it's basically the opposite of Nicole's good luck charms."

"Huh."

Black Dove motioned to the mortals. "They're not protected. I can turn them into cats and shove them in the crate together. Though the fat one might accidentally suffocate the baker."

"Rude," Cyrus accused.

Red Wolf shook his head, taking out his phone. "Cyrus is the greater threat. And I want Violet to know these two are her real, precious humans if we have to kill them."

"You mean have *Michelle* kill them, right?" Black Dove corrected.

"At this point, I genuinely do not care." He hit redial on the last number and drew a knife.

All three captives stiffened. The baker glared harder. "Listen, asshole, I know you think you're basically Batman or John Wick or whatever—"

"JC," Cyrus interrupted.

"—but once you start torturing people, it's really hard to see you as any sort of good guy."

"JC, shut up."

Red Wolf ignored them as the phone rang, and then was answered.

"Red Wolf," Violet greeted.

"I have your ward, your witch, and your baker," he said. "You gave one of them a rather powerful protection charm."

"Obviously. Are any of them injured?"

The baker's leg sluggishly bled from where Red Wolf had sliced them. Considering the bruise on Crescent's neck, he didn't feel a flicker of guilt for it.

"Cuts and bruises," he said. "They will remain uninjured if they and you do as you're told. Cyrus, remove your ring."

The blue fairy clenched his jaw. "No. You want it, you're going to have to use that."

He motioned to the knife.

"All right." Red Wolf flipped the knife over and drove it into the uninjured leg of Jennifer Charles.

The baker gasped, all the air pushed out of their lungs by pain and shock. Cyrus tried to lurch forward, but Michelle pushed him back easily, barely standing to do it, and Black Dove had her wand out and pointed at the mortal witch, not that she was much help, rocking back and forth and muttering some sort of mantra under her breath.

"Fucking hell," the baker hissed.

"Remove your ring," Red Wolf repeated.

Cyrus hesitated.

Red Wolf twisted the knife, metal carving through flesh. The baker groaned, but said through gritted teeth, "No..."

Cyrus wilted, as weak as his mentor. "All right–"

"You die for this."

Everyone in the van paused at the baker's words. "What?" Red Wolf asked.

The baker grinned at him, all teeth and barbarism. "You want it, you fucking pay for it."

"JC..." Cyrus argued.

"No. You're cool losing a finger. Wolfie boy's gotta be cool paying the price, too."

Red Wolf considered stabbing the other leg when Violet spoke up: "I agree with Jennifer Charles."

"Why am I not surprised?" he grumbled.

"How many of your people have already been killed for this?" she demanded. "How many of them are risking their lives? If you don't do the same, then why should they follow you?"

It was an old lesson. The first lesson she'd taught him. The lesson of loyalty and teamwork, the reason so many had been drawn to the Violet Princess in the first place.

Red Wolf looked to the young witch. She was all soft curves and edges, unused to a life of pain and cruelty. Easier to break. "Or perhaps I haven't tortured the right person yet."

The witch, still rocking and muttering, gave him an unnerving stare.

Then she *slammed* her head against the back of the van. Again. And again. And again.

Hard enough that everyone in the van winced in sympathy each time.

Hard enough that Black Dove yanked on her shoulder to stop her, only for the witch to pull free and hit her head again.

Hard enough that when she finally stopped, swaying a bit, that side of her face was washed in blood.

"...well, shit, they both make a really good point," Cyrus said faintly. "The ring stays on."

There was a difference, Red Wolf knew, between enduring pain caused by yourself, and enduring pain caused by others. Given enough time, he could probably get the three of them to bend to his will.

But he didn't have that time. He needed Cyrus neutralized and Violet broken.

"What just happened?" Violet asked, almost successful in hiding her concern through the phone.

Red Wolf yanked the knife out of the baker's leg, ignoring their strangled scream. "Very well. Cyrus, turn around."

Finally, the young fairy obeyed, exposing his bound hands.

Black Dove leaned into his ear, hissing, "You will be dead within seven days."

"Then you have seven days to find a way to undo such a curse," he said.

She shook her head. "You overestimate my skill."

"Then I die. When that day comes, I trust you to lead the others to finish the mission. Deliver Violet to her cell and ensure the complete and utter destruction of Gialdon." He gave a weak smile. "Our benefactor has plenty of other replacements for me. I am not indispensable."

Black Dove swallowed and nodded.

Red Wolf cleaned the red from the knife. Pure iron, for a cleaner cut on a Fae. He pretended it was a courtesy, to minimize the chance of infection on his subject, and not time needed to brace himself. Come to terms with this. He'd gone into battle several times before, situations where he *could* die, but it was never a guarantee. This was much more final.

And he realized he was all right with it.

He leaned toward Cyrus. The boy met his gaze, but couldn't quite hide his fear.

"Save us the trouble and take off the ring," Red Wolf said quietly.

The boy's face twisted in defiance. "You want it, you pay for it."

Red Wolf chuckled, handing the phone to Michelle.

"Put it on speaker. I don't want Violet to miss a thing."

§

They tossed Cyrus's finger and the ring out the window. Red Wolf—unattuned to magic though he was—could still feel reality shift around him, the curse settling over his skin like a thin film. Black Dove transformed Cyrus into a tabby cat and shoved him snarling into the kennel, locking him in. The van only became slightly less claustrophobic. Michelle handed Red Wolf the phone.

"Here's what's going to happen," he said. "I am taking these three to Black Beach. If you are not there within two hours, I'll have my mercenary kill the baker. At three hours, she kills the witch. At four, I take Cyrus into the Fae Realm as a replacement for you. Do you understand?"

For a moment, all he could hear was Violet's breathing. The rumble of the van. The air hissing in and out of the baker's teeth as blood leaked down their legs, turning the metal floor sticky.

When Violet finally spoke, her voice had an icy edge he'd only ever heard during executions: "Is this what you really want?"

"You turned yourself into a monster," he said. "Monsters need to be put down or broken."

"...then why should I stop?"

He frowned. "Pardon?"

She gave a cold, humorless laugh. "If I am going to be treated as a monster even as I do everything in my power to become good, then why should I stop acting monstrously?"

He didn't say anything, his stomach sinking to his feet.

"I'll see you in two hours."

the exile

Excerpt from *Round-Ears: A History of
Gialdon and Humans in the Fae Realm*

During the Gialdonian War, most of the Violet
Princess's enemies claimed that she was only
assisting the mortals for her own power and
ambition. That she wanted to create a kingdom to rival
her grandfather's and use it to one day take his throne.
These rumors were mostly used as propaganda to dissuade anyone—mortal and immortal—from joining
her cause. And many did believe it. At the very least,
they thought that the Violet Princess would become

the Violet Senator, or Speaker, or Chief Magistrate. The most popular theory was that she would become the Chief Commander of the new fledgling country, as that had been her rank and duty in Ivae.

And yet, she achieved no position. She did not run for any office within the Senate, and there is very little evidence that she asked for one. Perhaps she intended to manipulate others and rule from the shadows?

Yet that rumor had barely begun to circulate when the shocking news dropped: the Violet Princess had been exiled from Gialdon.

This decree—given by Speaker Aster and agreed upon near-unanimously by the First Senate—is meticulously recorded by Aster himself, the Senate scribes, and many of the Senators' own private journals. Given the complete lack of surprise shown by the Violet Princess, it's probable that this was talked about before the Senate meeting, possibly even before the war ended. She may have even suggested it herself.

Some point to the fact that she drew her blades against Speaker Aster and Chief Magistrate Coral as proof that she was hungry for power. That she intended to take revenge and only stopped when she realized she couldn't escape with her life—or, for the more dramatically inclined, because of some romantic love for one or both of the Senators (never mind that there is no evidence of such a relationship or feelings on either side).

This is almost certainly false. She likely drew her blades to make a point, as her final advice of "Get yourself some bodyguards" was a lot more poignant when every Senator could see how close and how swift danger could be, even after the war. (This advice was immediately followed; to this day, the Senatorial Guard is considered one of the best security forces in the Fae Realm.) The Violet Princess, as we have seen numerous times in this text alone, possessed a flare for the dramatic.

The greatest question people ask is *why* the Violet Princess was exiled. She wasn't even paid for her efforts, and had in fact bankrupted herself over the course of the war, funding the Gialdons. Again, people like to think this was a preventive measure to keep her from claiming power at a later date, or perhaps revenge for her earlier actions against humanity.

The most likely reason was the final step of reconciliation between the Violet Princess and those she had so egregiously wronged. Yes, she had risked her life to win mortal liberation in the Fae Realm, and lost much: her friends, her family, her position, her wealth, her reputation. Yet, she was still called the Hammer of Ivae and the Iron Witch, and the memory of her oppressions could not be so easily erased.

It is an unfortunate truth that sometimes, for some deeds, forgiveness is simply unattainable. This is likely why many Gialdonians wanted to see the Violet Princess executed for her past crimes against them and their ancestors. But that would have caused several diplomatic issues. Despite being an enemy and traitor of Ivae and all other Fae kingdoms, the Violet Princess was still an immortal fairy, and royalty. Killing her—especially after she had helped them—could very easily have re-started the war Gialdon had just fought so hard to win, and might enable future defectors.

Even without that, many Gialdonian Senators did not want the Violet Princess to die. Speaker Aster wrote in his memoir, *I did not see how another corpse would bring us any peace or ease any suffering. There are few Fae policies that I agree with, but their aversion to killing—even state-sponsored executions—is one of them. What good does it do besides give us a false sense of righteous achievement?*

Thus, exile. The old adage "Time heals all wounds" is incomplete and inaccurate. Time *and distance* will heal *some* wounds. At the very least, it makes recovering from the trauma easier. And Gialdon decided that it needed time and distance to recover from the wounds caused by the Violet Princess before her defection. She gave them that.

Perhaps she wished to heal, as well.

Pictured *the Violet Princess leaving Gialdon, likely for another Realm entirely, although it's unclear exactly where she went. Although this carving depicts her as alone, contemporary sources state that she left with a Fae boy orphaned in the war.*

who's dying tonight

Red Wolf's work had been quick. Cyrus had only screamed for a few seconds before it was replaced with a pained cat's mewling, staticky through the phone.

O'Brian, Nelson, Swanson, and Hendricks had all paled when they'd realized what was happening. Violet had spent the time texting on the same phone the sounds of torture came from.

Now, she returned the phone to its owner, letting the cold rage wash over her. "I'll take it from here."

"Whoa, hold on." Hendricks chased after her down the narrow hall, to the exit. "Violet, we've got two hours. I can have a whole team of police officers, state troopers, SWAT—"

"No. This is my mess. I'm cleaning it up." She shouldn't have spent the last day trying to reach Red Wolf, trying to pull him along her own path of inner peace, if not redemption.

She should've just put an iron sword in his heart and called it a day.

"They invaded a police station," Hendricks argued as they made it outside. "Mind- controlled civilians. Tortured other civilians on fucking speakerphone! Let us handle it."

"No."

He grabbed her arm. "I will arrest you."

She raised an eyebrow. "For what?"

"Obstruction of justice."

"Be sure to add assaulting a police officer, too."

"...why?"

"Because if you don't remove your hand, I will break it."

She could see the exact instant he recalled fairies could not lie. Or bluff. He removed the hand.

"They have at least two wands," Swanson called, joining them. "What's your plan for that?"

"That's my concern. Not yours," she said.

"This is *my* case. It's been my case for months. Those wands are mine."

"They'll be surrendered to the proper authorities," she assured him. "I just want my people."

"Your people are as good as dead."

Hendricks glared at him. "*Swanson.*"

The detective gave a helpless shrug. "I'm sorry, but it's true. You think anyone outside of the Twin Cities is equipped to handle those fairies? Even radioing it in now, the soonest they'd get there is three, three-and-a-half hours. Someone's dying tonight. But at least we can snatch those wands before they do any more damage."

"You are correct," Violet said. "Someone *is* dying tonight. Probably multiple someones."

"Violet..." Hendricks warned. "Let the professionals handle this."

She couldn't help it. "*Child,*" she laughed. "What do you think I did for seven *centuries* in the Fae Realm?"

Both men gave her an uneasy look.

"How are you even going to get there?" Nelson called from the doorway. "You don't have a car!"

Violet heard it, first, looking up at the sky. Eventually, the humans could hear it, too: wing beats cutting through the summer's night sky.

It was impossible to see the dark-scaled beast. Not until they landed on the pavement, gray and black scales gleaming from the station's orange lights. Their body was as long as a school bus, claws digging into the cracked concrete.

Nelson drew her gun with a swear. The dragon hissed smoke through its teeth, crimson eyes bright as they tracked the pistol. "Cute," they rumbled.

"Don't," Hendricks said, holding up a hand. "Dragon scales are bulletproof."

Swanson's face lost all color. "I thought there *weren't* any dragons in Minnesota."

"You thought wrong," Violet said, stepping into the parking lot in her bare feet. "Rethu," she greeted.

"Violet," they replied, showing off their rows of sword-like teeth in a feral grin. "So. Who's dying tonight?"

bad guys don't get happy endings

Blood dripped down JC's legs, staining their khakis during the long-ass drive to Black Beach. A red puddle formed and grew beneath their shoes, and finally they asked, "I don't suppose I could get a Band-Aid?"

"No," Red Wolf said. Black Dove had turned herself into a dog and curled around Cyrus's bloodstained crate. At least it gave the rest of them crammed in the back some breathing room.

"Well, then, you're cleaning out this van."

"The van has no use in the Fae Realm."

"Did you not pack a first aid kit?"

"We packed all-heal. You are not worthy of it."

"Ouch," JC muttered. "How about a cigarette? You got one of those?"

"No."

"Also no," Michelle added. "I gave that shit up years ago."

"Insulin? I'm diabetic." They were already feeling light-headed. Fuck that Officer O'Brian.

"Nope."

JC sighed, leaning against the van wall. "You're all terrible."

The back of the van had no windows, but the front obviously did, and JC could just barely make out a cop car idling by the side of the dark road—a speed trap. They held their breath. *Come on, someone must have reported this van...*

They drove by. The cop did not follow.

Red Wolf must have noticed their disappointment, because he chuckled. "Black Dove glamoured the exterior of the van, including the license plates. Nobody's coming to rescue you."

"Fan-fucking-tastic," they grumbled, glancing beside them. Nicole had been silent since Cyrus got turned into a cat, still rocking back and forth. The blood had dried against her skull and locs. "How you doing?"

She shrugged, still rocking. After a long moment—long enough for JC to think she'd gone back into that total nonverbal state—she quietly admitted, "I think I gave myself a concussion."

That wasn't good. Escaping would be hard enough with everyone in top form. But with Cyrus as a cat, JC stabbed in both legs, and Nicole's brain turned to scrambled eggs, those odds weren't great.

"Do you need a bucket?" they asked.

"...maybe."

Michelle stood and carefully walked along the moving van, slightly hunched over, until she found a trash can stashed in the corner behind Black Dove's tail. She shoved it between Nicole's legs.

"Thank you," Nicole said.

"Blood is a lot more pleasant to clean off my clothes than vomit," the mercenary grumbled.

"Agreed," JC said.

For a moment, they considered trying to open the back door, roll out, and run for help. But that intrusive thought was absolutely useless. Their hands were zip-tied behind their back, so they'd be fumbling for the handle for a while, long enough for someone to pull them back. If they did manage to get the door free, they'd be falling out of a van moving at least fifty miles an hour. JC wasn't a doctor or scientist, but that'd probably be fatal. If they survived and kept most of their bones intact, then they'd be in the middle of bumfuck nowhere with the sun down. And while they were running around for help in the middle of the cornfields with two gaping leg wounds, who knew what would happen to Nicole and Cyrus?

At least the van had air conditioning.

"Why'd you frame me?" they asked.

"Why not?" Red Wolf replied, way too chill for a torturer. "We needed a smoke screen to throw off law enforcement, and you have a record."

Made sense. Still, "That was a dick move."

Michelle snorted. "So is shooting a guy coming out of a gym."

JC made a face at her. Nicole hurled in the bucket.

Everyone looked away or groaned as the smell swelled in the van. JC was just glad that Nicole had her locs held back by a scrunchie.

Red Wolf called a halt, and the driver said that there was a gas station a mile up.

"Don't get any ideas," he said, before JC could even think of an escape plan. "The van is enchanted to hide whatever's inside from prying eyes and ears. And if either of you escape, Michelle will kill you both."

"As if you're not going to do that anyway," they retorted.

Red Wolf didn't answer, and that was all the confirmation they needed.

§

One of the fairies–the indigo-skinned Crescent–took the puke-filled plastic bag from the trash bin and went to toss and replace it. Michelle got out of the van, stretching but staying close, pistol in its holster on her side. Red Wolf had gone to use the restroom. The only fairies in the van were Cyrus the cat and Black Dove the dog.

"You feeling better or worse?" JC whispered, knowing that the fairies could hear them anyway.

"Better," Nicole grumbled. "The fact that there aren't windows back here isn't helpful. I'll probably throw up again."

"Serves them right."

"Mostly I'm annoyed by the headache, but I can't really blame them for that."

JC chuckled. "Not gonna lie, that was really badass."

Black Dove lifted her head and growled at them. JC shrugged. "What? It was."

Nicole blew a stray lock from her face. "Why did you shoot someone in a gym?"

JC's smile fell. "Ah. Well…"

They sighed. They were all going to die in a few hours anyway. Might as well come clean.

"You know I'm a recovering drug addict. Before the 'recovering' part, I cooked for the Bobcats. One day, a marmair shipment goes missing. I was pissed, because I was running low on my own personal stash. We were pretty sure this other gang, the Minneapolis Brotherhood, took it. So, I used up the last of my stash because I didn't have the guts to face them sober, grabbed my gun, and went to their neck of the woods. Found one of them coming out of a gym—his name was Markus, we'd gotten into a few fights before—and saw that he was carrying a duffel bag. 'Cause, you know, he'd just come out of the gym. I convinced myself that he'd stashed our marmairs in there and just...emptied my clip. Right there on the sidewalk. Took the duffel and ran. When I finally looked inside, it was just gym clothes."

Nicole let out a breath, but didn't say anything. JC continued: "Cops busted me the next day. Wasn't a hard case to crack. The fact that I was high helped my case, but since I was high on an illegal drug, killed someone, and also the gun I used was stolen from my dad, I got sentenced to fifteen years."

She frowned. "You served six."

JC's smile was a fleeting thing. "Good behavior plus overcrowding, and a bit of bureaucratic magic. Been clean ever since, but I guess that's not enough."

"What do you mean?"

"I mean shit was bound to catch up to me eventually, right? Bad guys don't get happy endings."

"You're not a bad person," she stressed.

"Did you miss the part where I shot a man in the street?"

"Did you miss the part where you've put yourself in harm's way multiple times to try to rescue a woman you barely know and to whom you owe nothing?"

"I wouldn't say *nothing*..."

"Good and evil exists in everyone, and you've been actively choosing good since prison," Nicole said. "The past doesn't matter nearly as much as the present, and you've been kind to everyone who hasn't tried to hurt or kill you. You're breaking your cycle of violence, and that's a good thing."

JC took in her earnest face, her blazing brown eyes, and the adorable tap tap tapping of her fingers against the van wall, and said, "You really do have a concussion."

She kissed their cheek. "And you have no self-worth."

"Not really." Their face burned where she'd kissed them. Somehow that felt more intimate than the actual sex they'd had. "I'm sorry you got roped into this with us."

"I chose to do this," Nicole stressed. "And so did you, even when you didn't have to. That alone makes you at least a not-bad person."

gotta try

As soon as Violet flew off on the dragon, Hendricks started making calls, warning the state's northern precincts about what was going to happen and where.

"Come on," he said, motioning for Nelson. The Moose Lake precinct would soon be swarming with state troopers to investigate the murder and impersonation of police officers. "We've gotta go."

"We're not gonna make it in time," Nelson argued.

"We've gotta try."

"If Violet wants to get herself killed, let her."

He glared at her. "We've gotta try."

§

The call went out: *All units, be advised: We have a triple 10-134 in progress. Repeat: Triple 10-134 in progress. Suspects are heading to Black Beach in a van, ETA two hours. Suspects are Fae, skilled with glamour, armed with firearms, wands, and other dangerous...*

my sins

What would have been at least a one-hour drive, Rethu turned into a 20-minute flight.

The dragon landed on Bernier's Main Street, the yellow lights from the street lamp reflecting off their gray and black scales. Violet slid from their back and hurried to her café.

"What the–Violet?"

She paused, smiled. "Hello, Caroline."

The elderly yarn shop owner stared down at them from the second story window of her apartment. "Are yuh hurt, baby? You got kidnapped!"

"I'm fine. Just have to handle a few things."

Rethu shrank down into human form, keeping the wings, horns, and tail on their tall, pale human body. Their clothes–jeans, Star of David necklace, and a beaten-up V-neck– had likely been enchanted to work with such transformations rather than shredding with the change. Dragons were, by and large, genderfluid, and Rethu usually used gendered pins to note the identity of the day. But they must have been in a rush, because there was none on their shirt.

Violet had bespelled the doors of her café. She never had to bring a key, because as soon as her hand touched the door, it unlocked for her.

Being back in her domain normally soothed her, even if her café was closed and dark, lit only by a couple of back lights, everything tucked away and shut down.

But the people who should be in her domain, safe and sound, weren't. And that could not stand.

"Nice place," Rethu complimented, trailing after her. "Why not stash your stuff at your house?"

"Some of it *is* stored in my house, among other locations. I don't put all my eggs in one basket." Violet pulled up the loose floorboard in the corner of the dining area, revealing a small box. Or as Cyrus called it, her "box of holding." It did have a similar enchantment to the Dungeons and Dragons' Bag of Holding, though any magical scholar would tell you that the Fae had invented it first.

Someone knocked on the door.

"That's probably Caroline come to fuss," Violet said, not looking up.

Rethu answered it. "You're not the old lady."

"Uh, no?"

Violet looked up. Jack stood on her doorstep, waving sheepishly. He'd added a hoodie and baseball cap to his outfight, hiding his face and auburn curls. "You said that I knew where you worked, and I figured no one would come looking for me here, so..."

"Bring him inside," Violet ordered, setting the box on the table.

Rethu pulled Jack in and closed the door behind him.

"I don't have your money or charm yet," she said. "I need to rescue some people, first."

"Right. Cool. So..."

"Most of your coworkers are dead. Michelle remains out of police custody, but she is not my priority. If she lives, so be it."

Jack balked. "If she survives, she'll kill me! She hunts down everyone who backstabs her! And their families!"

"Then I suggest you invest in a few new identities," Violet said. "That, or come along."

Rethu scoffed, a bit of smoke curling from their mouth. "Do we need him?"

"No. But we could use a third pair of hands, and he can see Michelle dead with his own eyes." She pressed her hands to the table, meeting Jack's frustrated gaze. "And I'll add an additional five million dollars if you help."

Frustration and fear turned to near-delight. "Sold. What's the plan? Do I get to turn into a unicorn again?"

"No. Rethu will fly us there to beat Red Wolf's deadline. Ideally, we'll get there first so we can put everyone in position and ambush them."

"That'll be tough, but doable," Rethu said, tail flicking behind their heels.

"I don't have any weapons on me, but Michelle rented out a warehouse with a few emergency guns," Jack offered.

"Sounds like a good pit stop."

"And what's in here?" he asked.

Violet opened the box, revealing her old armor, two of her swords, and an Elemental Wand. "My sins."

mortals and metal

"I see the dragon," Crescent called after over an hour of silent driving with one more unplanned stop to clear the vomit from the trash can. His knuckles tightened on the steering wheel. "It's circling around."

"We've got a bigger problem," Michelle said.

Red Wolf left his seat to get to the mesh divider. He was immediately washed in gaudy red and blue lights.

They'd been following a highway that trailed along Lake Superior, which was vast enough to almost trick Red Wolf into thinking he was seeing an ocean. All that was missing was the pungent, salty smell. They'd taken an exit to get to Black Beach, only to find the road leading to the forest and water beyond blocked by police vehicles.

"We can glamour?" Crescent suggested.

Michelle shook her head. "They've already seen us."

"Silver Bay Police," someone announced over a speakerphone. "Please step out of your vehicles with your hands up."

The other Fae and mercenary cars flanked Red Wolf's van. His phone rang. He answered.

"I can probably handle them," Crow Moon offered through the speakerphone. "The lightning boots will let me disarm and knock them all out in seconds. Then Mouse can move the cars."

A decent plan. But Red Wolf wasn't jeopardizing anymore Fae lives if he could help it.

"I was thinking of something a little more ostentatious," Red Wolf mused. "Black Dove. Are we close enough to the lake?"

Black Dove shifted from dog to fairy and pulled out her Elemental Wand. "Barely, yes."

She moved the wand in a back-and-forth manner, akin to the tides, as a couple of police officers cautiously approached them, guns out. They were ten feet from the van when their colleagues called out in alarm.

A wall of water formed behind the police barricade, rising from the lake as if it had a mind of its own.

"Get down!" the baker and Michelle ordered at the same time. Michelle grabbed Red Wolf and yanked him to the floor as the baker shoved their whole body against the witch to get her down. Not a heartbeat later, the police fired on the van, correctly assuming the sorcerer was within.

Glass shattered. Cyrus yowled. Bullets hit metal, but not flesh. Red Wolf's final good luck charm fell from his ring finger, and he gritted his teeth.

Black Dove flicked her wand.

Red Wolf couldn't see it from the floor, but he heard it: the wall of water crashing into mortals and metal, washing them clean off the road and into the trees.

He hauled himself up. The wall of water was twelve feet high, contained to the stretch of road that had been formerly occupied by police. Black Dove flicked her wand again, and all the water went back into the lake, leaving a few tree branches behind but no sign of the mortals. Not even their cars.

Crescent silently drove on. Red Wolf blinked at the carnage. "...I think you killed some of them."

Black Dove swallowed, black skin turning gray.

He cleared his throat. "They're just mortals, anyway."

"No one's blaming you," Crescent piped up. "It had to be done. Just like taking out the trash."

She smiled weakly.

§

They reached the parking lot of the beach and hauled their mortal and cat cargo out. The baker slowed them down, grumbling about "the giant holes in my legs," and largely had to lean against Michelle, who kept her pistol out in a clear threat. All the hostages were surrounded by the remaining mortal mercenaries: Michelle, Quentin, Roger, David, and Alex, who held Cyrus's cat-carrier.

Black Beach was a beach of tiny, sharp stones, not sand. When the mercenaries pulled out their flashlights, Red Wolf could see that it had earned its name. They followed the narrow strip of dark pebbles to its triangular point, the little crimson island topped with trees just barely connected to the landmass by a thin finger of black and red rocks. Blue picnic tables were scattered across the beach, some knocked over or pushed into trees from Black Dove's wave.

"Damn," the baker breathed, staring at the endless water as it reflected the moonlight. "Hell of a view. Look, you can even see stars!"

Red Wolf silently agreed. This was the first place he'd seen in the last two months that wasn't tangled in concrete and rebar. The black rocks obviously weren't natural, but they were folded into the natural beauty of the place in a truly unique way that he'd never seen before, and couldn't bring himself to criticize. He could imagine people—mortals, mostly, but perhaps fairies, too—having lunch at the tables, climbing the island's red rocks, children and adolescents daring each other to go into the frigid water.

For the first time on Earth—ever—Red Wolf wanted to hesitate. Wanted to linger. Wanted to see what this place looked like in the sunlight.

"Yeah," the witch agreed. "My parents once took me further north. It's even more beautiful and peaceful up there."

"Is this what the ocean looks like?" the baker asked with childlike wonder.

"Very similar, yes. But with a smell of deviled eggs gone bad."

"It's louder, too," Red Wolf added quietly. "The waves are larger, and you can hear each one crash against the shore. It's not quiet like this."

"Huh," the baker said. "Not a bad last thing to see."

Red Wolf shook himself and moved, nudging the group along.

"Black Dove, I hope you're not tired, because the cops will be back," Michelle warned. "And they'll probably bring helicopters this time."

"No worries," the sorceress said, pulling out her druidic wand, now holding a magical item in each hand.

"Well, I hope you plan on carrying me," the baker grumbled. They'd gotten paler and sweatier as the trip progressed. Whether it was from blood loss or that "diabetes" they'd mentioned, Red Wolf did not know or care.

He ignored them. "Black Dove, I think we'll need wings–"

Crow Moon dropped, a pale gold hole in her forehead. The *BANG* came half a second later.

Everyone instinctively crouched. "Get to cover!" Red Wolf ordered.

Black Dove conjured a wall of water to shield them as they moved back to the trees. But then something roared, shaking the air, before it crashed onto the beach in front of them.

The gray and black dragon blocked their retreat, trapping them against the cliffs of the island. And on its back was a fully armed, fully armored, and very angry Iron Witch.

made of iron

JC thought that the bus-sized dragon with horns, claws, and teeth as big as swords would be the scariest thing they'd seen. But Violet on its back somehow managed to look more intimidating. Her cloth under-suit was either black, gray, or dark purple—hard to tell in the night—with knee-length chainmail that glowed silver in the moonlight. Over *that* she had a breastplate and gauntlets that JC would bet a month's pay were made of iron. She looked like a nightmare stepped out of a history book.

Except she didn't wear a helmet. Just a headband with metal links sewn into the fabric.

Michelle dropped JC on the rocks and fired her pistol. Twice.

The bullets got so close to Violet's head that a few wisps of dark hair moved. Two of the several *dozen* metal links fell from her headband. She gave Michelle an unimpressed look and raised a wooden wand.

A stream of fire shot out, and Michelle burst into flames.

The screams, the *sounds* she made were not human. JC scrambled as best they could on the ground, away from the flames as Michelle staggered, then crumpled, but the fire did not spread. It remained on her until there was nothing but charred bone.

Violet didn't say anything. Her face did not change. She was as impassive as watching the coffeemaker.

There was half a second where nobody moved. Shock from the death. Fear. JC wanted the dragon—or Violet—to deliver some more fire, but with Nicole, Cyrus, and themselves stuck in the middle of the group, that'd end up frying them, too.

Black Dove waved her wand. More water rushed up and out of the lake, creating a larger circle around the fairies and mercenaries to protect them from Rethu, Violet, and the shooter. The water layer was so thick and moving so fast that if JC jumped in, they wouldn't make it to the other side, they'd just get caught up and drown in the current.

"Kill the baker!" Red Wolf ordered, just barely heard over the sounds of chaos.

JC, hands still tied behind their back and a hole in each leg, couldn't do much besides try to wiggle away as Alex turned her sights on them.

Nicole kicked the Canadian in the back, sending her stumbling. But the mercenary quickly regained her footing and back-hand-slapped the witch to the ground.

Thanks, anyway, JC thought, trapped between the water, the mercenary, and their own injuries.

And then...

There was that familiar pop of reality, the echo of Violet's voice–though this time, JC couldn't make out any of the words she said.

The cat-carrier exploded. Cyrus burst out in full fairy form, landing on his feet, and JC recalled how much magic a fairy could do with your true, full name. Of *course*, Violet would know Cyrus's.

Cyrus elbowed Alex in the back of the head, sending her down to the black rocks before hauling Nicole to her feet. He put himself firmly between JC–whose back was inches away from the wall of water–and the other mercenaries.

"Careful now," he goaded as they aimed their guns. "*I'm* the valuable hostage, remember?"

"Rude," JC grumbled as Nicole tried to help them to their feet–not that either of them were much help, both their hands tied behind their backs. And JC was swamped by the familiar fatigue, dizziness, and sweating that meant they needed insulin *yesterday*.

The mercenaries hesitated.

The massive gray dragon punched their head through the powerful water current, smoke hissing out of their mouth.

Mouse snatched their upper and lower jaw and, somehow, through some quirk of magic, managed to keep them together, stopping Rethu from breathing fire.

Black Dove waved her wand again, and all the water that had surrounded the group coiled up and smashed into Rethu, pushing them back. JC breathed a little easier, no longer surrounded by a liquid cell.

Violet had dismounted the dragon at some point. She marched across the black sand and waved her fire wand. Flames shot out, aiming for Red Wolf and missing only because Crescent tackled him out of the way.

Black Dove smacked Gold with her other wand—the druidic wand.

Gold's fairy body bloated and hardened, covered in white scales and golden horns, until they stretched into a full dragon. Rethu shook off the water and roared at them, so loud and deafening that the black rocks shook and JC's ribs rattled.

Gold launched themself at Rethu. Black Dove tapped Crescent, turning him into a dark blue dragon. He spread his wings and flew away from the fight, toward the island where the sniper shot had come from.

Violet neatly stepped around the dragons fighting—right as they flew up into the sky to have a proper airborne battle—and tossed a bundle to Cyrus before focusing on Red Wolf and Black Dove.

the right thing

Violet tossed Cyrus his belt—with several knives sheathed in it—and focused on Red Wolf, Black Dove, and Mouse.

Further ahead, Crescent breathed fire, lighting the entire island with its wild portal ablaze, unable to find Jack in the dark with his borrowed invisibility cloak. Hopefully, he'd made it out.

Black Dove sent a wave of water crashing after Violet, and she countered with an inferno, turning the water wall into steam. The Elemental Wand grew hot in her hand, would have already blistered her skin if she weren't wearing gloves specifically designed and enchanted to counter that. She drew her sword as fire and water clashed, recognizing the diversion tactic.

Mouse came running at her from around the elemental battle, Red Wolf from the other side. Violet dropped the inferno and rolled toward Mouse, getting sprayed but not blasted with the edges of Black Dove's water. The short strongman tried to swipe at her, every blow as deadly as a vampire's.

But strength wasn't as valuable as speed, and had the unfortunate side effect of making its bearer believe themselves invincible, when they were just as flesh and blood as everyone else.

Violet dodged another blow and jabbed Mouse's calf with her sword—the pure iron one, not the one she'd reclaimed from Red Wolf and surrendered to evidence bags. He gasped in pain, giving her the opportunity to slice through the Achilles' tendon on the other leg, bringing him down to his knees. She pivoted to a better position and brought her sword on his green neck, cutting off his head and sending it rolling to Red Wolf's feet.

On the mortal side of the field, Cyrus threw a knife straight through Roger's bald head before he could use his rifle, and used another to slice through Nicole's bindings. He pressed the blade into her hands to free Jennifer Charles before re-arming himself against Alex, Quentin, and David.

Above their heads, Rethu clashed with Gold and Crescent, who had abandoned the burning island to help his companion. Gold breathed a torrent of flame at Rethu; it did no damage. Neither did David's bullets when he tried to shoot at them with a rifle, the metal harmlessly bouncing off thick dragon scales, until Cyrus commanded the bookworm's attention by disarming Alex and slicing Quentin's side, spraying his blood across the black sand.

Violet turned her attention to her own foes.

Red Wolf had re-armed himself—*Always bring a spare weapon, preferably two,* Violet had trained her apprentices—and Black Dove, who chose her Water Wand over glamour. Smart.

"You didn't tell me you'd made friends with a dragon," Red Wolf said, glancing up at the aerial fight over Lake Superior.

"It never came up," she replied.

He looked at her sadly, and she saw all the battles fought together and against each other, the quiet hours spent talking and dreaming and laughing and crying, all the bodies buried back then and in the next hour.

"You were never going to do the right thing and come with me, were you?" he asked.

What might have been a laugh came out in a little huff. "The fact that you still think that's the right thing..."

He cracked his neck, and Black Dove readied another wave of water.

screaming dragons

Nicole cut JC free and hauled them to their feet. The dragons, Violet's fight with Red Wolf and Black Dove, they tuned those out as Cyrus went toe-to-toe against four—whoop, make that three; bye, Roger—armed mercenaries.

JC took a step to help, instead crumpling against Nicole as their legs screamed in protest. Little black rocks clung to their skin and clothes. "Fuck! We've gotta go. We're sitting ducks."

"Let's get to the trees," Nicole agreed, pulling them along.

"Won't they just burn it down?"

"Fairies don't hurt the land."

"*Um...*" They waved a hand to the burning island, the wildfire lighting the whole beach.

"That's an isolated island! The flames won't spread. Now, do you have a better idea?"

Between the dragons, the fairies whipping water and fire and swords at each other, and the knife vs. gun fight happening ten feet away?

"...no I do not," JC said. "Start running."

Nicole did not run. She half-dragged JC down the beach, pausing only when they swooped down to pick up Alex's dropped handgun. They glanced over their shoulder, seeing Cyrus break Quentin's arm and yank him in front of him as a human shield in time to catch David's bullets.

The two of them had to pass the trio of fairies trying to kill each other in a swirl of fire, water, and blades. JC had seen dozens, hundreds of fights in their short life: fist fights, knife fights, gun fights. They had *never* seen anything like this. Violet and Red Wolf clashed with swords, swiping and dodging and pivoting.

He managed to draw a thin line of golden blood on her cheek while she nicked his ear. He tried to swing at her head, she blocked with her metal-covered arm...

But she was doing it all one-handed. The other had the Fire Wand, which she used to evaporate Black Dove's hose attempts. Violet tried to send a fireball at Red Wolf, only for the other sorceress to defend him with a cyclone of water that she sent after Violet, who turned the gallons and gallons of water into steam and smoke with white-hot flames.

All of this happened on the thin stretch of black sand that went from the forest to its tip at the burning island: Cyrus's fight was on the thinnest stretch of land closest to the island, while Violet's had only slightly more wiggle room.

Nicole and JC sloshed through the water, going up to their knees to give the fighters as wide a berth as possible. JC sucked in a breath at how cold it was, even in summer. They'd pulled warmer drinks from refrigerators. A quick glance over the shoulder showed that Cyrus was still standing: David had run out of bullets and Alex had reverted to a knife, and the fairy kept both of them busy with his own blades, managing to stab David in the gut before Alex tossed him over her shoulder and into the water.

Seeing a clear shot, JC stopped Nicole, aimed, and fired their handgun.

Alex flinched at the hit to her arm, but stayed standing.

"This fucking dizziness," JC grumbled. That should have been a fatal shot.

Cyrus took full advantage of the distraction, though, shoving a knife into Alex's kneecap to bring her down into the water with him, and then slitting her throat.

Nicole hauled JC along, almost getting sucked into Violet's fight when Black Dove summoned more water.

They had no idea why Nicole didn't just bail. "I'm slowing you down. Just—"

"If you tell me to leave you behind, I will paint a penis on your face with glitter," Nicole snapped.

JC stared at the woman, scowling at them in ice-cold, knee-deep water, lit up by fire and still with blood stuck to her nose and forehead, and it was the most cliché thing in the world, but she really was the most beautiful being JC had ever seen. They giggled at the absurdity. "Okay."

Nicole hauled them along, skirting around the edge of the fight. Violet's eyes met JC's for about half a second, and she very briefly smiled before slapping Red Wolf's sword away and shooting fire at Black Dove, only to be blocked by a wave of water that almost swept the two mortals off their feet and onto the rocks. If JC had had a clear shot, they would've taken it, but all three of them were moving too much, too fast.

"Just a few more yards," Nicole panted.

A dragon *screamed*.

Screaming dragons sounded different from roaring dragons. When Rethu had roared, it had been a challenge. A deep bolt of thunder that swelled through the air.

The scream was somehow louder, higher-pitched, and terrifying, because JC could hear the pain.

Two dragons crashed onto the ground, spraying black rocks and water everywhere, and blocking the mortals' path to the trees. Rethu was on top of Crescent's back, digging their teeth and claws into blue scales and ripping, until Crescent's wing dangled freely from their mouth. They spit it out like a chicken bone.

JC and Nicole scrambled back, trying not to get crushed by the two squirming behemoths.

Gold slammed down onto Rethu, shrieking. The gray dragon rolled with the movement, off Crescent, and shot into the air, Gold in hot pursuit, leaving the one-wigged Crescent in the mortals' path.

"Swim around?" JC suggested.

"I think so," Nicole agreed. "Can you swim?"

"Not really."

"How do you *not* know how to swim?"

"The lessons were too expensive!"

Crescent hissed, lifting his head and meeting their eyes. The two stepped back, but heat from Violet's wand prevented them from going any further.

JC fired their handgun, emptying the clip.

All three bullets pinged harmlessly off thick blue scales.

"...fuck."

Crescent inhaled, throat glowing with fire, and JC knew there was no getting out of this. The water wasn't deep enough to protect them from incineration. They were dead.

And then, a bubble of reality popped.

In the heartbeats before Crescent's inferno, they heard Violet's voice, whispering in their ear, clear as day: "Jennifer Charles Maria Frederick Scott, you are a dragon."

feel my pain

Getting glamoured into a dragon was *weird*. In the literal blink of an eye, JC's entire body bloated and hardened, scales thicker than Kevlar coating their skin like dried Super Glue. They dimly heard Nicole yelp as wings sprouted awkwardly from their back, and they thought they'd shit their pants before realizing that no, they'd just grown a tail.

Crescent breathed his fire, a wall of heat, and JC immediately curled their SUV-sized body around Nicole—because even as a dragon, they were short as shit. The fires licked at their scales, harmless as a kitten. Nicole buried her face in JC's new scales, clinging to their new reptilian skin.

Across the beach, Cyrus finished off David, yanking his knife out of his skull from where he'd shoved it through his eye. Violet—despite enchanting JC—hadn't missed a beat in her fight, though she'd been pushed back closer to the burning island and was breathing hard.

Rethu had managed to get above Gold and overtake them from behind, using teeth and claws to rip the smaller golden dragon to shreds, scattering entrails across the waters of Lake Superior as the body—or what was left of it—shrank back into Fae form.

JC was surprised they'd lasted that long. Sure, two-on-one sounded like great odds, but JC was awkward and clumsy in their new body, whole new limbs twitching in weird ways. Gold and Crescent might have gotten an upgrade, but Rethu had been a dragon their whole life, and they clearly knew how to fight as one.

Crescent stopped breathing his inferno, pissed that his target was both still alive and had also gotten the scaly upgrade.

JC shifted their weight, wincing in pain and dizziness. Scales, yes. Leg injuries and diabetes, also yes. Glamour couldn't fix that, apparently.

Fire, yes?

Before they could test that, Nicole darted out of the safety of JC's arms and wings, hands up. "I'm not going to hurt you. But Violet and Rethu *will*, if you keep attacking. You're outnumbered, and you've lost a wing. *Please* stop. Do you honestly think you can win?"

Crescent studied her. It couldn't have been more than two seconds, but with Rethu flying back, and the three fairies still clashing, it was an eternity.

He shrank, morphing back into a blue-skinned fairy with a huge gash on his back. It was hard to tell beneath the clothes, but JC thought some of his flesh might've even been missing as he turned and limped into the forest, disappearing into the dark trees.

"You *are* the smart one," JC praised, their voice oddly deep in their bigger body. Nicole shrugged.

They turned their attention to the last fight. Violet, Red Wolf, and Black Dove were all out of breath, but JC didn't think they'd be sensible like Crescent, even with Rethu coming in as backup...

And then Black Dove spotted Cyrus sprinting to help Violet, and smirked.

Violet was busy with Red Wolf, who had a few more cuts and nicks from where he hadn't been able to block or dodge quickly enough. Black Dove summoned another wave, and Violet raised her wand, but instead of sending the water at her, Black Dove sent it careening into Cyrus.

Violet was surprised enough that she almost got her arm sliced off by Red Wolf. Black Dove rolled Cyrus into a water cocoon, creating a cyclone of rapids that made it impossible for him to escape—or breathe.

"Maybe we don't have to bring you back to Fae," Black Dove snarled. "Maybe I just want you to feel my pain for the rest of your miserable—"

JC had heard enough.

They lurched forward, getting into the fight much more quickly than they'd thought even with the wounds—yay for longer legs—and used their door-sized snout to bite Black Dove. She didn't even have time to scream.

The sorceress's blood gushed in their mouth as they plucked her from the ground, legs kicking against their chops. The water dropped, sending Cyrus sputtering to the ground. JC chewed— once, twice, three times before calling it good and spitting her out, her body as limp and crumpled as a used tissue.

Red Wolf's face darkened with rage. He lunged at Violet with a war cry, but never made it to her.

She shot a fireball into his face. And without his pet sorceress, there was nothing to stop him from catching fire.

the original exiled princess

The moments after a battle are some of the most surreal experiences. A combination of disbelief, relief, and grief.

Violet studied the charred corpse of her protégé for a long moment before sheathing her sword and putting away her wand. Times like this, she wished she truly did have the iron heart her family and courtiers had accused her of having. It would make everything so much easier.

But trying to be that cold, heartless fairy had granted her nothing but endless misery. This bout, at least, would be temporary, and soothed by the other people in her life.

"Cyrus," she called. "Injuries?"

"Besides my pride?" He squeezed water out of his shirt, tiny black rocks stuck along his side. His right pinky was gone, but she didn't see any blood. "Nothing to worry about. But Nicole's got a concussion and JC's legs—"

He dropped his shirt and pulled a knife, having heard what Violet saw: an invisible, glamoured figure moving toward them from the water.

Jack dropped the hood of his invisibility cloak as he reached the shore, holding up his hands. "I lost my sniper rifle."

Cyrus relaxed. Rethu landed, transforming back into a human as JC rinsed out their mouth, gargling and spitting cold lake water.

Glamouring others was Violet's preferred method over glamouring herself, as it didn't strain her body as much, and it allowed her to utilize others' strengths and better delegate. She checked over her work. Jennifer Charles was a small dragon, with denim-blue wings against tawny scales and deep gashes in their back legs, courtesy of Red Wolf.

They gargled and spat more water. "Ugh. Does it count as cannibalism if I didn't swallow?"

"That's a question for the philosophers," Violet said.

They swished more water. "Doesn't taste as tangy as human blood."

"That would be the lack of iron."

Rethu trudged up to her. "Sooooo, Elemental Wands are illegal, aren't they?"

"Yeah, the Supreme Court is fine with American citizens having a tank or flamethrower. But a *magic* flamethrower? That's off the table," Cyrus scoffed. "'Right to bear arms,' my ass."

"So how are we explaining all of this?"

Violet gave them a meaningful look.

The dragon sighed. "Fine. I guess I can keep the cops off your back. Just this once. But you owe me."

"Yes, I do," she agreed.

"Thank you, Rethu," Cyrus said in a childlike voice. "You're our favorite dragon."

"Damn right," they said.

Jennifer Charles spat a final mouthful of water and said, "Hey, Bob? This is cool and all, but can I be human again, please?"

"Of–"

Someone's phone rang.

"That's not me," Cyrus said.

The living patted themselves down–even Jennifer Charles the dragon–except Violet. She approached Red Wolf's charred corpse and pulled the phone out of his pocket. It was pristine; someone had enchanted the case.

She answered it. "This is Violet."

The woman on the other end sighed. "I was afraid of that."

Violet's lungs turned to ice. "Diamond. I should've guessed."

The others looked at her in confusion, except Cyrus. He stiffened.

"Yes, you should have," Diamond scolded. "Are any of my people still alive?"

"Nobody you care about."

"Pity."

"Did you really think he'd be able to bring me back?" Violet demanded.

"I figured he had even odds. Either he succeeds and you return. Or he doesn't, and I get a very good look at your defenses. See you around, Violet." She hung up.

Violet glared at the phone, then pocketed it.

"Who was that?" Rethu asked, crimson gaze curious.

"That would be my cousin. The *original* Exiled Princess."

paperwork

Hendricks, Swanson, and Nelson came to Black Beach to find three police officers dead, five more injured, seven dead suspects (with half of an eighth washing up an hour later), and six civilians in various states of shock.

They loaded Jennifer Charles, Nicole, and a pinky-less Cyrus onto ambulances. Violet insisted on going with her ward.

"I need to talk to you, first," Hendricks protested.

"Rethu will tell you what happened."

"And what *did* happen?"

"Red Wolf died. The hostages were saved. That's all you need."

He frowned, studying her jeans and sweater that she hadn't been wearing before and would bet they were glamoured. Glamoured from *what*, though, he didn't know.

"We'll catch up with you later," he said, waving her on. She joined Cyrus's ambulance.

Rethu—who refused to give any other name or even a last name—gave a bare-bones statement: "Violet told me what was going down, so I came here to protect my turf. Red Wolf's people got violent with the hostages, so I stepped in to prevent those hostages from dying. It got messy."

The final civilian—Jack Johnson—corroborated it. He was in hiking clothes, but was wet, his auburn curls limp against his forehead. "I couldn't sleep, so I went out for a walk. Heard the commotion and watched everything from the trees. I thought those fairies would kill those people, but then the dragon swooped in and started lighting everyone on fire. Went in the water to avoid getting hit."

Hendricks took a picture of Jack's ID, which stated he was from Wisconsin, in a town at least a six-hour drive away. Jack said he was visiting, "getting away from it all."

The next day, he checked with the local hotels. None of them had a room rented out to "Jack Johnson." And the young man was in the wind.

Hendricks pursued a warrant for his arrest, but he sincerely doubted it'd go anywhere. At the end of the day, Swanson had the Elemental Water Wand and druidic wand; the fairies that had attacked Bernier were dead or in custody except for one, known as Crescent; and all those who had been kidnapped were alive and accounted for.

He wasn't going to get anything else, save for a mountain of paperwork.

re-opening

Violet gave everyone the week off. JC spent the first day mostly in bed, exhausted and in pain from the stupid stab wounds in their stupid legs. The EMTs had given them an insulin shot, probably only a couple hours before they would've gone into a coma, and Elizabeth had been the one to pick them up from the hospital. She wrote them up for breaking curfew—again. JC didn't have it in them to fight her over it.

The next day, Violet called and said, "I have some all-heal. Did you want some for your injuries?"

"Uh...yeah, if you're willing to haul it up here," they said, still in their tiny twin-sized bed with its ancient mattress, worn blankets, and three other beds in the room. Alku had won Best Parolee of the Year and Best Goblin by fetching them their meals so they wouldn't have to stand.

"If you take enough, it might cure your diabetes, too."

JC stared at the speckled ceiling. "How much would that take?"

"Hard to say. All-heal is something of a misnomer, as it's not designed for diseases. I imagine it would take a lot."

"Then no. It's not worth it."

"Jennifer Charles..."

"It's not."

Violet sighed. "Very well. I'll send Cyrus up."

"Elizabeth!" JC hollered after the call. "I'm expecting a guest!"

"You are not," Elizabeth said firmly, coming into the bedroom. "I'll not have reporters in this house."

"He's not a reporter."

"If you're too injured for chores, then you're too injured for—"

"He's my lawyer."

She scowled, but gritted out, "Fine," and left.

§

"How's Nicole?" JC asked as Cyrus unscrewed the lid off the all-heal jar.

"Don't you have her number?" he asked.

"Well, yeah, but you've probably actually seen her."

"Not much. She's mostly been hounded by her family. As soon as they saw her name on the news, they came to see if she's okay."

JC focused on taking a fingerful of all-heal and rubbing it against the two sewed-up wounds. It was a little awkward, sitting on their bed in their t-shirt and underwear while Cyrus hovered, but they'd lost all sense of personal privacy in prison.

"That's good," they said, and only felt a tiny pinch of jealousy. Their only family check-in had been from their younger sister Kelly, who'd sent a text saying, *Not dead?*

They'd responded, *No, not dead*, and had gotten only a *K* in return.

"The movie theater has five-dollar tickets on Tuesdays," Cyrus said, taking the jar back as JC's legs sealed themselves back up. It felt itchy.

"...okay?"

"Just saying. They probably have something playing you'd both like."

They scowled at him. He grinned, screwing the lid back on and sitting next to them on the bed. A flick of his hand turned one of his pins into a tiny knife, which he used to cut the thread of their stitches and pull them through—which was a *feeling*. He still only had three fingers (plus the thumb) in that hand, a new black ring on his only remaining pinky.

"Boss says she understands if you don't want to work at the café anymore," he said out of the blue.

JC frowned. "But...my name debt..."

"Is cleared. You risked life and limb to bring her back. That's worth a name change, don't you think? It's even worth a decent good luck charm, if you're worried about finding a job afterwards. One that doesn't have a boss who's going to have to deal with some...interesting family drama."

"What's the deal with her cousin, anyway? If she's a princess like Bob, does that mean the whole country is in on this?"

Cyrus shook his head. "No. Well, probably not. If Ivae wanted Boss that badly, they'd have sent more than Red Wolf after her. Diamond is...unique. I don't know all the details, this happened way before my time. But you know how Boss is sometimes called the Exiled Princess?"

"Yeah..."

"Diamond was the *first* Exiled Princess. The OG. And I'm pretty sure that banishment is because of Boss. Not sure if it's because she exposed something bad that Diamond was actually doing, or..."

"Or," JC finished. With Violet, who had burned people alive just two nights ago without flinching, anything was possible. She could've framed this cousin. Could have fought a whole other war against her. Or Diamond could be a total bitch and Violet in the right.

He nodded. "Yeah. So. No hard feelings if you decide it's too much trouble. Debt's cleared. You'll get set up somewhere else. And Nicole's definitely still interested, so you won't lose that, either."

JC thought about it. Really made themselves consider the option. A decent-paying job for them would probably be cooking at a Perkins or helping with some ma-and-pa diner. They'd be fine there. They'd make a living.

But if it was outside of Bernier, there was a higher chance of slipping off the wagon.

And the people would look at JC with fear and suspicion as soon as they found out their history. No friendly smiles. No banter. No real second chance.

No understanding or compassion from someone who *got it.* Who was also struggling to claw her way out of a pit that was probably bottomless, but that wasn't going to stop her from climbing.

"When is she re-opening?" they asked.

"Next Monday."

"Since my debt's cleared, I want her original offer of twenty bucks an hour."

He smirked. "Done."

§

Cyrus left them with their insulin pump ("Finally got it back from Moose Lake. Lemme know if you want to sue.") and a tinfoil pan full of chicken casserole ("From Caroline and Andy. They both say get better soon.")

JC took a deep, deep breath and dialed Nicole's number. This would've been better in person, but phone would have to do. They certainly weren't going to chicken out and do it over text.

...maybe they should've done it over text.

"Hello?"

"Hey," JC said, clearing their throat. "Are you busy? I can call back."

"No. I'm taking a break from painting. Cyrus came by with a bit of all-heal so I can do it without the headache."

"Nice," they cheered. Nicole's voice was steady, deep, and monotonous, but they could still hear the genuine joy in it. "So... um...were you still interested in that third-ish date? Or did you want to step back and...chill? For a bit."

There was a beat of silence. JC rushed to fill it: "Because I totally understand if you need time. *I'm* used to people trying to kill me and having to...you know, protect myself like that—"

They had spent an hour brushing their teeth as soon as they were at the halfway house. Alku had just wordlessly loaned them his mouthwash.

"—but that was kind of all new for you—"

"It was," Nicole interrupted. "It was...intense. But I don't think it will be the last time."

JC grimaced. "Don't think as in gut feeling, or don't think as in..."

"Visions. I've been getting visions."

"Great."

456

"Yeah."

JC moved to cross their arms, but couldn't because they were holding the phone, so one arm was tucked awkwardly over their chest. "You might...I mean, if you don't want to deal with that, I'm sure Violet wouldn't mind you leaving Bernier. She'd probably even help you."

"She offered. I said no."

They smiled. "Yeah. I said no, too."

"She was very annoyed. But. Also a little proud, I think?"

"That sounds right. I think she wants us to be smart enough to run away from the fight. But if that's the case, she definitely shouldn't have hired me."

"Friends don't let friends deal with problems alone," Nicole agreed. "I want to show you something."

Something shuffled on the other end, and then JC's phone dinged with a text.

Nicole had taken a photo of her open sketchbook, where she and JC were drawn in messy watercolor, arm in arm, giggling like children. Their sides were pressed close together, arms locked together, sharing the same space, heads bent close enough that they shared the same air.

JC's mouth went dry. Not just because they wanted Nicole. They just hadn't ever seen themselves so...happy. They didn't know how she'd managed it, but somehow sketch-JC had real joy, and not just because they were on the arm of a cute girl. There was a confidence there that they had only dreamed of. The world could've been burning down around them, and that JC would've shrugged it off and powered through.

"Is..." They cleared their throat. "Is that a vision?"

"...maybe," Nicole said. "Do you want it to be?"

More than anything in the world.

They bit the words back, instead asking, "You free Tuesday?"

crackers

"If you try to convince me to bail on you one more time, I'm going to eat your entire box of favorite crackers before you get any of them," Cyrus threatened as soon as he came back from the Cities. He hadn't even taken off his sneakers.

Violet closed the mouth she had opened and looked meaningfully at his missing pinky.

He rolled his eyes. "Honestly, Boss, you're acting like I haven't been to war before."

He had. Even when she'd done her best to keep him out of it, he'd been in the middle of far too much blood and suffering. He'd already had to bury more friends and comrades than most people made in an entire lifetime.

"Officer Hendricks called," she said instead. "They're closing the case. Government officials will be returning the Fae bodies to Ivae."

"Good. JC says they'll see you on Monday. Twenty bucks an hour."

Of course they did, Violet thought, biting back a smile.

"Did that guy you bribed show up?" he asked.

"He took his first payment about half an hour before you arrived."

Jack had been solemn when he'd accepted his first cash payment: twenty pounds worth of $500 bills in a small cardboard box, hidden under a few books in case he got pulled over while driving.

"I truly mean it when I say don't spend it all at once," she'd warned.

His smile had been wan. "Yeah..."

"Are you all right?"

"Just...those people weren't really my friends, but they..." He'd shook his head. "I guess I still feel bad."

Violet could relate. "It was a difficult decision either way." She motioned to the box. "What will do you with it?"

"You'll laugh."

"Try me."

"Well, my sister's going to college, that'll take a chunk. But also...my mom works as a cleaning lady, but we've always talked about opening up a gardening and landscaping business. I'm bad at money, so I'll probably just give it to her and then work for her."

Violet had nodded her head in approval. "If you don't want her to know *how* you got your money, I'd recommend contacting a few launderers."

Now, she said to Cyrus, "You should visit Patrick soon."

Cyrus strolled past her. "I'm getting the crackers."

"We could use the allies," she added.

He paused.

"What Diamond is planning, it won't be pretty," she warned. "At the very least, we need to warn anyone associated with us. They're targets now."

"You're worried about collateral?" he asked, leaning against the wall. The two of them had repainted it a deep, warm blue just a couple years ago. Violet wondered if the house would survive what was coming.

She shook her head. "That implies accidental damage. Red Wolf may not have cared about who he hurt, but his wrath was targeted on me, and me alone. Diamond won't settle for that. She's going to go after everything and everyone I've ever touched, and pull them out root and stem. She'll spend centuries doing it if she must."

Cyrus didn't say anything, absorbing that.

"Of course, if you'd rather avoid her wrath, it'd be easy enough to get you a secret identity—"

"I'm eating *all the crackers*."

***

Others Books by
C. M. Alongi:

Citadel

*The Witch Who
Trades with Death*

*The Blackwing
novella series:*

To Kill a Necromancer

Hetgarib's Curse

The Horned Guardian

Ghost Peak

The Slain Princess

www.ingramcontent.com/pod-product-compliance
Ingram Content Group UK Ltd.
Pitfield, Milton Keynes, MK11 3LW, UK
UKHW041917290925
8134UKWH00013B/66/J